continued . . .

P9-DCD-907

LORD
RAKEHELL

Virginia Henley

A SIGNET ECLIPSE BOOK

SIGNET ECLIPSE
Published by the Penguin Group
Penguin Group (USA) LLC, 375 Hudson Street,
New York, New York 10014

USA | Canada | UK | Ireland | Australia | New Zealand | India | South Africa | China
penguin.com
A Penguin Random House Company

Published by Signet Eclipse, an imprint of New American Library, a division of
Penguin Group (USA) LLC. Previously published in a Signet Eclipse trade pa-
perback edition.

Signet Eclipse Mass Market Printing, December 2014

ISBN 978-0-451-41503-5

Printed in the United States of America
10 9 8 7 6 5 4 3 2 1

For Paula,
my grandson Daryl's beautiful wife

ACKNOWLEDGMENTS

I am indebted to the following historical and biographical sources on Victorian England's society, monarchy, government, and noble families, including the Hamiltons and the Curzon-Howes.

- Kenneth Rose: *Who's Who in the Royal House of Windsor*
- John Pearson: *Stags & Serpents*
- J. Preest Lord: *John Russell*
- Joseph J. Schroeder, Jr. (Ed.): *The Wonderful World of Ladies' Fashion: 1850–1920*
- History Learning Site: American Civil War December, 1863
- Victorian Web: Literature, History, & Culture in the Age of Victoria
- *The Morning Post* (London): February 19, 1863, and November 11, 1863
- *Illustrated London News*: March 7, 1863
- Encyclopaedia Britannica Online
- Library of the Commonwealth: Secretariat, situated at Marlborough House (Online)
- English Heritage (www.english-heritage.org.uk): Chiswick House and Gardens
- Sandringham (www.sandringhamestate.co.uk): Managing Sandringham Estate

Prologue

"Harry, you look radiant!" Lord James Hamilton kissed his sister Harriet's cheek. "There's something about marriage that makes females thrive." James winked at his brother-in-law, Thomas, Earl of Lichfield. "Can't imagine what it could be."

"It's the bed play," Harry declared.

Thomas closed his eyes, summoning forbearance.

James hooted with laughter. "How do you put up with the outrageous baggage?"

Thomas shook his head. "I swear there is something in the air at weddings that makes the fair sex giddy beyond control."

"It has the opposite effect on males. The groom wears black, along with a stunned expression, and the rest of our sex silently commiserate with the poor devil."

"James, I warrant on the inside you are laughing at the narrow escape you managed. Just think, you could have been Lady Emily Curzon-Howe's bridegroom today."

Lord Hamilton sobered. "Bite your tongue, Harry. I've an acre of wild oats to sow before I contemplate the institution of marriage."

"Surely a member of Parliament would benefit from a wife?"

"Since I am the *youngest* member of the House, I believe the disadvantages of matrimony far outweigh the benefits."

"You're heading in the wrong direction. St. George's Chapel is this way."

"I'm attending the Prince of Wales today. I'll likely find him in the billiard room."

"Ah, your partner in crime," Harry teased. "You were named one of his attendants because you are older and wiser. His misguided parents no doubt believe you will have a profound effect on the randy young devil."

"And so I shall. I'm three years older and abundantly wise in the ways of women, thanks to having seven saucy sisters."

"I'm not simply saucy; I'm also salacious."

Her husband rolled his eyes. "You are a scandalous baggage."

"How the devil do you keep from doing her violence?" James asked.

The corners of Harry's mouth went up. "He loves me to distraction."

Her husband changed the subject. "I hear the prince is eager for a military career."

"No chance of that at present. His father won't even consider it until he completes at least two years at Oxford. The prince is champing at the bit, and I can't blame him. His parents and tutors have had the poor devil in leading strings his entire life."

"Better watch out, James," his sister warned. "If they ever let Teddy out of his cage and he gets a taste of freedom, he may run off the rails."

James winked. "I shall make it my priority to see that he does so."

The nuptials of Lady Emily Curzon-Howe and her bridegroom, Colonel Robert Kingscote, were taking place in Windsor Castle's chapel because the bride was a lady-in-waiting to Her Gracious Majesty Queen Victoria, and the groom had recently been appointed as an equerry to Albert, the queen's prince consort.

All the invited guests belonged to the upper echelons of Society. The bride's father, Earl Howe, had been lord chamberlain to the late Queen Adelaide. The bride's oldest sister was married to the Duke of Beaufort, who was master of the horse, and another sister was married to the Earl of Westmorland, who, along with the bridegroom, had risen to the rank of colonel in the army.

Lord Hamilton's parents, the Duke and Duchess of Abercorn, were invited guests not only because they were friends of the Curzon-Howes, but also because Abercorn was Prince Albert's groom of the stole, and Abercorn's son, Lord James Hamilton, had just been appointed as an attendant to the young Prince of Wales.

James Hamilton strode off with purpose. His sister's words had reminded him of his brief infatuation with Lady Emily several years ago. *She took advantage of an inexperienced sixteen-year-old.* He smiled, remembering. *Lord God, I thought myself such a rake wallowing in the sexual favors of an older woman.*

Hamilton's thoughts were interrupted as two young people came barreling through the arcade of the Horseshoe Cloister and collided with him. The impact knocked off his silk top hat and sent it sailing across the ancient cobblestones.

"Now, see what you've done!" the boy accused the girl. He looked apologetically at James and ran to retrieve the hat. "I'm sorry, Lord Hamilton."

James recognized Lady Emily's young brother. "Hello, Montagu. What's the trouble here?" His glance swept over the young female, who was sobbing her heart out.

"It's my sister Anne. She's crying over nothing."

The girl stopped sobbing and raised her head. "I'm not crying over *nothing*. She hates me! She called me an ugly Irish maggot!"

"Well, she calls me a little Irish turd, but you don't see me crying over it," Montagu pointed out reasonably.

James hid his amusement. "Who is flinging these crude insults at you?"

"Our sister Emily," Montagu informed him.

"Our *half* sister," Anne cried passionately.

James understood the situation immediately. Their father, Richard Curzon-Howe, had been married twice and had produced a family with each wife. Lady Emily, her exalted sisters, and seven noble brothers had been born to the earl's first wife, who had been English. The pair of siblings before James at the moment had been born to his second wife, Lady Anne Gore, who was Irish.

James addressed the distraught female. "I'm sure Emily didn't mean it. I cannot imagine her being that cruel."

"Yes, she is," Montagu said matter-of-factly. "She hates us because we're Irish."

Anne blinked as crystal tears fell from her lashes and rolled down her cheeks. "She's the one who insisted I wear this childish bridesmaid's dress. I can't help being Irish and having ugly red hair."

"I'm Irish," James informed her, "and damned proud of it." He gazed down at the exquisite young female with her profusion of red-gold curls. Her green eyes sparkled with unshed tears. "If you stop crying, I'll let you in on a secret about Emily."

Anne gazed up at the handsome lord before her with the wavy black hair and warm brown eyes. She wiped her nose with the back of her hand and rubbed it down her frilly bridesmaid's gown. "A secret?"

"Emily doesn't hate you at all. When she looks at you, she is consumed with jealousy."

"Why is she jealous?"

James took his handkerchief from his pocket, gently cupped Anne's chin, and wiped away her tears. "Because you are as beautiful as a wild Irish rose."

After the ceremony, the guests made their way to Windsor Castle's grandiose banqueting chamber, decorated to commemorate England's victory over Napoleon at Waterloo.

"That wedding gave me the shudders," the Prince of Wales informed James Hamilton and Charles Carrington, his other attendant. "My parents are making a list of future brides for me—all fat and all German. I don't fancy sitting through a formal wedding banquet. Is there a place we can escape to, James?"

"How about the barrack rooms? The castle guards enjoy a lively card game on Saturday nights." James was eager to evade the clutches of Lady Emily. If he stayed at the reception, a dance with the blushing bride would be obligatory.

Prince Teddy thumped James on the shoulder. "How the devil would I manage without you, old man? Let's get away while the getting is good."

Lady Anne gazed about the banqueting chamber with both hope and apprehension. She was longing to encounter Lord Hamilton again, yet worried that she would be tongue-tied if he spoke to her. He had been so kind to her, comforting her as she'd lost herself in anger, and she found that she couldn't stop thinking about him. When she spotted her friends the Hamilton sisters, she joined them and sat down between Lady Frances and Lady Maud. Anne idealized the Hamiltons. Their household was harmonious, and compared with the acrimony and rivalry in her own family, their lives seemed perfect. She took dancing lessons with Frances and they were looking forward to putting into practice what they had learned.

Anne summoned her courage, took a deep breath, and casually inquired, "Will your older brother be joining you?"

"Perhaps he will if we save a seat for him." Frances searched the crowd of guests entering the chamber. "There he is!" She stood up, waved, and beckoned him over.

Anne's heart began to race with excitement. *I hope I don't faint.*

When a tall, dark young man joined them, Anne stared

at him blankly and an uncomfortable silence stretched between them. Finally, she blurted, "You're not James."

"Indeed, I am not, Lady Anne." The sixteen-year-old masked his disappointment at the young beauty's reaction. "I am James's brother John Claud Hamilton." He reached for her hand and took it to his lips. "At your service, mistress."

Anne swallowed her disappointment and tried to make amends for her rude reception.

"I am delighted to meet you, John Claud."

"But obviously meeting James would delight you more," he said dryly.

"Of course not. I simply wanted to congratulate him on becoming the member of Parliament for County Donegal," Anne improvised quickly. "It's quite an accomplishment to be the youngest member of the House of Commons."

John Claud had been unfavorably compared with his older brother, James, since childhood and felt fiercely competitive toward him. "In a couple of years I intend to run for the Conservative seat for Londonderry."

"I've never visited Ireland, though my mother was born in Kilkenny."

Frances cut in. "Oh, please let's not talk politics." She frowned at John Claud. "It is all my brothers ever speak about. This is Anne's sister's wedding and we intend to celebrate." She turned her back on John Claud and focused on Anne. "Will Maud and I be invited to your birthday party next month? You are invited to mine."

"Of course." Anne licked her lips, and asked softly, "Will James be there?"

"I very much doubt it. Since he's been appointed a gentleman of the bedchamber to the Prince of Wales, he's seldom at home."

Lady Anne was amazed at the young noble's accomplishments. "You must be very proud of him." Her eyes shone with the overwhelming admiration she felt for Lord Hamilton. "He was exceptionally kind to me before the wedding, when I was in a state of distress. His words took away my unhappiness and filled me with joy."

There was pity in the look that John Claud gave her. "Believe me, Lady Anne, he's no knight in shining armor. As a matter of fact he is gaining an unsavory reputation—one that is well earned, I warrant."

Lady Anne smiled her secret smile. *John Claud, I believe you are jealous of James.*

Chapter 1

Dublin Harbor
June 1861

"Free at last! I swear those dreary years at Oxford were worse than being buried alive."

The Prince of Wales was joining the Grenadier Guards at the Curragh army camp in Kildare for ten weeks of military training. He stood with his two attendants on the bow of the *Connaught*. As well as James Hamilton, his other gentleman of the bedchamber, Charles Carrington, had been allowed to accompany him.

"Last night I had a bloody nightmare that I was at Windsor Castle being married!" He shuddered. "My parents still can't wait to saddle me with a German princess."

"To quote Herrick: *Gather ye rosebuds while ye may*," James Hamilton advised, as the port of Kingstown, Ireland, came into view. When the steamer rounded the pierhead, a deafening gun salute sounded from the man-of-war *Ajax*. "You spoke of freedom too soon, Your Highness." James pointed to the military officials gathered at the pier to welcome the royal prince. "Your escort awaits."

"And wait they shall! It's Saturday, for God's sake, and I intend to spend the weekend in Dublin enjoying

myself before they inter me in Curragh's garrison. Be
firm with them, James, I'm depending on you."

"You may safely leave it in my hands, Your Highness."

Once the prince and his gentlemen disembarked, the
mayor of Kingstown and his welcoming committee greeted
them. Lieutenant Colonel Bradshaw along with a dozen
Grenadier Guards, who had been dispatched to escort the
Prince of Wales to the Kildare army camp, saluted His
Royal Highness and informed him that the commander in
chief, General George Brown, awaited his arrival.

The prince shook Colonel Bradshaw's hand, thanked
him, and moved forward to offer a greeting to each of
the dozen mounted and uniformed guards and admire
their horses.

James Hamilton introduced himself to the lieutenant
colonel. "His Royal Highness has been entrusted to
carry a private message from Her Gracious Majesty the
Queen to Ireland's viceroy, George Howard, Earl of
Carlisle. The prince plans to proceed to Dublin today
and in all likelihood will be ready to journey to Curragh
Camp to begin his military training on Tuesday."

After a moment's consternation, Bradshaw acqui-
esced to the new plan. "I shall dispatch a guard to the
commander in chief with the prince's itinerary, Lord
Hamilton. I and my men are at your service to escort you
to Dublin."

On the short carriage ride from Kingstown to the
capital, Prince Teddy thanked his friend profusely. "You
are a silver-tongued devil, James. I don't know how you
do it."

"It's second nature. I learned diplomacy at my father's knee."

"I'm amazed that bloody old Major General Bruce
wasn't awaiting me with a muzzle and a noose." Bruce,
the prince's governor who had kept him on a tight rein in
Oxford, had preceded him to the Curragh Camp to in-
spect his quarters and lay out a course of military exercises he deemed suitable for the royal heir to the throne.

"At the risk of being presumptuous, Your Highness, I

advise you to take a firmer stance with Bruce. You are a royal. You outrank him by miles. Bruce may advise you, but by no means should you allow him to rule you. He is the *servant* and you are the *master*. In my experience, if you stand up to a bully, he will invariably back down."

"By God, James, you give me hope." The prince's mind turned to another problem.

"What possible excuse can I give to the viceroy for coming to Dublin unannounced?"

"Let him know you are doing him a great service. Tell him, in strictest confidence of course, that Her Majesty the Queen and Prince Albert may decide to make a short visit to Ireland to observe your military training at Curragh Camp. Carlisle will be forever in your debt that you have tipped him off to such a possibility."

Prince Teddy blanched. "Christ Almighty, it's more than a possibility. Father keeps me on such a tight leash, he could seek proof with his own eyes that I am performing my military duties with Teutonic perfection."

"Have no fear. My father will send me word if Prince Albert decides to come."

"It must be wonderful to have a warm, close relationship with one's father." The prince gave James a wistful glance. "I've always been deathly afraid of *my* father."

Charles Carrington nodded in agreement. "He puts the fear of God in me too."

"For the next three days at least, you may cast your cares and worries aside. In Dublin there will be no governors, no tutors, and no spies to report your every move," James pointed out. "Let's make a pact to drain the cup of life to the dregs."

"Hear, hear, James. You are a man after my own heart."

"Your Royal Highness, you must forgive me. I am totally unprepared for your visit."

George Howard, Earl of Carlisle, stood in the elegant reception hall of the viceregal lodge in Phoenix Park, trying to disguise the panic he was feeling.

Prince Teddy shook his hand heartily and smiled. "My

dear fellow, I abhor formality. The last thing I need is another reception of dignitaries." He handed his hat to a hovering footman and introduced his gentlemen attendants.

Carlisle summoned his majordomo and gave him orders for the kitchen staff to prepare dinner and the housekeeper to plenish chambers for the prince's party, as well as his escort of a dozen Grenadier Guards.

James Hamilton cut in smoothly, "There is no need to throw your household into turmoil, Lord Carlisle. His Highness would much prefer to stay the weekend at Dublin Castle. I shall direct the lieutenant colonel to take his guards there, with your permission. The castle can accommodate soldiers far easier than Phoenix Park."

Prince Teddy nodded his agreement. "This is just a short, *private* visit. We can share a drink and a cigar, then be on our way with none the wiser."

The look of relief on Carlisle's face as he ushered them to the library amused James.

Poor devil! The look of panic will return the moment Teddy confides that Victoria and Albert may drop in on him sometime this summer.

"This is more like it." Prince Teddy removed his coat and tossed it onto a gilded chair in the luxuriously appointed state apartment of Dublin Castle.

"Fit for a prince," James declared as he threw open the French doors that led out onto the balcony, which provided a delightful view of the River Liffey.

The castle chamberlain entered and bowed low to the prince. "Your Highness, if you would be good enough to order what you would like for dinner, I shall relay your preferences to the kitchen staff."

"My dear fellow, whatever they are serving to the castle garrison will be perfectly fine for us. Would it be too much trouble to bring us some Irish whiskey?"

"I shall plenish your chambers with the finest wines and whiskey to be found in the castle's cellars, Your Highness. I'll dispatch a servant immediately to unpack for you."

"No need for that," James Hamilton declared. "Carrington and I are the prince's official gentlemen of the bedchamber. Actually, he desires this visit be kept as quiet as possible. While the prince is here, he would prefer that you refer to him as *Baron Renfrew*. I'm sure we can rely upon your discretion?"

"Absolutely, Lord Hamilton." The chamberlain hurried out to spread the word that *Baron Renfrew* and his friends were up to no good, and were in Dublin this weekend strictly for fun and games.

"I believe you enjoyed the garrison's food more than the stuff they dish out at Buckingham Palace," James observed as he drained his tankard of ale.

"I did! My tastes are decidedly unroyal, and the company is far superior to that of my usual dining companion. In fact, Governor Bruce would have an apoplectic fit if he saw me imbibing this whiskey." Prince Teddy lit a cigar and exhaled a cloud of blue smoke.

James smiled. "Would you like to visit the Theatre Royal in Smock Alley, or would you prefer to visit a music hall? There's one handy in Fishamble Street, I believe."

"Since I've never been to a music hall, ladies singing popular songs is my choice."

"I seriously doubt if any of them will be ladies," James pointed out.

"All the more reason to attend." The prince stubbed out his cigar and laughed at his ribald remark. "Do you suppose we could walk? Just the three of us on the streets of Dublin would be a rare occurrence for me."

"I'm already a bit unsteady on my feet," Charles Carrington confessed.

"Then the fresh air will sober you up," James decided.

By the time the trio left the castle, dark had descended and Dublin's cobbled streets were filled with men and women wending their way to the myriad places that offered an evening's entertainment. Voices and laughter filled the air, proving that on Saturday night the first order of business for Dubliners was enjoyment.

When they arrived at the Fishamble Music Hall,

James paid for front row seats, and as they stepped inside, the lights went down and the curtains opened. The three well-dressed gentlemen didn't garner too much attention, as all eyes were focused on the stage.

The orchestra began to play and a beautiful female with long red hair came soaring across the stage on a swing, which continued to glide out over the front row of the audience. The rush of air caused her skirt to fly up and expose a pair of shapely legs clad in flesh-colored tights. Her voice was full-throated and filled with innuendo as she sang the slightly altered lyrics to the popular song:

> She floats through the air with the greatest of ease,
> The daring young girl on the flying trapeze,
> Her movements are graceful, all the men she does
>   please,
> And my love she has stolen away.
> Oh, the man that I loved he was handsome,
> And I tried everything him to please,
> But I could not please him one half as much,
> As the girl on the flying trapeze. . . .
> Ooooooh, she flies through the air. . . .

By this time, most of the audience was singing the chorus and swaying from side to side in time with the music and the undulations of the pretty girl on the swing.

James didn't need to watch Teddy to know he was thoroughly enjoying himself. *The poor devil has been deprived of a normal life, but he's hell-bent on catching up. He's nineteen and never had a woman.* James smiled knowingly. *All that is about to change.*

The curtains closed to reset the stage and James bought them each a bag of hot roasted chestnuts from a female vendor. This time when the curtains swung back, they revealed an Arabian scene with women reclining upon cushions. The girls wore filmy trousers and face veils, and a great cheer went up from the males in the audience. When the ladies arose to dance, the tiny bells on their bracelets and anklets tinkled merrily. The lead singer, who had a cloud of black hair decorated with beads, swayed her hips as she moved to the edge of the stage and pointed her finger at the gentlemen in the front row.

Come into the harem,
The old sultan's harem,
That's the only thing I crave.
The sultan's too old, for he's past eighty-two,
And his thousand wives need a fellow like you!
You'd never beat us
With kindness you'd treat us,
And all that I ask is a trial.
I know you'd be gallant
You're brimful of talent,
So come into the harem and smile.

She crooked her finger and beckoned, and men from the audience shouted, *I'll come, darlin',* and *I've got what you need, love.* She raised her arms. "All together now," and the entire audience sang the lyrics and swayed in time to the music.

The scenery changed with each song as colorfully painted backdrops were lowered and raised to add to the atmosphere. Amid tombstones, they sang "Goblins in the Churchyard," and a bawdy tavern setting followed this for "Bella Was a Barmaid."

The singers' costumes became scantier and the lyrics more suggestive with each successive song, until most of the audience were doubled over with laughter. The Irish loved nothing better than to sing and laugh, especially when the humor was irreverent.

In the finale, all the girls assembled onstage wearing Irish bowler hats and green tights. They sang rude words to the melody of "The Wearing of the Green":

The Corporation muck cart
Was loaded to the brim,
The driver fell in backward
And found he could not swim.

He sank right to the bottom
Just like a little stone,
And as he sank he gurgled
There's no place like home.

When Paddy went awalkin'
He wore his coat of blue,
The wind blew up his trouser leg
And showed his toodle-oo.
Oh, his toodle-oo was dirty,
He went to show the Queen,
The Queen she gave him half-a-crown
To go and get it clean!

The girls sang it again and the raucous audience
joined in. When the performance was over, they clapped
and whistled through three curtain calls. The females
formed a chorus line and did high kicks as they departed
for the final time.

James got to his feet, but the prince had enjoyed himself so much, he sat there reluctant to leave. Hamilton
smiled at his two companions. "Follow me!"

He led them backstage, where they wended their way
through props, ropes, pulleys, and scenery to the female
performers' dressing room. The door was opened before
he had a chance to knock, and the three men stepped
into the large room overflowing with costumes and chat-
tering women in various stages of undress.

Their voices went silent immediately as they gaped at
the trio. They were used to male visitors, but seldom did
such well-dressed, noble-looking gents come trawling.

The redhead who had opened the show smiled at
James. "Hello, luv! I'm Nellie. Looking for some company tonight, are you?"

"Indeed we are." James's glance traveled about the
room, quickly assessing the female pulchritude. His sense
of decency made him eliminate the youngest girls, and he
smiled at the shapely singers who looked to be in their
twenties.

Charles Carrington greeted a young woman with large breasts and dark golden hair.

"My name's Dora—how do ye do, m'lord?"

"Allow me to introduce Viscount Charles and Baron Renfrew. I'm Lord James."

"It's a pleasure to meet ye, Lord James." The dark-haired beauty gave him a saucy wink. "I'm Kitty. Is this yer first visit to the music hall?"

Baron Renfrew found his voice. "Our first of many, I sincerely hope."

"Nellie, Kitty, Dora, would you ladies care to join us for a late supper?"

The three *ladies* preened when they realized they had been chosen from the large selection available. "It would be our great pleasure, gentlemen," Nellie declared. "Would you kindly wait outside while we change?"

Prince Teddy bowed and led the way from the dressing room. "Well done, James!"

In a scant few minutes the three women emerged wearing cloaks and fashionable bonnets adorned with brilliant ostrich feathers.

"How does the Oyster Cellar in John's Lane sound?" James suggested. "It's close enough that we can walk."

"Sounds bleedin' good to me," Dora declared, slipping her arm through Carrington's.

"Sounds a real treat," Nellie said, and Kitty nodded her head in agreement.

Though it was after eleven at night, the streets were filled with people making their way from Dublin's many theaters to the various public houses that provided food, drink, laughter, and camaraderie.

Their party was shown to a table that seated six, and the women waited politely for the men to order. "What would you like, ladies?"

"What do you suggest, Lord James?" Nellie was being cautious. Though clearly the men were well-heeled, she didn't want to sound greedy.

"How about oysters and champagne?"

Three pairs of manicured eyebrows rose. Most men

were willing to spring for ale, or even gin, but never offered champagne. "Are you sure?" Nellie asked.

Renfrew smiled indulgently. "My dearest ladies, you may have anything you fancy."

"In that case, I'll have cowheels and champagne," Dora decided.

The prince had no idea that people actually consumed cows' heels, but he did not question her. Nellie ordered oysters and Kitty asked for prawns and champagne.

The men all wanted oysters, but only the prince ordered champagne. The other two preferred ale.

The Oyster Cellar had a pair of fiddlers and the customers' voices rang out with song. Since the trio of females from the music hall had already sung for their supper, they were content to eat, drink, and be merry.

James kept a casual eye on the prince, who he knew was having the time of his life. The prince had long been starved of fun and laughter and was making up for lost time. He ate more oysters, drank more champagne, and laughed longer and harder at the witty repartee than any other patron in the room.

Finally, when everything had been devoured, they were the only customers left in the cellar. James paid the reckoning and generously tipped their waiter.

"It would be fun to continue the party." Dora reached for her cloak, both ready and willing to pay the piper. "Where are you gentlemen staying?"

"At the castle." James stood and placed Kitty's cloak about her shoulders, then moved around the table to Nellie. "Would you care to join us?"

The females were momentarily silent, as their estimation of the English gentlemen shot up a few rungs. Each wondered hopefully if she was being entertained by royalty.

James murmured in Nellie's ear, "I'm holding auditions for a starring role."

She searched his face. "Then lead on, Macduff."

As the group got close to Dublin Castle, the females fell back to walk together so they could exchange their thoughts. Nellie confided what Lord James had said about holding auditions for a starring role, and Kitty cautioned that the nobles likely hadn't given their real names. Dora murmured, "I don't give a shyte who they are. They're important toffs, they've got money, and that's good enough fer yours truly."

"I think Viscount Charles has singled you out, Dora."

"I *know* he has! But I'll still audition for Lord Bleedin' James."

When the young women were ushered into the state apartments of Dublin Castle, they were agog at the luxurious chambers. They were invited to make themselves comfortable in the spacious drawing room, and they removed their cloaks and bonnets.

"Before you sit down, let me show you where the amenities are." James took the trio along a carpeted hall, which led to the wing that held the bedchambers and bathrooms.

Dora patted her curls into place, and her eyes lit with mischief. "I'll audition first."

James grinned. "By all means." He waited until Nellie and Kitty went into the bathroom to freshen up, then took Dora into a small private room. The moment the door shut, she closed the distance between them, slipped her arms about his neck, rubbed her breasts against his chest, and offered her mouth for his ravishment.

James cupped her breast with his palm, but he did not kiss her. "If you were given the choice between two young nobles, one with sexual experience and the other without, which would you prefer?"

Dora looked incredulous. "A noble without experience? There's no such animal!" Her hand moved down to stroke his cock, and proved her point.

James chuckled. "Would you be amenable to spending the night with Baron Renfrew, if you were invited?"

"I'd have no objection. But I think Viscount Charles was more smitten with me."

James nodded. "I rather think so too, Dora." He escorted her to the door. "Would you ask Nellie to join me?"

The beauteous redhead glided in and closed the door softly. "What is the role I'm auditioning for, Lord James?"

"I serve a gentleman who's had absolutely no experience with women. He needs a tutor who will guide him to assume the dominant role and make him feel like a man."

"He needs a bed partner who will be playful rather than aggressive?"

"Exactly."

"You are speaking of Baron Renfrew," she said shrewdly. "How old is he?"

"Nineteen. Do you believe you could fulfill this delicate role, Nellie?"

"Yes, I would have no difficulty. Who *is* Baron Renfrew?"

"That's rather confidential."

Nellie's eyes widened. "Oh Jaysus, is it *Bertie*, the quayn's son?"

"Never call him *Bertie*. It is what his mother calls him and he detests it. He prefers Teddy." James asked earnestly, "Will you provide the affection he so desperately seeks?"

"It would be my great honor, my lord."

"I am in your debt. What's your full name, my dear?"

"It's Nellie Clifden, singer and actress extraordinaire."

James winked. "I am counting on it."

When he opened the door, he saw that Kitty was still waiting, but Dora had returned to the drawing room. "Thank you, Nellie. Join the others and I'll be along shortly."

When he and Kitty were alone, she looked at him ruefully. "You've already chosen Nellie." Her dark lashes swept down, hiding the disappointment in her eyes. "Why didn't I get a chance at the role, Lord James?"

He lifted her fingers to his lips and as she raised her lashes, he smiled into her eyes.

"Because I was saving you for myself, sweetheart."

Chapter 2

"You've taken to this military camp like an otter takes to water." James handed Prince Teddy a glass of claret.

"A fortnight back when I was greeted by a salute fired by the field battery of Horse Artillery, followed by a grand review and a brigade review, I feared the Grenadier Guards would hate me to a man. But once all the blasted formality was out of the way, they welcomed me as one of them."

"It's because you don't put on royal airs. You love nothing better than to share a drink and a smoke with them, and are not averse to telling a lewd joke."

"They are good chaps. They don't even resent me getting these grand quarters that belonged to Lord Seaton when he was commander of the Irish forces."

Charles Carrington lit a cigar. "The only fly in the ointment is the pair of Grenadier Guards standing sentry outside the door."

James smiled. "They are no problem. A sovereign a day guarantees they will turn a blind eye to any illicit activity we care to indulge."

"I like being here. My life at Buckingham Palace is a prison compared to this. I enjoy the army exercises each morning. Riding and target practice are enjoyable, and even weapon cleaning and learning how to care for my own mount give me satisfaction."

"Racket ball in the afternoon and gambling in the evening aren't hard to take either," James declared.

"I had no idea that the Curragh Plain was used to train racehorses. The horseshoe-shaped course is a perfect six furlongs. I'm a good judge of horseflesh—I've won most of the bets I've placed," Teddy said proudly.

"Well, if you gentlemen will excuse me, I'm off to enjoy the hospitality of the *Wrens of the Curragh*." Carrington drained his claret. "Enjoy your card game."

Teddy stared after Charles as the door closed. "Are *Wrens* what I think they are?"

"Yes, they are prostitutes who service the military men." James noticed the speculative expression on Teddy's face. "I wouldn't recommend it, Your Highness—far too indiscreet. Why don't you send an invitation to Nellie?"

"By God, if you could arrange that, James, I would be forever in your debt."

Within twenty-four hours, Nellie Clifden arrived in a coach that Lord Hamilton provided. James made arrangements for the songbird to stay at the nearby Magdalene Abbey, and that night when dark descended, his fellow officers took great delight in conspiring to smuggle Nellie into the private quarters of the Prince of Wales.

By the end of a sennight the late visits became a routine part of Prince Teddy's military training schedule. The Grenadier Guards closed ranks to keep the royal secret from their commander in chief, and from the prince's governor, Major General Bruce.

"James, you reign supreme among gentlemen of the bedchamber." Teddy removed his uniform, and donned a smoking jacket. "I must think of a suitable reward."

"Well, there is something I've been meaning to ask, Your Highness. Now that you have settled in here, I would like your permission to visit my constituents in Donegal."

"By all means, James. Since you are in Ireland, it would be remiss to ignore the people you represent in Parliament. I can dispense with your services for a time, since you have provided me with all the creature comforts."

"Thank you. I warrant two or three weeks will be adequate to deal with my Donegal constituents' petitions. I should be back by the end of July, or early August at the latest."

"Your birthday is in August—we'll celebrate. How old will you be, James?"

"I shall be an old man of twenty-three."

"I wish I were twenty-three." The prince gazed into his glass of claret.

"Don't wish your life away, Teddy. Savor every day, and especially the nights."

The prince grinned. "I'll drink to that."

Grosvenor Square, London
July 23, 1861

"I'm eighteen today!" Lady Anne Howe welcomed Frances and Maud Hamilton to her birthday party. "Hello, John Claud." *Your name wasn't included on the invitation.*

"Are you sure you're eighteen, Anne?" Frances asked doubtfully. "I thought you were younger than I am. How old are you *really*?"

"It's rude to ask a lady her age," John Claud chastised his sister.

Frances Hamilton rolled her eyes. "He insisted on escorting us even though our house is just around the corner."

"My brother Montagu will be happy you came, John Claud. Spending the afternoon with a gaggle of debutantes is akin to torture on the rack to him. Ah, speak of the devil, and in a puff of brimstone, here he is."

"Hello, John Claud." Montagu shook hands. "Shall we take refuge in the library?"

"I hope your father joins us. I never tire of hearing about his years as lord chamberlain when he was in charge of Buckingham Palace, Windsor Castle, and all who held office. He is a well of information to anyone interested in a royal appointment."

The young ladies moved into the drawing room and greeted Anne's other friends, Florence Paget and her sister, who were the daughters of the Earl of Uxbridge. Though Lady Florence would soon be nineteen, she looked younger than the other girls because she was rather small.

Frances lowered her voice. "John Claud professes interest in your father, but I think he came to see you. My brother is smitten with you, even if you are only *seventeen*."

"You are quite wrong, Frances. I have decided to be eighteen," Anne informed her friend, "so that I shall be presented to the queen along with you this year."

"How the devil can you arrange that?"

"You forget, my sister Emily is lady-in-waiting to Queen Victoria." *The real truth is that Father has so many offspring he doesn't have the faintest idea how old I am. Last night when Mother announced it was my eighteenth birthday, everyone accepted it.*

Maud threw Anne a look of alarm. "Emily isn't coming to your party, is she?"

"Have no fear—she condescended to come last night to the family birthday dinner."

"Did she bring you a gift?"

"Unfortunately, yes. She gave me a wine-colored shawl that clashes with my screamy-colored hair, knowing full well it will make me look hideous. Tomorrow I shall take it back to Madame Mantalini's and exchange it for one of pale lavender."

The Hamilton sisters greatly admired Anne. She was unconventional and passionate about everything from friendship to fashion, and even designed some of her own clothes.

"Did Emily bring any gossip from Buckingham Palace?" Frances asked avidly.

"As a matter of fact she did. She loves nothing better than impressing her older brothers and their wives with royal gossip." Anne lowered her voice. "She said that the queen and the Princess Royal are conspiring to find a bride for the Prince of Wales. Emily says the queen and Albert favor a German princess, but Princess Vicky disagrees. She wrote that the *Danish* royal family has lovely daughters."

"The Prince of Wales is very young, but then Princess Vicky was married when she was barely seventeen. She was engaged to Frederick of Prussia when she was fourteen."

"My own mother was married when she was sixteen," Anne confided. "Father was more than *three* times her age. He truly robbed the cradle."

"Do you think it was a love match?" eleven-year-old Maud asked innocently.

"Well, I don't doubt that Father was enamored of *her*, but I warrant she would have preferred a young husband over one who was on the wrong side of fifty, and had a grown family of ten from his first wife, to boot."

"You're more fortunate than us," Florence Paget pointed out. "Our father has had *three* wives. Our new stepmother is shockingly young."

"We must be the exception," Frances Hamilton said. "I think our father is only a year older than Mother."

"You are lucky. Your parents have a *perfect* marriage. It's obvious theirs was a love match. I warrant Lady Lu and the duke are *still* in love. That's the kind of marriage I want!" Anne declared passionately. Ever since Anne met James at Windsor Castle, she always found her mind drifting to thoughts of him. He seemed to embody everything she wanted in a man, unlike anyone else she'd ever met. Though she hadn't seen him for three years, an image of her friends' brother Lord Hamilton came full-blown to her, evoking a wistful sigh. "When will your brother James be home from Ireland?"

"At the end of August, I believe. He'll certainly be back before Parliament goes into session. Why don't the two of us make a trip to the visitors' gallery?"

"Oh, Frances, I would love to attend. That's so thoughtful of you," Anne said.

"She isn't being thoughtful," Maud declared. "She wants to look over all the eligible bachelors who are members of Parliament, if I know my sister."

"Exactly!" Frances declared. "By then Anne and I will have been presented to the queen and will be eligible to attend all the balls of the fashionable winter Season."

Anne caught her breath, recognizing the opportunity that the ball presented. One that she had been thinking about for quite some time. *Lord James will definitely be in attendance at the Hamiltons' annual ball. I must find a way to make him partner me in a dance. I shall count the hours until I see him again.*

Curragh Camp
Kildare, Ireland

"Good God, James, I've been counting the hours until you got back." Prince Teddy grabbed Hamilton by the shoulders. "Something disastrous has happened. Bloody old Bruce wrote a report to my father and told him about Nellie Clifden. My parents are on their way to Ireland. What in *hellfire* am I going to do?"

"Don't panic, Your Highness. I'll think of something." James opened a letter from his father informing him of Victoria and Albert's visit. *Better late than never, I warrant.* "I presume Nellie is safely back in Dublin?"

The look of dismay on Teddy's face told James that Miss Clifden was still within fucking distance. "The first order of business is to get rid of the evidence, so I'll take it from here." James glanced at Carrington and tried to overlook his uselessness.

"Welcome to Ireland, Your Gracious Majesty." James Hamilton bowed low before Queen Victoria. Then he shook hands with Prince Albert and bowed his head. "His Highness the Prince of Wales insisted on moving into mess quarters so you would be able to enjoy the best suite of rooms that Curragh Camp has to offer."

The queen gave a tight-lipped smile, and Albert said, "Thank you, Lord Hamilton. Bertie should have been here to greet us. Kindly tell him to present himself."

James lowered his voice confidentially. "The Prince of Wales was part of the field battery of the Horse Artillery who fired the welcome salute when you arrived." James noted that Prince Albert failed to look impressed. "I'm sure His Highness will be here the moment his commander dismisses him." He smiled disarmingly. "I'll attend him and let him know how pleased you are with the accommodation."

James found Prince Teddy watching a horse race. He gave him the unwelcome news that his parents had arrived and were asking to see him. He told him that he had placated his father with the lie about him being part of the welcome salute.

The prince paled. "I wish I didn't have to see them! Stay with me, James. I need you for support."

It's high time you replaced that wishbone with a backbone, milado.

James nodded to the guards standing sentry outside the suite, opened the door, and allowed the prince to precede him.

Teddy bowed to the queen. "Mother, welcome to Curragh." He looked at his father and nodded his head respectfully. "Your visit is a pleasant surprise."

Victoria pressed her lips together. "We doubt that, Bertie. Your father wishes to discuss a certain disturbing matter that has come to our attention. I shall withdraw until the distasteful business is resolved."

Albert waited until the queen left the room. "Major General Bruce has reported your immoral behavior. I am shocked you would disgrace the royal family by consorting with a woman of ill repute. You will cease and desist immediately!"

The prince's face turned red. "It is a pack of lies!"

James immediately stepped forward. "Your Highness, I feel compelled to confess that the female involved was here at my invitation. The prince nobly took the blame for my indiscretion. I assure you that my lapse in judgment will not be repeated."

The prince consort stared at James with moral outrage. "I see." His glance did not soften as it fell upon his son. "I am sure your mother will be vastly relieved when I explain the matter."

The young Prince of Wales and his attendants were scheduled to leave Ireland at the end of August. The night before they were to embark, James Hamilton lay in bed with his arms folded behind his head, contemplating his return to London.

Teddy will return to his royal apartment at Buckingham Palace, but it's past time for me to move from my family's home and set up my own establishment.

The reason he had been reluctant to do so long ago was John Claud. Since they were boys, James had taken on the protective role of guardian to his younger brother, but the words they'd exchanged the night before he left for Ireland clearly showed him that his brother was chafing at their relationship. *Now that John Claud is almost nineteen, he thinks himself a man, and rightly so.*

The scene of their last meeting rose up before him, and he winced at the words his brother had thrown at him in response to what James had thought a caring question:

"I'll be gone almost three months. Will you be all right?"

"You arrogant son of a bitch, James. I don't need the all-powerful Lord Bloody Hamilton to hold my hand. Have you any idea what it's like to be constantly compared with the gifted, accomplished heir, and come up wanting every time?"

James listened in stunned disbelief at his brother's animosity.

"Just because I had a couple of fits when I was a boy doesn't give you the right to act as my keeper for the rest of my life. I grew out of the bloody things by the time I was ten. I no longer need you to run interference for me!"

James held up his hand and said quietly, "I wasn't referring to fits. I wondered if you'd be all right for money."

"Oh." John Claud laughed, his anger melting away like snow in summer. "I'm sorry, James. It's not easy having an

older brother who excels at riding, shooting, fighting, and fucking."

James smiled into the darkness. *Once I remove myself from Hampden House, John Claud will come into his own.*

When James arrived in London, he leased a Georgian town house on the corner of White Horse Street that was close to the palace and Green Park. Then he went to Hampden House to inform his parents and to pack his clothes and belongings.

At dinner, his parents congratulated him on his wise decision. When his siblings could not hide their envy, he assured his brothers that their turn would come.

"Even before you went to Ireland, you spent more time at the palace than you did at home," his sister Frances remarked, "so we shall see no less of you than we always have."

"We shall see *more* of him," his mother declared. "James, darling, you have a standing invitation for dinner every Friday, or whatever night suits you."

"I accept your generous invitation, Mother. Now if you'll excuse me, the hour grows late and I must go up. I have a good deal of packing to do."

James Hamilton's dark brows drew together as he heard the scratching on his bedchamber door. The hour was close to midnight and he had assumed everyone, including the servants, had retired. He opened the door quietly and was surprised to see the young maid with an armful of shirts. "Jenny, you shouldn't still be working."

She slipped into the room. "I starched these just the way you like them, my lord."

"Thank you kindly." He took the shirts and set them on his dresser. "You should be abed."

"I . . . I just wanted to say good-bye. You bein' away in Ireland with the prince for three months and now that you have your own house, I may not see . . ." Her voice trailed off.

"Is something wrong, Jenny?"

"No . . . no . . . everything is perfect." Contradicting her words, her eyes flooded with tears.

James took her hands and led her to a chair. "Tell me," he urged.

"Everything is perfectly *awful*," she whispered miserably. "I . . . I'm in trouble."

James grasped the situation immediately. "Are you sure, Jenny?"

She nodded emphatically. "Very sure, my lord." She sought his eyes. "I can't stay here, it would cause a terrible scandal, but I have nowhere else to go."

"Have you told anyone?"

She pressed her lips together. "I thought about confiding in your mother. Lady Lu can be very understanding, but your father would go mad that one of his sons . . ."

James handed her his handkerchief, and Jenny blew her nose. "So I thought it best to wait until you got home, my lord."

"Yes, you did right, Jenny." He paced to the window, then paced back again. "It will be all right, my dear. I'll arrange a place for you at one of my married sisters'. They all have lots of babies and won't mind one more."

Jenny's eyes lit with hope. "Are you sure, my lord? I don't want to get you into trouble."

"Absolutely sure. Though I think it wisest to keep the details between ourselves. Now, which sister? You have two choices. Jane is Countess of Dalkeith with that great mansion in Whitehall, or there's Harry, Countess of Lichfield, who resides in St. James's Square. Jane is young and sweet-tempered, but Harry will do anything for me."

"I think . . . I think Lady Harriet would be more understanding, perhaps."

"And forgiving. Good choice . . . Harry it is. Go and pack a small bag and I'll take you round there tonight. Your other stuff can be forwarded later."

"Oh, Lord James, I thank you ever so much."

"No thanks, Jenny. Under the circumstances, it's the least I can do."

Chapter 3

Buckingham Palace
September 1, 1861

"Damn and blast it all! The bloody powers that be, namely, my mother the queen and my father the royal consort, have refused to let me join the Grenadier Guards."

James Hamilton already knew the outcome of the prince's audience with his parents. Though James's father, the Duke of Abercorn, had recommended the royal heir have a year or so of military service after his training in Ireland, Prince Albert decided it would afford his son too much freedom, when clearly discipline was what he needed.

"'Tis a great pity they deem the army unfitting for a royal prince of the realm. You have my sympathy, Teddy."

"To add insult to injury I'm being sent to study in Cambridge under the governorship of bloody Major General Bruce!" He kicked a footstool across the room and it hit the wall with a loud crash.

A moment later, a low knock came on the door, and the prince's sister Vicky, who was visiting from Germany, entered the room. "Someone's in a temper." She sent James a flirtatious smile.

He reciprocated immediately by taking her hand and bowing over it. Though the twenty-year-old Princess Royal had been married for three years, James knew she was still enamored of him.

Her brother snorted. "I'm in a temper because I'm being forced to attend Cambridge to further my studies, when what I want is a military career!"

"Since Father has been the chancellor of Cambridge University for over a dozen years, it is only natural he would like you to study there. However, I believe you can postpone Cambridge for a month by returning to Germany with me. I shall persuade Father to let you come to Strelitz to observe the military maneuvers."

Teddy's scowl was replaced with a look of calculation. "I am well aware that Father can refuse you nothing, but if I come, you must promise not to introduce me to any German princesses."

"No Germans. I swear on my honor."

"You have something up your sleeve," her brother said with suspicion.

"I'm trying my best to rid Father and Mother of their obsession that your future bride be German. There are other princesses in Europe, believe it or not."

"I'm nineteen. I don't wish to marry. The last thing I want is a fat, foreign bride."

"I'm not setting a trap for you, Teddy. Which will it be, Cambridge or Strelitz?"

"I'd love to come for the military maneuvers, Vicky, but only if you swear there will be no *matrimonial* maneuvers."

She smiled, walked to the door, and beckoned James. "Promise you'll accompany my brother?" she murmured.

"I must take my seat in Parliament this week," James evaded.

"Teddy is eager for the maneuvers. It would be a shame to disappoint him."

James smiled and acceded, knowing Vicky had her own maneuvers in mind.

*   *   *

On Friday evening, when James had dinner with his family, he greeted his mother with an affectionate kiss.

Lady Lu stroked his cheek. "It's lovely to see you, James. I missed you this summer. I'm glad you're back in England."

"Not for long." He waited until his sisters were seated, then sat down between his father and his brother John Claud. "I'm off to Germany with the Prince of Wales. His sister has invited him to Strelitz to observe military maneuvers."

"But Parliament opens tomorrow," John Claud pointed out.

Their mother laughed. "According to my brother Lord John, nothing much happens after summer recess. The members sniff each other like a pack of curs wondering who will be top dog, and which members will drink themselves to death before the year is up."

"I'm sorry that Prince Albert and the queen couldn't be persuaded to let Teddy join the military. I deem it a suitable occupation for the heir to the throne," Abercorn declared.

"He loathes the idea of returning to university under the governorship of Major General Bruce, so he jumped at Vicky's invitation to visit Strelitz, providing he doesn't have to meet any German princesses," James added with a grin.

His sister Frances, who had been listening avidly, cut in, "I heard some gossip from my friend Anne. Her sister Emily, lady-in-waiting to Queen Victoria, said she heard that Princess Vicky suggested that a princess from the Danish royal family would be a good match for the Prince of Wales, and she was eager to arrange a meeting between them."

"Well, I'll be damned. No wonder the queen gave permission for Teddy to go to Germany. The Princess Royal swore she had no ulterior motive."

Abercorn winked at James. "You should be onto Vicky's wicked ways by now."

John Claud laughed. He and James shared many secrets, and he knew all about his brother's indecent encounter with the sexually precocious princess. "Let's hope *she* is onto *James's* wicked ways."

"Oh, I'm sure she is," Lady Lu purred. "Now that she is safely married, she is allowed her peccadilloes."

After dinner, James joined his father and brother in the library to share a brandy and apprise them of the prince's training with the Grenadier Guards at Curragh Camp. "He did splendidly. He fit right in because he is open, kindhearted, and loves to laugh."

Abercorn nodded. "His father was so incensed when he got Bruce's report about his son consorting with the opposite sex that he rushed to Ireland."

"I took care of the matter. I believe I gave Prince Albert a satisfactory explanation."

John Claud was well aware of his brother's propensity for covering up indiscretions. "What really happened?"

"I took Teddy to the music hall and auditioned a bevy of songbirds to choose who would rid him of his virginity."

Abercorn's eyes crinkled with appreciation and John Claud choked on his brandy.

"Have you any idea how long I've anticipated this rendezvous?" Princess Vicky's possessive fingers toyed with the black curls on James's chest, and her tongue shot out to lick over a flat, copper nipple.

I have an inkling. James smiled lazily, demonstrating that he was in no hurry, though she was in a fever of need. His hand cupped her full breast; his thumb stroked the crest that had turned hard and erectile the moment he'd touched her. When he made no attempt to kiss her, she rubbed her mons against his hard thigh, and licked her lips in anticipation.

He bent his head, and when his mouth was just inches from hers, he murmured, "Tell me about the bride you have chosen for Teddy."

"I have no idea what you're talking about." She was panting, making her heavy breasts rise and fall.

"I think you do, my sweet."

Her fingers closed around his rampant cock. "I'll tell you . . . after," she gasped.

"Before."

She moaned softly, realizing he would not give her what she craved until he got what he wanted. "Frederick and I have become acquainted with the royal family of Denmark. I have made friends with one of their daughters, Princess Alexandra."

"A fat, foreign princess is anathema to your brother."

"Alix is slim as a reed. She is lovely, with a profusion of golden brown hair. She would be perfect for him in every way."

"And?" James prompted, reaching between her legs and slipping a finger into her hot, wet sheath.

She arched against him. All she could think of was having his magnificent cock inside her. "And what? Fuck me!"

"And you have arranged for Princess Alexandra to be in Strelitz for your own maneuvers."

"How did you guess?" she panted.

"You are as easy to read as a book," he teased.

She licked her lips. "The *Kama Sutra*?"

His cock stirred. "Is that what you've learned in Germany?"

"Oh, James, I just want Teddy to meet her. She's only sixteen, so there's no rush for her to marry. I'm just thinking of the future."

He grinned. "In that case, have at me." He lay back, and was most gratified that the voluptuous Crown Princess of Prussia did not hesitate. She lifted herself on him and plunged down with a cry that demonstrated her avid sensuality.

Buckingham Palace

Lady Anne Curzon-Howe's eyes sparkled with pleasure as she curtsied low before Her Royal Majesty Queen Victoria.

The queen's gaze traveled from the delicate gauze roses adorning the classic white gown, to the fashionable white ostrich feathers adorning the red-gold tresses of the debutante before her. "Welcome to our court, Lady Anne. I had no idea Lady Emily had such a lovely sister. Your gown is most elegant."

Hours of practice with the three-foot train had turned Anne's performance into perfection. "Thank you, Your Majesty. I designed it myself."

The queen looked impressed. "We could use a young lady with such talent at our court."

Anne bit her lip. *Curse my tongue. The last thing I want is to be one of your ladies-in-waiting.* A rush of relief swept over her as the queen nodded her dismissal, and she joined her friend Lady Frances Hamilton, who had been presented before her.

"I can't wait for your ball tomorrow night, since our mothers have invited exactly the same bachelors. I hope your brother Montagu asks me for a dance."

"If he doesn't, you must ask him," Anne advised.

"You are so unconventional. Would *you* dare do such a thing?"

"Just watch me. Next week at your ball I have decided to march up to your brother James and ask him to partner me."

"James won't be there. He's gone to Germany with the Prince of Wales and the Princess Royal."

Anne's face showed her dismay. "Oh damn, blast, and set fire to everything! I was so looking forward to seeing him again. Why did the prince have to go to Germany?"

"Supposedly to watch military maneuvers, but didn't your sister Emily mention a plan to introduce him to Princess Alexandra of Denmark?"

"So she did. I shall try to quiz Emily about it tomorrow night."

"She's coming, then?"

"Ha, she'll be there with bells on ready to criticize my mother's social skills. My other half sisters will be there too, looking down their long, condescending noses."

"Isn't Georgiana the Duchess of Beaufort?"

"Yes, the duke is such a dry stick! But my other brother-in-law the Earl of Westmorland is a different kettle of fish. Henry Fane owns racehorses and belongs to the Jockey Club. He's a good sport who isn't averse to placing a bet for me."

Frances's eyes widened. "You're allowed to gamble?"

"Of course I'm not allowed. It's all on the QT."

The Duchess of Abercorn stood conversing with Lady Curzon-Howe. "Being presented at court used to be such a prestigious social event. It was a gala evening at the palace, with everyone in formal attire, and the supper rooms offering endless buffets of desserts and imported wines." She glanced at the glass of punch she held and shuddered delicately. "These drawing rooms are abysmal. I feel rather sorry for today's debutantes. Fun and frivolity have fallen victim to Queen Victoria's one and only social rule: NO SCANDAL!"

The girls joined their mothers and overheard the last part of the conversation. Anne's eyes sparkled. "I adore your mother. She says the most outrageous things. I have decided to take her as my role model."

At her debut ball in the Grosvenor Square mansion, Lady Anne stood in the receiving line with her parents. Their majordomo, Jenkins, announced the names of their guests as they stepped into the ballroom. Anne wore her presentation gown, but she had embroidered brilliant green dragonflies to flit among the white roses. Emily was outraged that Anne wasn't in pristine white, and had voiced her feelings about the matter in no uncertain terms. She had arrived an hour before the ball was to begin, and had almost brought her younger sister to tears.

"You are never allowing your daughter to wear such an inappropriate gown to her debut ball?" Emily gave her stepmother a venomous look that showed exactly how much she disliked her father's young wife.

"I think Anne's gown is lovely."

"And *green* of all colors. It's as if you are advertising to all of London that she is Irish! As if the blatant color of her hair doesn't already shout it to the world."

"Her Majesty the Queen complimented her gown," Lady Howe said serenely.

"And that's another thing! She pushed herself forward and announced to the queen that she designed it herself...no doubt in the hope that she would be invited to become a royal lady-in-waiting. Let me assure you, there is little chance of that."

Anne closed her eyes and said a prayer of thanks.

At that moment, Earl Howe arrived on the scene. He kissed his wife and turned to Emily. "Isn't Anne the prettiest debutante you've ever seen?"

When Emily turned on her heel and left the room, the lump in Anne's throat miraculously dissolved. She went on tiptoe and kissed his brow. "Thank you, Father."

As the guests were announced, Anne received so many admiring glances that her anxiety was replaced by happiness, and she assured herself that Emily was envious.

When Lady Florence Paget and her parents arrived, Anne was able to see for herself how much older the Earl of Uxbridge looked than his new countess.

As custom demanded, Earl Howe partnered his daughter in her first dance, but in deference to his sixty-eight years, the musicians had been instructed to make it short. Then the young bachelors swarmed about Anne and filled up her dance card. Since she and Frances had spent an entire afternoon studying the list of eligible nobles, she had no trouble identifying George Churchill, Marquis of Blandford; Henry Fitzmaurice, the young Earl of Kerry; and Edward Turnour, Earl of Winterton.

The Hamiltons arrived fashionably late, and Anne crossed the ballroom to greet them. "Thank you so much for coming."

Gallant as always, the Duke of Abercorn kissed her hand. "It is our pleasure, Lady Anne." He lowered his voice. "I never miss a chance to dance with my wife."

Anne sighed. "Frances, your father is so romantic."

John Claud took possession of her hand. "It runs in the family."

"Here comes Montagu. He's been looking for you."

"Hello, Montagu. If you'll partner my sister, I'll partner yours."

Anne laughed and took back her hand. "John Claud, your gallantry overwhelms me, but I've promised this dance to Spencer Cavendish." She turned and smiled at the Marquis of Hartington, who was heir to the dukedom of Devonshire.

John Claud muttered, "Hartington's at least twenty-eight."

As a dutiful sister, Frances couldn't resist taunting him. "Anne admires older men." She smiled at Montagu and led him onto the ballroom floor.

John Claud made a mental note to stop taking Lady Anne for granted, and went in search of her father, Earl Howe, and her older brothers to curry favor.

Anne's second dance partner was young Henry Rawdon. He had already inherited a massive fortune in the previous year, when he became the 4th Marquis of Hastings. She soon learned that his hobby was purchasing expensive racehorses. "I have someone you must meet, Henry."

Anne took him by the hand and went in search of her brother-in-law. "Henry, meet Henry. Your Christian names aren't the only thing you have in common," she told the marquis. "This is my sister's husband, Henry Fane, Earl of Westmorland. He's the keenest judge of racehorse flesh in England."

Hastings eagerly shook Westmorland's hand. "Aren't you a member of the Jockey Club, my lord?"

"Indeed I am."

"The very chap I wanted to meet. By any chance do you suppose you could sponsor a new racehorse owner for membership?"

"Are you a betting man, Hastings?"

"Do dogs have fleas?" Henry laughed.

Anne tapped her brother-in-law on the shoulder. "Before you submerge yourselves in the dissolute sport of kings, I have a favor to ask. How about placing a bet for me in the St. Leger?"

"It would be my pleasure, sweetheart."

"Be warned. One of these days I intend to join you at Doncaster or Newmarket."

Fane winked, and rubbed the side of his nose to indicate her secret was safe.

The first ball of the fashionable winter Season attracted the crème de la crème of Society.

While the young people danced, their elders gathered in groups to converse. The males spoke of race meets and politics, while the females gossiped. Since the drink flowed freely, a good deal of laughter occasionally drowned out the music.

Anne's next partner was Henry Fitzmaurice, the young Earl of Kerry. Though he wasn't as tall as the Hamilton men, he had broad shoulders and brilliant blue eyes.

"So many gentlemen are called Henry that I think I shall call you Harry." Anne's eyes sparkled with mischief. "Harry Kerry has such a lovely ring to it."

"I don't much care for Henry either—my friends call me Fitz. Would you consider an outing with me, Lady Anne?"

"I most certainly would, Fitz. What do you have in mind?"

"We can do whatever would give you pleasure—the museum, the Tower, or how about the boating lake in Regent's Park?"

"They all sound wonderful, but by the width of your shoulders I warrant you enjoy rowing. If you take me to Regent's Park, I'll bring my sketchbook and draw some of the swans and herons."

"Lovely. I shall call for you Sunday afternoon, if that's convenient."

"You have your own perch phaeton, don't you, Fitz? Mother drives her own carriage in the park and taught me to drive last year. If you would be generous enough to let me take the reins, I would be forever in your debt."

*   *   *

After two hours of dancing, Anne, Frances, and Florence withdrew to powder their noses and compare notes. "You have such lovely, long legs, Anne. I have to stand on a stool to see in the mirror," Lady Florence complained.

"It doesn't stop you from dancing. My brother calls you the *Pocket Venus*."

"Which brother? You have eight," Florence pointed out.

"As far as I'm concerned, Montagu is my *only* brother. The other seven are half brothers. They look down their aristocratic noses at me, with the exception of Leicester. He's my youngest half brother, the only one who's unmarried."

"Is he the handsome devil in the dashing officer's green uniform?" Frances asked.

"Yes, he's an officer in the prestigious Prince Albert's Rifle Brigade."

"I find it hard to resist a man in a uniform," Frances confided.

"Blandford Churchill is a good dancer. He told me he has just joined the Horse Guards, if you are looking for a man in a uniform."

"Marlborough's heir is the best catch in London," Frances declared avidly.

Anne laughed. "He does remind me of a trout."

"Aren't you interested?"

"Not in the least."

"Good, then I shall put him on my list along with the Marquis of Hartington. By the way, who is that beautiful woman Harty was dancing with?"

"That's Louise, Duchess of Manchester. She used to be wardrobe mistress to the queen. The duke and my mother are distant cousins. Their family name is Montagu—that's where my brother gets his name." Anne gave her friend a quizzical glance. "Frances, do you *really* have a list?"

"Of course."

"Who are on this list?" Anne asked with amused curiosity.

"All the nobles who are first sons."

"Isn't that rather mercenary?"

"Oh, it's not the wealth, it is the title that is important. Since my sister Harry is the Countess of Lichfield, Trixy is Countess of Durham, and Jane is Countess of Dalkeith, I cannot let them outdo me."

"Then poor Montagu doesn't stand a chance?"

"He's an eighth son! I don't dare lose my heart to him."

"How on earth can you control your heart? I'm sure I couldn't, nor would I want to."

"Ah, but you have a passionate nature, Anne. I am more practical. My head will rule my emotions. I shall map out a plan and follow it."

"While I shall be swept away by a grand passion!" Anne declared dramatically. "And every woman in London will envy me."

"I certainly shall," Lady Florence bemoaned. "My parents are urging me to make a match with young Henry Chaplin. I won't get to choose."

"The viscount is heir to a fortune," Frances pointed out.

It tugged at Anne's heartstrings that her friend Florence would be pushed into an arranged marriage, and she tried her best to take the sting out of it. "Yes, Viscount Chaplin will inherit a great deal of land. Some in Lincolnshire, and some in Leicestershire that runs parallel to my father's country estate," Anne assured her.

Florence sighed. "I shouldn't complain. Most marriages are arranged."

Mine won't be arranged, Anne vowed passionately. *I shall choose my own husband!*

John Claud Hamilton waited impatiently for Lady Anne to return to the ballroom. She had danced continually with one eligible bachelor after another, and he decided he'd waited long enough. He crossed the floor and stopped before her. "I would like the pleasure of this dance, Lady Anne."

"I believe I promised it to John Beresford, my lord."
Anne looked at her dance card to make sure.

"Let me see." He captured her wrist and untied the
ribbon that held her dance card. He glanced at it, pretended to read it, then tore it into pieces.

She was amused by his audacity and when the orchestra began to play, she moved into his waiting arms. In
contrast to the lively quadrilles and cotillions played earlier, waltz music now filled the air. The slow, sweeping
movements of the dance made her feel languid. Anne
had the sensation that she was floating and she closed
her eyes, allowing the romantic music to flow about her.

Her heart began to beat in time to the music, and she
imagined that she was dancing with James Hamilton. His
arms tightened about her and she felt him draw her
close. With her eyelids lowered, she conjured his dark
image and was mesmerized by his closeness. As he bent
his head toward her, she shivered with anticipation and
opened her lips in invitation. When his mouth touched
hers, her eyelashes fluttered, and she whispered his name
with longing. "James."

She raised her lashes and gazed into the fierce eyes of
John Claud. She realized immediately what she had
done, and knew she must say something.

"How dare you kiss me?"

"How dare you mistake me for my profligate brother?"

"I did no such thing. I simply said his name to punish
you."

He smiled to cover his fury. "You are a beautiful little
liar!"

"What about *your* lies?"

"Mine?"

"You call your brother profligate with an unsavory
reputation."

He rolled his eyes. "You have no idea, my innocent."

"What makes you think I'm innocent?"

His mouth curved. "Because that was your very first
kiss."

"Oh dear, if it was that obvious, I need more practice."

"If you will allow me to escort you to supper, I'll see what I can do."

"You are a cheeky sod, John Claud."

He grinned. "Yes, I know. Would you come riding in the park with me after church on Sunday?"

"I would love to." She gave him an inviting glance. "If I didn't have a previous engagement."

"With whom?" he demanded.

Anne didn't answer his question. "Why don't we go to-morrow? On Saturday afternoon the park isn't as crowded."

After the ball, far too exhilarated to sleep, Anne sat propped up in bed, filling the pages of her journal with all the exciting details of her debut. She purposely left out any mention of Emily. The only member of her father's first family she put in her journal was her half brother Leicester.

I'm glad Leicester was on leave. He never fails to tell me how much I look like my beautiful mother. He's extremely dark and handsome and I'm surprised that he's still unmarried. There is a striking family resemblance between him and Montagu.

Next, Anne wrote down the names of all the young men with whom she'd danced, gave a thumbnail sketch of each, and described how she felt about them.

I seem to be attracted to young men with Irish ancestry. No doubt it's because I have Irish blood and it's "like" calling to "like." Or perhaps it gives me perverse satisfaction since the English nobility tend to look down on us Irish. I'm looking forward to my outing with Fitz Kerry. He has the boldest blue eyes.

She saved the best till last, but when she wrote down *John Claud Hamilton*, she lapsed into thought, wondering what to say. She realized her feelings about him were not simple; they were complex. He was the most attractive male at her ball, and he was fun to be with, but she found his proprietary behavior toward her disconcerting. Finally she wrote, *He kissed me, and it was heavenly until I realized it wasn't James.*

Chapter 4

"I much preferred the training at the Grenadier camp in Ireland to the methods they use in Germany. All that cold Teutonic discipline and stiff-legged marching seems rather soulless to me." The Prince of Wales and James Hamilton were returning to London aboard a Royal Navy ship.

"Well, at least it postponed your Cambridge studies, and you managed to leave unencumbered," James reminded him.

"Only thanks to your warning me what my sister was up to regarding the Danish princess."

"I thought Alexandra was rather sweet and innocent. Was there nothing about her that attracted you, Teddy?"

"What's to attract? She isn't a woman, she's a girl . . . a colorless slip of a thing. She was flat as a fluke, no breasts whatsoever, and a personality to match."

"Well, you didn't have to put up with her on many occasions. She didn't relentlessly pursue you. Unfortunately, I can't say the same for your sister Vicky. I'll be glad to be home to get some sleep."

"My sister and the young Danish princesses have absolutely opposite personalities. Why on earth do you suppose Vicky and Frederick are so thick with the family?"

James turned up his collar against the bitter cold wind of the North Sea, and reminded himself that Teddy was not a deep thinker with an analytical mind. "I'm afraid that Crown Prince Frederick and Princess Victoria have English views that clash with the authoritarian rule of President Bismarck. I would go as far as to say they loathe Germans. It is quite evident that they wish to align with Denmark as a buttress against Germany; hence their friendship with the Danish royal family."

"You explain it all so well, James. Ulterior motives and political maneuvering never occur to me."

Grosvenor Square, London

"It's all right, Jenkins, I'll get the door." Anne waited until the butler left before she opened it. "Frances, you're late. Florence is already here." Anne hung up her friend's cloak on the hall stand and led the way upstairs to the drawing room.

"I had to bide my time until John Claud went out. If he had known I was coming to Grosvenor Square, he would have insisted on joining me."

"I know I invited you to tea, but I believe something stronger is required to banish our inhibitions for this strategy session." She poured them each a glass of sherry. "We need a bold plan, if we are to make our Season count for anything. None of us want just any husband, or one our family chooses for us. We must each narrow it down to one man. If we don't pursue our dreams relentlessly, we will never achieve our goals."

Florence Paget took a tentative sip of her sherry. "But my family has already chosen a husband for me."

"Then we will have to thwart them," Anne declared firmly. "Bottoms up, Florence." She swallowed her sherry in one gulp and refilled her glass. "I warrant your family has chosen Viscount Henry Chaplin? Tell us truly, Florence, who is your heart's desire?"

"I have lost my heart to the Marquis of Hastings. But

it's a secret. No one knows; this is the first time I've ever whispered his name."

"Henry Rawdon? Well, I must admit he is rather dashing. He asked my brother-in-law Westmorland to nominate him for the Jockey Club."

"He's filthy rich as well as being a marquis," Frances added. "Very good choice, Florence. I'll make sure he gets an invitation to my parents' annual ball."

"But Henry Chaplin will be escorting me." Florence sighed unhappily.

"That's a perfect cover," Frances pointed out. "Anne will confide to Hastings that you find him attractive; then when he asks you to dance, it will give you the opportunity to secretly flirt with him. Your parents and Viscount Chaplin won't suspect a thing."

Florence drained her sherry. "I'll do it!" she vowed recklessly.

Anne looked expectantly at Frances Hamilton. "I know you have made a long list of eligible men, but whose name is at the very top?"

"The greatest title in England is the dukedom of Marlborough, so the name at the top of my list is the heir, Blandford Churchill."

"That's rather ambitious," Florence remarked faintly.

"That's the reason the three of us must form an alliance and swear an oath to succeed. Instead of merely wishful thinking, we decide here and now whom we shall marry, and from this day forward we will do everything in our power to make our choices reality," Anne declared passionately.

"A triple-threat alliance. One for all and all for one, like the Three Musketeers." Frances was eager for the plan. "What shall we call ourselves? The Fearless Debutantes?"

Anne laughed in derision. "The bloody Brass Monkeys if we want to be ridiculous. Next you'll be suggesting we sign the pact in blood."

"Well, when you put it that way, it does sound a bit childish, like something my sister Maud would come up with," Frances admitted.

"Anne, you haven't named *your* future husband," Florence pointed out.

"I'm going to marry Frances Hamilton's brother, of course."

"James isn't the marrying kind." Frances thought fleetingly of their maid Jenny, who was ripe with child. The girl had mysteriously disappeared from Hampden House and was now employed by her sister Harriet. It had happened when James came home from Ireland and Frances had put two and two together. "However, John Claud shouldn't prove difficult. He already worships at your feet, and he told me in confidence that your father as well as your older brothers think him the right husband for you."

Anne smiled her secret smile, and picked up the sherry decanter.

During October Anne attended many balls and entertainments, and she anticipated an encounter with Lord James Hamilton at every affair. She took special pains with her wardrobe, wanting to look elegant when they met. She daydreamed about him endlessly, and even practiced the things she would say. But each time, she was doomed to disappointment and poured out her heart on the pages of her journal. With each new invitation, however, her hope was renewed. When she was invited to the annual ball being given by Lord Hamilton's parents, the Duke and Duchess of Abercorn, at Hampden House, her heart soared with happiness. Anne reasoned that every member of the Hamilton family would be present at the Green Street mansion, including James.

When she arrived, Frances took her by the hand. "Come, I want to introduce you to my sister the Countess of Dalkeith. Jane has been invited to be a lady-in-waiting to the queen," Frances told Anne.

"Has she accepted?"

Frances lowered her voice. "She had no choice really. Over the years, Mother was asked twice by Victoria to be Mistress of the Robes, and turned her down both times.

My sister Jane has a sweet nature and accepted the post of lady-in-waiting to save face."

"I don't envy her sharing duties with my sister Emily. If as you say, the Countess of Dalkeith has a sweet nature, my bossy sister Emily will run roughshod over her."

When Anne curtsied to the countess, Jane immediately reached for her hands and raised her. "Oh, please, Lady Anne, there is no need for such formalities with me."

"Congratulations on your appointment to the queen." Anne tried to sound sincere.

"Ah, I can see Frances has given you all the details." The young countess couldn't hide her amusement. "I shall be joining your sister Emily at Buckingham Palace. I've been paying attention to all the fashionable gowns tonight, and I must tell you how much I've been admiring yours."

"Why, thank you. My status as a debutante decrees I wear white, but I seldom follow rules to the letter. I push the boundaries with my own designs."

"Your overskirt with the golden acorns is not only exquisite; it is very clever."

Music floated in the air and Frances pulled on Anne's sleeve. "Excuse us, Jane. I gave Mother a list of certain eligible bachelors. I hope they accepted."

Her sister smiled. "You won't know until you look in the ballroom. It was lovely to meet you, Lady Anne. I hope you enjoy the dancing."

The moment Anne entered the ballroom, the Marquis of Hastings made a beeline for her and asked her to dance.

"By any chance, do you suppose your brother-in-law Westmorland will be here tonight?"

"Let me guess. You want to know if he put your name in to the Jockey Club?"

"Precisely."

Anne saw her chance to kill two birds with one of cupid's arrows. "If he doesn't come tonight, we could drive out in your carriage to Curzon House and visit him on Sunday."

"That's extremely generous of you, Lady Anne."

"Not at all. I shall ask my dearest friend Florence Paget to come for the ride." She stood on tiptoe and whispered in his ear. "She is absolutely mad about you, Henry."

"The *Pocket Venus*? She's here tonight with Henry Chaplin."

"Chaplin is her parents' choice, not hers. I'm sure a marquis can easily outmaneuver a viscount if he puts his mind to it."

When the dance ended, Anne sought out Florence and told her what she'd planned. "I've done my part. The rest is up to you." She made her way back to Frances, who was surrounded by her three titled sisters and their attractive noble husbands. Anne found an immediate rapport with Harriet, recognizing instantly that they were kindred spirits.

"My friend Anne will most likely be our sister-in-law in the not too distant future. John Claud is madly in love with her, and tells everyone who will listen that he intends to marry her."

Speaking her mind as always, Harry said bluntly, "Anne would be wasted on John Claud. He's too immature. Anne, do you happen to know my brother James? He's a confirmed bachelor of course, but a beautiful wife is exactly what he needs. I shall put a bee in his ear if he shows up tonight."

Harry's words made Anne beam.

As it turned out, every member of the Hamilton family was there, barring James. After two hours, Anne gave up all hope. John Claud gave her his undivided attention. As they talked, and laughed, and danced together, she took special pains to hide her devastating disappointment.

Later that night, when she opened her journal, she sat for a long time. Her heart felt bruised because she was beginning to believe it was hopeless. She sighed deeply and wrote: *Fate is conspiring to keep us apart.*

*   *   *

Fate, however, was rather busy at the moment with the affairs, or rather *affair*, of the Prince of Wales. Upon his return from Germany, Teddy began his studies at Cambridge University. Governor Bruce leased a private residence in the town for the heir to the throne and realized his mistake almost immediately. Within a week, the red-haired actress who had visited the Grenadier Guards' camp in Ireland arrived. When Bruce registered his objection, the prince loftily informed him that Nellie Clifden was there at his royal invitation.

An alarmed Bruce reported the prince's indiscretions to his father. Bruce feared that the liaison could not be kept secret for long, and since Prince Albert was the highly esteemed chancellor of the university, the slightest whisper would sully the reputation of the royal family.

"I need your advice, Abercorn." Prince Albert was clearly agitated. He handed the letter from Bruce to the man who had been his groom of the stole, and his confidant, for fifteen years.

The duke, who knew the prince consort was under the weather from a recent bout of influenza, tried his best to downplay the situation. "On November ninth your son will be a man of twenty. This is likely his way of celebrating his rite of passage."

"The queen is beside herself that Bertie is consorting with a woman of ill repute. She fears that whispers will be leaked about this shocking liaison. Scandal, above all other things, is abhorrent to Victoria."

"I understand it is one of the queen's ironclad rules for Society, and she sets an impeccable example for all her people, but I doubt if your son's youthful indiscretion will become a full-blown scandal, Your Highness."

"Her Majesty worries about scandal, but I have deeper concerns such as *blackmail*!" Albert took out a handkerchief and wiped his brow.

Abercorn could see how agitated the prince consort was, and realized it would be impolitic to downplay the matter further. "Yes, better to be safe than sorry. If handled with discretion, I'm sure the young woman can be persuaded to return to Ireland, and none will be the wiser."

"We must put a stop to this sordid affair. Both the queen and I are in a panic that it could lead to *pregnancy*." He ran his hand over his receding hairline. "Your son James handled the situation at the Kildare military camp. He took the blame upon himself, which was most commendable. Unfortunately, Lord Hamilton is not attending the prince in Cambridge. He's taken his seat in Parliament, I believe."

"James will doubtless travel to Cambridge to celebrate the Prince of Wales's birthday. If you wish it, Your Highness, I'm sure he would not hesitate to go up a few days early and take care of this delicate matter. As lord of the bedchamber to your son, he considers it his sacred duty to serve and protect the heir to the throne."

"Thank you, Abercorn. We must nip this in the bud before the whispers begin." Prince Albert's haggard face was set in deep lines of worry. "I shall rely on his, and your, discretion."

When the session in the House ended, James Hamilton joined his uncle Lord John Russell. The grave topic of discussion was the American Civil War. Eleven states wanted an independent Confederacy, led by its president, Jefferson Davis.

"Though Britain depends on American cotton for our textile industry, we cannot extend diplomatic relations to the Confederates," John Russell declared.

"Prime Minister Palmerston is urging a policy of neutrality. War is an internal matter and should be settled by peaceful negotiation," James Hamilton agreed.

Abercorn arrived and placed a hand on each man's shoulder. "The Union wants to prevent us from recognizing the Confederacy. I agree that we must not take sides."

"Hello, Father, were you in the Lords today?"

"No, I've just come from an audience with Prince Albert about a personal matter."

John Russell excused himself and joined Prime Minister Palmerston.

James raised his eyebrows.

"It's the Prince of Wales. Seems he no sooner arrived in Cambridge than he sent for his Irish companion. Governor Bruce is agog over his playing house with the actress and has reported the matter to Prince Albert and Her Majesty. You know how abhorrent scandal is to the queen. She is adamant that this must not get out."

"If the prince has practiced discretion, gossip should have been avoided."

"Prince Albert is worried about blackmail, and both he and the queen are in a panic in case the young woman becomes pregnant."

"I'm going to Cambridge. He turns twenty this week; I will be expected at the celebration on Saturday."

"If I were you, I'd go tomorrow. Prince Albert is relying on you to put a stop to it before the whispers start."

"I'll see what I can do. I'll leave at first light."

"The prince may not listen to reason now that he's turning twenty."

"I'll handle it . . . one way or another. You may depend upon it, Father."

"James, you came early." Prince Teddy saluted Hamilton with his half-full glass of brandy. "We'll make a week of it!"

"Your Highness, let me be the first to wish you happy returns of the day." James threw Charles Carrington a look of censure and received a helpless shrug of the shoulders from the prince's attendant.

"You'll never guess who's here." The prince was beaming.

"Don't tell me your family arrived before me? I had no idea they would travel to Cambridge to celebrate your twentieth birthday with you, Teddy."

In spite of the spirits he'd imbibed, the prince sobered immediately. "My parents aren't coming, are they?" Teddy put the glass down and stood up. "Nellie's here!"

"I think it best if we move Miss Clifden from your residence to a hotel. Just in case members of your family arrive for your birthday."

"Excellent suggestion, James. Will you take care of the arrangements?"

"My pleasure." He saw Carrington motion with his head and grasped the significance. "I take it the lady is occupying the east wing?"

Teddy nodded. "Morning sun . . ."

I wager she doesn't see the light of day until afternoon.

James made his way to the east wing, tapped lightly on the first door, and entered.

Nellie, wearing a flimsy wrapper, was enjoying a full-course English breakfast. "Lord James! How lovely . . . you've come to celebrate *His Nibs's* birthday."

"Hello, Nellie. I'm here to rescue you."

She laughed. "From what, pray?"

"From yourself. Tell me, what would you do if Her Royal Majesty the Queen walked in and found you eating breakfast at three in the afternoon?"

Nellie blanched and set down her knife and fork. "She's coming?"

Though James knew that Queen Victoria would avoid Cambridge as she would an outbreak of bubonic plague, others were not to know that.

"Since the Prince of Wales celebrates his twentieth birthday this week, it is entirely within the realm of possibility that the royal family could descend en masse." He paused to let her digest his words along with the sausages. Then he smiled. "If you will pack your things, I'll take you to the Royal Cambridge Hotel and get you settled in a room."

Relief brought color back to her face. "Oh, thanks so much. That's a grand solution."

An hour later, James booked Nellie into the Royal Cambridge under the name of Mrs. Renfrew and carried up her two bags himself. He helped remove her cloak, offered her a chair, and sat down facing her. "Nellie, I feel we can speak plainly and there need be no subterfuge between us."

She nodded and looked at him with speculation.

James took out a leather billfold from his jacket pocket.

She threw him a coy glance, and the corners of her mouth went up. "You devil, James. My value has risen lately, but for you, ten quid." She stood up, and twirled about for his inspection, letting him see what a bargain he was getting.

James closed his eyes. "My dearest girl, I am not propositioning you. Let me explain the situation. In order to avert a scandal involving the Prince of Wales, you must return to Ireland."

"But I don't want to return to Ireland. I want to stay in Cambridge."

"That is impossible, Nellie. Prince Albert is the highly esteemed chancellor of Cambridge University. If it became known that the Prince of Wales was carrying on an illicit relationship with an actress, it would cause a scandal that would harm the royal family. Naturally, you won't be returning empty-handed. I'll make it worth your while."

"It's no secret. Everybody in Cambridge knows. Teddy isn't ashamed to be seen with an *actress*."

"Good *God*! No wonder the hotel clerk gave me a knowing look. Nellie, I give you no choice. You *will* listen to reason. The Prince of Wales is inexperienced in the ways of Society, while you are a *woman of the world*. This affair is over."

She raised her chin. "Perhaps not." She paused and gave him a calculating look.

James was shrewd enough to anticipate what Nellie was up to.

"I might be having a baby. How will you handle that, Lord James?"

"I will simply acknowledge paternity, and give your child my name." James reflected that it wouldn't be the first time he'd stepped in and taken the blame for an unwanted pregnancy.

Nellie stared at him in outrage. "What the hell would be the point of my having a baby if the world didn't know its father was the Prince of Wales?"

"Precisely," James said quietly.

The wind went out of her sails. "Then you might as well know I'm *not* having a baby."

"I think that's a wise decision, Nellie." His voice was kind.

"You said you'd make it worth my while?"

"Of course. You will be well rewarded. Five hundred pounds." He opened his leather billfold. "A hundred pounds now, and I will deposit the rest in the Bank of Ireland, in your name, to be withdrawn upon your return to Dublin."

By the surprised look on her face, James knew Nellie was impressed.

"Going back to Ireland?" Prince Teddy's voice was incredulous. "I don't want Nellie to leave!" He stood up. "Where's my coat?"

"Your Highness, please have a seat while I explain."

"Carrington, get my coat."

Charles threw James a helpless look and brought the overcoat.

The prince thrust his arms into the sleeves, then stood waiting for James to explain.

"Since your father has held the exalted position of chancellor of Cambridge University for more than a dozen years, it would be like a slap in the face if you caused a royal scandal to erupt in this hallowed town."

Teddy nodded. "Yes, a slap in the face."

Christus, this is payback for him denying you a military career. "It won't just reflect upon Prince Albert. Your mother, the queen, is head of the Church of England, she is the Defender of the Faith, and represents the moral authority in the kingdom. You must understand that as heir to the throne you have an almost sacred responsibility. You must never be the cause of a scandal that would undermine the queen's authority or blacken the reputation of the royal family."

"I promise to be discreet."

"You have already been totally *indiscreet*. Nellie says it's no secret—that everybody in Cambridge knows of the affair."

"She is no longer staying in my residence. My visits to the hotel will be clandestine—after dark—no one will know of them," Teddy insisted.

"Your Highness, a full-blown scandal can only be avoided by ending the liaison and having Miss Clifden leave the country." James poured the prince a small measure of brandy and handed it to him. "Your father is *livid*. He's in a towering rage. Under the circumstances you have only one option. You must *apologize* for your indiscretion, and vow it will never happen again."

Teddy turned red in the face and set down the glass of brandy. "Am I to be denied all female companionship?"

"Until this dies down, yes."

Teddy brightened. "Then Nellie can return?"

"Nellie is an actress with loose morals. She is totally unsuitable. Such an affair leaves you wide open to blackmail or worse. I take full blame for this. I should never have introduced you. But having a fling at an Irish army camp is a world apart from installing a whore at your residence in this hallowed city of learning. You must see that, Your Highness."

"What do other men do?"

"They make discreet arrangements with noble married ladies of their own class, whose husbands turn a blind eye. A well-bred mistress who doesn't flaunt herself is perfectly acceptable in high-class Society."

Teddy looked forlorn, and James realized that the inexperienced prince would not know how to approach such a woman. Nellie Clifden had been easy, and vulgar, and fun.

"Whatever shall I say to Nellie? How can I make her understand?"

"I have already explained the situation to her and she understands perfectly. Nellie has been well paid for her services. I feel confident she won't cause any trouble for you or the royal family."

The Prince of Wales sat down. "I was thoroughly looking forward to a celebration party on my birthday with my good friends. Not that I have many." His spirits were deflated, his face morose.

"A celebration party in Cambridge is out of the question," James declared. "But there's nothing to stop us from having a birthday bash somewhere out of town."

The prince brightened. "Where do you suggest?"

Suddenly, James's face lit up. "Why, Newmarket of course. It's less than ten miles away. Carrington and I both have carriages. We can do the rounds. Our first stop can be the White Hart Country Inn, only four miles from here. Then there's the Golden Boar, the Black Horse Inn, and the Olde Bull near Newmarket."

"The Rowley Mile Grandstand has *special events nights* that include an evening horse meet, followed by a musical concert," Carrington added.

"Next day, we could visit the training yards, and even take a look at Tattersall's sales ring. I can't think of a better gift than a new horse for your birthday."

"By Jove, that sounds just the ticket!" Teddy exclaimed with delight.

Chapter 5

In Grosvenor Square, Lady Anne sorted through the post on the entrance hall table, saw an envelope addressed to her from Curzon House, South Audley Street, Mayfair, and went in search of her mother.

"Here's an invitation from my sister Adelaide. The Earl and Countess of Westmorland are hosting a formal dinner on Thursday night; then next day the guests will be transported to Apethorpe Hall for the weekend."

"It's an annual party," her mother explained.

"Yes, but I've never been invited before," Anne pointed out.

"It coincides with Newmarket's last racehorse meet for the year. Henry Fane usually has one of his horses entered."

"How very fortunate for Henry that Apethorpe Hall is conveniently close to Newmarket. If you have no objection, Mother, I would love to accept this invitation."

"I'm sure your father would be delighted if you spent the weekend with your sister. Just don't ask me to join you, darling."

Anne laughed and kissed her mother's cheek. "I won't. Thankfully I don't need you to chaperone me at my sister's entertainments."

"Apethorpe Hall is exceedingly grand. Both Queen

Elizabeth the First and her successor King James were often entertained there. You had best pack your most elegant outfits. I shall lend you one of my furs for the races."

"Oh, lovely. I shall accept this invitation immediately."

"James, old man, how can I ever thank you?" Prince Teddy stood back to admire the huge bay gelding that his friend had bought for him at Tattersall's.

James had chosen the horse because it was almost identical to the one that the Prince of Wales had ridden at the army camp in Ireland.

The trio of males had quaffed and smoked their way to Newmarket the previous day, and James marveled at Teddy's capacity for brandy and cigars. He had begun to realize that his royal friend had a large appetite for all things, if the two plump barmaids he'd slept between at the Olde Bull were any indication. James was immensely thankful that the pair hadn't the faintest notion that the young bull was His Royal Highness the Prince of Wales. And though Teddy had told the ladies he would be back for more tonight, James thought it best that they move on to the Cadogan Hotel in Newmarket.

"I've arranged for Tattersall's to stable him until we return to Cambridge."

"You think of everything, James. I can't wait for the afternoon races."

James couldn't wait either. After the close proximity of Teddy's cigars he felt like a smoked kipper, and was looking forward to an afternoon in the fresh air of Suffolk.

Two hours later, while Teddy and Charles Carrington were watching the first race, James was at the betting window placing wagers. He nodded to Henry Fane and wondered if he was running one of his horses in the thousand-guinea race. James placed a bet for the prince and one for himself, then turned from the window in time to see Fane hand a ticket to his female companion.

She was a stunning beauty with a profusion of red-gold curls, and she was swathed in a luxurious, silver-gray fox fur. *You lucky bastard, Fane. Not only is she exquisite-looking; she's young enough to be your daughter. I wouldn't mind a piece of that tasty morsel!*

Anne's heart turned over in her breast and began to beat wildly. She did not dare believe that the sinfully handsome man who had greeted her brother-in-law was Lord Hamilton. She had seen him only once, more than three years ago, but the picture she carried in her mind greatly resembled the dark male who had nodded to Fane. Anne was so excited she couldn't breathe, couldn't hear, couldn't even think coherently.

Henry Fane held out two tickets. "You can take your choice between Lord Derby's horse Sagitta, or Lord Falmouth's Hurricane."

Anne blinked and tried to focus. "Lord Derby has such ridiculously bushy gray sideburns. I'll take Hurricane. Lord Falmouth is rather distinguished-looking."

Henry laughed. "The owner's looks is the strangest criterion for choosing a winner I've ever heard of. Still, some people throw darts at the names of the horses. To each his own, I suppose. Let's get back so we can watch the race."

"Let's not rejoin the old-boys club, Henry. Six disapproving brothers is more than I can stomach today. Why don't we just go down to the rail and watch the race?"

By the time they arrived, Anne was breathless with excitement. Still she managed to pose a casual question. "Who was that dark gentleman you greeted at the betting window?"

"That was young Hamilton. The Prince of Wales must be here this afternoon."

"Are you sure that was James Hamilton?" she gasped. He was even taller, darker, and more handsome than she remembered. "I know his sisters very well."

"Hamilton's a young rakehell. He's been seen in

brothels all over the country, and Ireland too. Rumor has it he's been showing the prince the ropes. Stay away from him, sweetheart."

Anne's heart contracted. All her happiness drained away. It felt as if Henry had stabbed her. *It cannot be true! John Claud has always insisted his brother is a rake, but I never, ever believed him. I've spent the last three and a half years of my life idolizing James Hamilton. Surely I haven't been wasting my time dreaming about a man who is nothing but a libertine?*

Because she had been true to him for almost four years, Anne could not help feeling that James had betrayed her somehow. She tried to banish him from her thoughts by focusing on the horse race. She watched Sagitta pull ahead of Hurricane, but in the stretch another horse passed both of them, and won by a nose.

It was declared that Nemisis was the official winner of the race.

"Oh dear, neither one of our horses won. You wasted your money, Henry."

"Hurricane came in third. You won a small amount, I warrant."

"Really? I shall go immediately and cash in my ticket."

"I can do that for you, my dear."

"Not a chance, Henry. I want to wallow in the thrill of victory!"

When she arrived at the ticket window, a line of men was before her. Suddenly, she came face-to-face with James Hamilton, who had just collected his winnings.

The dark devil swept her with an appraising look that took her breath away.

Hamilton tipped his hat. "You could do much better than Fane, sweetheart, unless you enjoy being an old man's darling."

Anne gasped, and drew her fur close, as if it would protect her. "Your reputation precedes you, *Lord Rakehell.*"

"You shouldn't believe any of the things you've heard

about me," he admonished solemnly. Then he winked. "Actually, they are much worse."

"You tempt me beyond belief." She gave him a freezing look of contempt.

James couldn't hide his amusement. "Debauched as I am, perhaps I could even thaw a beautiful *Ice Queen* like you. Allow me to buy you a drink and I'll show you that fire and ice are an irresistible combination."

Anne drew in a quivering breath. For years she had dreamed about this dark, handsome lord. She'd pined for just a glimpse of him, longed to meet him at a ball, imagined him dancing with her, and fantasized about his kisses. Now here he was before her in the flesh, with his eyes telling her he found her desirable. *Refuse the insolent devil!*

She licked her lips with the tip of her tongue. "I'd love a drink." She gave him a saucy, sideways glance. "But I warn you, it will take more than champagne to make me melt." *He hasn't the faintest idea I am a lady. In fact, he thinks I'm Henry Fane's mistress.* Rather than repel her, the thought excited her. *What fun!*

James ushered the young beauty inside the refreshment pavilion where libations were being served, and seated her at a small table. Then he pushed his way through the men at the stand-up bar to get their drinks. When he returned with the glass of champagne and mug of ale, he was not the least surprised to see she had attracted every male eye.

James sat down and raised his tankard. "I offer a toast to the loveliest lady attending the races today. I am the envy of every man here, and I don't even know your name."

She picked up her glass and took a dainty sip. "How devastating for you."

His eyes crinkled with laughter at the teasing game she was playing. "You enjoy being elusive."

She took another sip and shook her head. "I prefer being exclusive."

He caressed her with his eyes. "You have no idea what you are missing."

She ran her finger around the rim of her glass. "Nor do you, my lord." Her mouth curved with amusement and she whispered, "How devastating for you."

"If you won't give me your name, at least tell me where you live. I'd like to send you flowers."

She took another sip of champagne. "I live in London."

James masked his frustration with a lazy smile. "Such a fashionable beauty could live nowhere else. Could you be a little more specific?"

"And put you out of your misery?" she teased. "I'm afraid not."

It was a game, and though his vivid imagination conjured games he'd love to play with her, this particular game wasn't one of them. But she was so delectable, he couldn't take his eyes from her.

Suddenly, he realized the Earl of Westmorland was striding toward them.

"There you are! I've been looking everywhere for you. Sweetheart, I was concerned for your safety."

"Henry." With a fluid movement she slid to her feet and pulled her fur about her. She kissed his cheek affectionately. "Thank you for rescuing me, but I was in the very safe hands of Lord Hamilton." She gestured to the champagne and gave James a radiant smile. "I truly appreciate your gallantry, my lord."

He looked into her green eyes sparkling with mischief and knew he felt more than a passing attraction. The secretive beauty had quite taken his fancy. "It was my pleasure to be of service, *mistress*." He deliberately emphasized the last word, and he knew it amused her.

James watched her depart on Westmorland's proprietary arm. He was confident that it wouldn't take him long to find out the name of Henry Fane's latest ladylove.

Anne was on her way to her mother's sitting room for afternoon tea, and to share details of the exciting weekend she'd spent, when she heard her sister Emily's voice. Anne immediately returned to her room, and sat down to sketch a new winter dress.

Anne's mother, however, could not escape her step-daughter Emily's visit.

"I dropped in at Beaufort House this morning to visit my sister Georgiana. Since my duties to Her Majesty prevented me from accepting Adelaide's invitation to Apethorpe Hall, I knew Georgiana would describe the weekend in detail." Emily set her cup and saucer down with deliberation, and patted her lips primly with her linen napkin.

Her stepmother knew Emily had a bone of contention sticking in her craw, and waited patiently for her to voice her criticism.

"My sister told me that Anne attended without you chaperoning her, and she was actually wearing a fur coat."

"Your father isn't much of a racing enthusiast, as you know. But he encouraged Anne to accept the invitation. She hardly needs a chaperone when visiting her sister."

"But the fur coat. At her age, surely she doesn't own such a garment?"

"Actually she does. It was a gift from her father," the countess lied. "He didn't want her to be cold at the races."

"That's another thing that Georgiana told me, that I could hardly believe. The Newmarket race meet is usually attended by just the gentlemen. It gives the ladies the opportunity for a private get-together without the ever-intrusive male presence. Apparently Anne flaunted convention and swanned off to the races with Henry Fane." Emily stood up to take her leave. "I'm telling you this for your own good, my lady. If Anne gains a fast reputation, she will ruin her chances for a good marriage."

"It is so comforting to know that you have your sister's best interests at heart. Anne will be sorry to have missed your visit."

Five minutes after Emily departed, Anne joined her mother in her sitting room. "Thank heavens she's gone. She always has an ulterior motive when she visits."

"As we Irish say, she likes to stir the shyte!"

Anne laughed. "I love your irreverent humor, Mother."

"Poor Emily. I think she was feeling sorry for herself because she had to miss the weekend at Apethorpe Hall."

"Well, I'm certainly glad I went. I had a marvelous time."

"I've decided to let you keep the fur coat I lent you. I believe it's going to be a cold winter, darling."

House of Commons
November 12, 1861

William, Earl of Dalkeith, and member of Parliament for Midlothian, hailed his young brother-in-law at the end of the day's session. "Hello, James. This American Civil War will seriously affect our cotton supplies."

"Yes, the price of cotton will go sky-high."

"You haven't been in the House for a week. Nothing wrong, I hope?"

"I went to Cambridge for the Prince of Wales's birthday and we ended up in Newmarket for the last race meet of the year."

"Well, that sounds enjoyable, but I don't envy you playing nursemaid to Teddy."

James laughed. "Sometimes it gets complicated, but nothing I can't handle. I ran into Westmorland at the races. He had a most attractive young woman on his arm. Have you heard any rumors about a new mistress?"

"Haven't heard his name mentioned with any mistress, new or old. His obsession is horses. During the winter, when the racing season is over, he usually takes his seat in the Lords. Perhaps our brother-in-law Lichfield knows about his personal *affairs*."

"It's not important. Just a matter of idle curiosity, really."

"I'd better remind you that your sister's annual masked ball is coming up. You'll be getting your invitation shortly."

"Thanks for the warning, William. Although I know Jane sets great store by these things."

"All women do, and if you want to hear the latest gossip, about Henry Fane or anyone else, a ball is the ideal place."

As James left Parliament, he chided himself. *It's more than idle curiosity. I won't be satisfied until I find out who she is. I think I'll drop in at St. James's Street on my way home.*

At his sister's house, a footman let him in and he went upstairs unannounced, where six-year-old Thomas spotted him.

"Uncle James! Uncle James!" As he ran headlong down the hall that led from the schoolroom, his two younger brothers followed him and joined in the chant.

James swung Thomas in the air and laughed. "I always get the same welcoming committee." Georgie and young James, his namesake, each grabbed a leg and hung on as their favorite uncle staggered a few steps.

"For shame, you young hooligans," Rose, the head housekeeper, admonished. "Your fingers are still sticky from your tea. Go and wash your hands immediately. Your father will be home any minute."

"What's all the racket?" James's sister Harry emerged from the nursery carrying her baby daughter. "Oh, it's you. I thought it was Thomas." She turned and handed one-year-old Florence to her new nursemaid.

"Hello, Jenny. You seem to have settled in at the madhouse."

Jenny smiled and bobbed him a curtsy. "Lord James."

When she took the baby into the nursery, James again thanked his sister for providing a place in her household for Jenny.

"Oh, she's a godsend. We were desperately in need of another nanny."

"You don't think the boys will be too much in her condition?"

"Good heavens, Jenny isn't looking after the hooligans. She's my daughter's nursemaid. You mustn't worry about her, James. In January, when her time comes, we'll take very good care of her."

"You're very generous, Harry."

"As are you."

"Financially perhaps, but that doesn't compare with what you are doing."

"Oh, here's Thomas. Hello, darling. Look what the cat dragged in." As she lifted her face for her husband's kiss, her arms slipped up about his neck.

Harry's face radiated love and James thought for the thousandth time that they made an ideal couple.

"Will you stay for dinner, James?" Harry invited.

"No, no, I just dropped in for a word with Thomas."

"In that case, come into the library for a drink," his brother-in-law invited.

"I'll leave you to it, then. Oh, before I go, don't forget about Jane's masked ball on the twenty-ninth. You always manage to avoid your family's entertainments."

"*Mea culpa.* My social life is so demanding I have to juggle my invitations."

"And you conveniently manage to drop all the 'balls,'" Harry quipped.

In the library Thomas poured a measure of whiskey for each of them. The pair talked shop for a few minutes, discussing what was going on in the House and in the Lords; then casually Thomas mentioned that he'd seen Henry Fane at Newmarket.

"He attended the session today. He told me he had bumped into you. Asked me if you were engaged yet. I assured him you were a confirmed bachelor."

"He was squiring a young beauty. Perhaps he's worried that I'll lure her away."

Thomas raised his eyebrows. "And would you?"

"Damned right, given half the chance. I thought you might know who she is."

"Sorry, James. I haven't heard a thing."

*   *   *

House of Commons
November 18, 1861

Lady Anne sat in the visitors' gallery of the House all alone. It was far too cold and drafty to attract many ladies in November, and when the other two *Brass Monkeys* had declined her invitation to visit Parliament, she decided to go alone.

Anne had thoroughly enjoyed her encounter with Lord Hamilton a week ago and longed to see him again. The contact at Newmarket made her vow it would not be another three and a half years before she laid eyes on him again. And the most obvious place to see him was in the House. It would also add a fillip of intrigue that she could observe him at her leisure, while James would get nary a glimpse of her. It was an exciting game. While she knew his identity, he was totally in the dark about who she was.

Anne soon realized that the discussion on the floor concerned the American Civil War. Apparently, a large number of British vessels were being prevented from leaving Charleston Harbor because of a blockade by the Union forces.

Anne recognized Lord John Russell when he stood to speak. "The British consul for the Southern States demanded permission for the vessels to pass out on the grounds that when they entered Charleston Harbor, the blockade had not yet been established." Lord John raised his head, and rustled the communiqué in his hand. "He was *refused*!"

Prime Minister Palmerston glared at the members and challenged, "You may stand for this, but damned if I will!"

A member of the opposition jumped to his feet. "Our consul must be given precise instructions so we do not commit Britain to hostilities with the Northern States."

Lord John Russell replied, "No sane man can condone slavery, but British maritime commerce is being ruled by the cabinet of Washington."

Anne's heart began to hammer as she watched Lord James Hamilton get to his feet to add his voice to that of Russell, who was after all his uncle. "We cannot acquiesce in the capture and confiscation of British ships and their cargoes."

The members who agreed banged their shoes on their desks, and those who disagreed booed their dissent.

Prime Minister Palmerston raised his voice so he could be heard above the cacophony. "I propose we issue a direct order to the cabinet in Washington, demanding in the name of Her Majesty the Queen, and in no uncertain terms, that our ships be released immediately from Charleston Harbor. All in favor say 'aye.'"

Once again the members engaged in a contest to see which side could shout the louder. John Russell, who was still on his feet, said with satisfaction, "The ayes have it, Mr. Prime Minister."

As James Hamilton took his seat, a movement at the railing in the visitors' gallery caught his eye. He got a fleeting glimpse of red hair and gray fur, but the female stepped back immediately, as if she didn't want to be seen. A slow smile curved his mouth. It was the young beauty he'd been making inquiries about for a week now, and getting absolutely nowhere. His glance traveled over the members present, assessing and quickly eliminating every one of them. There was only one reason why she had come to the gallery, and *he* was that reason. He slipped quietly from his seat in the chamber, determined that his elusive quarry would not elude his pursuit. He grabbed his coat from the cloakroom, then strode toward the stairs that led down from the visitors' gallery. As she descended the marble steps, he gazed up at her with amusement dancing in his eyes.

"Caught in the act! How devastating for you."

"I haven't the faintest idea what you're talking about, my lord."

"You know exactly what I'm talking about. Your curiosity to observe me lured you like a lodestone."

"Not so," she said in a cool voice. "I came to see another."

James grinned. "Westmorland sits in the Lords, not the Commons."

"I took a detour."

He held her gloved hand and raised it to his lips. "That tells me you are impulsive, a most exciting quality in a woman."

She looked into his laughing eyes and abandoned all pretense. "I *did* come to observe you and I *did* get caught in the act. And you are right, I am incurably impulsive."

"In that case, could I tempt you to dine with me? The hour is early, but warm food and a glass of wine on such a cold afternoon would allow us to explore our curiosity about each other."

She hesitated. Her head told her to decline his offer. Her heart told her to accept. "It would have to be somewhere close by. Somewhere respectable," she cautioned.

"My dearest lady, you may put complete trust in me."

"Oh dear. How devastating for me," she teased.

"The Westminster Palace Hotel is close by Parliament and has a most respectable dining room."

"Then I shall obey my impulse and accept."

Hamilton shrugged into his overcoat and they emerged onto Parliament Square, where the November wind swirled about them furiously. James offered Anne his arm and she took it gladly as they made their way to the hotel. The surge of his blood told him her close proximity excited him. Before they entered the dining room, he checked his coat, but knew instinctively that his companion would be loath to relinquish her fur. They were shown to a table by the maître d'hôtel, who provided menus and hastened off for the bottle of claret that Hamilton ordered.

James moved behind her chair to help her remove her fur. "Gray fox shows off your glorious hair to perfection."

She was thrilled by his compliment. "Thank you, my lord."

"Call me James." He draped her fur over the back of her chair and his admiring glance swept over her gown with its lace ruffles at throat and wrist. "Lavender velvet suits you even better."

"I'm glad you like it. I designed it myself."

"You have exquisite taste and an eye for color; I shall add that to the vast store of knowledge I've learned about you."

She smiled into his eyes. "You haven't learned anything about me, have you?"

"I know that you are lovely, and that I enjoy your company. If you would tell me your name, that's all I need to know."

As she removed her gloves, she noticed their pearl buttons. *I refuse to call myself Pearl.* She glanced at the flowers on the table. "It's Lily." She picked up the menu and began to read.

"That's a pretty name. If I were a betting man, I'd wager you also have a surname."

The bottle of claret arrived and James poured the wine himself.

One of the items on the menu was roast leg of lamb. She glanced up and smiled disarmingly. "Lamb."

"There now, was that so difficult?" He raised his glass to salute her. "I am very pleased to make your acquaintance, Mistress Lamb."

She took a sip of wine and set her glass down. "Thank you, Lord Hamilton."

"I thought we agreed you would call me James. Do you see anything you fancy?"

Oh hell yes! With difficulty she lowered her eyes to the menu. "I think some leek soup would warm me nicely."

"Good idea. I'll have some too. What else will you have?"

"Dover sole," she said decisively.

He signaled the waiter, ordered the food, then leaned back in his chair to savor the view. "If you enjoy the theater, I'd love to take you tonight."

Her eyes sparkled. "I do enjoy the theater, but it's not possible tonight. I have a previous engagement." *There would be hell to pay if I arrived home at such a late hour.*

"Ah." He gave her a look of regret. "Another night, perhaps?"

"Perhaps."

The soup arrived and he noticed that the array of silverware did not daunt her in any way. She deftly handled the soup spoon with more grace than a member of the royal family. It was obvious that she was used to dining elegantly, and he wondered where the devil Henry Fane had found such a delightful female who had the poise of a fine lady.

Anne preferred to remain a mystery, so prompted him to talk about himself. "You are the member of Parliament for County Donegal, I believe."

"Yes. Politics is a family tradition. My father was the lord lieutenant of Donegal before his appointment to Prince Albert."

"And you are an attendant to his son the Prince of Wales. You obviously follow in your father's footsteps."

"You know everything about me. My life is an open book. I have no secrets."

She looked into his eyes. "Your *public* life is an open book. I know nothing about your private life. I'm willing to wager that you are a keeper of secrets, James—both your own and the secrets of others."

"People put their trust in me because I have learned *discretion*." He wanted her to know that he would be discreet about their meeting today, and any future encounters she would allow. He could not blame her for being cautious. If the Earl of Westmorland provided her with a house, servants, and a generous clothing allowance, it would take a good deal of persuasion on his part to have her risk losing it all for a fleeting liaison.

By the time the trifle arrived, she had eluded every invitation he suggested. "Perhaps the theater is too public a place to be seen together. I would be delighted if you would allow me to entertain you privately."

"At Hampden House?"

James threw back his head and laughed. "You have a sly wit. I no longer reside at the family home. I have a

Georgian town house on the corner of White Horse Street."

"How very convenient for you."

"Yes, it is within walking distance of Buckingham Palace, if that's what you mean."

"That isn't what I mean, as well you know." She finished her trifle and set her linen napkin beside her plate. "I enjoyed dining with you, James Hamilton. I'm sorry to refuse your invitation to the theater this evening. If I find it possible to attend sometime in the future, I will send a note to White Horse Street."

He threw her a rueful glance. "You expect me to be satisfied with that?"

"Not for a moment, my lord."

She smiled and he believed that her eyes held a promise.

"I really must go." She pulled on her gloves.

He simply couldn't tolerate her leaving without a plan to see her again. Suddenly an idea came to him, and he leaned forward. "Could I tempt you with a masked ball?"

Her green eyes sparkled. "Perhaps."

"My sister Jane is holding her annual masquerade ball on November twenty-ninth. In a costume and mask you could be completely incognito."

"You are speaking of the Countess of Dalkeith?"

"Yes. My sister Jane is married to the Earl of Dalkeith and the ball will be at Montagu House. Are you tempted?" James knew he should not invite this beautiful young courtesan to his sister's ball, but he simply didn't give a damn about what was appropriate at the moment.

"I am tempted beyond belief," she admitted. Only this morning she had received her invitation to the Dalkeith ball and had planned to attend with James's sister Frances.

"Then it's settled." He moved around the table to hold her fur while she slipped her arms into the sleeves. "I'll pick you up in my carriage."

She shook her head. "I prefer to meet you there."

He breathed in her fragrance and longed to bury his face in the fiery glory of her hair. He had never kept a mistress, preferring instead casual liaisons, but for the first time he realized that with the right female, a long-term exclusive relationship would be extremely rewarding. He watched her walk to the lobby as he settled the bill, but when he left the dining room to retrieve his overcoat, she was nowhere in sight. He hurried out onto the street, but as he feared, the young beauty had made good her escape.

Chapter 6

"Anne, I came to see if you got your invitation to the Dalkeiths' masked ball? I asked my sister Jane to send you one." Frances Hamilton handed her coat to the maid.

"Yes, thank you, it came in the post days ago. Come upstairs, I was just going through some picture books trying to get ideas for a costume."

"Riley, our coachman, is picking me up in half an hour to take me to the costume shop. Why don't you come with me?"

"My mother's dressmaker is coming this afternoon, so I think I'll take advantage of her expertise."

"I have no idea who I want to be. Costume balls are such fun for females. I can't understand why men look panic-stricken at the mere mention of them."

"Really, Frances? I think there is nothing more dangerous and seductive than a male wearing a mask."

"John Claud absolutely refuses to attend. *'A costume turns a man into a buffoon. A figure of fun for the ladies to laugh at behind their fans,'* he insists."

"Not all men think that way. I warrant your father will gallantly escort Lady Lu."

"Oh yes, Father's game for a bit of fun. And I insisted

Jane send an invitation to Blandford Churchill. How divine it would be if he wore his Horse Guard uniform."

"I would like to be someone exotic. I was thinking of Cleopatra."

"Oh, Anne, you always have such brilliant ideas! I'm the one with dark hair—I would love to be the Egyptian princess."

"You would make a most alluring Cleopatra, Frances. You need a turquoise robe and a gold mask, and see if the costumier has some snake jewelry."

"Are you sure you don't mind my stealing your idea, Anne?"

"Of course I don't mind. I'll come up with something else. I will most likely design my own costume. I would ask a favor of you, though. I want to be absolutely incognito at the ball, so even if you recognize me, I want you to pretend you don't know me."

"Oh, you are planning an intrigue! How exciting. I promise to completely ignore you, if you give me your sacred word to come round the next day and tell me all about it."

When Madam Olga arrived, she brought Anne's new winter gown for a fitting. "The skirt is finished and hemmed. You must decide on the bodice. I know we spoke of a low décolletage, my lady, but perhaps a square neck would be more suitable for a debutante."

"I'm so glad I chose white velvet. It is quite elegant." Anne gave the dressmaker a speculative look. "I'm invited to the Countess of Dalkeith's costume ball, and I would like nothing better than to dress as a Russian princess. This dress would be perfect if you could make it with long sleeves and a high collar that came up to my chin." Anne took a piece of paper and sketched the design she wanted.

When Madam Olga nodded, Anne began to get excited. "I shall sew crystal beads on the bodice. I'll need a white mask encrusted with crystal beads. Oh, and I just had a marvelous idea to complete the outfit . . . a white fur hat like the Cossacks wear!"

"That would be rather unusual, Lady Anne," she said faintly.

"Yes, wouldn't it?" Her voice was dreamy as she pictured herself at the ball in the spectacular outfit.

James Hamilton had attended his fair share of London's masked balls over the years, so they had lost their appeal for him long ago. When he started to feel excited about the masquerade at Montagu House, he realized the reason was Lily Lamb. He knew his costume would represent his intentions—not a raptor exactly, but definitely a hunter of some sort.

On the night of the ball, James wore a kilt of Hamilton hunting green tartan. He attached a lace stock to his linen shirt, and donned a black doublet and mask. He selected a silver dagger ornamented with a stag's head. A short hunting cloak completed the outfit.

James arrived early. That way, if the young beauty had any trouble gaining entrance to the elite affair at renowned Montagu House, he would be there to smooth her way.

His sister Jane was far too preoccupied playing hostess to recognize him, and when his parents arrived an hour later, they played along and at least pretended not to know his identity. James cooled his heels as he waited and watched for the beautiful girl who had captured his imagination. He had no desire to go into the ballroom and dance until his chosen partner arrived.

To pass the time he sampled all the delicacies laid out in the supper room and helped himself to a glass of champagne. Then he stationed himself in the opulent entrance hall, amusing himself by guessing the identities of the masked guests as they arrived.

When the front door stopped opening, it occurred to James that his fair Lily might not come. His excitement melted away and was replaced by acute disappointment, yet he could not dispel all hope. Eventually, he joined his brother-in-law William and Dalkeith's father, the Duke of Buccleuch, in the cardroom that Jane had thoughtfully set up, since most men preferred gambling to dancing.

Anne had decided that she would arrive fashionably late at the Dalkeith masquerade ball and it was after ten o'clock when she stepped into her family's coach. It took another half hour for the carriage to make its way from Grosvenor Square to the Pall Mall mansion. Anne thanked her father's driver and asked him to return for her no later than one o'clock.

She ran up the steps and before she could touch the bellpull, the massive front doors were opened by the liveried majordomo who accepted her invitation and hid his surprise that the lady was without an escort. A maid waited to take her upstairs to the dressing room that was being used for the guests' coats and cloaks.

As Anne ascended in the white velvet cloak, she drew stares and low gasps from the guests she encountered. When she removed her cloak in the dressing room to reveal the spectacular white velvet gown encrusted with crystals, a cry of delight escaped the maid.

She bobbed a curtsy to the Russian princess. "Oh, your ladyship, you are a vision."

Anne smiled her gratitude. "You are very kind." She had often heard about the grand staircase that led down into the central salon. It was top-lit with a large stained-glass dome, brilliantly illuminated to show off its magnificence, and when a female was descending, it displayed her to perfection.

Anne paused at the top of the grand staircase and gazed out at the crowd below. She saw a tall male wearing the uniform of a Horse Guard and sure enough the female beside him was Cleopatra. She was astounded when she saw them leave together. *That Brass Monkey is having an intrigue of her own!* Anne collected her thoughts, then began to slowly descend with dramatic flair.

                         *   *   *

James left the cardroom intending to search the crowded ball one last time before giving up and consigning all females to the devil. A vision in white velvet and fur stopped him in his tracks. The top-lit stained-glass dome made the crystals on her gown and mask glitter like diamonds. The sight of her stunned him like a bird flown into a wall. She was easily the most beautiful creature he had ever seen.

Slowly, as if his mind were playing tricks on him, he began to wonder if the exotic Russian princess could actually be the female he had invited to the ball. He stood mesmerized as step by step she descended the staircase until she was standing before him. When he saw her lovely green eyes through the slits of the glittering mask, it confirmed her identity, and when she smiled at him, his heart thudded wildly.

"I'm late," she murmured. "Have you been waiting long?"

"No, no. I only just arrived."

"Is that true, my lord?"

"No, it's a bloody lie. I've been waiting hours."

She began to laugh, and it was so infectious, he laughed with her, thoroughly enjoying himself.

He captured her hand and drew it to his lips. "Would you like to dance?"

"More than anything in the world."

James tucked her arm beneath his and led her into the crowded ballroom.

When James took Anne into his arms, she closed her eyes, savoring the moment. *I've dreamed about this for years. I can't believe it's finally happening.* Suddenly, she was jarred out of her reverie as another couple bumped into them. She opened her eyes and saw Napoleon partnering a lady in a powdered wig who looked suspiciously like Marie Antoinette. The pair's incongruity touched Anne's funny bone and she began to laugh.

James grinned at her. "You have a sly sense of humor that I fully appreciate."

Trying to keep a straight face, they started to dance again, but the floor was far too crowded to whirl about with grace. By mutual consent they staked out a corner of the ballroom, where James slipped a possessive arm about his princess so they could sway to the music. From this vantage point they were free to observe all the guests' costumes.

A matador danced by with a moon goddess. "From the ridiculous to the sublime," Anne whispered.

"With the emphasis on ridiculous," James countered. When a devil danced by them with a nun in his arms, they had to turn their faces away to hide their amusement.

As a wizard approached, Anne faced James. "If I watch anymore, I'll disgrace myself." She raised her mask and James took his handkerchief and wiped the mirthful tears from her cheeks.

They each took a deep breath and sobered. "We are no better than the rest of them, you know. I'm masquerading as a Russian princess and you're a hunter in a kilt!"

"You are an anomaly—a female who can poke fun at herself."

She leaned close. "Just to be authentic, I warrant you're naked beneath your kilt."

James was helpless with laughter. She'd hit the nail on the head. "You're an amazing judge of human nature. Come, I think we're in need of a drink." Just as he took her hand, a tall highwayman in slouch hat and mask blocked their way.

"Stand and deliver, James. You've monopolized the loveliest lady at the ball long enough."

"Father!" James was startled. The last thing he wanted was to turn Lily over to his shrewd parent. "We were just going for a drink."

"You do that, and I'll protect the princess from all the

lecherous devils on the prowl tonight." Abercorn offered his arms and Anne moved into them.

She did a remarkable job of holding her laughter inside at James's predicament. He didn't know who she was, but she suspected that Abercorn had identified her. He had seen her with his daughter Frances too often not to recognize her.

"Are you enjoying yourself, my lady?"

"Immeasurably, Your Grace."

"I take it Lord Rakehell has no inkling you're a debutante?"

She dissolved into laughter at the name he had given his son. It was the very same one she had thrown at Lord Hamilton at the races. "Oh, please don't spoil my fun by telling him."

"Your secret is safe with me, my dear."

James was back with the champagne before their dance was finished. When he saw them laughing together, he experienced a twinge of envy.

The music stopped and James's father, with a comical look of reluctance, relinquished the princess to his heir.

James held the glass to her lips, and she sipped some champagne before she took the crystal flute from him. He raised his own glass in a salute to her beauty, then drained it.

"The supper rooms aren't crowded at the moment, but come midnight we'll be buried in an avalanche of kings, queens, and knaves."

"Then what are we waiting for?" She took his hand and they left the ballroom.

"At midnight, when everyone makes a mad dash for food, we'll come back and dance our hearts out."

She smiled into his eyes. "What a romantic suggestion."

He bent close and whispered, "You'll find I'm full of them."

As they moved slowly past the long tables laden with delicacies, James watched her in fascination as she selected various things, popped them into her mouth, then rolled her eyes in ecstasy. She dipped a third lump of crab into drawn butter. "You absolutely have to try this. It's divine!"

"How in the name of God do you manage to eat crab, dripping with drawn butter, and not to get a drop on your white velvet?"

"There's a knack to it. I have a darting tongue."

James inwardly groaned.

They tried some of everything and took great delight feeding each other. He found it amusing that after enjoying macaroons and chocolate bonbons, she relished some black olives and an artichoke heart. "You're eating out of order."

"I'm often out of order. I love to flaunt the rules."

"And I'd love to flaunt them with you—all of them!"

"Uh-uh, here comes the avalanche. It must be midnight."

Hand in hand, they went against the tide of knights, pirates, shepherdesses, and winged fairies, not even bothering to mask their laughter.

As soon as their feet touched the ballroom floor, James swept her into his arms. The orchestra was playing a waltz and because the room was no longer packed, the music filled the space and reverberated around the walls and the high ceiling. The slow, sensual movements of the waltz made her feel desirable. Anne had the sensation that she was drifting in a sea of bliss and she closed her eyes, feeling the lovely, romantic music flow about her. Her pulse began to throb in time to the rhythm of the music. James's powerful arms tightened about her and she felt him draw her closer to his body. She pictured his dark, compelling image on the inside of her eyelids and was intoxicated by his nearness. As he bent his head toward her, she shuddered with desire and opened her lips in invitation. When his mouth touched her, her eyelashes fluttered and she whispered his name with longing. "James."

"I love the taste of my name on your lips," he murmured, then swept her into the next dance.

They became one with the music as he led her in great circles about the ballroom, floating on gossamer wings of magic. As the other guests came crowding back, they stood aside to watch the beautiful Russian princess in the arms of the kilted hunter.

As the dance ended, applause broke out, and they became aware that they were not alone. Anne's cheeks flushed, and she laughed self-consciously. Without missing a beat, James swept her out of the ballroom, then firmly took hold of her hand, led her through the grand salon, and began to ascend the magnificent staircase.

"Where are you taking me?" she asked breathlessly.

"Somewhere private where we won't draw every curious eye."

At the top of the staircase, he placed a proprietary hand at the small of her back, and urged her down a broad hallway, past the dressing room where she had left her cloak. He opened a chamber door and took her inside.

When James turned up the lamp, she saw that they were in a luxuriously furnished sitting room, with a deep-piled carpet. He removed her fur hat, unfastened her glittering mask, and laid them on the window seat. Then he led her to a softly cushioned love seat that sat in front of a cozy fire. "That's better." He removed his own eye mask and sent it sailing across the room. "Now I can see your beautiful face and your glorious hair."

He reached for a curl and rubbed the silken texture between his fingers. "I've been wanting to do this all night." He threaded his hands into the red-gold mass, and drew her face close. Then his mouth took possession of her lips in a sensual, lingering kiss.

"I could play with your hair for hours, and never tire of it." He lifted her hand to his mouth and placed a kiss on each finger. "Lily, you are an exquisite female." He removed his doublet and sat back and gazed at her. "You absolutely enchant me."

She smiled into his dark eyes. "Then I'm glad I decided to come." *I've daydreamed about being with you for years, but tonight is a thousand times more thrilling than any daydream.*

He traced a finger along the swansdown that trimmed her collar. "This high neck is far more sensual than any low-cut gown." He pictured her breasts beneath the velvet and desire rose up in him. He could feel the slow, heavy pulse in his groin. His lips traced a path from her ear to her chin. "Come home with me tonight?"

She could feel the texture of his linen shirt beneath her fingers, and see the crisp dark hair on his chest inside the open collar. His wicked suggestion tempted her beyond belief. It hung in the air between them for long, drawn-out minutes. "I can't do that, James."

He said ruefully, "I didn't think it would be that easy." He took possession of her hands and spoke seriously. "I want you, sweetheart. I'm determined we must come to an arrangement. Tell me what it will take. I will agree to whatever you ask of me."

She looked at him with her heart in her eyes, and sighed with regret. "You have no idea how much I wish that were possible, my lord."

His hands tightened. "I swear it! You may have carte blanche. I'll give you whatever you desire."

"No, you won't, James."

She suddenly felt extremely guilty over her deception. Gently she tried to remove her hands, but he would not let go. She shook her head sadly. "You will not give me what I desire, James."

"Name it!"

"Marriage," she whispered.

He stared at her in stunned silence and allowed her to take back her hands.

"I'm afraid I've deceived you, my lord. That day we met at the races, you assumed I was Henry Fane's mistress, and it amused me. It was just a game I played. In reality I am related to Westmorland through marriage. I am no man's mistress."

His emotions were suddenly at war. He was elated that she didn't belong to Westmorland, yet frustrated that she wasn't a demimonde. More than anything he longed to take her to bed and make love to her. He was also damned annoyed that she had deliberately concealed her identity from him. "If your name isn't Lily Lamb, what is it? I would like to know who you are."

"Ask your father."

He jumped to his feet. "My father knows you?"

"I am a lady, though tonight I truly wish it were otherwise, James." Regret made her voice husky. "My father's carriage is coming for me at one." She retrieved her mask and fur hat from the window seat. "Please try to forgive me."

James Hamilton stood at the window for a long time trying to make sense of things. His mind went back to the first time he'd seen the beautiful woman at the Newmarket races. *She said she was related to Westmorland. She must have been staying at Apethorpe Hall. Good God, what were my first words to her? I told her she could do much better than Fane unless she enjoyed being an old man's darling.* James flushed at the memory. *Her beauty hooked me like a damned trout and she agreed to go for a drink with me so she could reel me in!*

Damn it all, lady or no lady, she was attracted to me, or why would she seek me out at the House of Commons? Was it only a week ago that we dined together at the hotel? She was eager enough to accept tonight's invitation. She thoroughly enjoyed being in my arms dancing with me. She welcomed my kisses eagerly enough. Perhaps there's still a chance. She certainly wouldn't be the first lady to indulge in dalliance. I warrant she's deliberately playing hard to get.

James Hamilton's mood lightened considerably, and he went downstairs to seek out his father. He searched the ballroom and then the supper rooms. He found his sister Jane, who told him that he'd missed their parents by about five minutes. "Perhaps you'll catch them if you hurry out to Pall Mall, though you might find it a bit drafty if the wind catches your kilt."

"Would you enjoy me making a fool of myself, Jane?"

"Ah, James, you could never be that."

"I'm not so sure. I came within an inch of it tonight."

Her eyebrows went up in mocking amusement. "Only an inch?"

He grinned, his humor restored. "Well, perhaps six inches."

Anne didn't sleep well because her conscience pricked her about deceiving James Hamilton. In the morning, however, when she sat up in bed, she felt exceedingly happy. *How could I possibly have regrets about our evening together when it was so pleasurable? He was a magnificent dancing partner. We shared a good deal of laughter. We enjoyed feeding each other, and when he kissed me, I was in absolute heaven. But the best part, the very best part of all, is that James is attracted to me . . . so completely enamored that he offered me anything I desire if I'd agree to be his mistress. When he learns who I am, it shouldn't be too difficult to get him to court me.*

After breakfast, Anne glanced out the window. *It looks like it might snow.* Anne put on her jade green winter coat. Though Hampden House was only around the block, it was an extremely cold morning. She chose not to wear the matching jade bonnet, but instead donned the white fur hat she had worn to the ball. She decided that she wouldn't tell Frances too much about her intrigue, but was wildly curious about where her friend had gone with Blandford Churchill, the young noble Frances had marked as her prey.

"Anne, come upstairs. I have something exciting to tell you."

"Frances, I couldn't wait. I bolted my breakfast and rushed right over."

"If you were at the ball last night, I didn't recognize you."

"That's because I arrived late, and a wild guess tells me that you departed early."

"It's a secret! No one is supposed to know," Frances confessed. "How on earth?"

"I saw an Egyptian princess spiriting away a certain Horse Guard who shall remain nameless. Where did you take him? For a ride on your barge down the Nile?"

"He took me. But you're close. We went for a ride in his carriage along the Thames."

"Wherever did you find the courage to do such a scandalous thing?"

"Well, the ballroom was unbelievably crowded and hot, so when he suggested we get some fresh air, I thought it an excellent idea."

"I'll bet you did. You were ripe for the plucking."

"I have more good sense than to let him take too many liberties. My head rules my heart and always shall," Frances reminded her.

"How far did you go?"

"We went all the way to Windsor."

Anne threw back her head and laughed so hard, tears came to her eyes. "That isn't what I meant, but I'm glad to know that he stopped before he got to Maidenhead." She burst into laughter again.

"I'd recognize your lovely voice anywhere." John Claud strolled into the room.

"Anne and I were having a private conversation."

"Seems there are lots of private conversations this morning. James showed up first thing and dragged Father into the library."

Anne went pale and put her hand to her throat.

"Let me take your hat and coat."

"No! Thank you, John Claud, I was just leaving."

The library door opened, and Anne could hear Abercorn's and his son's voices as they approached the drawing room. She knew she was trapped.

"James, there's someone here I especially want you to meet." John Claud took Anne's elbow and turned her toward his brother. "This is Lady Anne Curzon-Howe. I believe you know her older sister Emily."

James stiffened in shock. The red-gold curls and white fur hat dazzled his senses. His dark eyes filled with fury.

"I've already had the pleasure. Lady Anne was masquerading under false pretenses last night."

"You attended Jane's ball?" John Claud asked James in surprise.

"Yes, much to my regret. I do not appreciate being made a fool of." His tone was icy.

"That's why I never go to costume balls. They turn grown men into idiots."

James's eyes narrowed. "Idiots indeed!"

"It was lovely to meet you again, Lord Hamilton." Anne licked her lips, which had suddenly gone dry. "I really must go."

"I'll walk you home," John Claud declared.

"No, please. It's only around the corner."

"I insist, Lady Anne. It would give me great pleasure."

She moved woodenly through the drawing room door toward the stairs, and John Claud followed her.

Anne's cheeks were so hot, the blast of cold air was a welcome relief.

"You encountered my brother James at the ball last night?"

Anne passed off John Claud's question as lightly as she could. "When he asked me to dance, he had no idea I was a lady."

"Of course not. James doesn't associate with ladies. He's constantly on the prowl, after only one thing. He's astonishingly handsome and gifted; women go mad over him. No matter how old or young, they flirt outrageously and throw themselves at him. His currency is seductiveness. He's like a graceful panther, ruthlessly stalking one prey after another."

"I must go in—I'm freezing." Anne bade John Claud a hasty good-bye. Inside, she ran straight upstairs to her bedchamber. She stood before her mirror and stared at her flaming cheeks. Slowly, hopelessly, she pulled off her fur hat. *James looked at me so coldly. He believes that I deliberately humiliated him.*

*   *   *

Back at Hampden House, James confronted his father with blazing eyes.

Abercorn held up his hands. "Last night, I gave Anne my word that I wouldn't let you know she was a debutante."

"A *debutante*? She's only eighteen?" James demanded in disbelief.

"I believe my friend Anne is only seventeen," Frances said. "She fibs about her age."

James was stunned. He felt as if his world had been turned upside down. Nothing seemed real. It was like a nightmare from which he prayed he would soon awaken.

Then suddenly he realized it didn't matter that she was a lady, and her age had absolutely nothing to do with the way he felt about her. *I must go after her.* He grabbed his coat and took the stairs two at a time.

He opened the front door and came face-to-face with John Claud.

"James, I'm so glad you finally met Lady Anne. She's the girl I'm going to marry!"

Chapter 7

Windsor Castle

I don't believe it. Prince Albert crumpled the letter from Major General Bruce in his fist. The female his son had been consorting with had not returned to Ireland after all. Bertie had moved the strumpet to the hotel in Cambridge, and according to Bruce, the sordid affair was common knowledge. *I assumed she'd be gone by Bertie's birthday, but it's now the end of November.* Albert wiped the perspiration from his brow. *If I want something done, I obviously have to do it myself, and by God, I shall!*

Prince Albert summoned his valet. "Pack me an overnight bag, and order my carriage." The prince consort made his way to Victoria's private sitting room and told the queen about the upsetting missive he had just received.

"I shall put an end to the scandalous affair, once and for all. In no uncertain terms I shall tell our son that both of us will disown him if he does not reform his evil, shameless way of life."

"Thank you, Albert. It is beyond belief that the heir to the throne would besmirch the Royal House of Windsor in general, and his mother, the Queen of England, in particular. He is an unnatural son, devoid of either love or obedience."

"Have no fear, my dearest Victoria, I shall bring him to heel."

What the devil is my father doing here? Teddy was thankful he had returned to Cambridge. At all costs he was determined to keep silent about gallivanting off to Newmarket for his birthday. He regretted that James Hamilton had returned to London—his friend was a dab hand at appeasing the prince consort.

"Let me help you off with your coat, sir."

"I shall keep it on." Prince Albert frowned darkly at Charles Carrington, then glared at his son. "Get your overcoat. I have something to discuss that is for your ears alone." He strode to the door and waited impatiently.

Outside, it had begun to snow, and the wind was bitter cold. The pair walked some distance in stony silence, before Albert declared in an ominous tone, "Nellie Clifden."

Oh, Christ, I feared that's why you came. What was it James advised me to do?

"Under the circumstances you have only one option. You must apologize for your indiscretion, and vow it will never happen again."

"I apologize for my indiscretion, Father. The lady returned to Ireland before my birthday. I swear on my honor, it will never happen again."

"You *have* no honor! You are lying to me. I have it from an impeccable source that the female is registered at the Royal Cambridge Hotel as *Mrs. Renfrew*, a name you use for dishonorable purposes, I've been informed."

"Father, I swear the lady in question has returned to Ireland. If you do not believe me, you may make inquiries at the hotel."

The snow turned from thick flakes to sleet as the temperature began to plummet.

"The life you have been leading is not only debauched and shameful; it is ungodly! The queen and I can never forgive you for this sordid behavior. I knew that you were thoughtless and weak, but I could not bring myself to believe you *depraved*, until now."

Teddy felt contrite, but at the same time he was also resentful. He was being honest, he had apologized, vowed it wouldn't happen again, and he didn't know what else to say. His father had a way of making him feel less than worthless. "You look ill, Father. I don't think you should be outside in this wet, freezing weather."

"This journey to Cambridge was only necessary because of your grossly immoral behavior. Marriage is the only cure. I shall begin negotiations immediately." Prince Albert turned and retraced his footsteps. When he got to the house, he strode toward his carriage.

"You are soaking wet, Father. Come in and get dry."

Prince Albert ignored him and climbed into his carriage for the six-hour return journey to Windsor Castle.

Teddy thrust his hands into his pockets. *He didn't even say good-bye.*

Windsor Castle
December 6, 1861

"Dr. Clark, my husband has been abed for an entire week, yet he doesn't seem to be improving. We would ask that you bring in another physician without delay." Queen Victoria used the royal *we* whenever she wished to assert her authority.

Dr. Clark bowed. "Your Gracious Majesty, I was about to suggest the very same thing. I will summon my colleague Dr. Henry Holland, with your permission, ma'am."

She nodded curtly and returned to the blue bedchamber, where Albert lay fevered. Victoria sat beside the bed and placed her hand over her husband's. "Clark is bringing Henry Holland to have a look at you. You should never have gone running off to Cambridge. Bertie is the cause of this!"

"As soon as I am up and about, I shall start negotiations for his marriage. It was the solution for Vicky, and it is the answer for Bertie." He raised his hand to his brow. "I'm so thirsty."

Victoria poured some barley water into a glass and offered it to him.

"Could I have a drink with lemons?"

Prince Albert's equerry jumped to attention.

The queen put up her hand. "I shall go to the kitchens and see to it myself." She swept regally from the blue bedchamber. She loved her husband dearly, and intended to sit at his bedside all night, if necessary.

The following day Dr. Clark and Dr. Holland stepped outside the blue bedroom to consult on a diagnosis. Clark thought Prince Albert had influenza, but Holland suspected typhoid and dosed him accordingly. In two days when there was no improvement, they brought in Dr. Thomas Watson, who was more concerned with breaking the patient's fever than naming the ailment that was causing it.

Queen Victoria was livid that the most professional doctors in London argued about a diagnosis rather than curing whatever was ailing her beloved Albert. It was obvious that he was growing weaker by the day; he could no longer eat; he did not sleep. He spoke seldom, and only in monosyllables.

Windsor Castle was awash in rumors. Both the queen's household staff and the prince consort's whispered that Albert's life was in grave danger. The queen's temper was short and none dared to approach her.

On Thursday, the Duke of Abercorn bearded the lioness in her den. "Your Majesty, I've seen the doctors arriving and departing the castle. Prince Albert must be ill indeed, since he hasn't been to his office for some time. Is there anything I can do to ease your burden, ma'am?"

"Oh, James, his doctors are useless! Do come upstairs and have a look at him. You must advise me what to do."

The duke had known Victoria for many years. Rather than have her lead the way, he took her arm and helped her up the stairs. When he saw Albert, he felt great alarm, although he did not allow the queen to see his dismay. "I recommend my own physician, William Jenner. In this case I believe many opinions will be better than one. Have you told your children how ill he is, ma'am? I would advise you to send word to Germany to Princess Vicky. Albert may rally if he sees his family surrounding him."

"I wanted to nurse him myself, but perhaps that's selfish of me."

"Not selfish, ma'am. But your children should be sharing your burden."

"Thank you, James. I pray your Dr. Jenner can help my poor darling Albert."

The following day, Dr. Jenner needed only a few minutes with the patient to know what the consort was suffering from. Prince Albert's lungs were filling, and his breathing was extremely labored. "Typhoid fever, complicated by pneumonia."

"My dear fellow, we dare not suggest to the queen that her husband has pneumonia. She will lose all hope," Dr. Clark declared. The other two physicians nodded sagely.

"Her Royal Majesty would be right to lose hope. In my opinion, Prince Albert's pneumonia, left too long without treatment, has allowed the typhoid to debilitate him to such a degree that he may not recover."

The three physicians who had attended the queen's consort for twelve days were filled with fear, and with dread of Victoria's reaction to the diagnosis, which they were beginning to believe, now that it had been pointed out to them in plain language.

The four medical men consulted, and Jenner declared, "I shall inform the queen."

Jenner thought Victoria took the news stoically, though she could very well be in denial or in shock.

The queen relayed the dire situation to Abercorn, who was Albert's groom of the stole. "James, would you handle the business of informing our children that their father is gravely ill, and tell them they should come to Windsor Castle without delay?"

"I will take care of it, ma'am."

Abercorn immediately dispatched a cable to Germany to the Princess Royal. Then he sent messengers to Madingley Hall summoning Princess Alice and Princess Helena.

Since Abercorn's son James usually came to dinner with the family on Friday night, he did not send a message to the Prince of Wales. He knew James would prefer to take the news to Cambridge himself.

It had been two whole weeks since the masked ball, yet to James Hamilton it seemed like only last night. He could not get the image of the Russian princess out of his mind. By day, she consumed his every waking thought, and by night his dreams were filled with her. *Lady Anne Howe, why am I obsessed with you?*

James knew the answer. Men always wanted the unobtainable. They desired it, craved it, longed for it, and without a doubt Lady Anne was unobtainable. If any other male had spoken for her, he would have laughed in his face and taken the prize. But it was John Claud, the brother he had protected all his life.

James was the privileged heir, who'd inherited the title Lord Hamilton at birth, along with the Scottish landholdings, and the wealth they produced. Because his father had been the lord lieutenant of County Donegal, Ireland, James had easily won the election to become the member of Parliament for Donegal. And shortly after, on top of everything else, he'd been appointed royal attendant to the Prince of Wales.

Since they were boys, John Claud had striven to emulate his older brother in every way, but his achievements in scholarship, athletics, and social skills always fell short. James knew if he pursued Lady Anne, it would be like rubbing John Claud's face in the dirt. His code of honor would not allow him to hurt his brother.

In a dilemma, James checked his watch. It was Friday night and he was expected at Hampden House for dinner. He hadn't shown up last week; the thought of sitting at the table with John Claud had been anathema under the circumstances. Tonight his gut knotted at the knowledge that he must force himself to mask his emotions and dine with his family.

James Hamilton didn't arrive for dinner until nine o'clock. "So sorry I'm late, Mother. You should have started without me." He could sense the atmosphere at Green Street was fraught with silent despair. His own problem was forgotten. "Whatever is wrong?"

"Prince Albert is gravely ill, James. Her Majesty has asked me to summon their children to Windsor."

James looked from his father to his mother. "Albert is only forty-two. Surely he's not in danger of dying?"

Abercorn solemnly shook his head. "I've spoken with Dr. Jenner. The prince has typhoid, complicated by pneumonia. He is slowly sinking, I'm afraid."

Lord Hamilton immediately realized that if Prince Albert died, the Royal House of Windsor would never be the same. Even his own family would be affected by the death. His father would lose his post, and the entire country would be thrown into deepest mourning.

"I feel certain Prince Albert must recover, but as a precaution I shall take my carriage to Cambridge and escort the Prince of Wales to Windsor."

"Thank you, James. Though I hope for the best, I fear the worst. Time is of the essence. Take my closed carriage and use post-horses rather than your own. It's a journey of sixty miles each way."

"I insist that you eat dinner before you set out," his mother said firmly. "It is such a bitter cold night, I don't want you coming down with pneumonia."

James drove with all the speed that the winter conditions allowed. His only stop was in Hertford to change the post-horses. Because the roads were empty after midnight, he made the journey in five hours. It was three in the morning when a sleepy manservant opened the front door of the Cambridge residence leased for the prince.

"This is an ungodly hour to come calling, Lord Hamilton," the elderly servant admonished. "I cannot awaken his Royal Highness without a good reason."

"The reason is confidential. I shall awaken him myself." James strode inside and headed for the stairs. Over his shoulder, he said, "Please light the lamps, and kindly rouse someone in the kitchen to make some coffee."

James gave the bedchamber door a perfunctory knock, walked straight in, and shook the prince's shoulder. "Teddy! Wake up, Teddy."

"James? Is that you, old man?"

James turned up the oil lamps and a golden light flooded the chamber.

Teddy sat up in bed. "What is it? Is something wrong?"

"I don't want to unnecessarily alarm you, but your father is ill and Her Majesty feels Prince Albert will benefit if his children come to Windsor."

"He wouldn't want *me* at his bedside." Teddy told James about his father's headlong rush to Cambridge to chastise him about Nellie Clifden. "He refused to believe that she had gone back to Ireland. My father and I are not even on speaking terms."

"That's irrelevant, Teddy. Your mother, the queen, has issued a summons to all of you. My father sent a cable to Vicky, your sisters Alice and Helena are on their way from Madingley Hall, and your brothers are being brought home from school as a precaution."

"But surely they should be kept away as a precaution against catching his influenza, or whatever is ailing him?"

A knock on the door brought the manservant with coffee. James took the tray from him and carried it to the bed. "Drink some of this. It's cold out there."

"James, I assure you, he won't want to see me."

James hesitated for a heartbeat, then made a decision. "Your father may be dying."

"Dying?" The prince jumped out of bed. "Why the devil didn't you say so? I should have realized. You drove all night to get here!"

James went down the hall to rouse Charles Carrington. He detected whiskey fumes and shook him until he knew he was cognizant before he explained the situation. "We must return the prince to Windsor without delay. Pack his bags. He may not be back for some time, if ever."

When he returned to the Prince of Wales, James saw that he was already dressed, and pacing up and down in distress. "What do the doctors say?"

"Typhoid fever complicated by pneumonia."

"Good God, then he really is in danger of dying."

"I'm afraid so, Teddy. Carrington is packing your bags. Drink some coffee. I'll get your overcoat." James moved to the wardrobe. "I think I'll take some of these blankets. It's damned cold out there and we could be in the carriage for six or seven hours."

Because of the snow-clogged roads, the carriage didn't arrive at Windsor Castle until two o'clock in the afternoon. James turned it over to Carrington and went with the Prince of Wales to his apartment. The corridors were inhabited by grim-faced servants, various members of Her Majesty's government, royal relatives, and medical attendants.

James helped the prince remove his overcoat and tweed jacket, and replaced them with a black morning coat. He poured him a small measure of brandy. "Drink this." Then they walked a direct path to the prince consort's bedchamber known as the Blue Room.

"Stay beside me, James," Teddy pleaded.

"I won't be allowed inside, Your Highness. . . . Family only." James placed a hand on his shoulder, turned the knob, and, when the door swung open, propelled the prince inside.

A strong smell of camphor, eucalyptus, and something Teddy couldn't identify pervaded the chamber. Four doctors conversing in whispers stood around a table that held a spirit lamp, medicine, stethoscopes, and other paraphernalia. To the left, members of the clergy stood with downcast eyes, their lips moving in silent prayer.

The prince saw the pale, frightened faces of his sisters

and the eyes of his young brothers staring with apprehensive disbelief at the figure lying unmoving in the center of the high bed. Each sibling sent their oldest brother a relieved glance of appreciation that he had at last arrived, which he gratefully returned. Not by the flicker of an eyelash did his mother acknowledge his presence. The queen sat stoically beside her husband, holding his hand.

Prince Teddy was deeply shocked at the state of his father. He had been brought from Cambridge because there was a possibility that his father might die, but one look at the still figure in the bed told him that death was a certainty. He had already sunk into unconsciousness, his breaths so shallow they were almost indiscernible.

More than anything Teddy wanted to apologize to his father, to offer him comfort, to be a loving son to him, but it was too late. It was too late to even say good-bye.

At nine o'clock, after a hurried whispered consultation with his colleagues, Dr. Jenner left the Blue Room to seek out Abercorn, who was sitting vigil in Prince Albert's office. "He's dying fast. I'm amazed he has lasted this long. You will know who must be officially notified, Your Grace."

"I will send a telegram to the City of London, and I will inform the secretary of state to start preparing the official notice from Whitehall. Let me know when it happens. A bulletin must be posted at Buckingham Palace. We must assure the country that Her Majesty the Queen, though overwhelmed with grief, bears her bereavement with calmness, and is not suffering in health."

Royal servants gathered in the corridor outside the Blue Room as news of Prince Albert's approaching demise spread throughout Windsor Castle. They stood their vigil in respectful silence, some in stunned disbelief, some in mournful sorrow, but all harboring fear for what this would do to Queen Victoria.

Albert drew his last breath ten minutes before eleven o'clock. Dr. Clark felt for a pulse and, when he found none, nodded solemnly to Victoria. She sat in silence, unmoving for long, drawn-out minutes; then without taking her eyes from her husband, she said, "Leave us."

The clergy hesitated, then slowly walked from the room, followed by the four doctors. One by one, Albert's sons and daughters filed past their father lying in the great bed. Teddy stood rooted to the spot where he had been waiting for almost eight hours. He did not dare approach the bed without permission from his mother. He took a deep breath as she finally raised her eyes and looked at him.

"You killed your father. I never wish to see your face again."

Her words pierced his heart as painfully as if she had plunged in a dagger. Teddy bowed his head, and slowly walked from the room.

James Hamilton was beside the Prince of Wales the moment he emerged from the Blue Room. He was prepared for Teddy's near collapse, and gave him full support as they ascended the stairs to his apartment. The prince's legs were shaking uncontrollably from standing so many hours. His heart was unbearably heavy from the burden of guilt, and his shoulders were stooped from his father's and mother's total rejection.

James closed the door and half carried him to a cushioned chair before the fire. He poured a measure of brandy into a glass and brought it to the prince. James knew that Teddy was exhausted and on the verge of collapse. Physically, he needed sleep, but James realized that mentally and emotionally he would first have to unburden himself to someone who would not judge him. More than anything, tonight the prince needed companionship and James sat down across from him ready, willing, and able to provide it.

They sat together quietly as the prince sipped his brandy. It was some time after the glass was empty that Teddy finally broke the silence. "It was my fault. If he hadn't come to Cambridge when he was ill, my father would still be alive."

"No, it was *not* your fault," James said firmly. "There

was no need for him to come rushing to Cambridge. You had ended the affair and Nellie was back in Ireland. If anyone is to blame, it is Major Bruce, whose false report was filled with vindictive lies."

Teddy shook his head. "Mother will always blame me."

"She has suffered an irreparable loss. Give her time to come to terms with it."

Teddy shook his head sadly. "She will never forgive me."

Queen Victoria refused to have a public funeral for her beloved husband. She insisted on privacy. Prince Albert's funeral and short procession took place at St. George's Chapel, Windsor, the day following the arrival of Princess Vicky from Germany.

James Hamilton stood beside the Prince of Wales in the chapel. Queen Victoria was attended by her ladies-in-waiting, and was surrounded by her eldest daughter and the rest of her children. Bertie was consigned to a pew behind the rest of the family, and was extremely grateful for James's unwavering support.

Lord Hamilton's glance searched the chapel until he found Lady Anne Howe. She was the only one wearing pale gray. *She looks beautiful and ethereal, and stands out amid this flock of black-clad crows.* James noted that she was with her parents, but directly behind her, his brother John Claud seemed to be standing guard over her. James watched her avidly throughout the entire funeral service, fully aware that it would be a long time before he would be given the opportunity to see her again.

Chapter 8

Buckingham Palace
August 1, 1862

"James, thank God, Parliament is recessed for the summer. On the days you sit in the House of Commons, I almost go mad. This apartment at Buckingham Palace has become my prison. Vicky is back in Germany, my other brothers and sisters are at school, and for the seven months since Father died, my mother hasn't even acknowledged my existence."

"She has withdrawn from public life, not just you, Teddy, and she vows to wear nothing but black mourning for the rest of her days. Everyone in London has been affected by your father's death. The full year's mourning that has been declared must be strictly adhered to by all Society."

"She relied on him for everything. My father read every letter, every dispatch, sat in on her meetings with her ministers, and advised her about running the country. If only she'd let me help her! I'm bored out of my mind, sitting here being useless."

"My father approached her about letting you help with dispatches and letters. He reminded her that you would be king one day, and it would be invaluable training for you. Though he can be most diplomatic and persuasive, Teddy, she won't hear of it. Though Abercorn thought he would lose his post, the queen is keeping him to handle the duties he performed for Prince Albert. She has also come to rely upon Prime Minister Palmerston for advice and has shut everyone else out."

The prince stood and paced back and forth like a caged animal. "It shames me to tell you, but she has cut off my money. I can't even afford to go into the country to ride or shoot. Here I am penniless. I tell you, James, I haven't a pot to piss in!"

"Tell you what, Teddy—it's Friday. I eat dinner at Hampden House with my family on Friday night. You are coming with me."

"It's a family affair. Abercorn won't want me at his table."

"That's what families have to do for entertainment these days. No parties, no balls. Can't even attend the theater or go to White's to gamble without being ostracized. The only socializing not frowned upon is families dining together. I insist that you come."

"James insisted that I come, Your Grace." A worried frown creased the Prince of Wales's brow when he saw the startled look on Lady Lu's face.

James's mother sketched a graceful curtsy. "Your Highness, this is such an unexpected honor. Welcome to our home."

"My dearest lady, if you would dispense with the formalities this evening, I would be forever in your debt."

"Consider it done." Lady Lu gave Teddy a warm embrace. "I shall treat you like one of the family." She contemplated telling him he wouldn't be the only dinner guest, but decided against it in case he bolted. "Dinner will be served at eight, so until then you'll find Abercorn in the library." The duchess made her way to the kitchen to ask Cook to add a few things to the menu. She knew the prince had a healthy appetite, and like most males preferred plain English food over fancy foreign delicacies.

In the library, Abercorn poured James and the prince a dram of Irish whiskey. The three men felt comfortable together and it loosened Teddy's tongue. "Thanks for inviting me. You've no idea how good it feels to have someone to talk to. I've felt totally isolated for the past eight months. I've no desire to return to Cambridge; I've spent more than enough years studying. Mother shuns me and refuses my offer of help with her royal tasks. Buckingham Palace cages me, yet I have no funds that would allow me to go elsewhere. I would love to visit Sandringham, the country estate my father bought in Norfolk just before he died, but Mother has forbidden me."

"Most likely she forbids you because your father never got to stay there."

His shoulders drooped. "I'm in total limbo. I don't see any way out of my prison."

Abercorn swirled the smoky whiskey around his glass. "There is a way, Your Highness." He hesitated, knowing how his suggestion would be received. "Marriage."

The prince recoiled. "That would be exchanging one purgatory for another."

Abercorn gave his son a speaking look, and James jumped in immediately. "You are so used to thinking of marriage in a negative way that you fail to see all the advantages it would bring. As a married man, your status would be immediately elevated. An unwed prince is considered a boy, under the authority of his mother. A married prince would become a man in his own right, and head of his own household."

"Not just a household, but a *royal* household," Abercorn emphasized.

James could see that though Teddy was far from being convinced, at least he was willing to listen to what they had to say.

"In three months, I come of age. Surely when I turn twenty-one, the queen will not be able to hold my money back. In fact, I believe my stipend from the Crown will increase."

"It will increase at twenty-five, not twenty-one, Your

Highness," Abercorn corrected, "unless of course you are a married man. That changes everything."

"Does it indeed? My education in royal affairs is sadly lacking. Tell me more."

"Since the fourteenth century, money for the Prince of Wales has been provided by the duchy of Cornwall and is overseen by the Treasury."

"Then how can the queen stop it?" Teddy demanded.

"Her Majesty has only stopped her allowance to you. The queen cannot stop your money from Cornwall. It comes to you annually to the tune of half a million pounds per year, but it is held in trust until you turn twenty-five, or marry, whichever comes first."

"Good God, that puts a different light on matters. I will be a wealthy man."

There was a discreet tap on the library door and the three men looked up expectantly.

The duchess opened the door and announced, "Our other guests have arrived, darling. I'm sure Earl Howe would enjoy joining you gentlemen until dinner is ready."

Abercorn smiled his welcome. "Do come in, Richard, you're just the man we need here, since you are a font of information on the royal households." He turned to the prince. "You know Earl Howe. I warrant introductions are unnecessary."

"Absolutely. How are you, my lord? I haven't seen you for some time."

"Your Royal Highness." The earl bowed his head formally.

"Please, none of that, Lord Howe." The prince shook his hand warmly.

Abercorn poured Richard a glass of Irish whiskey, then again addressed the prince. "George III, your great-great-grandfather, transferred the ownership of most royal residences to the British government. The royal family does not own Buckingham Palace or Windsor Castle."

"The royal residences don't belong to the queen?" the prince asked in disbelief.

Richard Howe grinned. "They do not. You, sir, happen to be a rare exception since you own the deed in your name to a royal residence."

"I do? How can that be? Which residence?"

Earl Howe was surprised that the young prince had been kept in ignorance. "Marlborough House," Richard informed him with relish.

James's eyes widened. "Marlborough House isn't owned by the Marlboroughs?"

"I'm sure you all know of the infamous friendship almost two centuries ago between Sarah Churchill, Duchess of Marlborough, and Queen Anne? Sarah talked the queen into building her a great mansion next door to St. James's Palace. It is fortuitous that Queen Anne, in spite of her infatuation with Sarah, was shrewd enough to keep ownership of the property in her name. Thus, Marlborough House has been passed down to each subsequent reigning monarch. When King William died, ownership passed to his widow, Queen Adelaide, whom I was fortunate enough to serve. When Victoria became queen, Adelaide vacated Buckingham Palace so your mother could reside there, and moved into Marlborough House. When Adelaide died, the ownership was passed to Victoria and Albert, who deeded the property to their son and heir, Edward, Prince of Wales, with a view to it becoming his residence when he came of age."

"I hadn't the faintest idea. No one ever told me." Teddy was clearly amazed.

"You were a child of eight when Queen Adelaide died. Your royal parents obviously gave their consent that the deed be put in your name."

"This is splendid news. I am astounded at my good fortune."

"Since it's close-by, right next door to St. James's Palace, I think we should go and have a look at it tomorrow," James suggested to the prince.

"My very thought, exactly!"

"For a few years Prince Albert allowed the Royal College of Art to lease it; then about ten years ago your father hired designer Sir James Pennethorne to substantially enlarge Marlborough House with a range of rooms on the north side, and two more stories were built onto the wings." Abercorn added, "Your father did this so you would have your own royal residence when you married."

"He never told me," the prince said wistfully.

"Perhaps because the discussion of marriage was always rather contentious between the two of you."

"That's true." Prince Teddy looked shamefaced, but at that moment Lady Lu tapped on the library door and announced, "Dinner is about to be served, gentlemen."

In the dining room James was shocked to come face-to-face with Lady Anne Howe. He schooled his face to mask his surprise. It had been more than seven long months since he had seen her at Prince Albert's funeral. *Good God, I should have known that if Earl Howe was a dinner guest, his family would be here.*

James stood aside as his mother introduced Countess Howe to the Prince of Wales; then she introduced the earl's daughter Anne, and his son Montagu.

The prince bowed to the ladies and kissed their hands. "I'm delighted to meet your lovely family, Lord Howe. I know your daughter Emily, who serves the queen so well."

"And I warrant you need no introduction to my son John Claud, or my daughter Frances, whom you've known since they were children. This young lady is my daughter Maud, who is far too grown up to be relegated to the nursery with the rest of our brood."

When the duchess indicated where each guest would sit, James watched his father hold his mother's chair, and saw Richard do the same for his wife. John Claud immediately stepped behind Anne to hold her chair. James's fists clenched, and he quickly looked away.

The first course served was sole poached in Chablis, and James's thoughts drifted to the dinner at the Westminster Palace Hotel. *Anne ordered Dover sole that day.* He wondered if the dish reminded her of their dinner together. *I loved watching her eat.* His glance moved toward the object of his desire, but he caught himself before he looked at her lovely face, and kept his gaze on her hands. He relived their meeting when she had come to watch him in Parliament from the visitors' gallery and remembered how exultant he'd felt when she agreed to join him for dinner.

When the roast lamb was served, James thought, *Lily Lamb. I was enchanted by the name, and over the moon that the beauty had finally identified herself.*

Then he heard her laugh. His father was a good host who entertained his guests with amusing conversation, but James heard none of it. His head was filled with memories of the masquerade ball where the two of them had laughed together at the other guests' outlandish costumes.

His gaze caressed her hands, and he remembered lifting one to his mouth and placing a kiss on each long, delicate finger. He recalled how it felt to take her into his arms and waltz with her. Toward the end of that first dance, his arms had tightened about her and he had drawn her close to his body for their first kiss. *It could not have been more perfect. When I withdrew my mouth from hers, she whispered "James" with longing. How I loved the taste of my name on her lips.* James felt his blood surge. *Come home with me tonight?* Then he felt the slow, heavy pulse in his groin, and his imagination swept him away as he relived a recurring fantasy in erotic detail:

Slowly, he took the pins from her glorious hair one at a time. The silken texture between his fingers made his desire flare. When the golden red mass came tumbling down, he could not resist burying his face in the fragrant curls. Then he lifted her high in the dominant position, so that the fiery tendrils fell upon his naked chest in a waterfall of splendor. He drew in a ragged breath of anticipation knowing the tips of her breasts would brush against the muscles of his chest as he pulled her down to him.

"What's the latest news in the House, James?" the earl asked.

James came out of his reverie and looked blankly at Richard Howe. "I'm sorry, my lord, I was a million miles away."

"The American Civil War," Richard prompted.

"Ah yes, since General Robert E. Lee assumed command of the Confederate army, they have been winning every battle."

"The Confederates certainly seem to have some superior generals."

"Yes, General Stonewall Jackson is advancing on the Union army near Washington. I believe General John Pope's soldiers will go down in defeat," James predicted.

Anne's presence, across the dinner table from him, was so distracting that James had great difficulty making intelligent conversation. He lapsed into silence, allowing the others to express their views, and nodded his head occasionally, pretending to follow the weighty subject of war. It wasn't long, however, before his imagination was filled with a far more enchanting subject.

In spite of her father's avid interest in war, Anne's attention was focused on more immediate concerns. Though she was sitting across the table from James Hamilton, she might just as well have been invisible for all the attention he paid her. *When Lady Lu told us the Prince of Wales would be dining with us tonight, I should have known James accompanied him, yet the thought never occurred to me. When I came face-to-face with him, my pulse began to race madly and my heart hammered in my breast so loudly it almost deafened me. Yet Lord Bloody Rakehell hardly glanced at me.*

James Hamilton's complete indifference stung her. She reluctantly admitted to herself that for almost eight long months she had been holding out hope that he would call on her or send her a note. The masquerade ball had been the most romantic night of her life, and a thousand times since she had regretted her refusal to go home with him. If she'd had a chance to relive that night and do it all over again, she would have kept her identity a secret and let him take her home. Now Anne cursed herself for being a fool.

It's time I grew up and faced reality. John Claud was right—James has no interest in ladies. It is utterly ridiculous to be infatuated with a man who will break my heart.

Anne glanced up at John Claud and found his possessive eyes on her. *In the past eight months our families have dined together more than a dozen times. I know my parents would be delighted with a match between us.* Her gaze traveled to the Duke and Duchess of Abercorn. *I would love to marry into this family, and I know they would welcome me as a daughter.* She glanced at John Claud again and this time she gifted him with a smile. *He's so devoted—perhaps I should give him a chance.* But deep down inside, her heart ached with longing, and Anne suspected that if she couldn't have James, she'd rather do without a husband.

Back in his apartment at Buckingham Palace, Prince Teddy was reluctant to have James leave. "I thoroughly enjoyed myself tonight, and got an education to boot. Bloody hell, I blush at my own ignorance."

"Well, I too was in ignorance. I had no idea that Marlborough House belonged to you."

"Best surprise I ever had in my life."

"You were due for a bit of good luck, I warrant," James said sincerely. "This calls for a toast." He poured them each a nightcap and they happily raised their glasses. "Here's to becoming head of your own household."

Teddy sipped his drink thoughtfully. "I want to be absolutely sure I have my facts straight, so correct me if I'm wrong. I'm free to move into Marlborough House when I turn twenty-five, and the Treasury will allow me to draw on my considerable fortune for its upkeep." He took another swallow. "The only fly in the ointment is that I won't celebrate my twenty-fifth birthday for another four years."

James nodded. "Four years and three months to be precise."

Teddy grimaced. "That's an eternity. Looking back over the last four years, the only time that was bearable was the three months I spent at the army camp in Ireland with the Grenadier Guards." He shook his head. "James, I'll never last another four years. I'm at the end of my rope now."

"So, let's explore the alternatives. The way I see it, you have three options. A quick death—slit your wrists; a slow one—drink yourself to death; or take a wife."

Teddy chuckled at his friend's dry wit. "When you put it so graphically, I really have no choice. Either I perish, or I marry."

"Well, look at it this way—sooner or later most men marry, and for a royal prince marriage is inevitable. You are the future king and your first and foremost duty to the country is to produce an heir to the throne." James drained his glass. "But you also have a duty to yourself. You must choose wisely for any chance at happiness."

"Though princes are *expected* to marry princesses, that isn't the law of the land. The lady I marry doesn't *have* to be royal."

"In theory that is true. But you must have the queen's consent before you can marry, and Her Majesty would never approve of a bride for you who wasn't a royal princess."

Teddy's shoulders drooped. "My choices are so limited."

"Especially since a German princess is anathema to you," James declared. "I thought Alexandra of Denmark was rather sweet."

"I found her colorless and childlike. She's not my idea of an attractive female."

"Well, I grant you that she is not like Nellie Clifden, and may I point out that if she were, she would not be acceptable."

"You are right, as always. Lady Anne Howe, who dined with us tonight, is a ravishing beauty. She seemed so vivid and filled with laughter. I warrant she'd be rewarding in bed." Teddy sighed. "I take it your brother is courting her?"

James stiffened at mention of Anne's name, and immediately tried to steer the Prince of Wales's thoughts away from her. "Our families have known each other for years. You don't have the luxury of years. If you want to establish your own household at Marlborough House, you need to marry as soon as your mourning period is over. Royal marriages take time to arrange. That means negotiations must begin as soon as you make your choice."

"How can I possibly decide who to marry? My choice is so limited."

"You must carefully weigh the qualities you want in a wife. First and foremost she should be a princess, and preferably one who is young and biddable."

"In other words someone childlike and colorless!" Teddy said with disgust.

"Bear with me for a moment, while I compare two princesses for you. Your sister Princess Victoria was indulged and thoroughly spoiled from the day she was born by doting parents who allowed her to have all her own way. She is vain, willful, demanding, extravagant, headstrong, and sexually precocious. She insists on having her own way about everything, and I'm willing to wager she rules her husband with an iron hand."

"You paint a graphic picture, James, but an exact one."

"Now compare Princess Victoria with Princess Alexandra, who is young, sweet, biddable, and above all innocent. It's quite obvious she has never been indulged and spoiled. Her father has never had money for an extravagant lifestyle. Such a young woman would be in awe of you, and would no doubt do her utmost to please you in every way. Would you prefer a wife who is aggressive or one who is passive? One who rules the roost, or one who would bow to your wishes? I warrant young Alexandra is malleable and can be molded to anything you desire her to be."

"I've been ruled long enough. The last thing I want is another woman ruling my life."

James set down his empty glass and went into the prince's study. His finger ran across the books in the bookcase until he found the one he wanted. "Here's a Genealogy of European Royalty." His glance searched the table of contents. "Princess Anna of Hesse, Princess Pauline of Mecklenburg, Princess Caroline of Schleswig-Holstein, and her gaggle of royal sisters, Princess Maria Alexandrovna, who's Russian rather than German." He handed the book to Teddy. "I shall bid you good night and tomorrow we'll visit Marlborough House."

"I am faced with an onerous task," Teddy lamented.

"Just remember, the lady you choose will be the next Queen of England."

"Thanks for making it easy for me."

"What are friends for?" James asked lightly.

Before Lady Anne climbed into bed, she opened her journal and dipped her pen in the inkwell. *I find it ironic that James Bloody Hamilton couldn't spare me a glance tonight, yet the most eligible bachelor in England, namely, His Royal Highness the Prince of Wales, couldn't take his eyes off me.*

However, I don't consider it a compliment, since Teddy looked at me with lust rather than admiration. According to John Claud, the Prince of Wales and James are both predators, constantly on the prowl for females willing to lift their skirts for them.

Tonight, I realized how foolish I've been to think James had a tendre *for me. When we saw each other again for the first time in almost eight months, for one mad moment my heart sang. Just one intimate glance would have told me I lingered in his thoughts, and would have kept my hope alive. But when James looked through me as if I were invisible, it was like a slap in the face—a slap I obviously needed.*

When this dreadful year of mourning is up, and social invitations to parties and balls are no longer frowned upon, I shall accept all of them. I will no longer discourage my admirers, I will collect them, and John Claud can get in line behind Fitz Kerry.

Anne closed her journal, turned out the lamp, and slipped into bed. Putting her thoughts on paper had given her a small measure of satisfaction. Her last thought before she drifted off to sleep was *I'll show him!*

"Marlborough House is absolutely magnificent. The interiors are far more grand than anything I imagined." Prince Teddy gazed about in amazement.

"Just look at this wall painting. I believe it's *The Battle of Blenheim* by Laguerre." James looked up at the ceiling where a cupola had been inserted and was surrounded by paintings. "All this magnificent artwork is a result of your father leasing the house to the Royal College of Art. Some of the greatest artists in the world have used the walls and staircases as if they were canvases, and turned it into a showplace."

"Every chamber takes my breath away. Look at all the marble, the chandeliers, the fireplaces. The tall windows were obviously designed to let in all this light."

"It was designed by Sir Christopher Wren. Is it any wonder he's considered England's greatest architect?"

"James, I can scarcely believe my great good fortune!"

"It's not just a mansion, it's more like a palace. Your Highness, this will become the social center of London. You will become the most famous host England has ever known. All Society will fight for an invitation to Marlborough House. You'll have more friends than you'll ever want or need," James predicted.

"That will be extremely gratifying for someone who's endured a rather lonely life."

"You can say good-bye to loneliness. Since Her Majesty the Queen has withdrawn from public life, all the focus will be on you. London has always looked to the royal family as the leaders of Society. Now that role will fall to you."

"I can't wait. I'd move in today if I could."

"You have to marry before that can happen," James reminded him. "Have you decided who will become the Princess of Wales?"

"By a process of elimination, I'm left with only one choice. It will have to be Princess Alexandra of Denmark. How do we start negotiations?"

"I'll consult my father. He has handled the royal family's business affairs for the past fifteen years."

"Thank you, James. What the devil would I do without you?"

I trust I'm not giving him false hope. Though Father is a miracle worker, God knows how long this will take. Teddy's been forced to live like a monk at Buckingham Palace.

"I have an idea. Here's the key to my town house on White Horse Street. Why don't you go and stay there for a couple of days? My servants are discreet, and won't blink an eye if you enjoy a little female companionship. I'll sleep at the palace."

Teddy accepted the key with gratitude. "You are the best friend a prince could ever have, James. Someday it will be within my power to grant you favors," he promised.

James Hamilton made his way to Abercorn's office at Buckingham Palace. He closed the door so they could speak in private. "Father, after seeing Marlborough House, the Prince of Wales is extremely eager to remove himself from Buckingham Palace. He has come to accept that he must take a wife, and realizes that negotiations must be started at once."

"That won't be easy. The year's mourning period isn't up for another four and a half months."

"Teddy's at the end of his tether. You must find a way to circumnavigate the mourning period. You are such an experienced diplomat, Father, surely you can come up with a way to get around it."

"It will certainly take some delicate maneuvering. Who is the lucky lady?"

"Princess Alexandra of Denmark, I'm happy to say."

"Is she his choice, or yours?" Abercorn asked shrewdly.

"Teddy's choice, with only a little manipulation from me."

Abercorn sighed heavily. "I shall certainly have to resort to manipulation when I approach Her Majesty on this matter. After all these months, she still considers it sacrilege for me to even utter her son's name."

"I believe that the only reason the queen gave her permission for the Prince of Wales to travel to Strelitz last year was so that he could meet Princess Alexandra."

"Yes, it was. For years, Victoria had her heart set on her son marrying Princess Anna of Hesse. It was Albert who suggested Princess Alexandra might be a better choice."

"And it was Albert's favorite daughter, Vicky, who persuaded him. She is a manipulator, par excellence."

"I'll rearrange my work schedule and give priority to this matter. The first hurdle will be getting an audience with Her Majesty. I'll put in a request today."

James grinned at his father. "The rest will be a piece of cake. According to Mother, Victoria has always fancied you. She'll be putty in your hands."

"Don't try to manipulate a manipulator, James."

"Your Majesty, forgive my intrusion, but I need your advice on a most delicate matter."

"My dear Abercorn, you never intrude. Please have a seat. You are so tall it strains my neck to look up at you."

"Thank you, ma'am." He took a seat and purposely rustled a paper in his hand. "As I said, I would appreciate your advice on some unfinished business that Prince Albert had begun with Prince Christian, heir to the King of Denmark."

"Was it in regard to his daughter Princess Alexandra?"

"It was indeed, ma'am. Prince Albert had made up his mind that the Prince of Wales should marry, and that Princess Alexandra of Denmark would be the chosen bride."

Victoria nodded. "My dearest Albert and I discussed it a few times."

"Your husband asked me to draft a letter that would open negotiations for the marriage, but alas, Prince Albert became too ill to finalize and sign the official letter."

"Is that the draft my husband dictated?"

Abercorn handed Victoria the draft that he had drawn up only this morning, and waited quietly while she read it.

The queen's eyes filled with tears. "Albert had such a way with words."

The duke cleared his throat. "Since it was your husband's wish that the marriage take place, would Your Majesty like me to prepare an official letter for your royal signature that will open negotiations?"

"That is an excellent suggestion, Abercorn. However, we cannot embark on such a mission during our year of mourning for our beloved Albert. It is unthinkable."

"I am loath to offend your sensibilities, ma'am, but such an eligible royal princess will be snapped up by some calculating, minor European royal the moment she turns eighteen. Her birthday is three months away, on December first. We could conduct our negotiations privately and in strictest confidentiality. After your year's mourning period is up would be the ideal time to announce the engagement, if we are fortunate enough to secure the marriage prize."

"You are overlooking the greatest obstacle to our plans, I'm afraid. The Prince of Wales adamantly refuses to even consider marriage. He is an unnatural son!"

"I believe the prince is so remorseful over his defiant behavior, he will eagerly fulfill his father's last wish. He has told me in confidence he will do anything to make amends."

The queen's lips tightened. "Leave us. We will think on the matter."

Within twenty-four hours Victoria summoned Abercorn and directed him to prepare an official letter to Prince

Christian of Denmark for her signature. "Would you be good enough to act as liaison with the Prince of Wales, my dear Abercorn? I'm sure that you understand how much my son's presence offends me. A wife is exactly what he needs to bring him into line. My dearest Albert had the answer. You have much experience with sons, and you have my authority to bring him to heel. You may inform him that it is our royal command, and he has no choice in the matter."

Abercorn, ever the diplomat, informed the prince that he'd persuaded the queen to immediately open negotiations for his marriage to Princess Alexandra of Denmark. "Actually, she had no choice in the matter. The decision was entirely yours, sire."

"By God, James, I think I like making my own decisions. I did a great deal of thinking when I had the freedom of your town house, and I concluded I need one of my own."

"A town house?" James puzzled.

"A perfect place to carry on a liaison. I've been suffering from night starvation for far too long. It isn't natural for a male to be abstinent. You'll have to put it in your name of course. I'm sorry that your reputation will be at risk, but I need total anonymity. It cannot be connected to me in any way."

"My reputation is already blackened beyond repair," James jested. "You may rely upon me to accommodate you, *Baron Renfrew*."

Chapter 9

"I'm actually looking forward to church today," Lady Anne remarked to her mother as they stepped from their carriage in Hanover Square and walked up the steps of St. George's. "These days it's one of the few places where I get to see all my friends. I hope Frances will come riding in Hyde Park this afternoon."

"I always enjoy my Sunday afternoon drives in the park and this weather is perfect. The autumn wind will arrive before we know it to strip the leaves from the trees."

Inside, Anne searched the congregation for Frances Hamilton and saw that she was sitting with Florence Paget. When they beckoned her, she slipped into the pew beside her friends. "Why don't the three of us go riding this afternoon?"

"Good idea. The park is one of the few places we can actually socialize with our male admirers until this wretched year of mourning is up," Frances declared.

"Speaking of admirers, I see that Henry Rawdon is here again. I warrant he only comes to flirt with Florence." Anne watched her friend's cheeks turn a pretty pink.

"Last week he surreptitiously passed her a note," Frances confided.

Anne rolled her eyes. "How very daring! Still, what better place than church to carry on a secret liaison?

Why don't I let Henry know we'll be riding in the park this afternoon? There are dozens of secluded trails that offer privacy."

"Thank you," Florence murmured.

Anne saw Fitz, the young Earl of Kerry, and when she smiled, he winked at her. *Fitz is always so obliging. When we visited the museum, he was a paragon of patience while I did some sketches of Egyptian artifacts, and when we went to the Tower, he took me to see the crown jewels when I warrant he would have much preferred to view the torture chambers and the artillery and cannons.*

The organ music soared and they stood to sing a hymn. Frances whispered to Anne, "I have some news to tell you about James, but it's secret."

Anne caught her breath at the mention of his name. She nodded her understanding, knowing Frances wouldn't tell her until they were completely alone. Her mind conjured a picture of the dark, handsome devil. She remembered watching him on the floor of the House of Commons from the visitors' gallery. *Perhaps I'll go again.* Then she recalled that Parliament was in recess until September. *Well, that saves me from making a bloody fool of myself!*

After the service everyone congregated outside the church, mingling with friends to exchange the latest gossip, commiserate with one another about how the royal mourning period was preventing them from enjoying any form of entertainment and how glad they would be to bid good-bye to the horrendous year of 1862.

Anne sought out Henry Rawdon, who was now laughing with Fitz Kerry. She casually mentioned that she would be riding in the park with Florence and Frances. "We usually meet at the Cumberland gate at two o'clock."

On the short carriage ride home, her mother asked if she was still planning to ride.

"Yes, Frances and Florence are meeting me at two. I think I'll skip lunch—I don't want to be late."

"I've changed my mind about driving in the park this afternoon. That sermon gave me a bit of a headache."

"I'm so sorry. Church would be much more enjoyable

without a sermon, in my opinion. Perhaps if you lie down, it will go away."

When they arrived home, Anne ran upstairs to change into a riding habit. She wrinkled her nose at the black skirt and jacket. *I'm so tired of wearing these drab funereal colors. In the spring I swear I'll design a new habit in a vivid shade of peacock.*

She pulled a riding boot from her wardrobe, but couldn't find its mate. *Where the devil could it be?* She looked under the bed, then did a more thorough search of the wardrobe. Anne knew if she didn't hurry, she would be late, so she went along to her mother's dressing room to borrow a pair of her boots.

Anne bent and picked up a letter from the floor that her mother must have dropped. On the dressing table was a velvet box that held about a dozen other letters. The envelope in her hand was addressed to Lady Anne Gore, Datchet, Berkshire, which was the Thames-side village near Windsor where her mother had lived before she was married. She looked at the postal date and realized it was the same year that her mother and father married. *She has kept these letters all these years. They must be love letters. I cannot imagine my father penning love letters.*

The temptation to read the letter she held was too great. She quickly slipped it from its envelope and unfolded it. She saw immediately that it was not from Richard. It was signed with the initial *L*. Guilt washed over her, and she quickly put the letter back in its envelope and put it with the others in the velvet box.

Anne forgot she had come to borrow riding boots and returned to her own room. She spied her missing boot behind her bedchamber door, pulled it on, then hurried to get her palfrey from the stables. She tried to push away thoughts of the letters, but her curiosity was piqued and she wondered who L could be.

The three friends met at Hyde Park's Cumberland gate and within minutes Henry Rawdon trotted up, pretending great surprise at the encounter. He maneuvered his horse close to Florence Paget's mount and the four riders cantered toward the Serpentine. It wasn't long before Rawdon veered into a wooded area and Florence followed.

"It's rather exciting playing Cupid," Frances declared.

Anne couldn't shake the uneasy feeling that had lingered since she had found her mother's letters. "Perhaps we shouldn't aid and abet Florence in these clandestine meetings with Rawdon."

"Surely she's entitled to a little romance before her parents marry her off to that dull Henry Chaplin. Mark my words, the moment this dreadful mourning for the prince consort is over, her parents will announce her engagement and she'll be a blushing bride before summer."

"It must be awful to marry someone you don't love."

Anne thought fleetingly of her mother, and pushed the unsettling meditation away.

"I warrant nine out of ten brides marry without love. Oh, that reminds me of the secret I learned. I overheard my brother James and Father discussing an arranged marriage. But you must promise on your life that you won't tell anyone."

James is discussing marriage? Anne experienced a sharp pain in her breast, as if her heart were being crushed. "Frances, please don't tell me—I don't want to know!"

"What's the point of my overhearing a delicious secret if I can't share it with my best friend? Besides, if I don't tell you, you'll never forgive me."

Perhaps it's better if I know. "Tell me, then." Anne took a deep breath and braced herself for the blow.

"James and the Prince of Wales are sailing to Belgium to visit the prince's uncle King Leopold on a highly confidential mission in September. Prince Teddy and Princess Alexandra of Denmark are to have a secret engagement at Leopold's Royal Castle of Laeken in Brussels. It won't be announced by Buckingham Palace until the mourning period is over."

Anne felt weak with relief. "Oh, that's absolutely marvelous, Frances. Thank you so much for sharing the secret with me. I promise I won't tell a soul."

"Just as I suspected, here comes John Claud. He knew I was going riding. If he pretends this is some sort of coincidence, I shall kick him in the shins. Still, I'm thankful your brother Montagu is with him. The afternoon won't be a total loss."

When John Claud maneuvered his mount next to hers, Anne saw Frances put a warning finger to her lips, and she nodded her understanding to her friend.

At that moment, Fitz Kerry came riding up from the opposite direction. Anne hid her amusement when she saw John Claud bristle with resentment, before he masked his anger.

"Lady Anne, I can think of no more rewarding way to spend the afternoon than riding with you at my side."

"You took the words from my mouth, Hamilton." Fitz maneuvered his horse to Anne's other side.

"Since you're both such devoted friends, I think it's time you called me Anne."

John Claud gave her an intimate glance. "I fully intend to be more than a friend."

Anne laughed. "Don't I know it!" She was aware his remark was meant as a warning to Fitz Kerry. "You're a cheeky sod, John Claud. I give you an inch and you take a mile."

"When I act like a gentleman, you are bored to tears and ignore me. When I act like a cheeky sod, you respond with laughter. I warrant this sedate trotting along the bridle path is another thing that bores you. Why don't we have a race?"

"I'm game for a race." Anne raised her eyebrows to Fitz.

"Me too," Kerry agreed. "You set the finish line, Hamilton."

"How about the Round Pond in Kensington Gardens?"

"You're on!" Anne wrapped the reins around her gloved hand and urged her mount into a gallop. Keeping pace with John Claud's hunter and Kerry's mare was no easy task. She lost the pins from her hair and it streamed behind her like a banner. A foul oath dropped from her lips as she saw both riders pull ahead and she doubled her efforts to catch them. But by the time she reached the Round Pond, both had beaten her soundly.

Anne threw back her head and laughed with delight. "Neither one of you has an ounce of gallantry, but if you had let me win just to curry favor, I would have despised you." She suddenly realized that the two males were far more interested in their rivalry than what she had to say.

John Claud was furious because Fitz had beaten him by a yard. He swallowed his wrath and turned to Anne. "Will you come riding with me again tomorrow?"

"Since the weather is so beautiful, why not?"

"I'd like us to ride alone. Let's not include the others," he said pointedly.

Anne asked innocently, "Do you mean your sister and my brother?" She looked around. "We seem to have lost them."

"Perhaps they lost us."

Anne shook her head. "Frances is attracted to Montagu, but her head rules her heart. She's only interested in first sons who are heirs to their fathers' titles."

His mouth tightened. "First sons are notorious rakehells," he said with disdain. It was a direct insult to the young Earl of Kerry.

Anne tried to deflect the offense. "You never miss a chance to blacken your brother's reputation!"

"I wasn't speaking of James," John Claud denied.

"Then who?" Kerry challenged. "Name a name."

John Claud knew Fitz Kerry was ready to fight him. If Anne hadn't been there, he would have planted the young earl a facer. He backed off a little. "Well, Devonshire's heir for one."

"The Marquis of Hartington? He's one of England's most eligible bachelors," Anne pointed out.

"He's profligate."

"Tell me," she begged.

"Of course I won't tell you. You shouldn't know of such things."

She remembered Hartington dancing with Louise, the Duke of Manchester's beautiful wife, at her debut ball. *Oh my God, I was right. They are having an affair!*

Anne was shocked that a married lady would have an affair. Then she thought of her mother. *Was she having a love affair with another man when she married Father?* She pushed the suspicion away. *It simply isn't possible!*

Anne was relieved to see her brother and Frances come riding up to them. In theory it was exciting to have two admirers vying for her favors, but in practice it was rather alarming. "Montagu, why don't you finish your ride with Fitz and John Claud? Frances and I must find our friend Florence Paget."

"Are you feeling better, Mother?" Anne had changed for dinner and tamed her wild mane of hair, which had been disheveled by the race.

"My headache didn't last long. Did you enjoy your ride?"

"Yes, I had a lovely time. Montagu and John Claud met us in the park. He invited me to go riding again tomorrow, and I accepted."

"I'm so glad you said yes. He makes no secret of the fact that he's enamored of you, darling. I want you to know that I fully approve of him as a suitor."

"He's a good friend, but he's rather young. I never think of him as a husband."

"Why ever not? You are just the right age for each other. There is little happiness in marrying an older man."

Her mother sounded wistful, and it gave Anne the courage to probe a little. "You were only sixteen when you married Father. How did you meet?" she asked softly.

"Come and sit down. I think you're old enough to hear my story. Perhaps it will help you make a wise decision when it comes to choosing a husband, or at least keep you from making a foolish mistake that could ruin your happiness."

Anne took a seat and looked into her mother's eyes. *Perhaps you'll tell me who wrote the love letters.*

"My father died when I was six. All I remember is that he was Irish and had red hair. Because he was an admiral in the navy, we lived in a village on the River Thames close to Windsor Castle. My mother, Georgiana, was a lady of the bedchamber to Queen Adelaide, and your father was the queen's lord chamberlain.

"After your father's first wife died, rumors began to surface that he was the queen's lover. Queen Adelaide spent a great deal of time at your father's country estate, Gopsall Hall, in Leicestershire. The queen decided the best way to put an end to the gossip was to find him a wife. My mother suggested me. Both the queen and Richard, Earl Curzon-Howe, thought it an excellent solution. My feelings were not taken into consideration. I was sixteen—I had no choice in the matter."

"Do you think the rumor of Father and the queen was true?" Anne asked, wide-eyed.

Her mother shrugged. "Where there's smoke, there is usually fire."

She believes my father was the queen's lover! No wonder she avoids going to his country estate in Leicestershire.

"I was in love with a young man who was just a little older than me. I should have listened to him when he begged me to elope. He warned me that my mother would conspire with Queen Adelaide to marry me to the lord chamberlain, but I refused to believe him."

"Who was he?"

Her mother hesitated. "He was a young officer in the army. He was immediately posted abroad, and I realized the queen and her chamberlain had a hand in it." She shook her head sadly. "Darling, I've always regretted that I did not have the courage to take my happiness in my own hands and marry the man with whom I was so deeply in love."

I wonder if you were lovers? I certainly hope you were.

At dinner, Anne noticed that Montagu looked preoccupied. His eyebrows were drawn together in a deep frown, which was unusual since her brother had a sunny nature.

She refrained from asking him questions in front of their parents, and decided to wait until the meal was over and she could get him alone.

After dinner their father went into his library, and their mother withdrew to her sitting room. Anne decided to question Montagu before he left the dining room.

"Did anything happen between John Claud and Fitz Kerry after I left?"

"No! Absolutely nothing. Why do you ask?"

Her brother's denial had come quickly . . . too quickly . . . and it raised a red flag. "Oh dear, they didn't come to blows, did they? John Claud hates my being friends with Fitz."

"They didn't come to blows." Montagu pressed his lips together.

"Well, something happened. You might as well tell me."

Montagu hesitated, then blurted, "John Claud told Fitz that he was wasting his time dangling after you because you were going to be his wife. Fitz Kerry laughed at him."

"That was the end of it?" Anne pressed.

Montagu said quickly, "Yes!" He bit his lip. "No."

"Good God, it's like trying to get blood from a stone!" When she said *blood*, her brother blanched.

"Anne, when Kerry laughed at John Claud, all hell broke loose!"

"So they *did* fight."

"Not yet."

"What do you mean?"

"They're going to fight at dawn tomorrow. John Claud challenged Fitz to a duel."

"Don't be ridiculous!"

"It's true. John Claud asked me to be his second."

"You may be an expert with a rifle, but you don't know anything about pistols."

"It's to be rapiers," he explained.

"Sword fights went out in the last century, you dolt."

"No, they didn't, Anne. The three of us attend fencing classes together. Tempers get pretty hot sometimes. John

Claud and Fitz have been sparring over you all summer. They are going to fight it out at dawn."

"Where?" she demanded.

"The Round Pond in Kensington Gardens."

"Idiot boys! They must be stopped."

"I tried to talk sense into John Claud, but it's gone too far. Neither of them will back down."

"I shall go to Kensington Gardens and stop the fools," she said decisively.

"Your presence would make it worse. It would be like throwing oil on flames. If you were there to watch, their rivalry would intensify and their pride of manhood would demand satisfaction."

"Well, someone must stop them. I shall go to John Claud's father."

"You can't tell Abercorn. Think of the shame it would bring to John Claud to be forbidden by his father. It would make him feel like a child!"

"Think of the guilt that I'll feel if either of them wounds the other. You'd better get over to Hampden House and talk some sense into him."

"I'll try, Anne. That's all I can promise."

She walked to the top of the stairs with him and watched him descend, but the moment he closed the front door, she knew that her brother would fail to deter the dominant John Claud. *I'll go and tell Lady Lu what her son is up to. She will soon put a stop to his nonsense!*

Anne hurried to her mother's sitting room. "Montagu and I are going round to the Hamiltons'."

"Have a lovely evening, darling. Say hello to Her Grace for me."

The minute Anne stepped out onto the pavement of Grosvenor Square, her steps faltered. *Telling John Claud's mother would be worse than telling his father. It would reduce him to a naughty little boy.*

She thought of James and knew immediately that if anyone could dissuade John Claud from his recklessness, it was his older brother. *Frances said he was going to Brussels.* Instinctively, she shied away from an encounter with James. *He's not going until September. It's only the end of August—he won't have sailed yet.*

Anne knew it would take courage to go to Lord Hamilton's town house in White Horse Street and ask him to intervene. Her reticence had nothing to do with the impropriety of visiting a bachelor alone, at night. She didn't give a fig for proper rules of behavior. It was the thought of going to him as a supplicant that was distasteful.

Since the shame of being a coward was far worse than swallowing her pride, Anne stiffened her backbone and walked briskly toward Hanover Square, where she knew there was a hansom cab stand.

Anne's pulse began to race when the cab turned off Piccadilly onto White Horse Street, and stopped in front of the Georgian house on the corner. She stepped out and spoke to the driver. "Would you be good enough to wait for me?"

The cabman touched his cap and Anne walked up to the door and lifted the brass knocker. After three taps the door was opened by a male servant.

"I'm here to see Lord Hamilton," she said breathlessly.

He opened the door wide. "May I tell his lordship who's calling, mistress?"

The servant, who had an Irish accent, gave her a knowing glance, and she was suddenly reluctant to give him her name. "I . . . I'd rather tell him myself."

He rolled his eyes. "Have a seat, while I see if himself is free."

James was in the library. He looked up from his desk. "Who is it, Grady?"

"Mrs. Currant Bread with a toffee on her head."

James laughed and stood up. "You irreverent sod. I take it it's a lady."

"Do ye know any ladies, m'lord?"

"Very few, thank God! You may show her up and make yourself scarce."

"Don't I always, m'lord?"

James followed Grady from the library, and went into

the drawing room to await his visitor. When he saw who his guest was, his eyes widened with surprised pleasure. "Anne! You finally came. My precious beauty, I am absolutely delighted." He strode to the doorway where she stood tentatively and ushered her into the room.

Her mouth was dry and her heart was beating wildly at the sight of him. She licked her lips. "My lord . . . James . . . you won't be delighted when you know why I came."

She looked so forlorn he wanted to enfold her in his arms. He resisted the impulse, took her hands, and searched her face. "Something's wrong. Tell me." He could feel her hands quiver. "Come and sit down."

He led her to a comfortable sofa and moved across the room to pour her a glass of claret. He handed it to her and sat in a leather chair facing her. "Drink up."

Anne had two good swallows, then took a deep breath. "This will sound utterly preposterous. I want you to stop a duel."

"A duel?"

"John Claud has challenged Fitz . . . Henry Fitzmaurice to a sword fight at dawn tomorrow. Montagu said they are meeting at the Round Pond in Kensington Gardens.

"I sent my brother to Hampden House to talk some sense into him, but John Claud is far too dominant and determined to listen to Montagu."

James felt a pang of resentment that the two young men obviously fancied themselves in love with Anne. Yet he was the one she had come to for help.

"How did it start? Were you there when they quarreled?"

"After church, your sister and I were riding in the park when John Claud and Montagu arrived. Next thing I knew Fitz Kerry rode up and their rivalry started immediately. Your brother suggested a race, and when Kerry won, John Claud was furious. After I left, Montagu told me that John Claud informed Fitz that he was wasting his time, because he was the man I was going to marry. When Kerry laughed at him, that's when John Claud challenged him to a duel."

"You fear that John Claud will be wounded?"

"I would be guilt-ridden if *either* of them were wounded! I came to you, because I believe you are the only one who can overrule John Claud."

"You did the right thing, Anne." His dark eyes caressed her face. "I'll take care of it."

"Thank you so much, James. I was afraid you wouldn't take me seriously."

He smiled. "John Claud's a Hamilton. There's a bit of a mad streak that runs through all of us." Suddenly, James couldn't bear to see her leave. "I'll take you home."

"I have a hansom cab waiting." She flushed slightly. "I have no money to pay him."

"I'll take care of it."

They went downstairs and James opened the cab door and helped her inside. He told the driver to take them to Grosvenor Square, then climbed in and took the seat across from Anne.

In the enclosed cab, his compelling presence was overwhelming. They sat in silence until the driver turned off Piccadilly onto Park Lane; then James spoke. "Will you marry John Claud?"

I don't want to marry him. I want to marry you. "He often talks about marriage, though he has never formally proposed to me. He simply takes it for granted that I will be his wife."

"And will you be his wife?"

"I don't know. My parents totally approve of John Claud, but I refuse to let their choice influence my decision. He's a good friend, and I feel great affection for him, but his proprietary attitude exasperates me. Most likely that's because I have always vowed that I will choose my own husband."

In the darkness, his mouth curved. "You are a free spirit. You don't want the man to do the choosing. Yet it's a man's world, and most accept that it's a man's choice."

"It certainly was in my father's case. Mother had no

say in the matter, but I intend to have a say. My husband will be *my* choice."

When the carriage stopped, James jumped out and held the door open while she alighted. "Good night, Anne. You mustn't worry, I really will take care of the matter."

"Thank you, James."

When Fitz Kerry left his house in Berkeley Square an hour before dawn, James Hamilton was waiting for him. "Good morning, Lord Kerry. I'm here to save you the trouble of meeting my brother at the Round Pond."

Kerry's brows drew together. "Lord Hamilton—did John Claud send you?"

"On behalf of my brother, I offer his apologies. The duel has been called off."

"Perhaps by you, my lord, but not John Claud. He will be there, and so will I."

"Do you not realize that if a duel were fought during the mourning period the queen has declared for her beloved Albert, it would bring the wrath of the monarchy down upon your head?"

Kerry raised his chin. "I'm willing to take the risk."

Fitzmaurice had played his card and James had no option but to trump it. "Lord Kerry, it is considered bad form to accept a challenge from a man of lesser rank. Need I remind you that you are an earl of the realm?"

"Damn and blast!" The wind went out of Kerry's sails.

James nodded his thanks. "Good day, my lord."

Dawn had just begun to lighten the sky when James Hamilton arrived at the Round Pond in Kensington Gardens. He saw his brother was there before him. He watched him remove his jacket and hand it to his friend Montagu. Then James stepped from the shadows. "Good morning."

"What the devil are *you* doing here?" John Claud demanded.

"I came to tell you that Fitz Kerry won't be meeting you."

"Damned coward!" He lowered the tip of his rapier to the ground. "Too bad the duel has to be called off. I was in the mood for a sword fight."

"The duel hasn't been called off. You'll be fighting me." James took off his coat, dropped it to the ground, and unsheathed his small sword.

"I'm not going to fight my brother."

James's eyes narrowed. "You owe me, John Claud." He brought the blade to his nose in the traditional salute. "First blood." He advanced one step. *"En garde!"*

Both brothers were tall and had a long reach, but James had a skill and quickness that John Claud lacked. As James began to thrust aggressively, his sibling was forced to parry. The blades slid against each other with a slithering, metallic sound, and John Claud retreated a step. He recovered, extended, and lunged. James caught his brother's blade and knocked it wide. Strong legs moved the men back and forth with agile speed. Then James began to advance, and a panting John Claud faltered for one split second. In a flash, James saw his opening and slid the tip of his rapier across his brother's forearm. He disengaged immediately as the sleeve of his brother's shirt turned red with blood.

"Are you satisfied?" John Claud demanded.

"I'll claim satisfaction when you stop bandying Lady Anne's name about." James sheathed his sword, picked up his coat, and departed without a backward glance.

John Claud turned to Montagu. "I never thought Kerry would go sniveling to James."

Montagu wasn't sure it was Kerry, but he decided not to confess to his friend that he'd told Anne about the duel. "Why on earth would James take Fitz Kerry's place?"

John Claud held his wounded arm and winced. "It was an old score my brother decided to settle. I had it coming. But I hope I can trust you to keep your mouth shut about this."

Chapter 10

Lady Anne stood at the window of her bedchamber watching the snowflakes pile up on her windowsill. She was in a pensive mood as she drew the drapes, then sat down at her desk and opened her journal. She turned the pages back to September and reread her entries for the last four months. She had only briefly mentioned the quarrel between her rivals, and that she had gone to James Hamilton to prevent John Claud from dueling, but she remembered every moment of her visit to White Horse Street. He had seemed so delighted to see her that she had hoped James's attraction would be rekindled, but her hopes had been dashed. She had not seen or heard from him since that night.

She saw that John Claud's name was on almost every page. She admitted that though she hadn't encouraged him to court her, she hadn't discouraged him either. Because of her friendship with Frances and John Claud, she spent a considerable amount of time at Hampden House. So much, in fact, that the Hamiltons now spoke freely in front of her, as if she were one of the family. Anne sighed.

Unfortunately, John Claud takes it for granted that I will be one of the family.

Anne dipped her pen in the inkwell and wrote: *Because of the imposed mourning for the late prince consort, there has been no winter Season, nor will there be a glittering, festive Christmas to look forward to. There is to be a dull family Christmas dinner that I dread because Emily will make disparaging comments about everything from my mother's social skills to my choice of gown.*

Anne scribbled one dreary sentence after another, and when she reread her words she suddenly began to laugh. "Hell's teeth, I'm filling the pages with gloom and doom!" Her mood lightened. "At the Christmas dinner I shall give Emily something to gnash her teeth about. I shall wear my white velvet gown with the brilliant crystal beads on the bodice. She will be wearing some dreadful funereal color that Queen Victoria insists upon. When she sees me, I hope it makes her swallow her bloody tongue!"

Anne redipped her pen and wrote: *There is a pent-up feeling of anticipation building. Everyone is so sick and tired of this dreary year of mourning. Once the year is over and 1863 is ushered in, Society will go mad and kick over the traces. There will be so many balls, entertainments, and weddings to celebrate that there won't be enough nights in the week to accommodate them all. The restaurants and theaters will be packed, and the fashions will change overnight.*

The most exciting thing of all is that London will celebrate the nuptials of the Prince and Princess of Wales. Nothing has been announced yet, but Frances told me in confidence that when James returned from Brussels, he assured the family that Prince Teddy was formally betrothed to Princess Alexandra and she will be brought to England for a wedding in the spring. After they are married, they will take up residence at Marlborough House. Frances and I speculate that the newlyweds will eclipse Queen Victoria's influence, and they will become the leaders of fashionable Society. Hallelujah, I cannot wait!

Anne turned out her lamp and got into bed. About an hour after she drifted into sleep, she began to dream.

She was standing at the entrance to St. George's Chapel at Windsor Castle. She was wearing her white velvet dress, whose bodice was encrusted with glittering crystals, but the gown now boasted a long train. On her head Anne was wearing a magnificent jeweled crown, and she suddenly realized she was a princess.

Her father took her arm and began to lead her down the aisle. Her bridegroom, who was wearing a kilt, awaited her at the altar, and her heart lifted with joy when she saw that it was His Royal Highness Prince James.

The archbishop of Canterbury said, "Princess Anne, your gown is most elegant."

She smiled. "Thank you. I designed it myself."

The archbishop performed the royal nuptials, and the prince and princess exchanged their wedding vows.

"I now pronounce you man and wife. You may kiss the bride."

Prince James lifted her veil and smiled into her eyes. "That's better. Now I can see your beautiful face and your glorious hair."

He drew her close, and as he bent his head toward her, she closed her eyes and opened her lips in invitation. When his mouth touched hers, her eyelashes fluttered, and she whispered his name with longing. "James."

Anne raised her lashes and gazed into a pair of fierce eyes. "You're not James!"

"Indeed I am not. I am your husband, John Claud Hamilton."

"But I married James!" she protested.

"James is not the marrying kind. First sons are notorious rakehells. James is profligate."

Anne felt as if her heart were being crushed inside her breast. Then her sorrow turned to red-hot anger. She raised her hand and slapped John Claud's face; then she turned to the archbishop of Canterbury and slapped him too. "The marriage isn't legal. I was only masquerading as a Russian princess!"

*   *   *

The hour was late when James Hamilton arrived at his town house in White Horse Street. He had spent Christmas Eve with his family at Hampden House. It had been a madhouse of overexcited children, not only his three young brothers, but his sister Harry's three boys, and his sister Beatrix's twins, plus her three other male offspring.

When his sisters had told him in no uncertain terms that it was time he married and produced an heir of his own, he had jested that spending the day with ten hooligans, all under the age of nine, had put him off siring children for a lifetime.

"Don't hold your breath waiting for James to take a wife. I shall be the next one married," John Claud had announced to the entire family.

As James lit his bedside lamp, he cursed Fate that both he and his brother desired Lady Anne Howe. He picked up the glass snow globe he had bought in Belgium, and turned it upside down to make it snow. Inside the globe was a horse-drawn sleigh that held a female figure wearing a fur hat and coat. When James had seen it in the shop in Brussels, he knew he had to have it.

He sat gazing into the tiny winter scene as the snowflakes settled about the lady in the sleigh, and suddenly he wanted Anne to have it. Impulsively, he searched for the globe's original box and found it in a desk drawer. He wrapped it up and wrote on the package: *Happy Christmas, Lady Anne.* Then he summoned Grady, asked him to deliver it to Grosvenor Square in the morning, and gave him a generous Christmas bonus.

James stripped and climbed into bed, but sleep was kept at bay by his thoughts. He regretted that his sweet sister Jane, the Countess of Dalkeith, had been absent from the Christmas Eve festivities with the rest of the family because she was on duty with the queen. He acknowledged that Victoria's first Christmas without Albert would be an emotional time for her, but then he thought of the unconscionable way she treated her son

Teddy and thought, *It's no wonder the Irish refer to her as the "Auld Bitch of a Quayne"!*

James was reconciled to spending Christmas Day with the prince, and not just because it was his royal duty. He did not want Teddy to feel bereft and lonely. He had rented a town house in his own name on Jermyn Street, where the prince spent at least one night each week, presumably enjoying the services of a courtesan, or titled wife of a complacent friend. He didn't know, and he didn't want to know. But Christmas Day was different and should be spent with someone who truly cared about you. Most of the morning would be spent in church. After that, James decided, they would go to Marlborough House, where the Prince of Wales could relish his freedom and make plans for the future.

His last waking thought, as it was most nights, was how much he regretted not stealing Anne away from the masquerade ball. *If I had made love to her that night, it would have removed John Claud from the picture.*

The moment he drifted into sleep the beautiful object of his desire was there with him. *They were sitting close on a love seat before a cozy fire. James took the pins from Anne's hair one by one, until the red-gold tresses tumbled about her shoulders. He threaded his fingers into the silken mass and set his lips to the tendrils that curled so enticingly on her brow.*

Her green eyes sparkled with mischief "I warrant you're naked beneath that kilt."

James began to laugh. "You are an amazing judge of human nature."

"Take it off and show me," she challenged. "I've never seen a naked man."

"Since you're incurably impulsive, why don't you undress me, then I'll return the favor. That will allow us to explore our curiosity about each other."

Anne, bubbling with laughter, unwound the green tartan from his hips. She sat back and gazed wide-eyed at his rampant cock, rising from the black curls between his legs.

He lifted a tress of bright hair from her shoulder and

rubbed it between his fingers. "I warrant the curls on your mons are as silky soft as this one. You have no idea how often I've seen them and touched them in my dreams, sweetheart."

"I've dreamed about you too, James, but I must confess the real flesh and blood man puts my daydreams to shame."

The moment James raised his hands to unfasten her gown, John Claud arrived on the scene. "James, I'm glad you finally met Lady Anne. She's the girl I'm going to marry."

"I'll fight you for her." James was naked, save for his rapier. Miraculously, John Claud had a sword in his hand.

"First blood," John Claud declared.

"Nay." James shook his head. "Last blood!"

With a swift parry, his brother's weapon arced into the air; then James thrust, aiming straight for the heart.

On Christmas Day, the Curzon-Howes gathered at the mansion in Grosvenor Square. The tree had been set up in the ballroom, because that was the only room large enough to accommodate the earl's plethora of sons and daughters and their families.

Anne had difficulty keeping them all straight. She knew that her father's oldest son, George, was married to Harriet and they had a sixteen-year-old daughter, Alice. The rest of her father's sons by his first wife were all military men, and she could hardly keep their names straight, let alone their ranks.

Her father's daughter Georgiana, who was married to the Duke of Beaufort, had four sons ranging in age from nine to fifteen, but the only child Anne liked was eight-year-old Blanche. Her father's daughter Adelaide, who was married to Henry Fane, Earl of Westmorland, was the only sibling who treated Anne like a sister, and as a consequence Anne loved their four-year-old son, Anthony.

Anne, holding young Blanche and Anthony by the hand, led them around a table laden with fruit, nuts, biscuits, chocolate bonbons, and sweetmeats. She tried one of everything and encouraged them to do the same. She winked at them. "Don't get sick, or I shall get the blame." She took them to look at all the presents piled under the tree.

"I want a pony," Anthony declared.

Blanche murmured in confidence, "I saw a big box with a rocking horse in it."

Anthony frowned, "Don't want a rocking horse!"

"You are a frightful boy," Blanche declared. She glanced over at her brothers, who were roughhousing in a corner. "I don't like boys much," she confided to Anne.

Her aunt laughed. "You only have four brothers. Pity me, I have eight." She spied Henry Fane and led Anthony to his father. "He says he wants a pony."

Henry picked up his son. "I bought you a pony. It's in the stable at Apethorpe."

"Can I see him today?" Anthony begged.

"No, you little blighter. You'll have to be patient," he admonished.

"Tomorrow, then?"

Fane winked at Anne. "Go and pester your mother. I'm just as eager to go to Apethorpe as you are, milado." When Anthony ran off to find his mother, Fane confided, "Adelaide will have a bloody fit when she learns I bought a four-year-old a pony."

Anne whispered, "You have horse piss in your veins!"

Fane threw back his head and roared with laughter. "You have a wicked Irish wit, m'dear. 'Tis a thing to be cherished."

"What's so funny?" Leicester Howe asked.

"I'll never tell," Fane replied, with another wink.

Leicester's glance swept Anne from head to toe. "May I say your beautiful gown makes you look like a glittering Christmas angel."

Anne laughed. "Henry will attest that I am no angel. You were very lucky to get leave at Christmas, Leicester. Aren't you stationed in the Ionian Islands?"

"Not anymore, my dear. I take it you heard that King

Otto was deposed and Greece is now ruled by King George. Since the new king is friendly to Britain, we are transferring the Ionian Islands to Greece. They will no longer be under British protection, so I won't be going back."

"Have you any idea where you'll be stationed next?"

Leicester's eyes crinkled in a confidential smile. "I have my eye on Ireland."

"There you are, Leicester." Montagu was delighted to see his half brother. He was hell-bent on joining the prestigious Rifle Brigade, and Leicester had promised to help him.

"I think it must be the *green jackets* he can't resist," Anne teased. As she watched Leicester and Montagu talk, she was struck once again at the family resemblance. They were like two peas in a pod and even shared the same mannerisms.

According to custom, the children opened their presents before Christmas dinner was served, and the adults opened their gifts after the meal. By the time the goose was ready to be served, the grown-ups were happy to troop to the dining room and leave the ballroom that was littered with toys and games. The servants had set up a children's table beside the Christmas tree, and Anne thought privately that the youngsters were glad to be rid of their parents for a few hours.

Emily eyed Anne's glittering gown with disapproval, and Anne returned the favor with a look of pity for her sister's drab dress, the color of which could best be described as *cat shit*. Anne caught her mother's eye, and both of them had to exercise constraint.

Emily, however, was simply bursting to share her news with the rest of her family. She waited until the soup was served, knowing everyone would be caught agog with their spoons halfway to their mouths. "His Royal Highness the Prince of Wales has become secretly engaged. Buckingham Palace will make the announcement in the New Year!"

"Oh, that is exciting news," Georgiana Beaufort declared. "Who is the lucky bride?"

"I shall tell you only because I know all of you will keep this in strict confidence." Emily paused, keeping everyone in suspense, basking in their undivided attention. "He is to marry Princess Alexandra of Denmark!"

"Poor princess," Lady Howe murmured.

"What on earth do you mean?" Emily demanded.

"She's so young, and coming to a strange country to a husband she doesn't know."

"In my humble opinion, there is nothing strange about England," Emily protested, "but then of course you're Irish."

"She never had a humble opinion in her life," Anne murmured to Henry Fane, and watched him cover his laughter with his napkin.

Henry's wife, Adelaide, said, "Well, Queen Victoria is so rigid and strict, I don't envy the young princess. Emily, didn't I hear you remark that Buckingham Palace is like a mausoleum these days?"

Anne simply couldn't resist. "The Prince and Princess of Wales won't be living at Buckingham Palace. They are to have their own establishment at Marlborough House."

Everyone spoke at once, save Emily, who sat with an open mouth. When she recovered, she demanded, "How did you come to possess such privy information?"

Anne's eyes sparkled with mischief. "I'm Irish. . . . I have second sight."

Everyone at the table laughed at the clever retort, except for Emily, who pressed her lips together in hatred.

Henry Fane remarked to Anne, "The prince is mad about horses and racing. Once he gets his own establishment and cuts the royal apron strings, he'll be a regular on the racing circuit."

"Yes, I recall that he was at Newmarket the day I attended the races with you."

That was one of the happiest days of my life. James stole my heart that day, and not for the first time.

The topic of the upcoming marriage between Prince Edward and Princess Alexandra lasted throughout the entire meal. Then the ladies withdrew to the drawing room while the men remained in the dining room to enjoy their port and cigars.

An hour later when the gentlemen joined the ladies, it was time for the adults to open their gifts. It was the custom for the men of the family to give their wives jewels. This was the first Christmas that Anne's niece Alice was old enough to join the adults. She opened a gift from her parents and eagerly showed the other ladies her seed-pearl brooch.

When Anne opened her present, she was thrilled to find an emerald bracelet. She knew it was her mother who had picked it out, though she also thanked her father profusely, knowing it was his money that had paid for it.

She watched her mother open her gift from her husband. It too was emeralds, a lovely matching set of necklace and earrings. Mother and daughter smiled into each other's eyes. "You have exquisite taste, Mother."

Montagu, who had been charged with the pleasant task of handing out the gifts, gave his sister a square box, and an oblong box to his mother.

Anne glanced down at the card that read: *Happy Christmas, Lady Anne.* The card gave no indication of whom the gift was from. Her mother opened her box first, and held up a carving of Poseidon, the God of the Sea, holding his trident.

"Oh, Leicester, how thoughtful. This is from the Ionian Islands. I shall treasure it."

Anne bent to pick up the card that had fallen from the gift, and when she glanced at it, she frowned. She tried to remember where she had seen the initial *L* before, and it came to her in a flash that it was precisely the same handwriting she'd seen on the love letter she'd found in her mother's dressing room. *That cannot be! My mother couldn't possibly have been in love with my father's son.* Anne dismissed the thought. She firmly told herself that such a wicked idea was unworthy of her.

She sat down to open her own present. She drew the snow globe from its box and sat gazing at it in wonder.

There was a tiny figure of herself, sitting in a horse-drawn sleigh. It was even wearing a white fur Cossack hat. She tipped it up and watched in delight as the snowflakes swirled about in a frenzied snowstorm. She read the card again:

Happy Christmas, Lady Anne. Because of the white fur hat she had worn to the masquerade ball, she knew that it could be from only one person: *James!*

Where on earth did he find such a treasure? Anne examined the box, and saw the words *Made in Belgium.* She felt the warmth from her cheeks slowly spread to her heart. She put the globe back in its box. She suddenly felt very possessive about it and didn't want to share it with anyone. Besides, there would be all sorts of questions about who had given her such a lovely present, and why, and she didn't want to answer them.

Anne didn't remove the snow globe from its box until she was safely in her bedchamber for the night, after all the Christmas festivities were over. She tipped it upside down and delighted in the flurry of snowflakes. She set it on the table beside her bed so that she could see it and touch it, and, yes, daydream about the man who had bought it for her.

After she got into bed, she reached over half a dozen times to stir up the snowstorm inside the magical glass globe and knew without a doubt it was the most precious gift she had ever received. She lifted the card and read it again: *Happy Christmas, Lady Anne.*

She suddenly remembered her mother's card from Leicester that bore the distinctive letter *L.* Her mother's voice floated back to her: *I was in love with a man who was just a little older than me. He warned me that my mother would conspire with Queen Adelaide to marry me to the lord chamberlain. He was a young officer in the army.*

Anne knew that Leicester and her mother were about the same age, and he was certainly an army officer. She suddenly thought of her brother's marked resemblance to Leicester. *Oh my God, what if Mother was having*

Leicester's child when he was posted abroad? Perhaps that's the reason she allowed her mother to coerce her into marrying my father. Anne's thoughts were so shockingly sordid, she instinctively denied them.

Mother couldn't possibly have been intimate with both a man and his son. But the forbidden thoughts came back again and again. Anne thumped her pillow and turned over. *It's wicked to think such vile thoughts. I adore my mother; she couldn't possibly have been involved in something so scandalous.*

Chapter 11

"I haven't received even one proposal of marriage, and Florence has received two!" Frances Hamilton put up her umbrella as she and Anne Howe walked briskly to the waiting carriage. The friends had been shopping on Oxford Street with the bride-to-be.

As expected, Lady Florence Paget's engagement to Viscount Henry Chaplin had been announced in mid-January, and the wedding was planned for Saturday, February 21.

"She said Henry Rawdon is begging her to elope." Anne opened the carriage door and both young women hopped in out of the rain. "Florence really should call off her wedding to Chaplin. I know it will take a great deal of courage, but she'll have no chance of happiness marrying a man she doesn't love."

As the carriage rolled along on its way to Hampden House, Anne remembered her mother's words: *I should have listened to him when he begged me to elope. I've always regretted that I did not have the courage to take my happiness in my own hands and marry the man with whom I was so deeply in love.*

"Do you think Florence has the courage to elope?" Frances asked.

"I don't know. She doesn't seem the impulsive type," Anne replied doubtfully.

When the carriage stopped at Hampden House, Frances invited Anne to come in.

"You might as well wait until the rain stops."

Lady Lu came to the top of the stairs when she heard them arrive. "I'm so glad you're back. Come and have a look at the *Illustrated London News*. Buckingham Palace has finally announced the engagement of the Prince of Wales!"

Frances and Anne hurried up and went into the dining room, where the duchess had laid out the newspaper on the long table. They were extremely curious about Princess Alexandra and pored over the newspaper engagement photographs with great interest.

"The setting is beautiful, but her gown is rather plain for an engagement."

"I think it's better to be too plain, rather than too frilly and fussy, Frances. That way everyone will look at her and not her dress. She has a sweet face," Anne said.

"When the princess and her family live in Denmark, I wonder why the engagement took place in Belgium," Frances asked.

"That's what I asked your father," Lady Lu confided. "Apparently, when he wrote the official letter to Prince Christian of Denmark, they were thrown into a dilemma. The family lived in rather Spartan circumstances. They didn't want the Prince of Wales to see Princess Alexandra in this setting. Unbelievably, she shared an attic bedroom with her sister Dagmar, and the girls made their own clothes. Abercorn immediately wrote to King Leopold of Belgium, and of course Prince Teddy's uncle was more than happy to offer the splendid hospitality of his Royal Castle of Laeken in Brussels."

"I had no idea a princess could be poverty-stricken," Anne declared. "My heart goes out to her."

"Her circumstances are about to change dramatically. According to James, the inside of Marlborough House is positively opulent. He and Prince Teddy are busy interviewing a legion of servants to run the place. He says the grand mansion will be the envy of Society and everyone will vie for an invitation. Personally, I can't wait."

"It says the royal wedding is to take place at Windsor on Tuesday, March tenth." Anne finished reading the article. "St. George's Chapel isn't very large."

"Queen Victoria insists on a small wedding because she's still in mourning. There are going to be a lot of disappointed people when they learn they haven't been invited."

"How long will the queen be in mourning?" Frances asked her mother.

Lady Lu rolled her eyes. "For the rest of her life would be my guess. The woman is obsessed. It's unnatural and unhealthy—she absolutely wallows in it!"

"My sister Jane tells us that the queen insists that the servants take hot water into Albert's dressing room every morning, and lay out fresh clothes for him, just as if he were still alive. Doesn't your sister Emily find Victoria's behavior obsessive?"

"I doubt that Emily would ever criticize the queen," Anne confided. "Her husband was an equerry to Prince Albert, and when the consort died, Victoria appointed him her groom-in-waiting as a special accommodation to my sister."

"Jane told me that Princess Alexandra's wedding gown is being designed by Charles Frederick Worth, and fashioned after Queen Victoria's," Lady Lu confided.

"Good heavens, won't the princess have any say in the matter?" Anne asked in disbelief. "What if she doesn't like the gown when she sees it?"

"Since it's to be fashioned after Victoria's wedding gown, how could she like it?" Lady Lu asked wryly. "I thank my lucky stars every day that I turned down the position of Victoria's Mistress of the Robes."

"You say the most deliciously outrageous things, Your Grace. I have taken you as my role model."

Lady Lu winked at Anne. "You could do worse."

*   *   *

"Here it is on the front page." James had an armful of newspapers, all announcing the Prince of Wales's engagement, but the *Illustrated London News* had produced the best photographs.

"Newspaper pictures are anything but flattering." Prince Teddy frowned.

"Don't worry. Everyone knows what you look like. All eyes will be on the princess."

"I think I like this one best, James, where Alexandra is sitting."

"Yes, the princess is smiling in that one."

"March seems so far away. I detest Buckingham Palace. I can't wait to move out."

"I've been thinking about that. Now that your official engagement has been announced, I see no reason why you shouldn't move into Marlborough House. Since we've hired a full staff of servants, it will give them a chance to get to know you and vice versa."

"But, James, my money doesn't come through until I'm a married man."

"That shouldn't prove a problem. We'll just forward the bills for all the expenses to Sir William Knollys at the Treasury Department. He's been named your comptroller, and I doubt he will question your expenditures."

Teddy's face lit up. "By God, James, do you think we could go today?"

"I don't see why not. Let's have the servants in to begin your packing."

"I can't wait to start entertaining in my own establishment."

"And why should you wait? Why don't we start working on a list of gentlemen you can invite to your bachelor's party?"

"But my mother . . ."

James held up his hand. "Your mother will object to everything you do. The queen seems determined to be sad, sour, and solitary. My advice is to start out as you mean to carry on. From now on you are your own man—a man who makes his own decisions, and let the devil take the hindmost!"

"You are a marvel, James. What on earth would I do without you? Henry Chaplin, a friend of mine from Oxford, just got engaged. I'll drop him a note of congratulations and invite him to the celebration. Chaplin owns racehorses, so that's another thing we have in common."

"I predict there will be a multitude of weddings this year. You will set the fashion."

"What about you, James? Are you ever tempted to take on a wife?"

"London's loveliest ladies will soon be flocking to Marlborough House. I'll be able to take my pick." He thought wistfully of Lady Anne Howe, but he knew that if he dwelled on her too much, she evoked a feeling of longing that was difficult to dispel. *Stop deluding yourself. You only want her because you can't have her.*

The minute that the prince moved into Marlborough House, and was away from the scrutiny of the queen and her loyal Buckingham Palace servants, Teddy was ready to kick over the traces. During January and February the Prince of Wales began to indulge in scandalous behavior. Accompanied by his close friends James Hamilton and Charles Carrington, he frequented Evan's Music Hall in Covent Garden, and began to attend Cremorne Gardens at Vauxhall for assignations in their notorious private supper rooms.

The orgies and celebrations, replete with nymphs of the pavement and courtesans, lasted into the small hours. The ale and whiskey flowed freely, and the prince's amorous escapades erupted each night along with the firework displays.

Gossip about the Prince of Wales and his gentlemen attendants spread like wildfire, and their reputations as rakes and libertines grew apace. James attended to keep an eye on Teddy and to make sure he was not exposed to any real danger. He gave little thought to his own reputation, and was perversely amused that his good qualities were obscured by a facade of ill repute.

James indulged Teddy, believing that the repressed prince should get it all out of his system before his royal marriage to Princess Alexandra.

On February 14, Lady Anne received three valentines in the morning post. John Claud's card was a huge red heart decorated with real lace, and a romantic verse asking if she would be his valentine. A second card from Fitz Kerry showed a bouquet of red roses, tied with real satin ribbon. The verse told her that she had stolen his heart.

Anne held her breath as she opened the third envelope. Her hopes were dashed when she saw that it was from Edward Turnour, Earl of Winterton. *Perhaps I'll get one in the afternoon post. But perhaps not. I'll be the last person James will be thinking about today.* Montagu had told her that the Prince of Wales and James Hamilton were hosting a bachelor's party at Marlborough House tonight and that he and John Claud were going.

"Oh, how lovely!" Anne's mother was holding a large bouquet of red roses. "These must be for you, darling. Open the card quickly, I can't wait to see who sent them."

Anne's heartbeat quickened as she took the bouquet from her mother and breathed in the heady rose fragrance with appreciation. She opened the tiny card with trembling fingers. "Ah, John Claud." She immediately covered her disappointment.

"He's a lovely young man. You are lucky to have such a devoted suitor."

"I'm going to visit Frances this afternoon, so I'll be able to thank him for the flowers. Our friend Florence is coming to discuss last-minute arrangements for her wedding next Saturday."

"I'm surprised she didn't ask you to be a bridesmaid, darling."

"Well, I know she would have liked both Frances Hamilton and me to be bridesmaids, but she has half sisters to consider. Her father has been married three times and had large families with his first two wives."

"Like father, like son! The Earl of Uxbridge divorced his first wife. Poor lady was never accepted at Victoria's court after that. The queen always had one set of rules for gentlemen and another for ladies. She wouldn't dream of banning Uxbridge because he was divorced, but his poor wife was persona non grata."

"The Duchess of Abercorn believes the court of Buckingham Palace has fallen out of fashion. From now on Marlborough House will be where Society gathers."

"Montagu is attending a bachelor party there tonight. But of course, ladies won't be invited until Alexandra takes up residence as the Princess of Wales."

"I'll put my lovely roses in water. This afternoon I'll take my valentine cards to show Frances. I hope she got some."

"I would imagine every fortune hunter in London will have sent a valentine to Abercorn's daughter."

Mother seems envious of the Hamiltons, but if I'm being truthful, I too am envious. They are such a perfect family.

"I've brought my valentines to show you." Anne took the three cards from their envelopes, and spread them out on the tea table in the Hampden House drawing room.

"May I see them?" Frances's sister Maud asked.

"Of course. This one with the lovely red heart is from John Claud, and this one with the ribbons is from Fitz Kerry."

Maud gasped. "The Earl of Kerry? Oh, I think he is divine!" She sighed. "I would be over the moon if he sent me a valentine, or even looked at me. But he doesn't know I exist."

"You're only twelve," Frances pointed out. "It would be scandalous if you received valentines."

Maud put her hands on her hips. "I shall be thirteen this year, and if Anne can add a year to her age, so can I.

That makes me fourteen!" She picked up the valentine from Fitz Kerry and pressed it to her heart.

"You may have it if you like, Maud," Anne offered.

"Truly? You're not in love with him?"

Anne smiled wistfully. "No, I'm not in love with him."

"Thank you. I shall take it up to my room and put it on my pillow."

When she left, Frances looked at Anne's third valentine and began to laugh. "Such an amazing coincidence. I too got one from Winterton!" She produced the card.

Anne joined in her friend's laughter. "I didn't know he was interested in women. I thought his only love was cricket. This makes for a sticky wicket."

"The post brought me something far more exciting than valentine cards. The queen has asked me to be one of Princess Alexandra's bridesmaids. I accepted immediately."

"Oh, you lucky monkey, Frances! I thought we were fortunate to be invited to the wedding, but to be a bridesmaid is such a special privilege."

"I'm not deluding myself. Victoria only asked me because of Father's close association with Prince Albert."

Just then Florence Paget arrived. They took one look at her and saw that she was fairly bursting to tell them something.

"Catch your breath and tell us," Anne urged.

"First, you have to promise on your lives to keep this secret!"

"Of course we promise," Frances vowed. "We never divulge your secrets."

"Wild horses couldn't drag it out of us," Anne declared.

"I'm going to be married!" Florence ran to the drawing room door and closed it.

"Yes, we know . . . next Saturday . . . a week from today,"

"No, Anne. I'm going to be married on Wednesday at St. George's Chapel, Hanover Square. We're going to elope. Henry has arranged a special license."

"Are you talking about Henry Rawdon?" Anne asked with disbelief.

"Yes! Isn't it exciting? You must both help me concoct a plan for Wednesday."

"What sort of a plan?" Frances asked, wide-eyed.

"I need an excuse to get away from home on Wednesday morning, and I need a place to meet Henry."

"You've left it rather late. Wednesday is only four days before you're supposed to marry Henry Chaplin," Anne pointed out. "Your wedding gown has been fitted, and all the guests invited. This will cause a terrible scandal, Florence. Are you sure?"

"Absolutely sure. We are madly in love. On Wednesday, Henry will make me the Marchioness of Hastings."

"Rawdon lives in St. James's Place. Can't you meet him at his house?" Frances asked.

"Henry Chaplin insists on taking me in his carriage wherever I need to go. I can hardly ask him to take me to St. James's Place."

"Well, you could ask him to take you to Oxford Street, on the pretense that you need last-minute shopping for the wedding," Frances suggested.

"That's a splendid idea. Marshall and Snelgrove made my traveling outfit. If you two would wait for me at the front door of the store, I'll meet you there. Then I can slip out the back door into the marquis's carriage."

Anne was aghast at her friend's plans. "Henry Chaplin and your family will be devastated, Florence. Have you thought this through?"

"I've decided that it's better to jilt Chaplin than marry him without love. As for my family, I don't give a fig about my meddling stepmother who talked my father into arranging my marriage."

"Anne Howe, you are the one who declared we must form an alliance to choose our own husbands, and do everything in our power to make our choice reality," Frances pointed out. "You are the one who urged us to be *Brass Monkeys*."

"I just want Florence to be sure. What time do you

want us to meet you at Marshall and Snelgrove?" Anne asked faintly.

The ladies fell silent as John Claud opened the door and entered. He was dressed in evening clothes in anticipation of the Prince of Wales's celebration.

Anne gifted him with a smile. "You look very smart, John Claud."

He performed an exaggerated bow. "Why, thank you."

"No, it is I who must thank you. The red roses you sent me are beautiful and much appreciated."

"It was my pleasure, Anne. Did you receive any other flowers?"

His question sounded casual, but Anne knew it was anything but. He simply could not prevent himself from being possessive.

"Yours were the only ones," she assured him. *Though I wish it were otherwise.*

"Your brother and I are going to Marlborough House tonight. I'd invite you to go with us, but it's gentlemen only."

A mischievous light came into her eyes. "Yes, I was just suggesting to your sister that we should dress up as males and crash the party."

His face showed alarm. "You mustn't do that. You would be mistaken for . . . for . . . ladies of the night," he finished lamely.

"Ha, is that what goes on at these affairs?" Anne teased.

"Since my brother James made all the arrangements, it wouldn't surprise me."

Anne kept the smile on her face and said lightly, "You needn't blacken Lord Rakehell's reputation. He can manage without your help."

Marlborough House
February 14, 1863

"I can't believe how many accepted my invitation!" The Prince of Wales lifted another glass of champagne from the silver tray of one of his very own liveried footmen.

"There are far more here than invited guests. Every man we invited brought at least two friends with him," James pointed out.

"The more the merrier! I'm on my way to the card-room. Do you know if those cigars arrived?"

"They did indeed. Would you like a footman to hand them out?"

"Good idea. Smoking, drinking, and gambling, an irresistible combination that just may lure them back to Marlborough House."

"Lure them back?" James laughed. "You'll have a hard time getting shut of them."

Most of the young nobles present knew one another, and since it was males only, they didn't need to watch their language, or limit the number of drinks they consumed. Viscount Henry Chaplin rubbed elbows with Henry Rawdon, Marquis of Hastings, never dreaming that Rawdon was planning to snatch the viscount's bride from under his nose and elope with her in four days' time.

George Churchill, Marquis of Blandford, who had attended Oxford with the Prince of Wales, brought his young brother, Lord Randolph, who was only fifteen. The young noble was already addicted to alcohol and often rolled home at breakfast time, drunk as a lord. Randolph was thick as thieves with Lord John Redesdale, a notorious womanizer, addicted to nymphs of the pavement.

James wasn't surprised to see his three noble brothers-in-law, Thomas Anson, Earl of Lichfield, D'Arcy Lambton, Earl of Durham, and William Montagu, Earl of Dalkeith, arrive together. Anson, who was an art expert, was amazed at the magnificent paintings on the walls. He shunned the cardroom, and instead asked James to give him a tour of all the splendorous chambers of Marlborough House. "James, you are a lucky devil to be one of the prince's gentlemen and treat this place as your second home."

James grinned at Thomas. "Luck had nothing to do

with it. I began currying favor with Teddy when we were both in knee britches. When he is the King of England, I shall be one of the powers behind the throne."

"You are very loyal to him—it can't be an easy task."

James winked. "It has its privileges." He greeted his brother John Claud, who had arrived with Montagu Howe. When he saw Anne's brother, a full-blown picture of his heart's desire filled his thoughts. *Montagu's dark coloring is so different from Anne's.* Whenever he imagined her, a need rose up in him to thread his fingers through her red-gold tresses. He banished the thought quickly.

"Thomas, keep an eye on these two young devils while I check to see that all is well in the cardroom."

"You didn't invite Father, did you?" John Claud asked James.

"Actually, I did, but he graciously declined. By the way, Fitz Kerry is here tonight. I hope I can count on you not to issue any further challenges?"

James headed to the cardroom and saw Charles Carrington accompanying Christopher Sykes. Prince Teddy recognized Christopher immediately. "Sykes, as I live and breathe. I haven't seen you since Cambridge. How are you faring these days?"

"Very well, Your Highness. Perhaps you heard that my father passed away recently?"

Tatton Sykes bred blooded horses, but he was an authoritarian who bullied his sons. Since misery loved company, Christopher and the Prince of Wales had much in common. "When the Doncaster races start, you must allow me to entertain you at Brantingham Thorpe."

"I accept your hospitality, Sykes. I'm thoroughly looking forward to Doncaster. Have a seat and we'll play baccarat."

"I thought baccarat was banned in England, Your Highness."

Prince Teddy laughed. "It is, but who the devil is going to challenge me in my own house? Hartington can be the dealer—his pockets are deep."

"Since Marlborough House is the only venue in England where I'm allowed to play baccarat, I will gladly deal and provide the first bank," Lord Hartington agreed.

James shook his head and reminded himself to exercise patience. *More fodder for the gossip mills. Tomorrow it will be the talk of London that the Prince of Wales allows baccarat at Marlborough House. Damn good thing I drew the line at inviting a flock of delectable doves to flutter their wings. The twin vices of drinking and gambling will cause enough scandal, without adding the indulgence of whoring under his own roof.*

James recognized Charles Mordaunt, who sat in the House of Commons, but as he moved about among the guests, he realized that half of them were members of Parliament. Tonight, however, the conversations were not about politics. As usual, when England's nobles got together the main topics were horses, races, and wagers.

He stopped to greet Henry Fane, who remarked, "It won't be long before the prince buys his own stable of racehorses, and applies to be a member of the Jockey Club."

"I have no doubt of it," James said with a wink. "A married man needs diversions." *Once Teddy gets his money, he'll be like a child let loose in a toffee shop.*

The new majordomo, whom James had lured away from Prime Minister Palmerston, approached. "Lord Hamilton, the chef has all the food prepared, and I would like your permission for the footmen to begin setting up the buffet in the dining room."

"This will certainly be a trial by fire for the new chef."

"From what I've seen in the kitchen, I believe he'll pass with flying colors, m'lord."

"Excellent. You may announce supper at midnight."

"James!" The Prince of Wales looked ashen as he hailed his friend, who had just returned from a vote in the House of Commons. "The comptroller from the Treasury is here asking to see me. I'm sure it doesn't bode well and I warrant you would be far better at answering his questions than I."

"Your comptroller's name is Sir William Knollys. We'll see him together."

When they entered the library, James held out his hand. "Sir William, welcome to Marlborough House."

Knollys bowed his head. "Your Highness, Lord Hamilton." He opened a leather case and took out a sheaf of what looked like bills. He cleared his throat. "I have invoices that I must approve, and the thing is, I must verify that the goods were actually delivered."

James immediately realized that the man could prove to be foe or ally, and it was up to him to smooth the way for approval of all future expenditures. He held out his hand for the sheaf of papers, and even at a glance he could see the exorbitant costs of Prince Teddy's bachelor party. "I can confirm that these things were delivered, but my dear fellow, what an onerous position if every time His Highness puts in a request for something, you must come running to Marlborough House to verify its legitimacy."

"Unfortunately, that is among the tasks of a comptroller, Lord Hamilton."

"Sir William, since you are the comptroller of the Prince of Wales's household, wouldn't it make sense if you became a part of that household?" James saw his eyes dilate as the bait was dangled before him.

"You mean that I should reside at Marlborough House?"

"For the convenience of your office, it makes sense to me." He turned to the prince. "Do you not agree, Your Highness?"

"Perfect sense." Teddy nodded.

When Knollys hesitated, James sensed something was holding him back from jumping at the golden opportunity he had just been offered. "Is there a problem, Sir William?"

"The opportunity to reside at Marlborough House is something I would deem a high honor, Lord Hamilton, though it would necessitate that I live apart from my wife, Elizabeth."

James clearly saw that the man who would control the

prince's purse strings had taken the bait, but he could still slip off the line, unless he reeled him in quickly.

"Not at all. The future Princess of Wales will need ladies-in-waiting to attend her, as well as a social secretary to help with her engagements once she takes up residence at Marlborough House."

Knollys could not believe his good fortune. He stuffed the invoices back into his leather case, and bowed his head to the prince. "Your Highness, your generosity overwhelms me."

James said smoothly, "Generosity begets generosity, Sir William."

Chapter 12

THE MORNING POST

Thursday, February 19, 1863

A surprise marriage took place Wednesday, February 18, between Lady Florence Paget and Henry Rawdon, Marquis of Hastings, at St. George's, Hanover Square. *The marriage was hurried and unexpected, more particularly to the connections of her ladyship, none of whom were witnesses to the ceremony. The couple then proceeded to Donington Hall, Leicestershire, the ancestral home of Rawdon-Hastings.*

Lady Florence, a petite beauty known as the "Pocket Venus," was engaged to Viscount Henry Chaplin, and the nuptials set for Saturday, February 21st. The esclandre *has stunned London Society.*

"Your friend Florence Paget has eloped!" Anne's mother looked up from the morning newspaper with an astonished expression on her face.

"Yes, I know." Anne felt a rush of guilt. "If it's in the newspaper, everyone in London will know. Florence promised to send a letter to Henry Chaplin, begging his forgiveness for jilting him."

Lady Howe set the newspaper on the breakfast table between them. "What a courageous thing to do, to elope with the man she loved, rather than marry the man her parents chose."

Anne was surprised at her mother's reaction. *I shouldn't be surprised. Mother wishes she'd had the courage to do what Florence has done.*

"Did you help her carry out her secret plan, darling?"

"Yes," Anne confessed. "She told Frances and me her plans on Valentine's Day and asked us to meet her yesterday morning at Marshall and Snelgrove's Oxford Street entrance. She left by way of Vere Street, where Henry Rawdon was waiting with his carriage."

"How very clever!"

Anne bit her lip. "Poor Henry Chaplin brought her to the shop and waited for her. I thought it an extremely shabby trick to play on him."

"Don't feel guilty, darling. You helped her marry the man she loves."

"You think the end justifies the means, but I'm not so sure. I feel guilty because I *am* guilty. I just hope she made the right choice, or I shall feel even worse."

"God in heaven above! Your friend Florence Paget eloped with the Marquis of Hastings yesterday!" The Duchess of Abercorn put down the morning paper and gave her daughter Frances a look of accusation. "What part did you play in this disgraceful deception?"

"I knew nothing about it until yesterday. It was our friend Anne Howe who aided and abetted her, and has been encouraging her to choose her own husband, rather than marry Henry Chaplin, who was her parents' choice."

"The scandal will be devastating for them. We and everyone else the Earl and Countess of Uxbridge invited to the wedding of their daughter on Saturday will be outraged. What a selfish, childish thing to do. Florence was only here on Saturday. Are you telling me you weren't part of this conspiracy?"

"She ... she swore us to secrecy, and I gave her my word."

John Claud gave his sister a cold look of disapproval. "No good will come of this. Hastings is a womanizer, addicted to gambling and drink."

Frances tossed her head. "He's just inherited a fortune and he's a peer of the realm."

John Claud looked disgusted. "Why don't debutantes realize that most heirs are notorious rakehells?"

"It will be a long time before Florence is accepted by polite society, if ever," Lady Lu declared. "Gossip lingers and scandal clings like the smell of a cesspool."

"I'm afraid the standard will no longer be set by Queen Victoria, Mother," John Claud predicted. "Unfortunately, Society will look to the Prince of Wales and Marlborough House."

"That doesn't sound unfortunate to me," Frances declared, "especially when our brother has so much influence with Prince Teddy."

John Claud gave her a pitying glance. "The moral standard will be lowered."

"Don't be so self-righteous, John Claud," his mother scolded. "I don't know where you get it from; both your father and I are decidedly liberal, even a little licentious at times."

"Ah, so James didn't breed out?" Frances teased.

Lady Lu laughed. "Going back to the matter of your friend's scandalous elopement, at least the timing is in her favor. In a fortnight when Princess Alexandra arrives in England, no one will be talking or even *thinking* of Florence-what's-her-name!"

Grosvenor Square
March 7, 1863

"Oh, how young, and pale, and frightened, she looks," Anne passed the *Illustrated London News* to her mother.

The newspaper had ensured a reporter and photographer were waiting at Gravesend to snatch the first photograph of Princess Alexandra's arrival, and they rushed it into print for Londoners to see the same morning.

"I bought two papers." Montagu handed Anne the second newspaper. "I didn't want you to fight over it."

The black-and-white photograph showed a slim, pale-faced girl, nervously clinging to the rail of the *Victoria and Albert* royal yacht.

Anne looked at Alexandra's dark topcoat with its high, enclosed neckline and old-fashioned bonnet, and her heart went out to her. Montagu was escorting her and their mother to the parade route. She had a new spring hat for the occasion, with cream roses and pale violet ribbons, and as she looked into the hatbox, she felt guilty because the princess wore shabby clothes.

"The paper shows the route of the procession. Where do you think will be the most advantageous place for us to view her?" Lady Howe traced her finger along the Strand.

"Trafalgar Square will be packed with humanity. It will be a madhouse," Anne declared. "I think our best plan would be to get as close as we can to Paddington Railway Station, where she will leave the carriage and take the train to Windsor Castle."

"Montagu, what's the estimated time?"

"The train is scheduled to arrive in London at two this afternoon; then the carriages will slowly make their way along the parade route. When I went out to get the papers, people were already starting to gather. It will take them hours to get through London."

"So, if we are in our places by four o'clock, that should be plenty of time."

"Good. We'll have an early lunch and that will give us ample time to dress."

All three looked up as they heard feet pounding up the stairs. Emily came rushing into the morning room, breathless and disheveled.

"I'm here on an urgent mission for Her Majesty the

Queen," Emily gasped. "She took one look at that dreadful newspaper photograph and almost suffered an apoplexy."

"Newspaper pictures are never flattering," Anne explained lamely.

"Queen Victoria thinks the princess looks hideous. She has given me the task of finding the girl a fashionable hat. Her Majesty cannot allow the bride-to-be to parade through London looking like a scullery maid!"

"Why on earth did you come here?" the countess asked. "I would advise you to go to Redfern's. They buy from the finest milliners in London."

Emily raised her chin. "I thought about Anne's fashion sense. I was sure she would help me choose something to make Alexandra look more like a princess."

Emily was lying, of course. Lady Anne was Queen Victoria's suggestion, and when her sister's name was brought up, another of the queen's ladies-in-waiting, Jane, Countess of Dalkeith, had said: "I highly recommend Lady Anne's fashion sense, and moreover she is the same age as Princess Alexandra, and will know exactly what will be flattering."

Emily's eyes fell on the hatbox. "What's this?"

"It's my new spring hat. I'm going to wear it today." Anne lifted it from the box.

"Put it back in the box," Emily ordered. "I'll take it."

"Take it where?" Anne demanded.

"I have a carriage waiting. I'm to rush the hat to Southwark Rail Station where the royal party will be arriving from Gravesend. I cannot fail, I must carry out the queen's orders to make Alexandra look less of a sow's ear."

"That is a spiteful thing to say." Anne put her new hat back in its box. "Take it. I will consider it an honor to have the princess wear a hat that I chose."

Emily put the lid on the hatbox. "I must rush. I have to get to Southwark Rail Station before two o'clock."

Montagu looked at his sister as if she were deranged. "Why the devil did you let that hateful bitch take your new hat? Emily would never do *you* any favors."

Anne smiled wistfully. "I did it for the princess, not for Emily."

Earlier, on Saturday at dawn, James Hamilton accompanied the Prince of Wales to Gravesend. At first light, from their carriage, they watched the royal yacht, *Victoria and Albert*, dock. Within minutes a crowd began to gather on the pier, and shortly after figures appeared on deck.

"There she is." James pointed to a female clad in a warm topcoat with a high collar. Her face beneath the bonnet was pale, as she clung to the ship's rail with apprehension. Four Royal Navy sailors let out the gangway and attached it safely to the stanchions on the dock.

The mayor of Gravesend and his official greeting committee arrived and pushed their way through the throng of Sixty Fair Maids of Kent, who had been selected to scatter spring flowers before Princess Alexandra to welcome her.

"She looks frightened," James said. "If you run up the gangplank and give her a smile and a welcoming hug, Alexandra will be forever grateful, Teddy. Let the mayor cool his heels. Your bride needs your attention at this moment."

The prince abandoned protocol and royal dignity as he sprinted forward. Whether his eagerness stemmed from a desire to get it over with, or from a genuine feeling of anticipation, none would ever question his touching display of affection.

Alexandra gave the prince a tremulous smile and clung to his hands. "I'm so glad to see you, Your Highness."

"You must call me Teddy."

She nodded. "Could you possibly call me Alix?"

The princess's mother, Louise, dipped her knee. "Your Royal Highness."

He kissed her hand. "I hope you had a smooth voyage, Your Highness." Teddy turned to see Prince Christian of Denmark, and shook his hand. "Welcome to England, Your Highness." Teddy greeted the siblings of his bride-to-be. "No doubt the Channel was cold and windy, but spring has arrived in England."

Alexandra licked her lips nervously. "So many cheering people—they love you very much, Your Highness."

"The cheers are for you, my dear."

Her pale cheeks tinted a delicate pink.

The prince glanced about at the members of the Danish royal family. "If everyone is ready, we can disembark." He took his future bride's arm and led the way to the gangplank. When they reached the dock, a brass band began to play a welcoming march, and as Teddy led her along Terrace Pier, the glee girls who were ranged on each side of the pier began to toss primroses and sprigs of myrtle in her path.

Wearing white crinoline dresses and broad-brimmed straw hats with leafy garlands, holding their dainty baskets of wildflowers to scatter at the feet of the royal lady, they made a stark contrast to the way Princess Alexandra was dressed.

At the end of the pier a carriage stood waiting to transport them to the railway station. The Prince of Wales handed Alexandra into the open carriage, and motioned for her family to follow. Then he stepped forward to shake hands with the mayor of Gravesend, and all listened attentively as the dignitary delivered the welcome message.

The band struck up again and the air was rent with boisterous cheers.

James directed the driver of the prince's carriage to join the one holding the Danish royals and the two landaus slowly made their way through the jubilant crowds.

The train journey from Gravesend to London took only an hour, and they arrived at Southwark Station at two o'clock as scheduled. From this point on the timetable ceased being workable.

James Hamilton was first off the train; then he returned to the prince. "Everything is in readiness. There are six landaus drawn up and waiting. The queen has her ladies-in-waiting in the first carriage. Until Princess Alexandra is a married lady, she must ride in a carriage with ladies only. Prince Christian will ride beside you in the second carriage, and the third landau is for Alexandra's mother and sisters. Behind them will be Alexandra's four brothers: Frederick, Valdemar, Christian, and George."

"James, I don't know how you do it. You already know everyone's name. Will you ride with me? Otherwise I won't know what to talk about."

"I'll stay close until you actually get into the landau and we'll direct everyone to the appointed seats in the open carriages. If you get stuck for something to say, just point out London's landmarks—London Bridge, and the Mansion House, where the lady mayoress resides, and all. You'll be just fine. I'll meet with you at Paddington Rail Station, so we can take the train to Windsor."

James and the prince led the way off the train, where they encountered Emily, the queen's lady-in-waiting.

She sketched a curtsy to the prince, then put her hand on Hamilton's arm. "James, Her Majesty has ordered me to get that hideous bonnet off Princess Alexandra." She indicated the hatbox she carried. "She must change into this hat before she is paraded through London."

"Lady Emily." James smiled. "Wait beside the prince and me, and when Princess Alexandra alights from the train, curtsy to her and say, 'Her Majesty the Queen has sent you this welcoming gift and would be most honored if you would wear it today.'"

"Thank you, James." She gave him a coy glance. "Diplomacy is your second long suit." She removed the lid of the hatbox in preparation.

James pretended the double entendre had gone over his head.

"What a lovely hat!" Princess Alexandra lifted it from its box with reverence. She untied the ribbons on her old-fashioned bonnet and handed it to Emily. Then she smoothed her light brown wavy hair and lifted the chapeau to her head. "Does it look right?"

"It looks perfect, Your Highness." Emily felt weak with relief that Princess Alexandra had not taken offense, but seemed genuinely delighted with the new hat.

When the Prince of Wales led his bride-to-be to the first landau, Lady Emily stuck like glue and followed the princess into the open carriage. The other ladies-in-waiting made room for the queen's preferred attendant, then with friendly smiles introduced themselves to the princess.

By this time a crowd of Londoners had gathered to get a glimpse of the young royal who would soon become their Princess of Wales. The cheering, laughing, jostling, and waving spectators made Alexandra nervous, and she sat stiffly, trying to take it all in.

When at last the entire royal party was seated in the six landaus, they set off toward London Bridge. Each carriage was pulled by four horses in polished harness, with their heads decorated by the Prince of Wales's feathered plumes. The bridge was ablaze with masses of flowers and garlands whose banners read THE ROSE OF THE NORTH.

Alexandra hesitantly asked Emily, "Am I the Rose of the North?"

"Of course—who else?" Emily replied. She stared at the erect, timid creature beside her and ordered, "Wave to the people!"

The crowd was more like a mob as the landau slowly made its way from London Bridge to the Mansion House, where the mayoress of London waited with a bouquet. The carriage stopped; the lady mayor presented Princess Alexandra with the flowers and gave her speech of welcome. The people were gathered so close to the carriage that the driver could not proceed. Then there was a scuffle when a few overenthusiastic Londoners tried to unharness the horses, so that they could take the shafts and pull the landau themselves.

The commotion and the shouting that ensued frightened Alexandra and she sat stiff as a ramrod, mortified that she was the cause of all this tumultuous disorder.

The five landaus behind were backed up to the bridge and sat waiting to move forward.

After sitting without moving for half an hour, James left his carriage, which was behind the last landau, and walked toward the Mansion House. He had to physically push his way through the noisy crowd that surrounded the princess's coach. He spoke to two or three policemen who were having a difficult time controlling the jubilant Londoners, and they formed a small group. They went to the horses and slowly led them forward, the crowds parting occasionally to let them pass.

As the landaus moved leisurely down Cheapside, the throng thinned a little and allowed the carriages to proceed at a walking pace. With James still holding the bridle of the lead horse, they moved past St. Paul's Cathedral to Ludgate Hill, then along Fleet Street and Temple Bar to the Old City Gate.

As Princess Alexandra rode beneath the gate, she looked up to see a beautiful statue. When Emily explained that it was a statue of Hymen, the princess blushed profusely.

They proceeded at a snail's pace along the Strand, and when the landau reached Trafalgar Square, the people clogged the entire roadway, and had to be cajoled, threatened, and finally ordered to allow the princess to pass.

Flowers were tossed inside the carriage from the jubilant spectators, and the queen's ladies-in-waiting gathered them together into bouquets. Alexandra could hardly breathe in her woolen topcoat. She undid the high neck and Lady Jane, Countess of Dalkeith, helped her to remove it. Her dress beneath the coat was extremely plain compared with the frilly gowns in vogue in London, but since she was sitting down, all that most people saw was her fashionable hat.

It had taken two full hours to get to Trafalgar Square. When they finally were allowed to proceed down Pall Mall, James stepped back and the driver was able to pick up speed. As the second landau carrying Prince Christian and the Prince of Wales passed him, Teddy shouted, "James, I've never seen anything like it!"

James could tell that Prince Teddy was bowled over by all the attention. He waved and shouted, "I'll see you at Paddington."

"Are you sure you want to wait longer?" Montagu asked his mother and sister. "We've been standing here at Paddington Station for an hour and a half, and still there's no sight of them."

"Look on the bright side," Anne admonished. "Half the people have left, so we are sure to get more than a glimpse."

"Well, darling, I'm game if you are," Anne's mother assured her.

"Speak of the devil—I hear cheering." Montagu winked. "Hang on to your hat!"

Anne gave a shout of laughter, since by choice she was hatless. Instead, she had pinned a bunch of violets into her red-gold hair to match her pale violet dress. Excitement bubbled up as she waited breathlessly for the first landau to drive up. Her eyes were focused on the young Danish princess who was indeed wearing her hat. "Oh, she's so sweet and pretty."

All at once Anne's glance traveled to the woman sitting beside Princess Alexandra. When she saw her sister Emily, waving like royalty, she whooped with laughter. "Oh my God, I'm going to pee!"

When the second landau rolled past, her mother said, "That's Prince Christian, who will soon be the King of Denmark."

The Prince of Wales nodded to Lady Anne and she wondered if he had actually recognized her. She cast her gaze on the ladies in the third carriage. She was particularly interested in seeing what Alexandra's sisters looked like. Anne smiled her secret smile.

Princess Alix was without doubt the beauty of the family.

The landaus began to slow as they reached the rail station, and much to Anne's amazement an open carriage came to a stop directly in front of her. She recognized Lord Hamilton immediately, and moreover James recognized her. The corners of her mouth lifted in a tremulous smile as her heart began to race wildly. On impulse she unpinned the violets from her tresses and tossed them into the carriage.

James Hamilton deftly caught the flowers, inhaled their fragrance with appreciation, and threw her a kiss. *Oh Lord, he's off to Windsor. I must wear something eye-catching when I attend the wedding in St. George's Chapel. It's the last time I'll get to see him for eons.*

When the train arrived at Windsor and once again the entire royal party had to disembark and climb into carriages to be transported to the castle, James urged the Prince of Wales to take the lead once they arrived at the ancient fortalice. "The princess has had an exhausting day and she still has the most daunting task of all ahead of her—being presented to the Queen of England for inspection."

"I'll stay beside her. That way if Mother has any criticism, it will be directed at me."

The landaus and carriages entered through the gate to the North Terrace in the Middle Ward and stopped before the state apartments. The Prince of Wales left his landau and instructed Prince Christian, "Gather your family and follow me."

He helped Alexandra from the carriage and kept hold of her hand. "That was quite an ordeal. Londoners can be extremely enthusiastic. You handled it very well."

Lady Emily gathered up Alexandra's coat and bonnet, sprang from the landau, and trotted after the prince and his bride-to-be before the other ladies-in-waiting could make a move. Prince Christian gathered his wife and family and they slowly followed Emily.

When the prince and princess entered the Audience Chamber outside the Queen's Drawing Room, they stopped and waited for the Danish royals to catch up.

Lady Emily walked to the adjoining door and spoke up. "I will inform Her Majesty the Queen that you have arrived." Without hesitation she opened the door, stepped inside, and firmly closed the door.

Emily curtsied to Victoria. "The princess and her family have arrived, Your Majesty."

"It is after seven o'clock," the queen said impatiently. "What on earth kept you?"

"The entire route from Southwark Station where I met the royal party was thronged with cheering crowds of people who slowed our progress to a crawl, Your Majesty. I have never seen anything like the welcome the Londoners gave Princess Alexandra."

Emily saw the queen's mouth turn sulky and knew she had said the wrong thing.

"What are you carrying?"

"Princess Alexandra's coat and bonnet, Your Majesty."

"The garments are hideous; burn them. What about the hat? Did your sister Lady Anne select one that's more suitable?"

"She chose one that is most fashionable, Your Majesty." If Victoria didn't like the hat, Emily wanted her sister to get the blame.

"The Prince of Wales and Princess Alexandra are in the Audience Chamber, Your Majesty, as are the entire Danish royal family. Shall I show them in, ma'am?"

"You may bring in Alexandra, but not my son. We have no desire to see him. The rest of the Danes can wait."

Lady Emily curtsied. Victoria was using the royal *we* and must be obeyed to the letter. "Yes, Your Majesty."

Emily emerged from the Queen's Drawing Room, and spoke directly to the Prince of Wales. "Her Majesty wishes to welcome the princess alone, Your Highness."

"Alix prefers that I remain beside her, Lady Emily." Edward set his jaw.

Emily pressed her lips together. "If the queen's orders are not obeyed to the letter, Bertie, you know there will be untoward consequences."

His mother's hated name for him sapped his manhood and reduced him to a boy. He freed Alexandra's hand. "She wants to see you alone, my dear. I'll wait here for you."

Emily handed the coat and bonnet to Alexandra's sister Dagmar and led the bride-to-be into the Queen's Drawing Room.

Princess Alexandra clasped her hands before her and approached Queen Victoria. She sank down into a stiff curtsy and lowered her eyes. The red walls, priceless portraits, gilt chairs, and rich Aubusson carpets were overwhelming enough without the presence of the squat, thick-figured commanding presence of the woman in black. "Your Gracious Majesty," Alix murmured breathlessly.

"Welcome to our England. We will be seated. We don't like people to tower over us."

Alix took the seat the queen indicated and waited for her to speak first.

"Your dress is unfashionably plain, but we'll soon remedy that. Your wedding gown has been designed by Worth and fashioned after my own. Tomorrow will be soon enough for your fitting. You are extremely slim—I hope you enjoy good health."

"Yes, Your Majesty." Alix spoke softly, timidly.

"You won't be slim long—you'll soon be in an unhappy condition. Still, your primary duty is to provide an heir to the throne of England. I was twenty when I wed, so I was in for it at once. It's all fine to talk of pride of giving life, but I felt more like an animal at such moments."

The young bride-to-be licked bloodless lips. She could think of nothing to say.

"Men are the cause of all our suffering, and your husband will be no different. We poor creatures are born for man's pleasure and amusement and suffer endlessly for it. Poor woman is bodily and morally the husband's slave. Childbirth turns merry young girls into ailing, aching wives. It is the penalty of marriage."

Victoria summoned Lady Emily, who had removed herself to an unobtrusive corner.

"Who chose the hat?"

Emily disclaimed all responsibility. "My sister Anne, Your Majesty."

"The mauve ribbons honored our mourning. Give our compliments to your sister." Victoria's stomach rolled noisily. "Let us have the rest of them in. Dinner will be served precisely at eight; we have waited long enough. Oh, and inform the Prince of Wales there will be no further contact with the princess until the wedding."

Chapter 13

"Is this your entire wardrobe, Your Highness?" Lady Emily had directed the servingwomen to unpack Princess Alexandra's trunks.

"Yes, my lady." *She cannot hide her disdain for my clothes. The queen's lady-in-waiting is as unkind as her mistress.*

"You had best wear the gray dress today. The style is sadly outdated, but at least it's an acceptable mourning color."

"Is the customary mourning period longer than one year here in England, my lady?"

"Her Majesty the Queen and her court are still very much in mourning for Prince Albert, no matter the custom. The wedding invitations state plainly that the ladies attending must wear muted shades of gray, lilac, or mauve."

"I didn't realize."

"Her Gracious Majesty no longer appears in public. At the wedding ceremony in St. George's Chapel here at Windsor, Queen Victoria will watch from above in Queen Katherine's Closet, where the guests won't be able to see her."

How very strange. "I must learn the customs of my new country."

"Indeed, that would be wise. Your Danish accent will undoubtedly set you apart."

I need an ally. Lady Emily will never befriend me. "Do you know if the prince's sister Vicky has arrived for the wedding?"

"I don't believe the Crown Princess of Prussia is here at Windsor as yet. Come along, or you will be late for your fittings. Punctuality is paramount at our royal court."

Alexandra followed Emily to a large chamber where a dozen sewing ladies were working on various garments. Clothing and bolts of material were piled high on tables and chairs, and in the center of the room stood a designer's mannequin dressed in the most ornate, ostentatious, embellished gown the princess had ever seen.

Her eyes widened with horror as it slowly dawned on her that this might possibly be her wedding dress. Alexandra's hand went to her head as a wave of dizziness came over her and she swayed on her feet.

Jane, Countess of Dalkeith, snatched up the clothes piled on the nearest chair. "Sit down, Your Highness. You have gone pale, my dear."

"She's quite overcome at the sight of the magnificent wedding gown," Emily explained.

Alexandra sat down quickly, and Lady Jane knelt down before her. "Did you not have breakfast, my dear?"

"She had a full English breakfast brought on a tray — eggs, ham, sausage, kidneys, fried bread — but hardly ate a thing." Emily rolled her eyes at Jane.

"Perhaps toast and a little fruit would be more to your taste, Your Highness?"

Alexandra managed a tight little smile, and Lady Jane assured her that tomorrow's breakfast tray would be more to her liking.

"There's no time to waste," Emily told the sewing women. "Take the wedding gown off the mannequin. Please stand, Your Highness, so I can remove your dress."

"I will do it myself," Alexandra said shyly. She removed her gray dress and stood in her plain linen shift, waiting for the women to lift the monstrosity over her head.

First they put on a whalebone and wire crinoline and fastened the tapes at her narrow waist. Then they lifted on the gown. "Oh dear, it gapes everywhere. It will have to be taken in a great deal. The princess is so slim," the head fitting woman declared.

"*Too* slim," Emily said. "Her Highness unfortunately has an unfashionable figure."

"Princess Alexandra has a girlish figure because she is still a girl," Jane said kindly.

Alix was vastly relieved when they removed the wedding dress, but almost immediately her anxiety returned as the fitting women urged her to try on some of her wedding trousseau. She shook her head as they held up one garment after another. "They are not my style," she whispered unhappily.

"And a good thing, since your style is dowdy and unfashionable," Emily declared.

Alexandra's eyes flooded with tears and she ran from the chamber.

"Well, did you ever?" Emily demanded to the room at large.

"Lady Emily, your words were most unkind," Jane protested. "Try to imagine yourself in her place; all this must seem extremely strange to her."

"She turned her nose up at everything that has been especially designed for her, at great cost to Her Majesty. Her reaction to the Worth wedding gown showed her lack of taste and breeding. Though it pains me deeply, it is my duty to inform Queen Victoria."

The Countess of Dalkeith followed Lady Emily from the chamber, determined to play advocate for the unhappy bride-to-be.

When Emily finished her diatribe to the dour-faced queen, Lady Jane spoke up.

"I'm afraid Princess Alexandra feels overwhelmed by all the royal trappings. She is young and unworldly, which is to be desired in a bride."

"And what is your solution to this dilemma, Lady Jane?" Victoria asked.

"I believe that Princess Alexandra would benefit from a couple of ladies-in-waiting who are her own age, Your Majesty. I take the liberty of recommending my own sister."

"You could be right, Jane. I am loath to share my ladies-in-waiting with Alexandra. Your loyalty to me must be paramount." Victoria looked directly at Emily. "Your sister Lady Anne, the one with the flair for elegant fashion, should serve the purpose."

"I don't believe my sister would be at all suitable, Your Gracious Majesty."

"You question our decision, Lady Emily?" The queen was not amused.

"Absolutely not, Your Majesty. I shall send for her immediately."

"Your father is going to Gopsall Hall for the lambing, and taking Montagu with him. It will likely be the last time your brother can go for some time, if he gets called up to his regiment."

"Oh, I'd love to go to Leicestershire. They won't go until after the royal wedding, will they? Do you think they will take me with them?"

"They will go on Wednesday, the day after the wedding. Of course you can accompany them, darling. You don't often get the chance to go into the country."

"I won't attend church today—instead I'll go and pack a bag for Leicestershire."

Anne chose two riding habits, and since the weather was springlike, she packed a few light day dresses. Before she was finished, her mother called her downstairs. When she arrived in the drawing room, she was surprised to see her dreaded sister Emily.

"Anne, I want you to know that I have recommended you to act as lady-in-waiting to Princess Alexandra. Queen Victoria thinks the young princess would benefit from a few ladies her own age, and I persuaded Her Majesty that you would be an ideal candidate."

Anne's eyes lit up. "I would be honored to be chosen as a lady-in-waiting."

"You are needed at Windsor Castle today. Alexandra must be fitted for her wedding gown and trousseau, and there are a hundred other tasks that need to be taken care of before Tuesday's wedding. You must hurry and pack; I have a carriage waiting."

Anne's mother spoke up. "I'll come and help you, darling. You'll need to take your outfit for the wedding. Perhaps you'll even get to go on the honeymoon—far more exciting than Leicestershire!"

Emily waited until the carriage entered the Upper Ward of Windsor Castle before she warned her sister. "I didn't tell you until now, Anne, but you are going to have your hands full, I'm afraid. The princess is not very biddable. She's childish, temperamental, and . . . well, *foreign*! And her accent isn't the most unattractive thing about her. That would be her wardrobe. Her clothes are shabby and old-fashioned, yet she turns up her nose at the lovely garments that have been especially designed for her. She's thin as a lat, yet refuses to eat the delicious food that's brought to her. I'm at my wit's end with the stupid girl!"

Anne felt dismay, but it lasted only a moment. Then she smiled to herself. *I can only imagine how Princess Alexandra feels about you, Emily.* "Thank you for warning me. I will try my best to cope with the difficult situation."

"I'll put you in a room in the same wing as Alexandra and her family, and I'll have a servant unpack your clothes. There isn't a moment to be lost, Anne. You must persuade her to go back to the fitting room and try on the wedding gown and the rest of her trousseau. Have a handkerchief ready; she bursts into tears without provocation."

Anne placed her luggage on the bed, and followed Emily down the castle corridor. When they stopped before a door and knocked, there was a long silence before the door was opened by Alexandra's sister. Emily almost pushed Anne into the bedchamber, and was immediately accosted by Dagmar.

"Are you the one who has been bullying my sister?"

"Please, Dagmar, don't make trouble," Alexandra pleaded.

Emily looked down her long nose at Dagmar, then spoke to Alexandra. "This is Lady Anne, especially chosen by Her Gracious Majesty to be one of your ladies-in-waiting. Kindly excuse me, I have important duties for the queen I must perform."

When Emily departed, Dagmar glared at Anne. "I will attend my sister."

"I'm so glad you have acted as your sister's champion, Princess Dagmar." She looked at Alexandra's pale face and red-rimmed eyes, and her heart went out to her. "Sisters don't always do that. Emily excels at bullying. She is my half sister, and it is a great wonder that I haven't murdered her in her sleep."

Alexandra laughed softly. Dagmar remained vigilant.

"What has made you so unhappy, Your Highness?"

Alexandra hesitated, then reluctantly admitted, "The wedding gown."

Anne smiled. "'Tis rumored that it has been styled after Queen Victoria's, so it's no wonder you find it repugnant."

"It has yards and yards of silk and lace, it has ruffle upon ruffle, and it is wreathed with swags of artificial flowers, and it is . . . it is . . ."

"Hideous," Anne supplied.

Alexandra laughed again, and even the dour Dagmar smiled.

"Try to keep in mind that you will only have to wear it for a couple of hours; then you never have to see it again. Once you are married, you may choose your own clothes for the rest of your life. After the wedding ceremony, you must make up your mind to never allow Queen Victoria to dictate to you again. However, until the nuptials are performed, it might be best for the sake of peace and harmony to give way a little."

Alexandra nodded hesitantly.

Anne smiled. "Let us gird our loins and go forth to the fitting room. From now on we will privately refer to the wedding dress as *the monstrosity*. Perhaps when I see it, I can make a few suggestions that will render it less hideous."

Alexandra was now giggling behind her hand and agreed to proceed to the fitting room to once again try on *the monstrosity*.

Ten minutes later when Alexandra stood before Anne in the wedding gown, her eyes were filled with a look that clearly begged, *Please help me!*

Wisely using discretion, Lady Anne spoke to the queen's sewing women. "Worth's design, incorporating roses, shamrocks, and thistles into the lace, is delightful. Unfortunately, Princess Alexandra's slight figure cannot do justice to so many ruffles. You ladies would improve his design immensely if you removed some of them and left only three at the most."

Mrs. Bale, the head sewing woman, agreed and set her helpers to undoing the stitches.

"The train will have four young ladies of the queen's choosing on each side. They will find it difficult to manage more than five feet each. If you cut the gown's train from thirty feet to twenty, it will be far less cumbersome. Charles Frederick Worth is a renowned designer, but when it comes right down to it, he is a man, and where wedding gowns are concerned, I believe a woman's ideas such as yours are superior."

"I couldn't agree with you more, Lady Anne." Mrs. Bale nodded decisively.

"I'd rather cut off my tongue than be critical, but don't you think that artificial flower garlands are in rather poor taste, Mrs. Bale? When fresh orange blossom and myrtle are available at this time of year, don't you

agree that the real thing will put artificial to shame?
They could be added an hour before the ceremony."

"Oh, I quite agree. And the fragrance of fresh orange
blossom will fill the chapel."

"Your ideas are amazing, Mrs. Bale," Anne said with
sincerity. As she helped the princess remove the wedding
gown, she whispered, "Off with *the monstrosity* and on
with the trousseau."

When Alexandra put her hand to her ear and shook
her head, Anne realized the princess could not hear
whispers, so she pointed to the garments waiting to be
tried on.

Princess Alexandra looked at the clothes that had
been especially designed for her wedding trip and sighed.

"Tell me, which do you hate the least?" Anne asked.

"I like the pale violet shade of this morning dress, I
think you call it, but I need a much higher neckline."
The princess blushed. "I . . . I have an ugly scar I must
cover up."

"It's hardly noticeable," Anne lied. "A necklace of
pearls is all that's necessary."

"I . . . I have no jewels," the princess shyly confessed.

"I'll see what I can do about changing that. The queen
has more royal jewels than she will ever be able to wear
in this lifetime. And if Her Majesty won't share, I will
lend you my pearls. Now, what about this blue traveling
suit? I think it will complement your delicate fair coloring. It needs taking in at the waist so it will fit you better."

Alexandra was persuaded to consider a dozen outfits,
and with Anne's suggestions of removing frills, braided
frogs, and fancy furbelows, the princess began to see the
garments with new eyes, and realized they wouldn't be
too hideous with a few alterations.

Lady Anne spoke with the sewing women. "I have no
idea why there are so many gray dresses. It is the queen
who is in mourning, not Princess Alexandra. If you ladies
would kindly put a pink sash on this one and trim the

sleeves on this other one with some primrose ribbons, I'm sure the bride will be forever grateful."

"Her Highness hasn't tried on the veil," Mrs. Bale pointed out.

"The floor-length veil depicting English roses is exquisite, but it is quite spoiled by this crown of wax orange blossoms. I'll speak with the florist who is providing the wedding bouquet and have them design a coronet that you can attach to the veil." Anne smiled. "You've all been so helpful. We'll be back tomorrow for the final fittings."

"My mother has decreed that I must have no contact with Alexandra until the wedding. She's like a fire-breathing dragon. I have no say in anything," Prince Teddy complained.

James Hamilton smiled. "In my experience, no male ever has any say when it comes to his wedding. Females take over and immerse themselves in all the details as if they were planning a military campaign. I feel sorry for Alexandra; she's also been excluded from the plans."

"We haven't exchanged more than a few words since she arrived."

"Why don't you write her a letter, and I'll deliver it for you? Females put great store in such things."

"Never wrote a letter in my life. I'm no good at such things," the prince declared.

"I'll write one if you like, and you can sign it," James offered.

"An excellent suggestion. What the devil would I do without you?"

James sat down immediately and put pen to paper.

My Dearest Alix,
   Though tradition prevents us from being together before we meet in the chapel for our wedding ceremony, it cannot keep my thoughts from you. I even dreamed of you last night.

> *Only a short time remains to keep us apart and
> I am counting the hours.*
>
>   *I often feel constrained by the royal court
> and look forward to escaping with you to the
> Isle of Wight. I am honored that you have
> consented to become my wife and the future
> Princess of Wales.*
>
>   *Fondest love,*
>   *Prince Teddy*

James took the love letter to the other side of Windsor Castle, where Princess Alexandra and her family were staying. A servant directed him to her chamber, and he knocked on the door lightly.

Anne opened it, expecting to see the florist who had been commissioned to do all the flowers for the royal wedding. When she saw James standing before her, she was taken off guard. "Lord Hamilton! I wasn't expecting you."

"Nor I you, Lady Anne." His warm eyes kindled. "This is such a pleasant surprise. What are you doing here?"

"I'm acting as lady-in-waiting to Her Highness Princess Alexandra. There is so much to be done, and so little time. . . . I've been asked to help."

James held up the envelope. "The Prince of Wales regrets that he must keep apart from his lovely bride until Tuesday, so he has done the next best thing and written her a letter. Would you see that she gets it?"

"What a lovely thing to do. The prince is extremely thoughtful. I know it will please the princess." Anne hesitated for a moment, then plunged in. "We have a problem that perhaps you can help to solve, Lord Hamilton."

His eyes drank in her beauty. "I will try my utmost."

"Princess Alexandra has no jewelry. She needs a pearl necklace. A wide one like a collar, if possible. Do you suppose the Prince of Wales can supply one in time for the wedding ceremony?"

His mouth curved into a smile. "You may count upon it, Lady Anne."

She returned his smile. "Thank you, James."

Anne handed Alexandra the envelope. "Lord Hamilton, an attendant of the Prince of Wales, brought this letter for you."

"I am acquainted with Lord Hamilton, and like him very much. He insists that I call him James." The princess tore open the envelope, read the brief letter, and blushed. "The prince writes about escaping to the Isle of Wight."

"I've never been there, but I hear that Osborne House is lovely, and the gardens will be ablaze with spring flowers. The estate is comprised of three hundred and fifty acres. You will be able to ride and the prince will be able to hunt."

"Lady Anne, I'd like you to come with me. You won't abandon me, will you?"

"I would be honored to attend you on your wedding journey to the Isle of Wight."

Anne suddenly felt a wave of excitement sweep over her. *James will be attending Prince Teddy! Too bad the trip is only for three weeks.*

"You will need riding habits. I'll go to the fitting room and bring a couple back for you to try on. If you don't like them, I can lend you my new habit. We are the same size."

"Thank you so much, Lady Anne."

"Please call me Anne."

"I will if you'll call me Alix."

"I can only do that in private. If I addressed you as Alix in public, I would soon be dismissed from being your lady-in-waiting."

Alexandra's eyes kindled. "Once I am the Princess of Wales, I will decide these things for myself, Anne."

Aha! I believe there is a free spirit waiting to be released, and I am more than ready to aid and abet it.

Monday proved to be an extremely busy day. The bride took Anne to her parents' suite and introduced her. She warned her that her mother, Louise, was stone deaf, and Anne felt sad because she realized Alexandra had inherited her deafness, which would likely get worse in years to come.

Anne had breakfast with the Danish royal family; then it was back to the fitting room to make sure the bridal finery fit to perfection, and to choose which outfits must be packed for the honeymoon on the Isle of Wight.

At lunch the princess was introduced to the eight young girls from prominent noble families who had been chosen by Queen Victoria to be her bridesmaids and carry her train. Anne knew most of them personally, but when Lady Frances Hamilton curtsied before the princess, Anne told Alexandra that Frances was her best friend. "If you need another lady-in-waiting, Your Highness, I can highly recommend her."

"Hamilton? Is James your brother?" Alix asked.

"He is, Your Highness."

"Lord Hamilton is such a fine gentleman. I would be honored if you would consent to be one of my ladies-in-waiting."

"The honor is mine, Your Highness."

"Thank you, Lady Frances. When the prince and I return from our wedding trip, we will be moving into Marlborough House." The princess looked from Frances to Anne. "Will that be convenient, ladies?"

As Frances replied to the princess, Anne's heart began to beat wildly. *It never occurred to me until this moment. . . . James and I will both be living at Marlborough House!*

After lunch with the bridesmaids, Princess Alexandra returned to her chamber and within five minutes Princess Vicky opened the door and stepped inside.

"Vicky, I'm so pleased to see you. Did you only just arrive?" Alix asked.

"I arrived two days ago, but I've been throwing up since crossing the Channel. It had better be seasickness.

If I'm off again, my temper will be in shreds. Baby Henry is only six months old!"

"I hope it was just *mal de mer*," Alix said. "Has your sickness abated?"

"Slightly. I didn't eat breakfast—I didn't want to take the chance."

"I'd like you to meet Lady Anne Howe. My very first lady-in-waiting."

Anne curtsied to the Crown Princess of Prussia. "Your Royal Highness."

"Howe? You cannot possibly be the sister of Emily, my mother's lady-in-waiting. Emily's coloring is as dark as mine."

Anne tried not to stare. Princess Vicky was short, and thick as a glass jam jar. She made Alix look like a piece of delicate crystal. "Emily is my half sister, Your Highness."

"Ah, yes. Different mothers. Men invariably wear out their first wives with childbearing. Take heed, Alix, and don't let that happen to you."

Princess Alexandra blushed, and Anne could not help but think that the queen's daughter was rather coarse.

"If you don't need me for anything at the moment, I will go to my room and give you some privacy to visit with Princess Victoria."

Just then a knock came on the door. "See who it is, please, Lady Anne."

When she opened the door, Anne was once again pleasantly surprised to see James Hamilton. He was holding a blue velvet jewel case tied with silver ribbon.

"I have been entrusted to present Princess Alexandra with the Prince of Wales's wedding gift."

"I'd know that voice anywhere," Princess Vicky declared huskily as she advanced to the door. "James! It's been a year and a half since Strelitz. Do come in."

"Your Royal Highness." James bowed his head and proceeded into the room.

"Such formality, James. I won't have it."

Good God, Princess Vicky has gone all kittenish at the sight of him. Anne spoke to Alix. "Lord Hamilton has brought the groom's wedding present to his bride."

"Oh, it's a jewel case," Alix gasped. She took the blue velvet box and with trembling fingers undid the silver ribbon. She opened the hinged case to reveal a pearl collar necklace, with matching earrings and brooch. "Ah, how exquisite. These are my very first jewels. James, please tell the Prince of Wales that I thank him with all my heart."

"I'm sure these jewels will be the first of many, Your Highness."

"James, you are a silver-tongued devil!" Vicky gave him a coy, sidewise glance.

Well, I'll be damned. . . . She's slavering over him!

Chapter 14

*S*he's late! What on earth could have happened? Anne
Howe stood with her parents and her brother Montagu in St. George's Chapel at Windsor. The pews were
filled with waiting, invited guests. The court officials and
the heralds were all in place. The Prince of Wales, wearing the uniform of a general along with the Garter
Robes, stood waiting at the altar with the archbishop of
Canterbury, Thomas Longley.

People began to clear their throats, and a few coughs
penetrated the awkward silence.

John Claud Hamilton moved into the pew beside
Anne. "You look lovely, though your gown isn't a muted
shade," he whispered.

She glanced down with amused eyes at her seafoam
green silk. "It's muted for me."

"You flaunt the rules."

"Always." *I spent over an hour placing the fresh flowers in her coronet, and making sure her veil was in place.
When I left them, the bridesmaids were all holding her
train in readiness—don't tell me Alix is having a nervous
panic. I should have stayed with her until she started to
move down the aisle.* Anne glanced up toward Queen
Katherine's Closet. *Victoria will be incensed that the princess is late and keeping everyone waiting!*

After an interval of ten minutes that seemed more like an hour, the trumpets sounded and Prince Christian of Denmark led his daughter, swathed in white silk and silver lace, down the nave of the chapel toward the altar and her waiting groom.

James Hamilton, sitting in the second pew behind the Prince of Wales's royal siblings, turned to watch the bride approach. She was completely hidden inside her cocoon of silk and lace, and his eyes strayed to the guests, searching for a certain female.

He found her easily, but disappointment clouded his eager mood of anticipation when he saw that John Claud was her escort. It was so easy to forget that his brother was courting Anne, but seeing them together as a couple was a sobering reminder that the lady was out of bounds to him.

"Dearly beloved, we are gathered together here in the sight of God, and in the face of this congregation, to join together this man and this woman in holy Matrimony—"

The words of the archbishop, echoing in the vaulted chapel, brought James out of his reverie. He had attended many weddings, including those of three of his sisters, and the Solemnization of Matrimony was familiar.

"Albert Edward, wilt thou have this woman to thy wedded wife, to live together after God's ordinance in the holy estate of Matrimony? Wilt thou love her, comfort her, honor, and keep her, in sickness and in health, and, forsaking all others, keep thee only unto her, so long as ye both shall live?"

At that precise moment a ray of sunlight shone through the eastern stained-glass window and enveloped Queen Katherine's Closet in a halo of light. Prince Edward was so awed by Queen Victoria's power that he was unable to answer the archbishop. He swallowed hard and nodded his assent.

The archbishop of Canterbury, the only person in the chapel not overawed by the queen's authority, charged the princess with the same question.

"I will," Alexandra answered in a clear, sweet voice.

"Who giveth this woman to be married to this man?" the archbishop demanded.

Prince Christian placed his daughter's hand in Longley's and stepped back to stand beside his wife.

Find your voice quickly, Teddy. You must pledge your vows, like it or not.

The archbishop placed the bride's hand in her groom's right hand. "Repeat after me: I, Albert Edward, take thee, Alexandra Caroline, to my wedded wife . . ."

After a moment's hesitation, the Prince of Wales found his lost voice, and James Hamilton, along with the entire congregation, heaved a silent sigh of relief.

After the royal couple exchanged all their vows, Canterbury addressed the congregation. "Those whom God hath joined together let no man put asunder. For as much as Albert Edward and Alexandra Caroline have consented together in holy wedlock, and have witnessed the same before God and this company, and thereto have given and pledged their troth either to other, and have declared the same by giving and receiving of a ring, and by joining of hands; I pronounce that they be man and wife together, in the name of the Father, and of the Son, and of the Holy Ghost. Amen."

The archbishop read two psalms and some traditional prayers, and finally the Anthem was sung by Jenny Lind, who truly had the voice of a nightingale. Her performance was marred by loud sobs from Queen Victoria. The Anthem had been written by her late, beloved Albert, and she lost her composure and broke down.

Good God, here come the waterworks, James lamented. When many of the guests followed the queen's lead, James knew how uncomfortable the Prince of Wales must feel.

It's mass hysteria. Heaven be praised we are at the end of this ceremonial circus!

James should have known there was worse to come. A temporary banquet hall had been erected, opening out of the west door of the chapel, and as the multitude of invited guests followed the bridal party into the huge tentlike chamber, the pecking order was called into question. Members of the government vied with the nobility, who in turn took umbrage that foreign royals were shown precedence over British peers. Sarcastic comments, bruised feelings, and outright hostilities pervaded the air. Order and manners fell by the wayside as pushing and shoving became prevalent. The size of the fortune spent on this royal wedding should have guaranteed an atmosphere of love and joy; instead, it produced the opposite.

John Claud found seats for Anne, Montagu, and their parents. "I brought my carriage. I'll give you a ride home, Lord Howe. The train from Windsor back to London this evening will be a mad scramble for seats."

"Very kind of you, my boy, but we also brought our carriage. Montagu and I are off to Leicestershire this evening. We're going to Gopsall Hall for the lambing."

John Claud nodded his understanding; he knew that Montagu had joined the Rifle Brigade and would soon be called up. He smiled at Anne. "It would make me happy if you would allow me to drive you back to London."

"I'm sorry, John Claud, but Princess Alexandra has asked me to accompany her to the Isle of Wight."

"On her honeymoon? Surely that's highly irregular?"

"I think she invited me because she feels she needs an ally. She's chosen me as one of her ladies-in-waiting, and when we return to London, your sister Frances will be joining us at Marlborough House."

John Claud frowned. "You won't be living there full-time, will you?"

"I imagine I will spend certain days of the week there, and some at home. Just as your sister Jane, Countess of Dalkeith, spends certain days at Buckingham Palace in her capacity as lady-in-waiting to the queen, and then returns home for part of the week. It will be up to the Princess of Wales to decide our schedule."

His brow was still furrowed with disapproval. "I

would appreciate it if you would let me know when you will next be at home, Anne. I'm trying to court you, but it's proving rather difficult."

Anne's eyes filled with amusement. "Poor John Claud, first it's Fitz Kerry, now it's the Princess of Wales. Rivals are the very devil."

"Those aren't the rivals I worry about," he said dryly.

Though his brother's name had not been mentioned, Anne knew he was thinking of James. Her pulse quickened. *We'll be together at Osborne House and then at Marlborough House.* Anne blushed as she recalled that she had tossed her violets into Lord Hamilton's carriage. *From now on I must treat James with cool indifference, or he will assume I am throwing myself at him, like the voluptuous Princess Vicky ... and all the other females who lay eyes on him.*

Anne bade good-bye to her parents when they decided to leave the reception early without waiting for the wedding cake. She kissed her father. "Have a safe trip to Leicestershire."

John Claud shook hands with her father and kissed her mother's hand. He knew they approved of him as a suitor to their daughter and he intended to keep it that way. After they left, he turned his attention to the guests who were members of Parliament. "Did you see the look Lady Churchill gave Disraeli's wife? I thought she was going to have hysterics when she saw that she was an invited guest."

"The duchess thinks she's superior to the rest of the nobility, so it doesn't surprise me she's outraged that people who aren't in the peerage have been invited."

"MPs in my humble opinion are far more important than aging aristocrats."

Anne's eyes sparkled. "You have no *humble* opinions, John Claud."

"I'm off to Ireland soon to run for the Londonderry seat. When I return, the youngest member of Parliament will have a proposal to put to you."

"You take it for granted you'll win the seat."

"Absolutely!"

"And you take it for granted that I'll say yes, you cocky devil. I'm afraid you are in for a rude awakening, John Claud."

They both looked up as James Hamilton approached. Anne caught her breath.

James greeted his brother, then turned to Anne. "Her Majesty has commanded that the newlyweds join her in the royal apartments to have their photographs taken with her and a bust of Prince Albert."

"How . . . inventive," Anne murmured.

"Teddy's had enough domination to last him a lifetime," James said quietly. "We are going to secretly smuggle the couple back to Marlborough House tonight. Sometime tomorrow we'll take the train from London to Portsmouth, then sail across the Solent to Osborne House. I'll give you a signal when we're ready to leave."

Anne nodded. She agreed that Alexandra would be much happier once she was away from her new mother-in-law, Queen Victoria. "I'll be ready, Lord Hamilton."

It was more than an hour later when James returned to the reception without the newlyweds and waved his hand. Anne bade good-bye to John Claud. "When I'm next at home, I will drop in at Hampden House. Thank you for your escort today." *If I remind him that I did not seek his escort, it would hurt his feelings, but I truly wish he wasn't such a devoted swain.*

When Anne arrived at Marlborough House, the chamberlain assigned her a chamber in the wing where Alexandra had her private quarters, which were apart from those the princess would share with the Prince of Wales. She did not see the newlyweds, who were already ensconced in the master suite.

Anne decided to leave her trunk unpacked, since she'd be leaving sometime tomorrow for the Isle of Wight. She opened the lid to get out a nightdress and realized she should have brought more clothes. Since the honeymoon would last for three weeks, she would be hard-pressed to find a different outfit each day.

I should have brought my sketching supplies so I could design some dresses for Alix. She really didn't care for many of the outfits that had been designed for her trousseau.

She heard a light tap on the door and was surprised when she opened it to find James Hamilton.

"We don't expect the newlyweds to emerge early, so I've arranged for us to depart on the afternoon train to Portsmouth." He smiled. "No need for you to arise at dawn."

An idea came into her head. "Do you suppose I would have time to go home in the morning and collect a few more things?"

"Of course, Lady Anne. I'll arrange a carriage for you at nine o'clock. Good night."

Anne was an early riser and awoke at seven. Her chamber was elegantly furnished, and the deep-piled Turkish carpet was more costly than the one in her bedchamber at home. She was pleased with the flat-topped writing desk where she could work on her design sketches. She drew back the brocade drapes and was delighted with her view of St. James's Park.

When she answered a light tap on the door, there were two female servants, one with hot water and the other with her breakfast on a tray. "Thank you for the service. I wasn't expecting a tray."

The maid bobbed a curtsy. "Lord Hamilton ordered it for you, my lady. He said you would be pressed for time this morning."

How very thoughtful of him. I'll eat now before I get dressed. She sat down and lifted the silver cover. There was a Dover sole with parsley and lemon. *Did he order this to remind me of the meal we shared at the hotel that day?* She saw the lily in the crystal vase, and smiled her secret smile. *He remembered every detail. I think I'll bring my lovely fur coat. We'll likely have some cool evenings on the Isle of Wight.*

*   *   *

It was after ten o'clock when Anne stepped from the carriage, ran lightly up the steps to the Grosvenor Square house, and opened the door with her key. The house was quiet; there were no servants about, not even Jenkins, and she wondered if her mother had gone out. *I don't have much time, but it won't take long to get my sketchbook and pack a couple of outfits. I won't pack my fur coat, I'll wear it.*

Upstairs, she opened her wardrobe and selected three outfits. One was cream brocade, whose bodice she'd embroidered with black-and-gold honeybees. Another was a mauve linen walking dress, and the third was a teal velvet riding habit. She folded them into an overnight bag and slipped on her fur coat. She glanced at the sketchbook on her desk, then heard her mother's laughter.

Anne went down the hall to her mother's dressing room, but when she recognized a man's voice, she stopped. *Father and Montagu have gone to Gopsall. Who could be in Mother's bedchamber?*

"Leicester, darling, let's stay abed all day. I want to reward you for getting Montagu accepted into the prestigious Rifle Brigade."

Anne's hand flew to her mouth. She'd suspected that her mother had been in love with Leicester before she'd been married, but was shocked to her bones that they were still lovers.

"He's my son—it's the least I could do, sweetheart."

Anne began to shake. On unsteady legs she walked quietly back to her own chamber.

With trembling hands she slipped her sketchbook into her overnight bag, and crept out of the house. She sat stunned in the carriage as it returned to Marlborough House. As she leaned back against the velvet squabs, she did not recall leaving her mother's dressing room, only the sound of Leicester's voice.

Montagu is Leicester's son. Anne felt her stomach knot. *Mother's lover is her husband's son.* She shook her head in denial. Surely, her mother could not be so depraved? *That would mean she has been sleeping with both for twenty years!*

When the carriage stopped, Anne sat in a trance. *No one must ever find out about Mother's wicked secret. Oh my God, if Emily ever got scent of such a scandalous thing, she would destroy us. Father would divorce my mother and neither she nor I would be accepted in polite society. The Hamiltons would withdraw their friendship. Any whiff of scandal is such anathema to Queen Victoria that we would be "beyond the pale."*

"Are you feeling all right, my lady?"

Anne blinked at the driver who had opened the carriage door. She moistened dry, bloodless lips. "Perfectly all right," she murmured, as a footman came out of Marlborough House to take her bag.

She followed him inside and glanced at the tall clock in the reception hall. She couldn't believe that it was only a few minutes past eleven. In the space of one brief hour, her world had been turned upside down.

When Anne glimpsed Alexandra's pale, anxious face as she descended the staircase, she pushed thoughts of her mother's shocking affair aside. *Oh dear, Alix doesn't look like a happy bride.* "I've been on an errand, Your Highness. I was just going up to make sure the servants have packed everything you want to take to Osborne House."

"Please call me Alix," she pleaded. "Yes, everything is packed and ready."

You don't look ready. "Are you going to lunch?"

"I'm not sure where the dining room is."

Anne gave her a reassuring smile. "We'll find it together, Alix."

It wasn't difficult to locate, as liveried footmen and the prince's gentlemen were headed in that direction. "Do you think I may sit here by the window?"

"You may sit anywhere you fancy, Alix. This house belongs to you."

"I couldn't manage any breakfast, but I think I should

eat something before the long journey. I feel almost faint," she confessed shyly.

Anne's stomach was in a knot, and the last thing she wanted was food. "I had breakfast, so I'm not very hungry," she told the liveried server. "Perhaps some soup."

"May I take the liberty of suggesting mushroom bisque, my lady?"

"Yes, that would be lovely, thank you."

"I'd like some too," the princess said softly.

"Certainly, Your Highness." The server bowed and departed.

"You look lovely in that shade of lilac, Alix."

"I like any shade of purple or mauve, and it is an approved mourning color." Her hand went to her pearl necklace. "I wore my wedding jewels. Am I being too ostentatious?" she asked anxiously.

"Not at all. Not only are they perfect for a royal princess; they are your husband's wedding gift to you. He will be most pleased that you have chosen to wear them."

"I hope he's pleased."

Anne heard the wistful note in her voice. *I can tell she is too reticent to say more.* "Ah, good, here's the soup. I'm sure it will make us both feel better." For Alix's sake, Anne forced herself to pick up the spoon and pretend to relish the mushroom bisque.

Just as they were finishing their soup, the Prince of Wales, accompanied by James Hamilton, arrived. The moment he saw his bride, Teddy stopped in his tracks. Then in a great show of conviviality, he moved forward, kissed his bride's hand, and sat down beside her.

Anne, expecting a blush on Alix's cheeks, saw her turn white.

"We have a renowned chef at Marlborough House," Teddy declared. "What have you ordered, my dear? Perhaps I'll have the same!"

"Lady Anne and I have finished our lunch. We were just leaving."

Anne glanced at James, set her linen napkin on the

table, and arose. She sketched a curtsy to the prince.
"Good morning, Your Highness."

"I insist we dispense with this wretched formality. All
this bowing and scraping makes me damned uncomfortable. Off you go, ladies. Lord Hamilton and I must fortify
ourselves for the long train ride. Do sit down, James."

James bowed his head to the Princess of Wales and,
after they left, sat down. He kept a wise silence, knowing
that Teddy would soon voice his dissatisfaction over
what had happened, or likely what had *not* happened, on
his wedding night.

The prince ate in silence, while James was amazed at
the amount of food Teddy consumed. He started on the
third course before he was ready to talk. "My wedding
night was rather uneventful. Alix is a decidedly cool female, I'm afraid."

"The sea voyage, and all the wedding preparations, to
say nothing of being scrutinized by the queen and the
royal family, must have been overwhelming. She will
need a little time to overcome her exhaustion, sire."

"You are distancing yourself from me when you call
me *sire*. Don't do it."

"Sorry, Teddy." James helped himself to some grapes
and a bit of Stilton.

The prince finished his partridge and wiped his fingers.
"Well, what's done is done, and can't be undone. But in
my way of thinking, a bride should be *eager.*"

"And in my way of thinking, a bride should be innocent."

The prince stared at his friend. "So, your advice
would be?"

"Patience."

Teddy picked up a spoon and dug into his whiskey
bread pudding.

On the train ride to Portsmouth, Anne had hours to
think about what she had discovered at her home in
Grosvenor Square earlier in the day. *How could Mother*

*risk such disgrace? And having an affair with your hus-
band's son is disgraceful in the extreme!*

Anne knew that discovery would be ruinous, not only
to her mother, but to her marriage, and to the son and
daughter of that marriage. The risk of being found out
was gargantuan. The danger of arousing suspicion was
even greater. *Why on earth would Mother put herself in
such jeopardy?*

Anne had always had a close bond with her mother,
and as her shock began to lessen, her thoughts softened.
*She must be deeply in love. Over the years, her longing
must have been unbearable. They don't see each other often because he's posted abroad, and when he returns to
England, her yearning to be with him must overcome the
risk.*

Anne's thoughts diverged. *That doesn't make it right.
She's having an affair with her stepson. It's almost inces-
tuous!* Another thought came. *It's Leicester's fault. How
could he put her in such an untenable, dangerous position?*

Excuses came readily. *He was in love with her, and
begged her to elope. She was having his child. His feelings
have never wavered. He must love his son, Montagu, as
deeply as he loves her.*

The focus of her thoughts shifted to her father. *How
could he have conspired with Queen Adelaide to send
Leicester abroad so that he could marry my mother? If
she was having a baby, no wonder she gave in.* A more
damning thought occurred to her.

*What if Father knew they were lovers? What if he knew
she was having his son's child?*

*What if he knows of their twenty-year affair? That is a
far worse sin.*

Anne recoiled at the thought that her father might
knowingly share his wife with his son. *Perhaps Richard
Curzon-Howe isn't my father!*

Chapter 15

"The queen has sent some of her ladies to serve you," Anne explained the group waiting to board the yacht. She sent up a silent prayer of thanks that Emily was not among them.

"I wish she had not," Alix murmured.

"Well, you need a couple of lady's maids and someone to do your hair. The queen must have dispatched them on an earlier train. When you return to London, you will be able to choose your own servingwomen."

On the voyage across the Solent, Anne did not have time to ruminate on her own problems. The Princess of Wales was not a good sailor and suffered from a bout of *mal de mer*. Anne stayed with her in her cabin and tended to her needs. When they arrived on the Isle of Wight, carriages awaited the royal party. As a new bride, the princess shared the prince's carriage for the short ride to Osborne House.

Teddy made small talk. "This is East Cowes. I hope you enjoy it here. The seaside palace is lovely. The estate encompasses over three hundred acres, and the hunting is exceptional."

"I'm sure I shall enjoy it, Edward. It looks as if spring has arrived before us."

At Osborne House the carriages drew up before the pavilion of private apartments.

Anne left the carriage she'd shared with the other ladies, and since the prince did not step forward to carry his bride across the threshold of Osborne House, Anne accompanied the Princess of Wales inside.

The chamberlain met them. He bowed to the Princess of Wales. "Your Highness, my name is Mathews. If you will kindly follow me, I will take you to the royal apartments, up on the first floor."

"Thank you." Alix and Anne glanced about the ground floor, where the dining room, drawing room, and billiard room were located, before they ascended the stairs.

"This is the master bedchamber, Your Highness. I'll have your luggage brought up."

Anne saw the pinched look on Alix's face. "My name is Anne, the princess's lady-in-waiting. In addition to this chamber, Her Highness would appreciate a separate bedchamber, with a dressing room." She was rewarded by a grateful look from the bride.

The chamberlain took them to an adjoining wing and opened double doors to reveal a lady's boudoir complete with dressing room.

"This is lovely. Kindly have Princess Alexandra's luggage brought here."

"There is a small chamber two doors down the hall that will accommodate you nicely, Lady Anne. Dinner is served at eight here at Osborne House."

"Thank you, Mathews, you have been very helpful." When he left, Anne said, "This will give you a little breathing space. When the queen's ladies arrive, I'll tell them that I will unpack for you."

"Thank you, Anne. I don't feel ill, I just feel . . ."

Anne suggested the word she was reaching for. "You feel a little apprehensive."

Alix nodded. "I hope Edward isn't expecting me in the master bedchamber."

"It will be a hive of activity in there for hours. His Highness has a mountain of luggage. He has brought two valets with him, as well as his gentlemen attendants. If I know anything of men, the first order of business will be changing into riding clothes and inspecting the horses in the stables."

Alix let out a long breath of relief.

When the luggage arrived, Anne unpacked for the princess, and hung everything in the large wardrobe. After a quick consultation, she laid out a blue dinner gown with matching shoes, and a mother-of-pearl fan. Then she retired down the hall to her own bedchamber to unpack her clothes.

At precisely seven Anne returned to help Alix dress for dinner; she herself was wearing the seafoam green silk she had worn to the wedding. When the princess saw her reflection wearing the blue dinner gown, she changed her mind. Anne helped her don an ecru lace that boasted a bustle. Alix seemed happy until she turned sideways; then she decided it would be awkward to sit in at dinner. "Perhaps the blue will be better after all."

First she decided she wanted to wear elbow-length, cream gloves. Then she exchanged them for gray, and finally discarded the idea of gloves completely. She sat down at the dressing table and asked Anne to help her put up her hair. When her lovely fair hair was brushed upward and pinned into place, she declared that it made her look too plain.

Anne suddenly realized that Alexandra was doing whatever she could to delay going down to dine. She glanced at the mantel clock and saw that it was eight o'clock. "You have some lovely mother-of-pearl hair ornaments in your jewel case that will match your fan perfectly. Let me get them."

Anne pinned the ornaments into her coiffure and handed her the fan. When she saw the look of indecision on the face of the princess, she knew the reason that the bride had been late for her wedding. She also knew that being late gave Alix a tiny bit of control in a situation where she had very little. Anne said gently, "You cannot hold back time, Alix."

"It's all so daunting," she whispered.

"It will get easier. You will dazzle everyone with your beauty. Your gown is lovely and you can rest easy knowing you never have to wear *the monstrosity* ever again."

Alix laughed behind her fan. "Lead the way."

When the two ladies entered the dining room, all the gentlemen stood and bowed their heads in welcome. The prince took longer to get to his feet, but made up for it by indicating an empty chair. "Come and sit beside me, Alix. The first course is about to be served. The sea air gives me quite an appetite."

The princess sat down between Teddy and James Hamilton. Anne took a seat across the table so that Alix could make eye contact with her if she felt the need. She smiled at Charles Carrington, who would be sitting beside her, and nodded to Lady Emma Lascelles and Lady Theresa Digby, two of the queen's ladies-in-waiting who had been assigned to attend the bride on her honeymoon.

The prince included everyone in his conversation, rather than exchanging private words with his new wife, and Anne saw Alix relax a little when they all joined in.

During the second course, Prince Teddy announced with great enthusiasm, "Tomorrow morning we are hunting! I can't tell you how much I've been looking forward to it. We'll get you mounted first thing, Alix."

The princess patted her lips with her linen napkin. "I love to ride, but I'm afraid I don't enjoy hunting, Edward."

The prince looked astounded. "It's only fox and hares, my dear, no big game."

The princess opened her mouth to protest, but nothing came out, and a momentary silence filled the room.

James Hamilton smoothly filled the pause in conversation. "It would give me great pleasure to accompany you on a riding tour of the estate, Your Highness. There are many acres of woodlands, a home farm, a pair of Italianate towers, and some lovely views of passing ships in the Solent."

"It's most generous of you to forgo the hunting, James." Teddy picked up his claret. "I salute you."

James, whose attention was focused on Anne, saw the relieved look she and Princess Alexandra exchanged. *Teddy hasn't the faintest idea that his priority should be pleasing his bride rather than pleasing himself.*

James was free to watch Anne, as she conversed with Carrington. *She seems reserved tonight, not bubbling with her usual mischief. I doubt it's because she's dining with the Prince of Wales—she's supped with him before.*

He noticed that neither she nor Alix touched her claret, and when the next course was served, he addressed Teddy. "Perhaps the ladies would prefer a lighter wine, Chablis?"

"Let's have some champagne. I believe I could develop a taste for the stuff myself."

James received a grateful smile from Alix, but Anne did not spare him a glance. *She's pensive. I wonder what she's thinking about. She seems oblivious that I'm even here.*

Anne was very much aware of Lord Hamilton. He covered the prince's lapses in manners and hospitality, and did it so smoothly that Teddy's gaucheness went unnoticed by the other ladies and gentlemen at the table.

It was just after ten o'clock when the fruit and cheese were placed on the table and the footmen brought in the whiskey. Teddy pulled his cigar case from his pocket. "No need for the ladies to withdraw tonight. The men are off to the billiard room."

James masked his thoughts. *Most bridegrooms cannot wait to be alone with their new brides. Let's hope the ladies think he's being considerate. I know better.*

When the gentlemen departed, Princess Alexandra thanked the queen's ladies for their attendance. "You may have the rest of the night off, whatever is left of it."

Anne accompanied Alix to her private bedroom. The princess paced about restlessly. "This bed looks very inviting," she said wistfully, "but I must sleep in the master bedchamber."

"Perhaps if you took a bath, it would help you relax, and also pass the time." *Teddy may not tire of billiards until after midnight.*

"That sounds very tempting, but I hate to put the servants to work this late."

"Ten thirty isn't late. I know they are eager to serve you."

Anne helped Alix remove her blue gown and she put the garments away in the wardrobe. Then she waited patiently until the princess chose a nightgown, slippers, and robe from the huge selection that had been handmade for the royal honeymoon.

It was midnight before Anne accompanied the princess to the master chamber and bade her good night. Then she retraced her steps back to the wing where her own chamber was located.

Anne didn't light her lamp. Instead she walked to the window and stood gazing out into the darkened garden. At last she was alone with her thoughts, and she knew they would keep her from sleep. She stood there for a long time, trying to keep the darklings at bay. She glanced ruefully at the bed and knew there was no point undressing.

On impulse, she took her fur coat from the wardrobe, tucked it under her arm, and made her way to the ground floor. She stepped outside into the shadowed garden, where her green gown made her almost invisible.

James opened his bedchamber window, letting in the cool breeze, hoping it would banish the smell of Teddy's cigars. He stood looking out at the shadowed garden as he took deep breaths of fresh air. Across the vast dark lawn, a figure suddenly became visible. He narrowed his eyes and saw it was a female who had just donned a pale gray fur. He'd seen that coat before and knew immediately that it was Anne. *I didn't see her until she put on the fur because her gown blended into the greenery. Why is she wandering in the dark?*

James watched the figure as it moved beyond the pond with its ornamental fountain until it disappeared inside the latticed summerhouse. His first instinct was to go out to the garden and join her there. *She couldn't sleep. But perhaps if something is troubling her, she needs solitude.* He forced himself to leave her be and stood watch at the window waiting for her to return to the house. He couldn't dispel a feeling of longing that stole over him as he looked at the summerhouse. The emotions she evoked were new to him. *Anne awakens the unknown inside me.*

At least half an hour elapsed before he saw her emerge and return across the lawn.

James undressed slowly and climbed into bed. His last thoughts before he slept were of Anne, and when his dream began, he was free to be with her, without the impediment of John Claud's presence.

When the Prince of Wales opened his eyes, he was vastly relieved that his wife had already left the bed and departed the master bedchamber. His valet entered and laid out his hunting attire and boots. Teddy declined a bath, but accepted the hot water a footman delivered.

James arrived to accompany him to breakfast. "I trust you had a good night, sire."

Teddy grimaced. "*Sire* did not have a good night."

Though James did not wish to hear the details, he resigned himself to the prince's complaints.

"I said she was *cool*, but *cold* is a more accurate description. She simply lay there and initiated absolutely nothing!"

James kept a wise silence, knowing a reply would encourage Teddy to elaborate, but elaborate he did. "Your advice to be patient didn't work. If I'd waited all night, she wouldn't have taken the first step."

James swallowed his exasperation. "An innocent, uninitiated young bride must be awakened."

"Oh, she wasn't asleep. She was staring at the ceiling."

James glanced at Teddy's face to see if he was making a jest. *He's serious, begod.*

"What do you suggest?"

"You should go slowly and be gentle. Once you take off her nightgown, don't jump on her. Instead, caress her and woo her with words; tell her how lovely she is."

"I tried to remove her nightgown, but when she resisted, I simply pulled it up and got on with the business. She showed little reaction—no laughter, no tears. I enjoy fun and games. I don't know what the devil is wrong with the girl."

Princess Alexandra is likely in shock. Your previous sexual partners have always been vastly experienced and trained to take the lead, while you lie back and let them. Likely I'm to blame—I've helped create a monster. "The weather is splendid. You should have a good hunt."

At last Teddy smiled. "I can't wait! Let's go and eat."

At the stables, once the prince was in the saddle, he was impatient to loose the hunting dogs so the hunt could get under way. "Alix, my dear, you may rely completely on Lord Hamilton to mount you suitably and escort you wherever you wish to go. I shall see you at dinner."

"Thank you, Edward." The princess schooled her expression so the others wouldn't guess she was glad to be rid of him. At breakfast she had graciously invited Lady Emma and Lady Theresa to join her on her ride to explore the estate, and they hovered at the entrance to the stable, awaiting the horses that would be saddled for them by the grooms.

James gave Alix an encouraging smile. "Do you prefer a palfrey, or a hunter, Your Highness?"

"I don't need a horse with an easy gait, my lord. I prefer a mare with a little spirit."

"Brava . . . you and Lady Anne will get along famously." He nodded his head in Anne's direction. She had taken the lead and was walking past the stalls to select a mount for herself.

"I think I'll take the gray," Alix decided. She colored slightly. "I'm used to a regular saddle, if that's permissible."

Anne overheard her. "Whatever you decide is permissible, Your Highness. I'll take the black hunter with a regular saddle." She led the black from its stall and handed it over to a groom. "I believe the queen's ladies will expect sidesaddles," she confided.

Out of consideration for the ladies, James chose a gelding. He helped the princess into the saddle and before he mounted, he caught his breath as Anne approached him.

"Alix has a slight hearing problem," she confided in a murmur, then led her black from the stables, mounted, and fell in behind the princess and James.

I should have known Anne's thoughts were not focused on me.

Two grooms joined the party and Anne indicated that they should attend the queen's ladies, who were primly perched upon their sidesaddles.

Alix turned her head toward James. "Are you up to a full-out gallop?"

He laughed. "Be my guest."

The Princess of Wales took off at a gallop and James stayed close beside her. They crossed an open field filled with buttercups, and when they came to a small stream, she didn't hesitate but rode straight through it.

Anne kept pace with the pair before her, but they left the two ladies and their grooms far behind. When the home farm came into view, they drew rein and slowed to a trot.

Alix beckoned Anne. "Ride beside me while we explore this amazing farm. James tells me it provides everything that Osborne House needs." She laughed at the hens and geese clucking and honking as the horses approached. "The farm reminds me of my childhood. I love the animals and the smells."

Anne pointed out some newly born lambs who seemed to be skipping among the ewes. It made her think of the lambing at Gopsall Hall, and her father.

James saw the look of delight on Anne's face suddenly vanish and an anguished expression take its place. *Her thoughts steal her happiness.*

They were served lunch in the farm kitchen and Anne was delighted that the princess enjoyed every mouthful of the plain fare. The queen's ladies, however, looked completely out of place in the rustic setting.

After the tour of the farm, James led the way to the Solent. "This is a private beach. The water is never really cold. It's warmed by a gulf stream."

"We can come and swim one afternoon, if you like," Anne offered.

"That would be lovely. The sea in Denmark is far too cold for swimming. Whatever is that?" Alix pointed to a huge canvas box on wheels.

"Ah, that is Her Majesty's bathing machine," James said.

Anne explained further. "It allows a lady to go into the water without being seen. It gives the queen complete privacy from prying eyes."

Both young women, picturing Victoria working the ridiculous contraption, went off into peals of laughter.

The corners of James's mouth lifted as he joined in their amusement. He was relieved to see Anne laugh. But it was short-lived, and in repose she looked sad.

From the beach they rode east on the property where a miniature fort complete with barracks had been built in a previous century. "I warrant the fort was built as protection from wicked European invaders, yet here I am." Alix laughed in jest, and both Anne and James realized that the Princess of Wales had a sense of humor that surfaced when she felt safe.

In the late afternoon they visited the Swiss cottage that sat in a meadow of beautiful wildflowers where red squirrels scampered. Instead of tea, they were served hot Swiss chocolate and buttery hamantaschen pastries.

That night at dinner, Teddy described everything he'd bagged at the hunt in great detail. Dessert was being served before it occurred to him to ask his bride if she had enjoyed her day.

"I had a lovely day, thank you, Edward. We visited the home farm where everything for Osborne House is grown. The greenhouse even produced these delicious strawberries we are eating for dessert."

Prince Teddy frowned. "I hate the farm. When I was a boy, my parents insisted I grow a vegetable patch. Father inspected it regularly and always found fault."

Once again it was midnight before Anne bade the princess good night at the door to the master bedchamber. Though the day had been filled with activity from dawn till dusk, Anne knew that she would once again take a walk through the garden to the summerhouse. The solitude had brought her a measure of peace the previous night, so that she had been able to sleep.

Tonight she slipped on a velvet cloak over her dinner dress, and went down to the garden. As she passed the formal beds on her way to the summerhouse, she breathed in the heady scents of hyacinth and iris, and when she passed the pond, the unusual fragrance of marsh orchids stole to her. Early-blooming lilac bushes surrounded the summerhouse and their perfume filled the night air.

The moon looks as if it's sailing across the sky, but of course it's the clouds that are moving. Inside, moonlight shone through the white latticed walls making patterns across the wooden floor. Anne sat down and she was again consumed with thoughts of her mother's shameful affair. She and her mother had always been exceptionally close, more like bosom friends than mother and daughter, and she wanted to exonerate her of wickedness. But she knew that such a *ménage à trois* was decadent, so she laid the blame squarely at the feet of the men.

When I get back to London, I shall confront Leicester and ask him outright if I am his daughter. Now that her decision was made, she decided to push it to the back of her mind. She wouldn't think about her next step—that would depend upon his answer.

Anne looked up at the call of a nightjar, and a paper tucked into the lattice caught her eye. She stood up and took down the folded note. *I know something is troubling you.* It was signed with the initial *J.* Though there was nothing to indicate that it was intended for her, she knew that it was. *James must have seen me come here last night. He knows that I have been worrying. Thank God he doesn't know what it is.* A wave of comfort washed over her. *He cares about me. It isn't because he's on the prowl.* Anne's mouth curved. *Well, if I'm honest, he likely is on the prowl, but at the same time he does care about me.*

She tucked the note into her bodice between her breasts. *Next to my heart.* The thought banished the darklings and lingered until she undressed and slipped the note under her pillow. When her dream began, James was in bed with her, holding her fast.

Chapter 16

The following morning, the Prince of Wales was off on a shoot. The estate had an abundance of pheasant, red-legged partridge, and wood pigeons. This time he insisted that James join the hunting party.

The ladies, left to their own devices, had no trouble finding enjoyable diversions.

"My mother taught me how to drive a carriage. Every week she takes a drive through Hyde Park. Let's ask the grooms to harness one of the carriage horses to a phaeton and we can take a ride," Anne suggested.

Alix's eyes lit up. "That sounds wonderful. I've driven a donkey cart—do you think you could teach me to drive a carriage?"

"Absolutely. It takes a bit of courage. My mother is fearless and I suppose I take after her. I believe that if you have the desire to do something, that's more than half the battle." To be polite, Anne asked the queen's ladies if they would care to join them, but was delighted when they declined.

Alix smiled and murmured, "We are free as larks for the rest of the day. I'm very relieved that Edward doesn't insist that I hunt."

"Yes, the prince has a passion for it and will likely hunt every day he is here. Lord Hamilton was coerced into joining him today, though he doesn't enjoy the sport."

"That's unusual. Gentlemen are usually avid hunters."

"The Hamiltons have an estate in Ireland, where hunting is frowned upon."

"Have you known James for a long time?" Alix inquired.

"Yes. Our families are friends and we live fairly close, although James no longer lives with his family. His sister Frances is my dear friend, and his younger brother John Claud has often partnered me at balls, and has accompanied me on rides in the park."

"John Claud is courting you?"

"Well, I cannot deny that he is very attentive, and makes no bones about how he feels about me, but I prefer that we remain good friends."

The groom led the horse and phaeton from the carriage shed and when the two ladies climbed up, he handed the reins to Anne. "I should accompany you, Your Highness. I'm sure Her Gracious Majesty would not approve of ladies driving alone."

Anne raised her chin. "I would be offended if you weren't so ridiculous. I drive a carriage in London, I'll have you know, so this is a doddle."

As Anne slapped the reins and the horse trotted forward, Alix giggled. "What is a doddle? I never heard that word before."

Anne grinned. "It's English slang. It means *easy*—like a baby's game."

"As well as teaching me how to drive, you can teach me English slang!"

"Done! Let's see, a man is a *bloke*, a horse is a *nag*, and a policeman is a *copper*."

Alix nodded. "That bloke was acting like a copper when he said ladies shouldn't drive nags alone." Both girls went off in peals of laughter.

Before the day was over, Alix was handling the reins with great confidence. Anne was both surprised and pleased to learn that the princess enjoyed speed and threw caution to the wind when she made turns.

"When we return to London, I shall ask for my own carriage and we will drive in this Hyde Park you speak about," Alix declared.

Anne grinned. "I'll borrow my mother's carriage and we'll have a race."

Alix laughed. "We'll have to watch out for the coppers!"

Anne assumed a haughty expression. "They wouldn't dare arrest the Princess of Wales. You will become the toast of London!"

When Anne bade Alix good night, she was glad to see that the princess no longer had a look of dread on her face. *She doesn't look exactly eager, more resigned than anything. It's so sad that it isn't a love match.* Anne immediately thought of her own parents' marriage and subdued a shudder. *I'll never marry without love,* she vowed.

The moment Anne entered her bedchamber, she knew she would once again walk to the summerhouse before she returned to sleep. As she reached for her cloak, she wondered if there would be another note for her, and her pulse began to race.

Tonight there was more cloud and the moon was only visible for fleeting moments.

The fragrance of the night-blooming stocks was heady, and she took deep breaths, savoring the scent.

When she entered the summerhouse, her glance went to the spot on the lattice where she had found the note. Though there was hardly any light, she was disappointed to see there was no folded paper tucked there.

"Don't be alarmed."

Anne didn't jump when she heard his voice. She was thrilled that he had been awaiting her. "You never alarm me, James." *You have a beautiful voice, like dark velvet.*

"You took the note I left for you. Will you share with me what is troubling you?"

"It's a personal family matter. It's nothing you can help me with, truly." Anne realized he wouldn't be satisfied unless she gave him something more concrete. "My brother Montagu is off to the army any day now and it won't be the same at home."

"But you'll be at Marlborough House most of the week. I sense there is something more that is troubling you."

Her mind searched for something plausible. "Well, if I'm being truthful, I have been concerned about Princess Alexandra. It's such a daunting, complex role she must fulfill as the Princess of Wales, Queen Victoria's daughter-in-law, and Edward's bride. I've advised her about the first two, but I'm at a loss about the third."

"Has she confided in you about her husband?"

Anne shook her head. "No. But I sense she's not an eager bride."

"The princess is young and innocent, and her bridegroom rather callow in spite of the fact that he's a royal prince."

"Has Teddy said anything to you about Alix?"

"I would never divulge the things he says to me in private, but I do try to advise him and make suggestions that I hope will ease their path and solve some of their difficulties."

"It's sad that they are not in love with each other."

"They may *never* fall in love," he warned gently.

"Marriage without love would be intolerable."

"Not many marriages are love matches, yet many are successful."

"Well, I hope they make a success of it, in spite of the fact that it was arranged. She could hardly turn down a marriage proposal from the British Prince of Wales."

"How about you, Anne? Have you turned down any marriage proposals?"

"Oh, dozens," she said lightly. "Most of them from your brother John Claud. Though it doesn't discourage him in the least."

"Are you serious?" James asked quietly.

"Nothing discourages him. He has informed me he will ask me again, when he wins the seat for Londonderry."

"I meant were you serious about turning him down?"

"Absolutely serious. I warned him he was in for a rude awakening."

"You have no intention of becoming his wife?" James asked carefully.

"I won't marry without love. I'm deeply fond of John Claud, but there is no . . ." She hesitated, searching for the right word.

"Desire," he finished the sentence for her.

Moonlight suddenly illuminated his face.

Anne caught her breath at its intensity.

James stepped closer and lifted a tendril of her red-gold hair. "There is desire between us . . . at least on my part," he murmured.

Anne shuddered. His closeness was so compelling, she felt mesmerized.

He ached to take her into his arms, yet hesitated. His reputation as a rakehell was legendary, and he didn't want Anne to think this was merely a passing flirtation. James stepped back. He took her hand and lifted her fingers to his lips. "If there is anything I can do for you or Princess Alix that would make your stay more enjoyable, please don't hesitate to ask." He bowed his dark head. "I am your devoted servant, Lady Anne."

Each day took on a pattern. A duck hunt or game shoot was arranged by Prince Teddy. The men returned at dusk, and after dinner stayed in the billiard room until midnight.

In the mornings, Anne designed dresses, gowns, and riding outfits for the princess, which would be made when they returned to London. And in the afternoon they either rode or drove in the phaeton about the estate, and even ventured farther about the island.

Anne did not again visit the summerhouse late at night. That would look like she was throwing herself at

James Hamilton. She did look forward to seeing him at dinner each evening, and thoroughly enjoyed the intimate glances he bestowed upon her.

After only one week, James knew that Teddy was becoming bored with the "honeymoon." While shooting billiard balls into pockets for small wagers, the prince spoke longingly of the entertainments he would host when he returned to London. The racing season was about to open and James knew Teddy would become a fixture at every racecourse within fifty miles of London.

"Why don't we make up a party and go into Cowes?" James suggested. "The weekends bring out the yachting crowd, and there will be lots of amateur enthusiasts as well as professional racers practicing for the Cowes Week Regatta."

"Splendid idea, James." The prince glanced round the table and beamed. "The ladies will enjoy it too. It'll give me a chance to show off the Princess of Wales to the crowds."

The following day, Saturday, three carriages transported the royal party into Cowes. Alix, garbed in a summery white dress and a straw leghorn to protect her from the sun, strolled about on the prince's arm, smiling and waving at the cheering crowds who had gathered to watch the yachts tacking about on the Solent.

James gallantly offered his arm to Anne and they sauntered along the promenade following the royal couple. When the two couples stopped to watch an impromptu race, it was left to James to answer Alix's questions.

"A spinnaker is the colorful round sail hoisted at the front of a yacht when it's running downwind. The Solent is a tricky course because of its double tides."

"I'd like to learn how to sail," Anne remarked. "With a good wind it would be exciting."

"The danger makes it exciting. If you're serious, I'll teach you," James offered.

Anne's pulse began to flutter. "Lord Hamilton's father, the Duke of Abercorn, keeps a yacht to take the family to their ancestral home in Ireland. Here at Cowes in August they hold a racing regatta known as Cowes Week."

"I have an idea." James looked at Teddy. "Why don't we make plans to return in August for Cowes Week? The crowds make merry with parties, and wagers, and there are marquees overflowing with food and drink. The public houses stay open all hours, and each night ends with a fireworks display. You could offer a 'Prince's Cup' to the winner of the yacht race. I believe it was your predecessor the Prince of Wales who started the racing regatta back in 1826."

"Jolly good idea, James. I shall leave the planning to you."

James caught the amused glance Anne gave him, and he grinned back, knowing she was thinking, *You walked into that one!*

The next day brought rain, and the Prince of Wales, prevented from his usual hunting, declared they would return to London on the morrow.

James cautioned him that it would be seen as cutting the honeymoon short. Eyebrows would be raised, and speculation might become rampant.

"I've had enough. Honeymoons aren't what they're cracked up to be, if you know what I mean, James."

Indeed I do know what you mean. The inexperienced Danish princess does not come close to satisfying your sexual needs.

On extremely short notice, plans were made to transport the royal party back to London. Princess Alexandra's trunks were packed hurriedly and she was at a loss to understand why the honeymoon had been abruptly curtailed. "We were supposed to stay until the end of the month. I hope the queen won't think I found fault with her plans for our wedding trip to the Isle of Wight. I think this seaside estate is delightful."

"I'm sure Her Majesty won't blame you, Alix. Lord Hamilton explained to her ladies that the Prince of Wales was eager to return to London to oversee some refurbishing at Marlborough House." Anne could see that the princess was not convinced. "The real reason is that Edward is easily bored. He has a passion for hunting, and since the rain curtailed that, he wants to be off on his next passion, which is horse racing."

Anne was both right and wrong. When he returned to London, Prince Teddy *was* off on his next passion, but it wasn't horse racing. The races didn't start until the first weekend in May at Newmarket. It was another sport that he pursued the moment he returned to Marlborough House.

"James, will you see that the Jermyn Street house is provisioned? Be sure there is champagne, as well as claret and sherry. Make sure there's a box of my favorite cigars—oh, and by the way, I'd like a couple of keys."

Good God, he intends to commit conjugal infidelity on his first night back in London.

"Yes, I'll see that all is in readiness, Your Highness." *I'd better send a note to the florists to have roses delivered to Princess Alexandra. Flowers would never occur to Teddy.*

While the Prince and Princess of Wales had been off on their honeymoon, their comptroller and his wife had taken up residence at Marlborough House. Anne was introduced to Lady Elizabeth, and she wondered how she would go about informing Alix that she had a lady-in-waiting who was not of her own choosing.

"Your Highness, allow me to introduce Lady Elizabeth, who is the wife of Prince Edward's comptroller, Sir William Knollys."

When Elizabeth curtsied, Alexandra took her hand. "I am delighted to meet you, Lady Elizabeth. I believe a comptroller approves all the expenditures. Will you be acting as *my* comptroller?"

"Good heavens, no, Your Highness. Sir William takes care of all that. I am here to serve you in any way I can."

"Do you think you could help me with my correspondence, Elizabeth? While I've been away, the post has brought dozens of letters addressed to me, and I haven't had a chance to open and read them yet."

"I would be delighted, Your Highness. I warrant that most of them will be supplications from various charities."

"Oh, I hadn't realized. It will be such a privilege to be in a position to help those less fortunate than myself. You can pass on the requests to Sir William for payment."

"I shall start reading the letters today. Then once you select the charities you wish to donate to, I'll present them to my husband, and write letters to the ones you decline."

"Oh, I won't decline any of them, Elizabeth. When I have been given so much, I feel it is my sacred duty to be generous."

The following day, Princess Alexandra received a summons from Queen Victoria to present herself at Buckingham Palace. With trepidation in her heart, Alix showed the note to her favorite lady-in-waiting. "Will you accompany me, Anne? I'm afraid I need your moral support."

"Of course, I'll come. But you must be prepared to go into Her Majesty's presence chamber alone. They likely won't admit me. Try not to let Victoria see that she intimidates you."

"Whatever shall I wear?"

"Since Her Majesty is in perpetual mourning and expects everyone else to follow her lead, I would advise you to wear a gray dress. Since the summons says you are to present yourself at one o'clock, you'd better change now."

Alexandra opened her wardrobe. "I like this pale lavender gown, and it is an accepted mourning shade."

"Yes, it is one of the few dresses from your trousseau that complements your delicate complexion and shows off your lovely golden hair to perfection. For that very reason, I would advise you not to wear it. The queen already resents your youth and your slim figure; you don't want your beauty and fashion sense to antagonize her."

Alexandra sighed, and reached for a nondescript gray.

Anne smiled. "The dull and dowdy *monstrosity* is a perfect choice."

At exactly one o'clock, Princess Alexandra and Lady Anne stood waiting outside Queen Victoria's presence chamber.

Anne was not the least surprised when her sister Emily opened the doors. Her critical glance swept over the two females; then she addressed the princess.

"Her Gracious Majesty wishes to see you alone, Your Highness."

"Thank you, Lady Emily."

Princess Alexandra looked serene, though she felt anything but as she approached the Queen of England. She swept into a graceful curtsy before the black-clad monarch, who was seated on a padded, gilt chair that resembled a throne.

"Do have a seat, my dear. I cannot bear people to tower over me."

"Thank you, Your Majesty." Alix sat down on the straight-backed chair indicated.

"Your honeymoon journey was curtailed. Did you find fault with Osborne House?"

"Not at all, Your Majesty. I found Osborne House delightful, and thoroughly enjoyed the Isle of Wight."

"Then why did you not stay until the end of the month?"

"It was my husband's decision, Your Majesty."

"The Prince of Wales often makes unwise decisions, though I commend you for honoring your marriage vows to obey."

"Thank you, Your Majesty," Alix murmured.

"Though we are in mourning and have withdrawn from public life, we will make an exception in your case, my dear. We will grant you an audience every month when you may present yourself to me here at the palace. We will set aside the same hour on the fifteenth day of the month."

Alexandra thought Victoria was using the royal *we* as

if she were dispensing queenly favors. But her heart sank as she realized she was being sentenced to a command performance every month, where she would have to present herself for inspection.

"That will be all."

When Alix rejoined Lady Anne, she murmured, "The monstrosity I'm wearing doesn't compare with the monstrosity I faced in the Audience Chamber."

Entertainment plans began immediately at Marlborough House. James hired a social secretary for the Prince of Wales and provided him with a list of titled young males and females of the nobility. The secretary's sole job would be sending out invitations to the parties and *drums*, as they were now called, and keeping track of the number of guests who accepted, which likely would be every invitee.

The curtailed honeymoon resulted in the inevitable whispers about the bride and groom and the state of their marriage, which in turn made some of the female guests who'd been invited conclude that Prince Teddy was ripe for plucking.

The fashionable designs that Anne had sketched for dresses and gowns were turned over to newly hired seamstresses, but because none of the garments could be finished for at least a week, Anne took Princess Alexandra to the London fashion house of Redfern's.

"I feel wicked selecting new clothes when I was provided with a large trousseau."

"But, Alix, you don't like any of the outfits that were made for you," Anne reasoned.

"My trousseau cost more than my sister and I spent on clothes in our entire lives," she murmured guiltily.

"Then it's high time you were indulged. A woman has so little control in her life; choosing her own wardrobe should be at the top of her list. Alix, not only will it bring you pleasure; it will give you self-confidence."

Alix smiled. "Self-confidence is exactly what the Princess of Wales needs."

With Anne's help, Alexandra chose a royal blue evening gown as well as a pretty shell pink, and another in her favorite shade of pale violet. She selected four day dresses and a riding habit with a new narrower skirt complete with a slit to show off her boots.

Anne realized that she must go home to Grosvenor Square so that she could transfer most of her clothes to Marlborough House. *I've been avoiding Mother, but I can put it off no longer.* When the princess informed her that her mother, Louise, and sisters were coming to spend the day with her, Anne asked permission to take the day off. "When I return, I shall bring Lady Frances Hamilton. You will need more than two ladies-in-waiting, Your Highness. All the daughters of the nobility will be vying for such enviable positions, so you'll be able to pick and choose."

"I will rely on your advice, Lady Anne. Her Majesty has sent me a list of suitable ladies. I know I'm being contrary, but I don't want anyone Queen Victoria recommends."

"That's not contrary, that's prudent. You don't want anyone who will carry tales to the palace, and neither does the prince, I warrant."

Anne asked her driver to stop at Hampden House on Green Street before he drove her home. She was greeted by Frances and the Duchess of Abercorn.

"So it's true, the newlyweds did curtail their honeymoon," Frances declared.

"Yes, they are back at Marlborough House and Princess Alexandra is in need of another lady-in-waiting, if you are free to come today."

"I can't wait. You must tell me all the juicy details of the wedding trip."

The duchess warned, "Frances, darling, you must be absolutely discreet and not bandy gossip about the princess." Lady Lu winked. "Of course you must tell me."

Anne smiled. "I'm on my way to Grosvenor Square to pack my wardrobe. Entertaining has already begun. Invitations have gone out for a dinner to be held Friday night as a welcome-home party. Frances, you will need all your evening gowns and fancy clothes. I'll come back for you this afternoon."

John Claud arrived in the drawing room and when he saw who their visitor was, without ceremony he picked her up and swung her around. "Anne! You kept your promise to visit the moment you returned to London. Did you miss me?"

I must discourage him from such possessive behavior. "It's been less than two weeks. You act as if I've been gone for months. My duties left me no time to miss anyone."

"Why is it fashionable for ladies to affect an aloof attitude to the opposite sex?"

"So we don't get 'picked up' and have to give gentlemen a 'set down' perhaps."

"You're in a bantering mood. Tell me all about the Isle of Wight."

"I'm on my way home to get my clothes, John Claud. But I'll be back to get Frances this afternoon. Perhaps I'll see you later."

"No perhaps about it . . . I shall be here."

"That's what I was afraid of," Anne said dryly.

John Claud frowned and his mother chided, "You have no sense of humor, my dear."

"I see nothing funny."

Lady Lu, Frances, and Anne looked at him and said in unison, "We do," and the three females enjoyed a good laugh at his expense.

Back in the carriage on the short ride to Grosvenor Square, Anne's mood underwent a drastic change. Her amusement was replaced by apprehension about seeing her mother with her newfound knowledge about the secret affair. Once again she began to conjure excuses. *She is in love. The affair has been going on for two decades. Mother was forced into an arranged marriage with a much older man. How can Leicester allow her to take such risks? He should be shot!*

Anne stepped out of the carriage and told the driver he could wait in the courtyard.

She ran up the front steps and opened the door with

her own key. She breathed a sigh of relief when she saw Jenkins. If he was there, there wasn't likely to be any dalliance afoot.

"Welcome home, Lady Anne."

"Thank you, Jenkins. I'm here to pack my clothes. I'll be off again shortly."

She didn't go directly to her own chamber, but entered the drawing room.

"Anne, darling, I'm so glad you arrived home early. It will give you a chance to say good-bye to Montagu. He joins his regiment today."

Her grinning brother was wearing the distinctive green uniform of the Rifle Brigade.

Anne's glance swept over him. "You look very smart, indeed. I'm here to pack most of my clothes; then I'm stopping to get Frances before I return to Marlborough House."

"I'll come with you. I can't wait to show off my uniform to John Claud."

Anne's mother noticed the dark smudges beneath her daughter's eyes. "I'll come and help you pack, and you can tell me all about the honeymoon." She summoned a servant and asked that a couple of trunks be brought down from the attic.

When they were alone in her bedchamber, her mother asked, "Are you feeling all right, Anne? You look pale. Is anything wrong?"

Anne opened her wardrobe doors and, pretending to survey her clothes, thought about bringing up the delicate subject of her mother's infidelity. *I can't do it. I don't want to see the trapped look on her face when she realizes I know her shocking secret.*

"I'm perfectly fine, Mother. There's so much to do at Marlborough House. The Prince of Wales is entertaining Friday night, and the gowns that the queen chose for Princess Alexandra are dreadful. They neither make her *look* good nor *feel* good. We spent hours yesterday at Redfern's; then I stayed up late sketching some new designs."

"Is the princess difficult to please?"

"Not in the least! Alix and I are extremely compatible. She's a little shy, but not around me. She's very sweet and unspoiled, and likes to laugh. I taught her how to drive a carriage at Osborne House, and soon I'll persuade her to venture into Hyde Park."

"The honeymoon was rather brief. Does she seem happy in her marriage?"

"She doesn't talk about her husband, but I know she isn't in love with him." Anne began to fold her garments and put them in one of the trunks the servant brought.

"How sad. My heart goes out to her." Her mother opened a dresser drawer and started to pack Anne's pretty undergarments.

Afraid her mother would declare how intolerable a marriage without love could be, Anne spoke up quickly. "Well, Teddy isn't exactly the most gallant bridegroom. He was off hunting every day, and after dinner played billiards until midnight. He gets bored easily and when the rain curtailed his hunting, he decided to return to London."

"The princess wasn't allowed to choose her husband. It was an arranged marriage and she will have to find her happiness in other things."

"Other things?" *I hope you're not suggesting she find a lover.*

"Her home, and children, not to mention all the royal estates she can visit."

"Of course." Anne smiled. "And I'll get to visit them too."

It was two hours before all her belongings were packed. Shoes and fans had to be matched with her gowns and day dresses; her jackets, coats, and cloaks were packed with riding skirts and boots; then she had to sort through all her hatboxes.

"I'll get Montagu to help carry these trunks down."

"You'll likely find him in the library, where your father's tallying the lambs born at Gopsall. It will give you a chance to say good-bye to your father." She sighed heavily. "The house will be so empty once you and Montagu leave today."

"Well, I'm not off to Outer Mongolia. I shall be home quite often, and I'll make sure you are on the invitation lists."

"That will be lovely." Her mother embraced her. "I shall miss you fiercely."

Anne's arms tightened about her and she whispered, "I love you, Mother."

The carriage pulled up in front of the house and Jenkins and Montagu loaded the large trunks and an extra piece of luggage that held her small jewel case, and her sketching pencils and watercolors she used for designing fashions. Anne's thoughts were still with her mother. *I'm such a coward. I should have broached the subject and listened to what she had to say.*

She got into the carriage and Montagu jumped in and closed the door. *I have to tell him.* Her lips trembled and she pressed them together trying to find the right words. *He has every right to know.* She took a deep breath and plunged in. "Montagu, I have something to tell you. And it's going to come as a shock. Your real father is Leicester Howe."

Dead silence filled the carriage.

Then Montagu said quietly, "Yes, I know."

Anne gasped in surprise. "How?"

"Leicester told me when I turned eighteen, but I'd suspected for many years." His voice was somber. "How did you find out, Anne?"

"I . . . I'm shamed to speak of it." She hesitated, then found the courage to tell him. "After you left for Gopsall, I came home to get some things. I . . . overheard them in Mother's bedchamber. She thanked him for getting you into the Rifle Brigade."

He took hold of her hands and looked into her eyes. "Anne, you must never breathe a word of this. Mother's life would be ruined."

"I am well aware of the horrendous scandal it would cause. I know it happened over twenty years ago, but they are still lovers. How can Leicester put her at such risk?"

The carriage stopped. "Where does Leicester stay when he's in London?" Anne continued.

"He leases a town house on Jermyn Street. But he's asked for a post in Ireland."

"Thank God for that!"

Montagu helped her from the carriage. "Smile, Anne; you look so woebegone. You don't want the Hamiltons asking questions."

They went into Hampden House together, and Montagu, in his green Rifle Brigade uniform, was the center of attention. It gave Anne a chance to recover somewhat from the distressing conversation she'd had with her brother.

"I'm almost ready," Frances promised.

"There's no hurry. Make sure you have everything you'll need," Anne said. "There's a dinner party Friday night."

John Claud's admiring glance moved from Montagu's uniform to Anne. "The post just delivered the invitation. I ask that you let me have the honor of acting as your escort."

Anne shook her head regretfully. "No, I'm sorry, John Claud, but I'll be in attendance on the princess. If she decides there will be dancing after dinner, I'll save you one."

"I'd prefer it if you'd save them all for me."

"And I'd prefer it if I didn't," she said firmly.

"John Claud, stop mooning over Anne and help me with my trunks," Frances said.

"I'm coming, but can't you see I'm trying to court her?"

"I can see that you're making a cake of yourself."

When the brother and sister left the room, Anne turned to Montagu. "We'll say our good-byes while we're alone. I'll miss you. Take good care of yourself."

He enfolded her in his arms and kissed her brow. "Don't let the family secret steal your happiness, Anne. All the worry in the world won't change things. The heart wants what it wants, right or wrong."

"You suddenly sound very wise. And that's a good thing. Be safe, Montagu."

Anne spent another sleepless night as her thoughts chased each other in endless circles. She had been completely taken off guard when Montagu had acknowledged that he knew Leicester was his father. She tossed and turned, chiding herself for her cowardice in not confronting her mother about her shocking secret affair, but an hour later she reversed her thinking and told herself that questioning her would have caused her mother unnecessary pain.

The one I should confront is Leicester Curzon-Howe! I swore I'd go to see him when I returned. Montagu said he resides in Jermyn Street when he's in London.

By the time dawn began to lighten the sky, Anne realized that she would never have peace of mind until she had braved the lion in his den. Jermyn Street was within walking distance of Marlborough House. The next two days would be a mad rush because of the dinner party, but she vowed that Monday morning she would somehow find the courage to pay Leicester a visit.

Chapter 17

James Hamilton, who tried to visit his family every week when he was in London, hadn't dined with his parents for almost two months. Because of John Claud, James had thought long and hard about keeping his distance from Lady Anne Howe, but at Osborne House, where he had seen her every day, he began to believe that his feelings for her were more than a passing fancy.

Anne told me she wasn't in love with John Claud, and has no desire to become his wife. Tonight, I'll put my cards on the table and give my brother fair warning that I intend to court her.

When James arrived at Hampden House, he was surrounded by his younger siblings who hadn't seen him for some time. Ronald and Frederick thanked him for the racing-yacht models he'd brought them from the Isle of Wight, and Maud was delighted with a book on the castles and royal residences of the island.

At dinner they talked about John Claud running for the parliamentary seat in Londonderry that had just become vacant.

"We'll be leaving for Ireland in a few days," Abercorn said. "If you can get away from your duties for a couple of weeks, your brother could use your help on the stump."

Lady Lu laughed. "James could kiss the wives for you."

"With his reputation, they'd do better to lock up their women," John Claud remarked. "If you don't mind, I'd rather do this myself. I don't need James to win the seat for me."

James didn't even raise his eyebrows. "Did you get your invitations to the dinner at Marlborough House tomorrow evening?"

"Yes, darling. But I don't think your father and I will be attending. I warrant the Prince and Princess of Wales want to surround themselves with a younger crowd."

Maud spoke up. "I didn't get an invitation, and I'm young."

"You're barely out of the nursery," John Claud declared.

"You got an invitation. If you were the least bit gallant, you'd escort me."

"I have another lady in mind."

"It's not fair! John Claud, James, and Frances will all be there."

"Maud, darling, sometimes life does seem unfair," her mother explained. "Just have patience and you'll be sixteen before you know it."

"By that time, Fitz, Earl Kerry, will be married to someone else!"

Everyone tried not to laugh.

"First sons are never eager to marry," John Claud warned. "Look at James."

"Though you assume my heart is encased in ice, I'm happy to inform you that a thaw has set in. Perhaps my aversion to marriage will melt away like snow in summer."

John Claud's brows drew together, while his mother's arced in speculation.

Abercorn, witty as always, said, "It must be the idyllic union of Edward and Alexandra that lightly turns your thoughts to love."

"In the Spring the wanton lapwing gets himself another crest," Lady Lu said, quoting another line of the

Tennyson poem. She was far too wise to press her son on the subject of his love life.

After dinner, James shared a glass of Irish whiskey with his father and brother in the library. Before he left, he took John Claud aside. "I am giving you notice that I no longer consider Lady Anne Howe your private preserve. Out of a misplaced sense of honor, I kept my distance, but now I give you fair warning that I intend to pursue her."

"Damn you, James. I told you she's the girl I intend to marry!"

"In the immortal words of the Bard, *Stiffen the sinews, and summon up the blood. The game's afoot.*"

"The royal blue gown makes you look regal, Your Highness, and for this first dinner party I urge you to wear your diamond coronet. It gives you a royal air and will make the prince feel extremely proud of you."

Anne fastened the wide pearl choker about Alix's slender neck. "There! Look in the mirror. Your hair looks elegant pinned up with one long curl on your shoulder."

"I'm nervous meeting my husband's friends for the first time. When you are dressed, please come back so we can descend the staircase together."

"I'll come back, but I've been told the Prince of Wales will escort you down."

Anne hurried along the hall that led to her own bedchamber. When she opened the door, the fragrance of flowers met her.

"These were delivered for you, but there was no card." Frances Hamilton, who was sharing the large luxurious bedchamber with her, until her own was assigned, was already dressed for the evening.

Anne caught her breath at the sight of the lovely bouquet on her dressing table. Her mouth curved into a smile. *Pink lilies. They can only be from James.* Her heart had been heavy since she'd said good-bye to Montagu, but magically the lilies banished the gloom and she was filled with a delicious feeling of anticipation.

"So far the princess hasn't given me any duties. My sister Jane finds Queen Victoria quite demanding, so I expected to be fetching and carrying by now."

"Tonight, all you have to do is be there. It's simply custom that a royal princess have ladies-in-waiting in attendance."

Anne threw open her wardrobe doors and changed her mind about which gown she would wear. Instead of the pale blue that would complement what Alexandra was wearing, she chose a pink silk embroidered with silver love knots. The back had a floating panel that fell from the shoulders into a short train.

Anne brushed her hair to one side and pinned one of the pink lilies above her ear. She opened her jewel case and donned a pair of silver cuff bracelets, then slipped on silver kid slippers with a small heel to complete the outfit.

"Anne, you look lovely. Your clothes are so much prettier than mine, but I suppose that's because you know exactly what suits you best."

"Thank you, Frances." When Anne saw her reflection in the mirror, she felt a tremor of excitement.

As the two friends walked from their wing of Marlborough House to the royal apartment, they could hear voices and laughter from the guests who were gathering below. Before Anne could tap on the double door, it opened and they stood to one side as Prince Teddy led his princess bride to the top of the sweeping staircase, paused for a moment, then descended as a murmur of approval rose up to meet them.

Lady Anne and Lady Frances followed a short distance behind the royal couple.

"I see Blandford Churchill," Frances whispered. "This is so exciting,"

As Anne mingled with the guests, she realized she knew a good many of them. The males greeted her with speculation in their eyes, and the females gravitated toward her, wanting to be presented to Princess Alexandra.

"I can't believe it.... Florence Paget, I mean *Lady Hastings*, just walked in with her new husband," Anne told Frances.

"So much for my mother's theory that it would be a long time before Florence was accepted in polite society," Frances murmured.

"What makes you think the Marlborough House guests are polite society? I just saw Henry Chaplin talking to Prince Teddy. Perhaps the fur will fly."

"Two dogs fighting over the same scandalous bone."

"Florence is our friend. Let's go and welcome her," Anne suggested.

Henry Rawdon greeted Anne and Frances and turned to his wife. "I shall leave you with your friends. I want to buy a horse from Sir Christopher Sykes, and I've just spotted him talking with the prince."

"Hello, Florence. You look lovely tonight," Anne said, kissing her cheek.

"You've been Lady Hastings for a month. How is married life?" Frances asked.

"My honeymoon in Leicestershire was wonderful, but now that we are back in London, I'm no longer the center of Henry's life. All he thinks about are horses—racing horses, wagering on horses, and buying horses."

"How fortuitous that Hastings inherited a fortune," Frances remarked.

Florence lowered her voice. "He never stops drinking."

"I'm so sorry, Florence." Anne asked with concern, "Do you regret eloping?"

"Yes ... no ... I don't know. I feel guilty about Henry Chaplin, and my family is angry."

"Give them a little time to forgive you. Come and I'll present you to the princess."

Anne led the way and found Alix standing with James Hamilton. The prince was surrounded by young men who had attended Oxford or Cambridge with him. At university the Prince of Wales had been kept on a leash and forbidden to carouse with the other young nobles, but now that he was a married man with his own royal residence, his acquaintances were more than eager to curry friendship with their future king.

"Princess Alexandra, may I present Lady Florence Hastings? She too is a new bride."

"Welcome to Marlborough House, Lady Hastings."

Florence curtsied. "Your Highness, I'm delighted to meet you. Thank you for the lovely invitation."

Alix turned to James. "Thank you for your company, Lord Hamilton."

"It was my pleasure, Your Highness. Excuse me, ladies."

"Frances, your brother is such a gallant gentleman," the princess declared. "Whenever my husband abandons me, James is always there to fill the breach."

Frances laughed. "My brother's reputation as a ladies' man is renowned."

"We'll stay together until dinner," Anne told Alix. "Everyone is extremely eager to be presented to their hostess. The lady coming toward us wearing taupe is Adelaide, Countess of Westmorland. She's my half sister."

"Ah, she's invited because her sister is Emily, the queen's lady-in-waiting."

Anne's eyes sparkled. "No, she's invited because her husband is a big noise in the Jockey Club, and therefore a particular favorite of the Prince of Wales."

"I'm beginning to realize the paramount topic of conversation among the gentlemen at these affairs will be horses."

Anne nodded. "The ladies prefer gossip and fashion, not necessarily in that order. I predict that at the next entertainment, every female will be wearing a wide pearl choker."

Alix laughed and touched her necklace. Then one by one the female guests made their curtsies to the Princess of Wales. Anne presented Louise, Duchess of Manchester, Edith, Countess of Aylesford, and Harriet, Countess of Lichfield, who was sister to Frances and James Hamilton.

While Harriet and the princess were enjoying a discussion about fashion, Frances asked Anne, "Do you know if the Duke of Devonshire's heir, Lord Hartington, is here?"

"Yes, he was in that group surrounding Prince Teddy."

Frances rolled her eyes. "I've decided to cross Hartington off my list. I believe the gossip that he's having an affair with the Duchess of Manchester. You never see one without the other, and they are both here tonight."

Anne nodded. "I've suspected that since I saw them dancing at my debut ball."

"It seems that suddenly affairs are all the fashion," Frances declared.

Anne's laugh was brittle. "You're wrong if you think affairs have only just come into vogue. They've always gone on, but because of Queen Victoria's strict moral standards, Society has become more adept at hiding them."

Just then a young woman greeted Frances warmly. "I hope your brother John Claud is coming tonight. I think he's divine." She placed her hand over her heart. "I persuaded my brother Fitzgerald to bring me. Frances, would you introduce me to Lady Anne? I don't believe we've actually met."

"Of course. This is Caroline Chandos, granddaughter of the Earl of Harrington."

"I'm delighted to meet you, Caroline."

"Lady Anne, I wonder if you would do me an immense favor? Could you put in a good word for me with the Princess of Wales? I have my heart set on becoming a lady-in-waiting to Her Highness, and I know the competition will be fierce."

"Well, first, let me introduce you to her. If you get on nicely, I will see what I can do." A calculating thought occurred to her. "I happen to know that John Claud will be without a dinner partner tonight. Perhaps you could sit next to him," Anne suggested.

A few minutes later when John Claud arrived, he walked a direct path to Anne. Almost on his heels, Prime

Minister Palmerston and his wife arrived. James had persuaded the prince that they should be invited since he was privy to all the queen's business, and should be cultivated as an ally.

After John Claud kissed Anne's hand, she said, "I shall leave you in the delightful company of Lady Caroline Chandos. I must present Princess Alexandra to the prime minister's wife and vice versa."

As Anne and Alix crossed the chamber, she explained that Emily, once known as Lady Cowper, was a social lioness who had been the leading lady of Almack's club.

"Lady Palmerston, it is my great honor to present you to Her Highness Alexandra, Princess of Wales."

"Thank you, Lady Anne. It is delightful to meet you, Princess Alexandra. How kind of you to invite the prime minister and me. I love to be around young people. I hope there will be dancing after dinner."

"There will, Lady Palmerston. The orchestra has already arrived in the ballroom."

"Your Highness, I shall give you the secret for being a great hostess. To make a ball successful you need to invite three men for every lady—one to dance, one to eat, and one to stare—that makes everything go off well."

The princess laughed. "Well, we have invited many gentlemen, but how do we get them to stop talking about horses?"

"A good supply of champagne and an ample display of breasts usually lure them to the ballroom."

Anne was glad that Alix was not shocked at the outspoken Lady Palmerston. "I believe dinner is about to be served, so I will return you to the Prince of Wales."

"She is an amusing lady, in spite of her age," Alix remarked.

"Everyone in Society still refers to her as Emily Cowper. She was Lord Palmerston's mistress for years. They couldn't marry until her elderly husband died."

"Oh dear, Queen Victoria must thoroughly disapprove of her."

"Lord Cowper died just as Victoria ascended the throne, and I very much doubt if anyone was indelicate enough to discuss Viscount Palmerston's scandalous past with the unwed queen."

The Prince of Wales took Princess Alexandra's hand and with their attendants following closely behind, Edward led the way to the dining room. Prime Minister Palmerston and his wife were seated close by, as were the royal couple's attendants. The rest of the guests chose their own seats and were free to ignore the rigid pecking order that prevailed at court functions.

Princess Alix sat between her husband and James Hamilton. Anne took her seat between James and Charles Carrington. Frances took the chair beside Carrington and was thrilled to bits when Blandford Churchill sat down beside her.

Anne glanced down the table and saw John Claud glowering at her because she was sitting next to James. But she was glad to see that Caroline Chandos had managed to secure the place beside him.

Prince Teddy's attention was focused on food rather than conversation when he dined, and James smoothly filled in, entertaining Alix with amusing anecdotes. Finally, he looked at Anne, and his glance lingered on the lily in her hair; then he smiled into her eyes. "Beautiful," he murmured.

Her green eyes sparkled. "I am particularly partial to lilies."

"Your brother-in-law Fane has invited the royal couple to stay at Apethorpe Hall for the Newmarket race in May. It will be a reunion for us," he teased.

"If I decide to go."

"Your sister will beg you to help her entertain the Princess of Wales."

"The Countess of Westmorland is my *half* sister."

"Then meet her halfway. . . . Meet *me* halfway."

James signaled a footman. "Princess Alexandra prefers champagne to claret."

Alix smiled up at him. "Thank you, James."

When the server returned with champagne, he said, "Lady Anne also."

Anne took a sip and laughed when the effervescent bubbles tickled her nose. "Will you buy me champagne again in Newmarket?"

"It would give me the greatest pleasure in the world."

She gave him a mischievous glance. "Lady Anne also."

By the end of the meal the guests were openly remarking on the excellent quality of the food, and the great variety of dishes to choose from. Word spread that the Prince of Wales had engaged the services of a renowned French chef, and most decided that all future invitations would be eagerly anticipated.

New customs were begun. Rather than the ladies retiring while the men stayed behind to drink and smoke, all left the dining room together. There was a staircase just for guests that led to rooms where they could refresh themselves.

The orchestra began to play and the music lured the ladies to the ballroom. Most of the men, including the Prince of Wales, followed reluctantly, knowing that after a token dance or two they could escape to the commodious gaming room, where brandy and cigars would accompany the high-stakes card games. If they were lucky, illegal baccarat would be included, and the main topic of conversation could return to horses, racing, and wagering.

Prince Edward dutifully led out Princess Alexandra in the first dance. The orchestra had been instructed to play a waltz, and to make it short. Then the dancers were invited to choose their partners for the new, popular promenade.

Anne's attention was drawn to the prince. Edith, Countess Aylesford, was standing on her toes, whispering in Prince Teddy's ear. *The brazen hussy is making a play for him! I hope Alexandra doesn't see the intimate byplay.*

Suddenly she heard John Claud cough. "How on earth did you manage to be standing opposite me when the music stopped?"

"Would you believe it was random chance?"

"Not for a moment. You are an expert at manipulation."

"Your compliments go to my head." He held out his arms and she moved into them. "I'm leaving for Ireland, day after tomorrow."

"I hadn't forgotten, John Claud. I sincerely hope you win your campaign."

"You are dancing with the next member of Parliament for Londonderry."

Anne smiled. "I'm glad that you are confident."

He drew her closer. "That's not the only thing I'm confident about."

Anne knew he was once again hinting at a proposal of marriage, and deftly changed the subject. "John Claud, will you do me a great favor? Princess Alexandra wants the dancing to be a success. When Prince Teddy leaves, please don't desert us for the gaming room?"

"I would never desert you, Anne." His arms tightened.

"That's what I'm afraid of," she said lightly. "The prince can count on his gentlemen to partner Princess Alix, but it would be most gallant if you invited her to dance."

"That's a misnomer; Teddy's gentlemen are not gentlemen—they are predators. I shall consider it an honor to partner the Princess of Wales, and a solemn duty to dance with the prime minister's wife."

Her eyes glittered. "You devious devil. You are already planning to curry favor for when you become a member of Parliament."

"I've had excellent teachers. Both my father and my brother have cultivated friendships in high places."

"You've cultivated a friendship with my father too, but I'm onto your tricks," she warned.

Anne wasn't onto all of them, however. John Claud partnered her half sister Adelaide. "I am paying court to Lady Anne, and I'm most fortunate that your father, Lord Howe, looks favorably on the match. Once I have secured my seat in Parliament, I intend to ask him for her hand in marriage."

"Anne is a particular favorite of the Princess of Wales. My husband has invited the royal couple to spend the weekend at Apethorpe Hall for the opening of Newmarket."

Hellfire! Anne and James will be thrown together again. I'll have to put a spoke in his wheel, or he will beat me to the prize.

When the dance ended, John Claud returned Adelaide to her husband. As the couple danced, he saw that they were discussing him, so he once more asked Anne to waltz. A short time later when he saw Fane depart the ballroom, he caught up to him. "Lord Westmorland, do you have a horse entered in the Guinea Stakes at Newmarket?"

"Absolutely, my boy. I'm running Eau de Vie. The Prince of Wales is coming. Will you be there?"

"Unfortunately, no. Day after tomorrow I leave to campaign in Ireland. But my brother will no doubt accompany His Highness." John Claud hesitated. "A word to the wise, your lordship. James is a bit of a rogue with the ladies. Your young sister-in-law Lady Anne would benefit from your protection."

"Ah, I understand you are courting Anne. No need to worry, my boy. I already put a flea in her ear about the young rakehell."

When John Claud returned to the ballroom, he was chagrined to see James dancing with Anne. Still, he took solace in the thought that Adelaide would inform everyone in the Curzon-Howe family that he was paying court to her sister Anne, with the intention of asking for her hand in marriage.

He spied Caroline Chandos talking with Fitz Kerry, walked a direct path to her, and asked her to dance. It gave him twofold satisfaction—it was a thumb in the eye to Kerry, and showed Anne that she had competition for his attention.

When the dance ended, he bowed his thanks to Caroline, and swept his gaze about the ballroom searching for Anne and James. *Where the devil are they?* He guessed that his brother had gone down to the gaming room. When he saw that his sister Frances was also missing, he assumed that she and Anne had gone to powder their noses. John Claud was mistaken on both counts.

Before the dance had ended, James suggested to Anne that they get some fresh air. Before she had a chance to decline, he took her hand and led her into a chamber that adjoined the ballroom. He opened French doors and guided her out onto a stone balcony.

"James, you know where all the secluded nooks lie hidden."

"It's a beautiful night. It would be a shame to waste it."

She tipped her head back to gaze at the night sky. "The stars are like glittering diamonds scattered on black velvet."

"Exquisite." James was gazing at Anne. He took the flower from above her ear and tucked it into the décolletage between her breasts. Then he threaded his fingers into her red-gold hair and brought her face close. His lips brushed hers softly; then his mouth took hers in a long, deep, lingering kiss.

When their lips finally parted, Anne shivered at the intimate closeness, and James slipped off his evening jacket, wrapped it about her shoulders, then pulled her against him. "I'll keep you warm, sweetheart."

She gazed up into his eyes. "I'm not cold, James." *I'm on fire.*

James knew his feelings for Anne were unique. She stirred his emotions, and touched something deep inside him, a secret place within, where he had never allowed any woman before. When he was alone, she filled his thoughts, and his fantasies always left him with a longing that made his heart ache.

"Anne, my feelings for you are so special. You never fail to delight me, and when we are apart, you linger in my thoughts." His hands cupped her face; then his lips sought hers again in a kiss so tender it touched her heart.

*James, I've thought about you that way for years, since
the very first time we met.* She stood on tiptoe and
threaded her arms about his neck, bringing her body
close to his in an intimate embrace.

When the kiss ended, Anne whispered, "I must go,
James. I'm supposed to be attending the princess tonight." Her mouth curved softly. "Perhaps I'll see you in
my dreams." *I'm not the naive girl I used to be. Absence
makes the heart grow fonder, and none know that better
than I.*

An hour later Anne saw James laughing with a young,
flirtatious female who was also extremely pretty. "Frances, who's the young lady talking with your brother?"

"That's Sarah Moncreiffe—she's Scottish, recently
married to Sir Charles Mordaunt, who sits in the Commons with James. Females throw themselves at my
brother; his conquests are legion."

"Perhaps it's not *absence*, but *presence*, that makes the
heart grow fonder."

"Or the cock harder," Frances jested outrageously.

On Monday morning, Anne and Frances took breakfast
with the princess, and Anne saw that Alexandra was perfectly at ease with James Hamilton's sister. She searched
her mind for a way she could excuse herself for a couple
of hours without arousing suspicion about her absence.

"Frances, if you will attend the princess this morning,
it will give me a chance to confer with the sewing women
about the fashions I've designed for Her Highness."

Alix smiled. "Thank you, Anne, for giving us an opportunity to get to know each other." She turned to
Frances. "Is it true that your mother had the courage to
turn down Queen Victoria when she was offered the
royal post of Mistress of the Robes?"

Anne left St. James's Park and walked briskly up St.
James's Street to Piccadilly. She crossed and continued
until she reached Jermyn Street. She turned the corner,
walked past a couple of town houses, and knew she
would have to make inquiries. She gathered her courage,

walked up the steps to the third house, and lifted the brass knocker. When a female servant opened the door, Anne said, "I'm sorry to trouble you, ma'am, but I'm looking for a gentleman by the name of Leicester Curzon-Howe. He leases a house on Jermyn Street, but I've forgotten the number."

The woman drew her brows together. "I don't know anyone by that name. I'm the housekeeper here, and this place is leased by Viscount Linsey. I'm sorry I can't help you."

Anne's heart sank. "Oh dear, he's been posted to Ireland and I was hoping to see him before he left."

"Ah, he's a military man, I take it."

"Yes, he's an officer in Prince Albert's Rifle Brigade."

"Oh, he must be the handsome officer in the dashing green uniform."

"Yes, yes, that's him."

"He lives across the street at number twenty-six. He's a treat to the eyes, that one. Every time I see him, I go weak in the knees."

"Thank you so much. You've been very helpful."

The woman looked her up and down. "Are you his ladylove?"

"No, no, he is a relative."

"Ah, pity," she said with a shrug, and closed the door.

Pity indeed, Anne thought.

She crossed the road and knocked on the door of number 26 before she lost her courage. It was opened by a manservant, and when she told him she was there to see her brother, he let her in and went upstairs to announce her.

Leicester greeted her warmly. "Anne, this is an unexpected pleasure. Come into the sitting room and we'll have some coffee."

"Unexpected perhaps, but hardly a pleasure," she said curtly.

He indicated a comfortable chair. "Please sit down. Tell me what's wrong. I can clearly see you are upset."

Suddenly, Anne's knees went weak and she sank

down into the chair. "I know about you and Mother. I know that Montagu is your son."

"Oh my dear, no wonder you are upset." He knelt before her. "Your mother and I were deeply in love. We planned to elope, but suddenly I was posted abroad, and a quick marriage was arranged for your mother by Queen Adelaide."

"Yes, Mother told me." Anne's heart was pounding as she braced herself for her next question. "For my own peace of mind I need to know, are you also *my* father?"

Leicester stared at her for long moments; then he took her hand. "My dearest Anne, I would never do or say anything that would ruin your peace of mind, or hurt you in any way. I could not possibly be your father. My love affair with your mother ended over twenty years ago when she married."

Impatiently, Anne put up her hand. "I overheard you in her bedchamber. You are lying to protect her."

He sat back on his heels, neither denying nor confirming her accusation.

"Leicester, please don't lie to protect *me*. I came here for the truth. Are you my father?"

He got to his feet and the look on his face told her that he was fighting with his conscience. Finally, he spoke. "Anne, the absolute truth is that I don't know. I cannot deny that the possibility exists. But for your own peace of mind, I believe it would be best if you think of Richard as your father, and me as your brother, as you always have."

"Thank you for telling me the truth, Leicester. I appreciate your candor." She stood up. "Since the choice is mine, I shall continue to think myself the daughter of an earl."

Anne walked to the door. "When do you leave for Ireland?"

"Since you insist upon the truth, my new posting is here in London."

Her eyes widened. "I see." *The possibility of Ireland never existed. The London posting is what you've both wanted for years.*

Anne walked briskly down Jermyn Street toward St. James's, deep in thought. She realized with a pang of regret that the things she'd discovered had robbed her of her trust. *How unworldly and naive I've been! Perhaps it's a good thing that my eyes have been opened. Far better than going through life in ignorance.*

She was momentarily disconcerted when she saw James Hamilton insert a key in the door of an elegant town house on the corner of Jermyn Street and go inside. *I wonder what he's doing?* Her chin went up. *Since he's a male, I warrant it's something illicit!*

Chapter 18

"I get the distinct impression that you are avoiding me." James lifted Anne's fingers to his lips. The ballroom at Marlborough House was crowded and he had waited impatiently as she had danced with three other partners.

"Whatever makes you think such a thing?"

"In the last month there have been a dozen grand entertainments thrown at Marlborough House, and you've danced with me exactly twice."

Anne's mouth curved in an enchanting smile. "I don't want to monopolize you, James. There are so many beautiful, noble ladies eager for your attention."

"There is only one lady I am interested in."

"Careful, James, or your reputation as a ladies' man will be in shreds. I'm not naive. The parties here at Marlborough House are rife with flirting and dalliance. I sometimes wonder if even the prince is faithful to his new bride."

You're right. His new hobby is adultery. "Anne, I am not in control of the prince's morals. All I ask is a chance to prove my devotion to you."

"How can I resist, when you ask so gallantly?"

He pulled her into his arms as waltz music filled the air. "Stop it! You are far too lovely to be brittle and mocking."

He drew her close and their bodies swayed together in the slow sensual movements of the waltz. As always when she danced with James, the music made her feel desirable. She closed her eyes and gave herself up to the pleasure of being in his arms. No other man had this mesmerizing effect on her.

James watched her face, saw her lashes sweep down, and her mouth curve softly. His desire flared and he suddenly felt possessive of her. When other men flirted or danced with her, it was becoming difficult for him to control his emotions, and he knew he was experiencing jealousy for the first time in his life.

She doesn't take me seriously when I profess my devotion. She suspects my words are empty flattery. From now on I must show her by my actions that I am sincere. He touched his lips to her brow where the red-gold tendrils curled so enticingly. *I won't simply court you, my beauty. I'll woo you with a vengeance,* he silently vowed.

During the following week, James gave Anne his undivided attention. When Princess Alexandra and her ladies attended the theater, he made sure he sat next to Anne. They shared a sense of humor that was infectious, laughing at the same witty lines in the comedy of errors being enacted onstage. During the intermission he brought Anne champagne and caressed her with his eyes as she sipped the intoxicating wine.

James, who regularly spent his days in Parliament, decided to skip a few sessions. When the princess and her ladies rode, as they did most days in the lovely spring weather, James joined the courtiers who acted as escort to the royal party, and unfailingly maneuvered his mount alongside Anne's. His attention did not go unnoticed by the others and when she saw their speculative glances, she smiled her secret smile.

When Frances informed her brother that the princess and her ladies were curious about Cremorne Gardens and would enjoy a visit, James made the arrangements. He chose an afternoon that included a hot-air balloon ascent, and afterward, while the Prince of Wales and his friends attended the famed equestrian exhibit, James escorted the ladies through the lovely public gardens that lay along the bank of the River Thames.

As evening descended, the families with children departed, and the fashionable people arrived to enjoy the myriad entertainments of stage plays, or to dance on the famous oval platform, lit artfully by gas chandeliers.

At ten o'clock the royal party dined elegantly in one of the infamous private supper rooms, then watched the brilliant firework display that ended at midnight. On the drive back to Marlborough House, James sought Anne's hand in the darkness of the carriage.

"Thank you for such a wonderful day," she murmured. "You put a lot of thought into it. The princess enjoyed every moment."

"It was my pleasure, sweetheart." He squeezed her hand and whispered in her ear, "You are my pleasure."

Princess Alexandra waited at Buckingham Palace for her monthly audience with Queen Victoria, but this time she had been determined to spare Anne from an encounter with her critical sister Emily, and had asked Frances to accompany her instead.

Her Majesty again wore black, accompanied by her usual dour expression, and Alix was glad that Anne had suggested she wear a dress in a drab shade of mushroom. She went through the motions of curtsying and sitting in the straight-backed chair and realized it was a ritual she had come to dread.

"My dear Alexandra, far be it from me to be critical; it is not in my nature. But when you entertain at Marlborough House, you must never forget that you represent the royal family. I would advise you to go over your guest list and eliminate any female whose name has been associated with scandal. It has come to my attention that a young woman by the name of Florence Rawdon attended one of your dinner parties. Are you not aware that she brought disgrace upon herself by eloping with the Marquis of Hastings?"

"Your Majesty, Lord Hastings was invited by my husband. They are friends who were at Oxford together, I believe."

"I have no objection to Hastings being entertained at Marlborough House. But females are held to a much higher standard, and I think it would be unwise in future to include his wife."

Alix was taken aback that the queen had one set of rules for men, and another for women, but decided to keep a wise silence in the face of such utter prejudice.

"Which brings us to another unfortunate incident. When I was told you attended Cremorne Pleasure Gardens, I could scarce believe my ears. As Queen of England, I have always held myself above the common masses, and I expect the same high standard from the Princess of Wales. I advise you to choose your pleasures wisely from now on."

When Alix returned to Marlborough House, she found Anne waiting with a decanter of sherry and an abundance of sympathy. "Was it very bad?"

"I'm afraid that someone is carrying tales to her about everything we do."

Anne immediately suspected her sister Emily, since she was the queen's confidante.

Princess Alexandra remarked, "I believe that the Irish refer to Victoria as the *Auld Bitch of a Quayne*, and now I understand why."

The following day, the prince and half a dozen of his sporting friends planned to attend Sandown races in nearby Surrey. When Alexandra confessed to her husband that she would rather visit Hampton Court Palace, which was close to Sandown, Teddy asked James if he would forgo the races and escort the princess and her ladies.

Alix was enchanted with the gardens, and spent far

more time outside by the river than she did inside the historic chambers of the palace.

James spirited Anne away from the others and they found a latticed bench beside a fountain in the knot garden, planted with herbs from the sixteenth century.

"It's rather gallant of you to give up Sandown races and act as escort to the princess."

"Not really gallant. I'd far rather spend the day with you than the Prince of Wales."

"I suspect that Alix is of like mind."

"Teddy has all of the vices of a prince and none of the virtues, I'm afraid." He bent and picked a sprig of rosemary and tucked it behind her ear.

"Rosemary is for remembrance. . . . I remember every detail of every encounter we've ever had, Anne."

Her eyes sparkled with mischief. "I wager you a kiss that you don't remember the first time we met."

His dark brows drew together. "It wasn't at the Newmarket races?"

She shook her head. "It was at Windsor Castle, under the arcade of the Horseshoe Cloister. I was about twelve."

His mind flew back in time and he suddenly remembered the red-gold curls, and the lovely green eyes flooded with tears.

"I'd been crying, and you said—"

James put his fingers to her lips to stop her words. His mouth curved. "You are as beautiful as a wild Irish rose."

"You remembered!"

"You owe me a kiss."

When his lips touched hers, she felt as if her heart would melt.

"The prince and his friends have been talking about the Newmarket races for weeks. The topic dominates every dinner conversation." Princess Alexandra was vastly relieved that her husband had chosen to travel with his male companions, leaving her free to share her carriage with her ladies-in-waiting.

"The *sport of kings* has become an obsession with the English nobility. The important races dominate the entire Season," Anne remarked.

"I can understand why gentlemen enjoy the races. Their horses compete against each other and the men indulge in high-stakes betting, but why does it appeal to ladies?"

"It's the fashionable thing to do, I suppose," Frances declared. "It provides an opportunity to parade about in gorgeous clothes and congregate with wealthy, eligible men. Husband hunters will find far more men at the races than on the dance floor."

"Well, I can understand the allure of the Royal Ascot—the racetrack adjoins Windsor's Great Park—but Newmarket requires an entire day of travel."

Anne noticed that the princess had gone very pale. "Are you feeling ill, Alix?"

"I'm afraid the swaying coach makes me nauseous," she confessed.

"We are close to Hertford, where the horses will be changed. We'll go into the coaching inn. Perhaps a drink will settle your stomach."

When the carriage stopped, the three ladies went inside, and Anne asked for a private room. She ordered tea with lemon, but after a few sips, Princess Alexandra declared, "I'm going to be sick!"

Anne grabbed the china bowl from the washstand and held it before the princess, who clutched her stomach and began to retch. When it was over, Anne brought fresh water and a towel and cleansed Alix's face.

"It must have been what you had for breakfast," Frances suggested.

Alix shook her head. "I haven't been able to face breakfast for a week. I . . . I think I may be having a baby."

"Oh, that's wonderful news," Anne declared.

"Yes, it makes me very happy, but I don't want anyone to know just yet. Will you help me keep my secret?" the princess pleaded.

"Of course we will," Anne promised. "But I know

your husband will be extremely proud, whenever you decide to tell him."

"I don't mind Edward knowing. I don't want Queen Victoria to find out. You know what she's like. . . . She will take over our lives."

"I understand completely. The tricky part will be keeping it from the other guests at Apethorpe Hall. But we'll manage," Anne promised. "It will be a conspiracy of three."

"I fully understand why you don't want to spend the summer attending one race after another," Frances commiserated.

"Perhaps if you tell the prince, he won't expect you to accompany him."

"That would be wonderful," Alix said wistfully. "I daydream about spending my summer in a beautiful garden by the river, like the one at Hampton Court."

"Where on earth have you been?" the Prince of Wales demanded when the carriage arrived at Apethorpe Hall. "Lady Westmorland ordered dinner for seven o'clock. We've been awaiting you for more than an hour!"

Anne stepped forward and gave Teddy a ravishing smile. "It was completely my fault, Your Highness. I was indisposed and Princess Alexandra insisted we stop until I was fully recovered. My sister Adelaide is such an accommodating hostess that late guests don't bother her in the least."

Adelaide curtsied to the princess. "Welcome to Apethorpe Hall, Your Highness. This is such an honor for the earl and me."

Princess Alexandra took her hand. "The honor is mine, my lady."

Anne kissed her sister's cheek. "Adelaide, why don't you take the Prince of Wales and your other guests in to dinner? I'm sure the princess would like to freshen up and change her gown. There is no need to inconvenience the gentlemen longer. We can join you for a late supper."

"Excellent suggestion," Teddy agreed.

*   *   *

"Alix, I recommend a relaxing bath, while Frances and I unpack for you. I'll pick out something pretty for you to wear that shows off your flawless complexion."

"Thank you, ladies. You are unfailingly kind to me."

Two hours later, the princess and her ladies joined the other guests. Alix was gowned in shell pink, her delicate cheeks rouged artfully to disguise her pallor.

Among the other guests was Lord Hartington, heir to the powerful Duke of Devonshire. Though he was a steward of the Jockey Club and owned a stable of racehorses, he relied upon Henry Fane's expert advice. Both men had horses running tomorrow and the conversation— centering on such edifying subjects as racing colors, jockeys, odds, and the amount of the purses—was interrupted by the arrival of the princess.

When the gentlemen stood to greet the ladies, the princess waved her hand, "Oh, please, carry on as you were. I find the subject of horse racing endlessly fascinating." Anne had advised her that all she had to do was relax in a comfortable chair, and pretend to listen with a rapt look on her face.

At eleven, when a footman announced the buffet supper, Hartington offered his arm to Lady Frances, who accepted gracefully, since the Duchess of Manchester was conspicuous by her absence.

James escorted Anne to the supper room. "I very much doubt if it was you who was indisposed. I suspect it was the princess."

"How did you guess?"

He smiled down at her. "That's the sort of thing I do for the prince."

"Yes," she murmured. "I've learned all sorts of tricks from you."

"These people are obsessed with racing. None more than Teddy. It's the risk of the high stakes—they can't resist. It becomes addictive."

"Poor Alix is dreading being dragged from one race to another all summer."

"What about you, Anne?"

"I'm not looking forward to it either. I enjoyed New-market last year, because I'd never attended a race before, and of course I enjoyed our encounter."

"Will you let me buy you champagne again?"

She smiled into his dark eyes. "The anticipation leaves me breathless."

"There you are, Anne." Henry Fane took her arm. "My duties as host compel me to keep a brotherly eye on you."

"Ah yes, and Lord Hamilton must do the same with his sister Frances. Your bosom friend Hartington is a lecher of the first water."

"Alix, for heaven's sake, you're not even dressed yet! I've been up for hours. When I returned from breakfast, I expected you to be ready." Teddy glanced at her break-fast tray and saw that it was untouched. "I don't want to be late for the races!"

"Surely the races don't start at this ungodly hour, Edward."

"That's not the point. There's so much going on long before the races start. I like to view all the horses entered, talk to the jockeys, consider the odds, and simply enjoy talking with my friends. All the other men are ready and raring to go. The very atmosphere at the New-market races is charged with excitement, and I don't want to miss a moment of it."

"I understand, Edward. I know you've been looking forward to it. Please don't wait for me. Go and enjoy yourself with your friends. I'll be along as soon as I'm ready."

"You don't seem to understand. We are invited guests of the Earl and Countess of Westmorland. We should arrive with our hosts, who will enjoy great prestige presenting the Prince and Princess of Wales to the crowds."

Edward answered a knock on the door. "Lady Anne, Her Highness needs help. She has no sense of urgency. See what you can do to speed things up." He turned back to his wife. "I'll wait a short time, but there is a limit to my patience, Alix."

He descended to the first floor and on his way to the stables encountered James. "Alexandra has no more enthusiasm for attending this race than flying to the moon."

"I believe racing appeals to males more than females, sire."

"But we don't have *any* interests in common. She makes me feel like I'm dragging her to these events against her will. Sykes has invited us to his country house in Yorkshire for the Doncaster races; then there's the Derby and the Royal Ascot. Fane has offered to sponsor me as a member of the Jockey Club, but Alix shows no enthusiasm for the sport whatever." He looked at his watch and impatiently tapped a riding crop against his boots. "To be totally truthful, James, I'd enjoy myself far more if she wasn't included."

"Then there's your answer. Attend the races without her. Why drag her along when she doesn't enjoy the sport?"

"Leave her behind at Marlborough House? It would reflect very badly on me. Nobody stays in London in the summer."

"The Duke of Devonshire owns a summer villa at Chiswick on the Thames. It's a palatial place with Italianate gardens. Females take great delight in these things. Since Hartington handles Devonshire's business affairs, why don't we sound him out about leasing it for the princess and her ladies for the summer?"

"By Jove, that sounds just the ticket. It would leave me free to travel about and enjoy my friends' hospitality, and allow me to appear generous and caring to my bride at the same time. Would you have a word with Hartington about it, James?"

"Leave it to me, Teddy. I'll arrange things so that everyone is happy."

In due time, Princess Alexandra emerged from Apethorpe Hall on the arm of her hostess, the Countess of Westmorland. The Prince of Wales had been pacing back and forth, while Fane stood patiently beside the open barouche.

Anne waited until Alix settled back against the velvet squabs, then handed her a stylish parasol. She was relieved that the princess's morning sickness had passed off and felt fairly confident that Alix would be free of nausea for the rest of the day.

Carriages had been arranged to transport the guests to and from the Newmarket racecourse. Anne waited for Frances, and when she arrived with her brother James, Anne's heart began to flutter.

As they waited for one of the carriages, Frances said firmly, "I will attend the princess today. It will give you and James a chance to spend a few hours together."

"That's very generous of you, Frances. I suspect that James suggested it."

He smiled down at Anne. "Of course I did. I'll meet you at the grandstand. I have some business to arrange with Hartington, so I'll share his carriage."

When Anne and Frances arrived, they were amazed at the throng that had gathered. The weekend in May that officially opened the racing season always drew a crowd at Newmarket, but the attendance of the Prince and Princess of Wales was an added attraction that swelled the attendance to double its usual number.

Anne soon spotted where Alix and Adelaide were sitting and she and Frances joined them in the grandstand. Anne wanted to see for herself that the princess looked well before she left. "I see your escorts have already deserted you," she said lightly.

The princess laughed. "They couldn't get away fast enough."

Adelaide waved her hand. "Fane never sits. He's taken His Highness to see Eau de Vie, the horse he has entered in the two-thousand-guinea stakes."

"I'll go and place a bet on Henry's horse myself, if I can fight through the crowd."

Adelaide raised her eyebrows. "That's rather daring, Anne."

"Downright brazen. Do wish me luck." She winked at Frances and hurried off.

Anne had no trouble spotting James in the milling crowd in front of the grandstand. He was so tall, he stood head and shoulders over most.

"There you are, my beauty. We owe Henry and Adelaide a debt of gratitude—they've taken our charges off our hands for a few hours. What would you like to do first?"

"I'd like to disappear in the crowd and observe all the ridiculous outfits people invariably wear when they attend the races."

Surreptitiously, he indicated a fellow in bright yellow pantaloons and a black-and-white houndstooth jacket.

Anne burst into laughter, while James tried to keep a straight face. Soon he could hide his amusement no longer as they rubbed shoulders with people who ran the gamut from the bland to the grand. "Donegal, the county I represent in Ireland, is famous for its tweed production, but the hodgepodge of mix-matched tweeds here today make the elite look like country bumpkins."

James bought hot roasted chestnuts and took great delight in peeling them and feeding them to her. The pair laughed their way from one end of the racecourse to the other, and ended up close to the betting windows. James pointed to a board with names posted for the first race. "Who do you fancy?"

"I like the sound of Black Irish—it reminds me of you."

"In that case I'll take Firebrand, for obvious reasons." He placed the bets, picked up a racing form, and handed Anne her ticket. "Let's make our way down to the rail—it's almost post time."

Breathless with anticipation, Anne pressed against the rail as the horses lunged from the starting gate. As they thundered past, she realized she knew neither the colors nor the numbers of the horses they'd chosen. She glanced up over her shoulder at James. "Damnation, there's so much I have to learn. Are we winning?"

He grinned down at her. "I know I am."

Her eyes sparkled. "I'm talking about the horses!"

"The number is on your ticket."

"Oh, so it is! How clever."

"Ingenious," he teased.

The winners' names were announced. "Oh, both our horses lost. I was going to take the money I won and bet it on the next race. I had such high hopes for Black Irish."

He handed her the racing form. "This time choose with your head, not your heart."

She ran her finger down the list of names for the thousand-guinea race. "Who on earth would name their horse Repulse?"

"It's owned by the Marquis of Hastings."

"He must have been drunk when he named it."

James nodded. "Hastings is seldom sober."

"I urged Florence to follow her heart. Now I think she regrets going against her family's wishes and marrying Henry Hastings."

"Don't feel guilty, Anne. You didn't choose him—she did. We are all responsible for our own decisions. This time use your head to pick a horse."

She studied the names on the racing form. "James, I can't. I'm simply not made that way. I'll always choose with my heart. Lady Augusta is a pretty name, and she's a filly."

"Come on, then, let's place our bets so we can come back and watch the race. My head tells me to bet on the favorite."

The betting windows were crowded, since it was an important race, and the pair amused themselves by people-watching as they joined a long line. Anne had to press her lips together to keep herself from laughing out loud, and James egged her on by indicating one outlandish punter after another.

At the window when James took out his wallet, she shook her head. "I want to bet my own money. The risk is what makes it fun," she asserted.

When she put down five pounds, James rolled his eyes. "Risk indeed," he teased.

"I don't have money to burn, and *I'm* not playing it safe by betting on the favorite, you craven devil."

"Craven, am I?" He turned to the window. "Fifty pounds to win on Lady Augusta."

They made their way down to the rail and used their elbows to persuade the crowd to make room. The anticipation for the thousand-guinea race was palpable, and a collective shout went up from the crush of spectators when the horses lunged from the starting gate.

The Thoroughbreds came thundering down the Rowley Mile. "Our horse is number six," she informed him in case he had forgotten to look at his ticket.

James glanced at the track a couple of times, but watching Anne's face gave him far more pleasure. Her look of anticipation was quickly replaced by excitement, then hope, then disbelief as Lady Augusta took the lead. An air of dread crossed her face as two other horses caught up and threatened to overtake her. James watched as she held her breath, then screamed, "Go, go, go!" as Lady Augusta pulled ahead and won by a nose.

Anne jumped up and down with happiness. Then she flung her arms around James and almost squeezed the breath out of him. "We won, we won! Oh, isn't it marvelous?" she cried. "We followed our hearts and we won!"

He gazed down at her and saw she was engulfed in triumph. She exuded an aura of pure joy, and in that moment James realized he had fallen in love.

Chapter 19

"I have the most wonderful news to share." Princess Alexandra's face glowed with happiness. She sat across from Anne and Frances as the carriage pulled away from Apethorpe Hall on its return journey to London.

"You've had a change of heart about attending the races?" Frances ventured.

"Even better." Her mouth curved in a smile. "My *husband* has had a change of heart about my attending the races."

"His Highness has agreed to go with his friends, and let you stay at home?" Anne was surprised that Teddy was suddenly being considerate.

"He's leased a villa on the Thames where I may spend the summer."

"Did you confide that you might be in a delicate condition?" Anne asked.

"No, I didn't mention it. He told me his conscience wouldn't let him leave me behind in London during the summer months, and since I don't share his interest in racing, he has decided to lease me a house on the river. It's at a place called Chiswick."

"Doesn't the Duke of Devonshire own a palatial villa at Chiswick on Thames with lovely Italian gardens? Anne, you must know the one I mean," Frances prompted.

"Indeed, I do." Anne smiled her secret smile. *So that was the business that James arranged with Hartington before the races. He never even hinted about it. He wanted it to be a special surprise for Alix from her husband.*

"Bless Edward. It will be so much easier to keep Queen Victoria from learning my secret if I live at Chiswick all summer."

"I'll design you some lovely new dresses."

"The weather here is so much warmer than in Denmark. I'd love some dresses that are light and loose."

"Muslin is exceedingly cool. It comes in elegant white and pastel shades, and for every day there is sprig muslin. I'll order some silk parasols too, and some fans."

"I can't wait to see the gardens. We'll start packing tomorrow," Alix declared. "Oh dear, I just remembered. . . . The queen informed Edward that we are to represent her at the opening exhibition of the Royal Academy of Arts on Wednesday. It marks the official opening of the London Season, so I've been told."

"It does," Anne confirmed. "Our families go every year, and for the Prince and Princess of Wales, it will be a command performance."

"We will get it out of the way and fervently hope we will be at Chiswick by the weekend. I am so looking forward to it."

"Your nausea seems to have abated," Anne remarked.

"Strangely, it began to disappear the moment Edward told me about the summerhouse." Her eyes twinkled. "Happiness seems to be a miracle cure."

The moment everyone returned to London from Newmarket, Emily made a point of visiting her sister Adelaide to see if her weekend entertaining the royal couple had been successful. She particularly wanted to know how close their half sister, Anne, was to Princess Alexandra.

"The weekend was a great success. Fane is sponsoring the Prince of Wales for membership in the Jockey Club. Regarding Anne, I was quite surprised that Princess Alexandra treats her more like a friend than a lady-in-waiting. There was another thing about Anne that raised my eyebrows."

"Do tell!" Emily waited with bated breath for any untoward behavior that she could relay to their father.

"At the reception at Marlborough House, John Claud Hamilton told me he was courting Anne, and that once he won the election, he intended to propose marriage. For a lady who was practically engaged, Anne spent an inordinate amount of time with James Hamilton, who's a known libertine."

Emily's stomach knotted with envy. "I've always believed she was willful and impulsive, and quite capable of scandalous behavior. Heaven only knows what goes on behind the closed doors of Marlborough House."

"I don't know very much about art," Princess Alexandra said by way of apology to her husband.

The Prince of Wales helped his bride alight from their carriage in Piccadilly as they joined the fashionable throng gathered at the Academy of Arts. "I warrant that most of the people here have come to see you, not look at the paintings."

"Large crowds make me nervous," Alix murmured as she took Edward's arm.

"Nonsense. Everyone we know will be here. All we have to do is stroll about and mingle with our friends."

When Alexandra saw Anne and Frances arrive, she felt immeasurably better. Their mere presence gave her confidence and she was able to relax and smile.

Anne, on the other hand, could not relax. Frances had told her that her family was back from Ireland, and as expected, John Claud had been elected member of Parliament for Londonderry.

Without a doubt Anne knew that the Duke and Duchess of Abercorn and John Claud, flush with his victory, would be here tonight. She had decided that if he even hinted at a proposal of marriage, it was only fair to make it plain, once and for all time, that they could never be more than *friends*.

"There they are," Frances declared, moving toward a large group gathered about the Hamiltons.

Anne was disconcerted to see her own parents were part of the gathering, offering their congratulations to John Claud on his victory in Ireland. Her face felt stiff as she smiled and greeted them.

"Here's Anne, come to congratulate you. I'm sure she's delighted at your achievement, though there was never any doubt that you would win the seat," Earl Howe declared.

John Claud stepped forward and raised Anne's fingers to his lips. His eyes were filled with triumph as he murmured, "The rude awakening you predicted never came to pass."

Not yet. "I am sincerely happy for you, John Claud."

"Thank you. Would you permit the youngest member of Parliament to escort you through the gallery?"

Anne licked her lips and looked at the smiling faces of both sets of parents. She realized it would be churlish to refuse. "Of course." He held out his arm and she had no option but to take it.

John Claud had a destination in mind, and guided her to the section that displayed the paintings of her favorite artist, Sir Thomas Gainsborough. He paused before the famous portrait of Georgiana Cavendish, the fifth Duchess of Devonshire.

"I am finally in a position to offer you a formal proposal of marriage. Will you marry me, Anne?"

Standing beneath the portrait of the beautiful, red-haired duchess gave her the courage she needed. *Georgiana married the wrong man and doomed herself to a lifetime of unhappiness.* "John Claud, my answer is no, as you knew it would be. I have told you many times that we can never be more than friends."

He sighed deeply, but seemed to accept her refusal calmly.

Anne was greatly relieved that John Claud didn't appear overly upset, and seemed to take it in his stride. She smiled up at him. "As one friend to another, I couldn't be happier that you won your seat in Parliament."

"It's a family tradition."

"Yes. They must be very proud that you have achieved your goal."

"This is just a first step. My ambition is *insatiable*."

"I believe you. When you set your mind on something, you are positively tenacious."

"There's Father, with the Prince of Wales. Let's join them."

As Anne and John Claud approached, the prince hailed him. "My dear fellow, I hear congratulations are in order. James told me your splendid news."

"Thank you, Your Highness."

"You couldn't do better than follow in your brother's footsteps. James is invaluable to me. No matter the task, he does it superbly."

Anne knew that John Claud would take no pleasure in hearing the prince sing his brother's praises, so she turned aside and joined Princess Alexandra, who was conversing with Lady Lu about Chiswick.

"You'll simply love the Palladian villa, Your Highness. The Devonshires threw garden parties there, until the duke became obsessed with making Eastbourne the most fashionable summer watering hole in England. The grounds are magnificent. There's an ornamental lake with grebes and swans. In June the gardens are ablaze with flowers, and the velvet lawns are shaded with lovely weeping willows."

"Perhaps I could have a garden party," Alix suggested.

"If you do, I predict invitations to Chiswick will be worth their weight in gold."

"Your Grace, did you happen to see which way my parents went? I want to tell Mother that we're moving to Chiswick for June and July."

"When I last saw them, they were heading in the direction of the Joshua Reynolds gallery. The Beauforts and your other sister, Emily, were with them."

Beaufort House is so close to the Royal Academy, I should have known Georgiana would be here. Normally, I'd avoid my half sisters, but I can't wait to see their faces when they learn I'll be spending the summer at Chiswick.

Anne excused herself and made her way through the crowd, seeing the look of relief on her mother's face when she found them. She greeted Georgiana and Emily, and without a hint of smugness in her voice said, "Mother, I didn't get a chance to tell you before. I shall be moving to Chiswick on Thames for the summer with the Princess of Wales while His Highness enjoys the racing season."

"And a damn good thing too!" Earl Howe declared harshly. "The prince has surrounded himself with dissolute friends. I hear the things that go on at Marlborough House are nothing short of scandalous. I am greatly relieved to hear that Princess Alexandra and her ladies will be spending the summer apart from Prince Edward and his racy friends."

Anne was taken off guard. *Emily has been filling Father's ears with gossip.* "You must have been listening to rumors that aren't true."

The Duke of Beaufort said, "Your father is right. The gossip about the prince is rife, to an increasing degree. I understand your father's concern about your living at Marlborough House."

Anne tried to control her anger. If she lost her temper, they would blame it on her Irish blood. In a cool voice she said, "Princess Alexandra's household is above reproach. Her moral standards are every bit as high as Queen Victoria's."

"I'm sure they are, darling," her mother agreed. "I'm delighted the princess will be spending the summer at Chiswick."

Anne smiled at her mother. "I believe plans are afoot for a June garden party. I'll make sure your name is on the invitation list." She turned to her half sister. "Georgiana, I won't put your name on the list, since you and Beaufort usually spend the summer in Gloucester." She gave Emily a pitying glance. "And of course, you'll be on duty to Her Gracious Majesty."

Anne made her way back to the Prince and Princess of Wales. She felt relieved when she saw that John Claud was no longer among the men surrounding Teddy.

Frances asked, "Did you find your parents in the Reynolds gallery?"

"Yes, but I predict they won't be there long. Georgiana and Emily were with them and I wager my mother made an excuse to get away from them the moment I left."

"John Claud was looking for you."

Anne winked at her friend. "Thankfully, he didn't find me."

John Claud, however, *had* found her. He stopped a short distance away, watching as she spoke with her family. And as he waited for her, he saw an opportunity to further his own interests. When she left, he did not follow her. Instead, he waited until she was out of sight. As the earl and his family strolled in the other direction, John Claud caught up with them.

"I was looking for Lady Anne."

"She just left, my dear fellow."

"I think she returned to the Princess of Wales," Lady Howe told him. "I don't know how you missed her."

He grinned boyishly. "My head is in the clouds." He lowered his voice confidentially. "A short time ago, I asked Anne to marry me."

"Well done!" Earl Howe declared. "Congratulations, John Claud."

"I must confess that she didn't say yes, at least not yet. But I have high hopes."

"James, it's so kind of you to take charge of our move to Chiswick." Alexandra stepped up into the carriage and sat down beside Anne. "I'm always nervous when I have to meet new people."

James took the seat beside his sister Frances. "The staff at the villa is overjoyed that you will be spending the summer there. Devonshire servants are well trained to be reliable and will most likely anticipate your every need." He reached into his pocket. "Here is a list of their names. The head housekeeper is Mrs. Bailey, the cook is Mrs. Gilbert, and the head gardener is Harry Hargrave."

"You think of everything." Alix smiled gratefully.

Sitting across from Anne gave James a chance to feast his eyes on her. *Those high-heeled kid slippers make her ankles look sensually delicate.* He imagined removing a silk stocking, raising her foot to his lips, and kissing her instep. It took a great deal of willpower to withdraw his attention from the object of his desire and address the princess.

"Your rooms have all been prepared, your luggage was dispatched earlier, and I brought your sewing ladies first thing this morning."

Frances asked, "Was there room in the stable for our horses?"

James nodded. "There were a dozen empty stalls and grooms aplenty to care for your mounts." He imagined taking Anne up before him on his saddle, felt her warm body between his thighs, and shuddered with longing when he envisioned her hair blowing in the wind and brushing against his throat. His fantasy dissolved as he heard Alexandra's voice. He focused on her words.

"My husband has promised to visit the villa frequently, but I don't honestly expect him to travel to Chiswick often."

"I think that's a wise assumption. The prince will be attending the Oaks at Epsom next weekend, and he's accepted an invitation to Yorkshire in the middle of June. He asked me to come to Chiswick and check on your welfare in his absence."

"That's very kind of you, James. You will receive a warm welcome whenever your duties in Parliament permit you to spend time with us," Alexandra assured him.

When James glanced at Anne, she lowered her lashes and her mouth curved into a smile. Her expression gave him hope that she too would welcome him warmly.

As the carriage bowled along the road that followed a curve in the river, the villa suddenly came into view.

Alexandra caught her breath at the exquisite domed two-story house in its jewellike setting. "It's a garden paradise."

The carriage drove through the main gate, which was guarded by carved sphinxes, and drove up to the villa, which was fronted by six Corinthian columns. James jumped out, and helped the princess alight; then he took Anne's hand and helped her from the carriage.

The roses that climbed up the Portland stone walls and framed the Venetian windows were in full bloom. They perfumed the air with their fragrant scent. Anne took a deep, appreciative breath. "It's far lovelier than I dared to imagine."

James squeezed her hand before he reluctantly released it. "Wait until you see the interiors." He opened the front door and the ladies went inside. "This first room on the ground floor is the Summer Parlor." He pointed to the ceiling where the central panel was painted with a huge, brilliant sunflower. "On the ground floor of the west wing is a conservatory. At the moment camellias are in bloom." James remembered placing the pink lily in the tempting valley between Anne's breasts, and pictured tucking a camellia against her porcelain skin.

Two women in crisp gray uniforms and white caps came forward and curtsied to the Princess of Wales. Alexandra smiled. "Mrs. Bailey, I am delighted to meet you." She was grateful that James had provided her with names.

"Your Highness, I have a staff of six: two parlormaids, two chambermaids, and two serving maids, all eager to serve you. We have no footmen at Chiswick." She stepped back and the second woman stepped forward.

"You must be Mrs. Gilbert." Alix smiled inwardly because the cook was plump.

"Your Highness, I have my own staff of kitchen and scullery maids. If you will provide me with a menu, I will see that they follow it to the letter."

"Please, Mrs. Gilbert, nothing so formal as that. My ladies and I have a few favorite dishes, but beyond that, you are free to decide the menu."

James immediately envisioned Anne sipping leek

soup. *I love to watch her eat. When she is enjoying the taste of something in her mouth, she always licks her lips.*

Mrs. Bailey again stepped forward. "Lord James, you are quite familiar with the villa. Would you be good enough to give the Princess of Wales and her ladies a tour of the second floor?"

"With the greatest pleasure." James led the way upstairs. "The villa has a unique design; all the upper rooms are connected to this central octagonal chamber. Every one of the ceilings is magnificently painted with copies of Italian masters." He opened a door. "This blue velvet room is the study. There's a red room and a green room, which I assume get their names from the colors of the lovely Venetian glass in their windows."

Anne traced her fingers over the Scottish thistles and fleurs-de-lys carved into the marble fireplace. "The artistry is exquisite!"

"Yes, and each fireplace is different. One has lions, one has owls, and another has small, winged cherubs. I think I should let you ladies discover the villa's charms on your own. The gardens abound with statues of Roman gods. There is even a pagan temple, and I have been told one of the buildings houses a Roman bath."

Anne laughed. "How very decadent. It lends credence to the rumors that the infamous Duchess of Devonshire swam naked upon occasion."

His imagination took flight. *I warrant you are impulsive enough to try it, my beauty.*

Princess Alexandra turned from the window. "Thank you so much, my lord. I deeply appreciate your time and attention."

"There are sixty-five acres to explore. Harry Hargrave is very proud of his gardens. I'm sure he will answer any questions you have about the estate. Good-bye, ladies. I trust you will enjoy every day you pass here at the villa."

James spent the morning in Parliament and he fully intended to return for the afternoon session to drum up support for an Irish bill he had presented a week ago to abolish the tax on salmon exports from County Donegal, but when he left for lunch, he noticed that there was a strong east wind, blowing in from the Channel. The clouds were scudding across the sunlit sky, and in spite of the stiff breeze, it was a beautiful day.

He suddenly lost all interest in going back to the House of Commons. He knew exactly where he would spend his afternoon. The allure of Anne at Chiswick on Thames was drawing him like a lodestone. He knew deep down in his bones that resistance was futile, for once he began to think about her, his longing became an ache in his heart.

Prince Teddy was attending the Tattersall horse auctions this week, and would shortly be off to Yorkshire so he could attend the races at Doncaster, where his friend Christopher Sykes had a breeding farm. Since the prince had asked James to spend a few evenings at Chiswick in his absence, James felt justified in passing the afternoon there as well.

As he drove his carriage down the Great West Road along the River Thames, his anticipation grew by leaps and bounds. When he arrived at the palatial summer villa, he stabled his horses and sprinted across the lawns to the mansion.

"James! How lovely to see you." Princess Alix, surrounded by her ladies and half a dozen other female staff, was busy planning a garden party.

He took her hand to his lips. "Your Highness, you are absolutely blooming. I promised the prince that I'd drop in to make sure all was well, but 'tis plain to see you are enjoying the villa."

James greeted his sister. "Where's Anne?"

"She's in the sewing room. She's designed us some exquisite summer dresses for the garden party, and she's gone to see if the parasols have arrived yet."

He strode into the villa and homed in on the sewing room. "Good afternoon, my beauty. Grab a warm jacket and come with me. There's a fair wind for sailing."

"James!" She set a blue silk parasol aside. "I thought I was the impulsive one."

"It must have rubbed off on me. I promised to teach you how to sail, and my word is my bond." He glanced down at her kid slippers. "You need sturdy leather shoes too."

Her pulse quickened. "I'll be back in a minute."

When Anne returned, she was wearing a green wool jacket and riding boots. She was too excited to care about how incongruous they looked with her pretty summer dress.

James grabbed her hand and they hurried down to the boathouse. Inside there were punts, rowboats, and small sailboats. He unfastened the rope on a sailboat, checked to see the rigging was intact, then braced his legs to hold it steady, while Anne climbed in beside him. Even in the shelter of the boathouse the water beneath them was choppy, making the boat rock from side to side.

"The first lesson is how to hoist the sail. You take it from the sail bag, then check the rigging to make sure the lines aren't fouled." When Anne's brow furrowed, he explained, "Make sure the ropes aren't tangled into knots."

When she nodded her understanding, he continued. "This is the jibstay—you attach it thus. This is the forestay." James hoisted the jib and allowed it to flap as he pushed the small sloop out into the river, head to wind, so he could attach the mainsail. "Sailors refer to this as a mainsheet. You attach it by these cleats; then you hoist it."

The wind caught the sail and the boat came alive instantly in the brisk breeze. Anne laughed with excitement. "Is it the same principle as a large yacht, where you run it up the mast?" she shouted.

"Exactly." He nodded and raised his voice above the wind. "This is the tiller. When I push on it, the boom comes around and you must remember to duck. Here, you try it."

Grinning, Anne took hold of the tiller, pushed on it,

and laughing, they ducked in unison. James moved close, so she could hear him. "You change course by turning into and through the wind. That's called *tacking*."

Her first attempt drenched them with a wave, but undeterred, she tried it again, guiding the sailboat over and around the small waves.

James hugged her to him and, grinning from ear to ear, gave her a thumbs-up. They positioned themselves close together, just aft of the middle, and the bow lifted and took them on a run to the center of the wide Thames, with the wind directly behind.

He showed her how to brace her feet, and lean her body windward for counterbalance. She threw her head back, as the sun blazed down, the brisk breeze played havoc with her damp, red-gold curls, and the spray wet their faces with deliciously cold, slightly salty water.

Anne closed her eyes. She felt as if nothing could compare with the feeling of freedom that sailing evoked. Floating between sky and water freed her imagination, and her mind.

Surely sailing was the most exciting, invigorating sport in the world. *And this is only the Thames. Imagine what it would be like in the Solent or the sea!*

James watched the rapture on her face. Being with Anne made him feel alive. The wind tempered and turned to a light breeze. He reached out his fingers to brush a damp tress of hair from her eyes, and was compelled to put voice to his feelings. "I want us to be together always. Will you marry me, Anne?"

"James!" She was breathless with exhilaration, and her eyes sparkled greener than the sea around them. "Of course I'll marry you." *I've been madly in love with you for years and years.*

"You've made me the happiest man on earth, Anne." He caressed her cheek tenderly. "Come on, you'd better get out of those wet clothes, before you take a chill."

Chapter 20

When James and Anne sat down to dinner with everyone, Anne's face was glowing with an inner joy. Princess Alexandra sensed her lady-in-waiting was hugging a secret to herself that she wasn't yet ready to share.

"Anne, your skin has a rosy blush tonight," Frances remarked.

Anne's cheeks turned even pinker. "That's from the wind out on the river. Sailing is exhilarating. I can only imagine how exciting it would be to be out in the sea."

Alix shuddered delicately. "I'm not a good sailor. Just crossing the Solent on our way to the Isle of Wight made me seasick."

James said, "Luckily, it's just a narrow strait that doesn't take long to navigate. The Irish Sea, on the other hand, can make a seasoned sailor sick, if a storm blows up."

"Did it ever make you sick, James?" Anne asked.

"I must admit that it never did."

Frances laughed. "James has what Father calls a *cast-iron gut*."

"That's rather graphic language for the dinner table. Her Highness is too well-mannered to take you to task, Frances."

"Anne and I are doing our best to remedy that, James."

"Well, I've always known that the Hamilton females

are far too outspoken for polite society, thanks to our unorthodox mother, but I had no idea Lady Anne was cut from the same cloth," he teased.

"Anne has taken our mother as her role model, I'll have you know."

Anne smiled into James's eyes. "I happen to adore Lady Lu."

He almost reached out to cover her hand, then realized it was too overt a gesture.

In spite of his reticence, Alexandra and Frances exchanged a speaking glance.

After dinner, the moon rose to bathe the lovely villa gardens in light and shadow. When James suggested a stroll to the ornamental lake, both the princess and Frances declined. Each, it seemed, needed a final fitting of the gowns they would wear to the royal garden party that had been planned for three days hence.

Without a word, Anne stood up, and the pair descended the villa's outside staircase that led down to the gardens. The air was filled with the fragrance of roses, and the heady aroma of night-scented stocks. James took her hand in his and they strolled toward the lake. "This garden is most conducive to romance. Do you think they are giving us the opportunity to be alone?"

Anne lifted her face to look up at him in the moonlight. "Frances has always known how I feel about you, James. Until today, she had no idea how you felt about me, but then neither did I," she said softly.

"Then let me make it perfectly plain." James enfolded her in his arms, lifted her off her feet, and kissed her while she was suspended in the air. She threaded her arms about his neck, and he swung her around, unable to curb his exuberance.

When they neared the lake, he bent to pluck a pink lily and tucked it into the décolletage of her gown. His thumbs caressed the delicate swell of her breasts; then he dipped his head to taste the silken skin of her throat.

With one arm about her back and the other beneath her knees, he lifted her and sat down on a latticed garden seat beneath a weeping willow. Then he kissed her fiercely, and with great abandon she kissed him back.

When their lips parted, she laughed softly. "With such gusto, we'll frighten the ducks off the pond."

"They've gone to nest."

"I wish we were snug in our nest."

"So do I, my beauty, but it won't be long. When we're apart, I ache for you." He threaded his fingers through her fiery curls and brought her mouth close to his.

Heat leaped between them, each longing to consummate the desire that left them burning with need. James kept a tight rein on his passion. He didn't want to frighten her, nor dishonor her. Anne was far too precious to him.

He set her on her feet, and took her hand. "I think we'd better go in. The night and the moonlight are luring us irresistibly down paths that are better explored by married lovers." He slipped his arm about her waist and led her toward the villa.

"James, must you leave tomorrow?"

"Yes, but if you are willing to rise at dawn, we can ride together. There are over sixty acres where we can lose ourselves for a few hours before the others are even awake."

Anne sighed. "What a romantic suggestion."

He bent close and whispered, "You'll find I'm full of them."

Anne slipped out of bed just as dawn was lighting the sky. She donned a riding skirt and linen shirt, and made her way to the stables. James was before her, already in the saddle, and her pulse began to race when she saw that he intended to share his mount with her.

She eagerly raised her arms, and he lifted her before him. He dropped a kiss on the top of her head, slid one arm about her waist to draw her close between his thighs, and, holding the reins in his other hand, urged the big chestnut gelding to gallop.

Anne laughed as a red squirrel ran up a tree and began to chatter. "He's scolding us because he thinks we might steal his chestnuts. How sweet he is."

James slowed the horse to a trot. "If you enjoy watching wildlife, we should have our honeymoon in Ireland at Barons Court. The house is old and rambling, but the countryside surrounding it is unsurpassed for its unspoiled beauty."

Anne leaned back against his powerful body, relishing the intimacy. His murmuring lips brushed against her ear and sent a delicious shiver down her spine. "I've always longed to go to Ireland. Tell me what it's like."

"Barons Court lies in a sheltered valley at the foot of the picturesque Sperrin Mountains. The air is softer, the grass greener, and because we've never allowed hunting, the wildlife is abundant and almost tame. Close by the house there is a string of connected lakes that glitter like a diamond necklace in the sunshine. Mother swears she fell in love with Father the first time he rowed her through the lakes."

"Tell me about the wildlife."

"Running across our lawns we have hares, and foxes with their kits. In the woods we have does with their fawns, and badgers that dance by the light of the moon. In the lakes we have minks and otters that are so playful they like to swim with you."

"I have a confession to make. I don't know how to swim."

"That's something that should be remedied immediately. If I'd known you couldn't swim, I wouldn't have given you a sailing lesson." He smiled. "It will give me the greatest pleasure in the world to teach you. I give you my word it will be second nature to an impulsive, adventurous female like you."

She laughed happily. "Is that how you see me?

"Yes." He rolled his eyes. "And naked, of course."

"In my dreams I've seen *you* naked," she confessed.

"Well, when we've finished our ride, you'll get your chance to see me in the flesh."

"You intend to teach me to swim in the lake?"

"Nothing so public, Lady Anne," he said formally.

Then he kissed her ear and whispered, "The Roman bath will give us complete privacy."

"Don't be afraid, there's no one here to see us." James pulled her inside the Roman bathhouse, shut the door, and put the iron bar across so nobody else could enter.

"I had no idea it was so beautiful." The square pool was lined with aqua tile, and the roof had octagonal panels of glass that allowed the sun to shine down on the water to make it glisten. Anne bent down to dip her hand in the water. "It's warm!"

"Yes, it's heated with hot-water pipes that run beneath the tile. The Romans were excellent engineers. That stone table in the alcove piled with towels was actually designed for massages, administered by bath slaves."

"That sounds rather decadent."

"The Romans didn't have Victorian attitudes. If the bathers were males, their bath attendants were females."

"And vice versa, I suppose?"

He nodded and rolled his eyes. "Naked, of course."

Her eyes glittered with mischief. "I'll let you be my bath slave."

"Don't tempt me. We're here to give you a swimming lesson, not play wicked games."

Anne gave the water a hesitant glance. "How deep do you think it is?"

"It's graduated. It starts out shallow, then deepens to about six feet." He waggled his eyebrows. "Are you game for a dip? Or does it intimidate you too much?"

Anne's look of hesitation vanished immediately. "Of course not. I trust you implicitly."

"Foolish wench. You can trust me not to drown you, but that's the only promise I'll make, my beauty."

"I would expect nothing more, Lord Rakehell. Turn your back while I remove my clothes."

James began to chuckle.

"You are laughing at me," she accused.

"I'm laughing at your innocence. You offer to let me

be your bath slave, then order me to turn my back while you undress."

Anne tossed her head. "On second thought, that's completely unnecessary." She took off her shirt, removed her riding skirt, and stood before him in a silk half corset and white drawers edged with lavender ruffles.

His appreciative glance swept over her. "If all your undergarments are this provocative, then God help me!"

Her mouth curved in a smile, and she gave him back his own words. "We are here to give me a swimming lesson, not play wicked games."

"Perhaps we can do both." James stripped down to his underdrawers and stepped into the water. "I would advise you to remove your riding boots."

"The sight of you taking off your clothes robbed me of my senses. I didn't realize I was still wearing them," she confessed. She took off her boots and sat down on the edge of the pool with her feet in the water.

James took hold of her corset strings and pulled her toward him. She opened her legs and wrapped them about his waist. His hands slid beneath her bum cheeks, and he carried her out into deeper water.

"It's so warm and inviting."

He brushed his lips against her brow. "Mmm, and the water feels lovely too." He groaned as he brushed his palm along her tempting thigh. "With your long legs wrapped about the small of my back, I could stay this way forever."

It was Anne's turn to groan. "You make me feel utterly desirable."

The wet slide of skin produced liquid tremors until they were both almost drowning with need. James was well aware that desire was capable of overcoming every scruple of what was right and proper. He forced himself to think of her innocence. This was supposed to be a swimming lesson, not an exercise in foreplay and arousal. He removed his hands from her thighs and spoke as a tutor rather than a lover. "I want you to learn how to float. I'll place my arms beneath your back so you won't sink. If you fill your lungs with air, it will make you buoyant."

She took a shuddering breath and tried to focus her thoughts on his instructions. When her body threatened to sink, she was immediately reassured when she felt her back come in contact with his strong arms.

"It's a matter of confidence. Put your head all the way back and trust me."

Within minutes, Anne was floating.

"To propel you backward or forward, gently waft your hands as if they were fins."

She did as he suggested, and to her amazement began to float away from him.

He followed her slowly and gave her a thumbs-up sign to add to her confidence. "You don't need me anymore. All you have to do, if you feel yourself start to sink, is put your feet on the bottom and stand up."

She began to laugh and brought her feet down. "How did such simple logic elude me?"

"Perhaps your thoughts were filled with flights of fancy rather than the task at hand."

She threw him a provocative smile. "You stole my senses."

"Can you recover them long enough for that swimming lesson?"

"Does it involve touching me?" she asked hopefully.

"Not intimately. I place my hand beneath your chin to keep you from swallowing water, while you move your limbs in imitation of a frog."

"Show me how."

As James cut smoothly through the water to the deep end of the pool and returned to her side, Anne watched him, mesmerized by his male beauty. *He could have posed for the Roman statues in the villa's gardens.*

"You make it look so easy."

"There's a first time for everything."

"Yes . . . I know," she teased. "I'm looking forward to all my lessons."

With infinite patience he instructed her until she was

able to take a few strokes on her own without sinking. He rewarded her with a lingering kiss. "You'll have to dry yourself, sweetheart. I don't trust myself with a towel."

When they arrived back at the villa, the servants were stirring and appetizing aromas were coming from the kitchen.

"If you hurry, you will have time to change and be in the breakfast room before Alexandra arises, and none will know the scandalous things we've been up to." He cupped her shoulders, drew her close, and pressed his lips to the damp curls on her brow.

"Must you leave now, James?"

"I must. I have things to do. I'm going to start looking for a house for us."

"You have a house."

"That's just a town house. I'm talking about a big house, with a garden, and stables, and a nursery of course. When you become Lady Hamilton, I want you to be a full-time wife and mother. Isn't that what you want, my beauty?"

"Yes. With all my heart."

Chapter 21

"It's out of the question!" Richard Curzon-Howe stared fiercely across his desk at James Hamilton. "How you have the barefaced effrontery to ask for my daughter's hand in marriage is beyond me."

Though James was both shocked and offended at Earl Howe's vehement reaction to his proposal of marriage, he masked his emotions. He remained silent in the face of the man's outrage, knowing that Anne's father had not finished his tirade.

"I have given approval for my daughter's marriage to John Claud Hamilton, with whom she has had an understanding for years."

"With due respect, my lord, Lady Anne has assured me that she has no intention of becoming my brother's wife," James stated firmly.

The earl's face contorted with anger. "It is obvious that during John Claud's absence in Ireland, you have gone behind his back and tried your utmost to seduce my daughter. 'Tis unconscionable!"

"I assure you, Lord Howe, that I would never attempt to seduce Lady Anne. I have only the highest respect for your daughter. I asked her to become my wife, and she has accepted my proposal."

The earl jumped to his feet and thumped his fist on

his polished desk. "And I, sir, am refusing it! I will never consent to a marriage between you. Your morals stink to high heaven; your reputation as a womanizer is as legendary as the profligate prince you serve."

James Hamilton stood up, and bowed his head politely. "Good day, my lord."

James felt as stunned as a bird flown into a wall as he left Grosvenor Square. This was in stark contrast to the way he had felt when he arrived for his appointment with Anne's father. He had been on top of the world, brimming with confidence that he had finally decided to marry the beauty with whom he was in love. The decision felt so right; he wanted to spend the rest of his life with Anne, and he was overjoyed that she felt the same way.

As he made his way to his town house in White Horse Street, he laid the blame for his thwarted plans squarely on the rigid shoulders of Richard Curzon-Howe. James was highly offended at the accusations the earl had hurled at him, and self-righteously denied that he was in any way to blame for the scandalous things that were circulated about him.

By the time night descended, however, his innate honesty forced him to admit that there was perhaps a grain of truth in the fact that his morals had not always been of the highest standard. Where Anne was concerned, however, his intentions were above reproach, and he truly believed that it was completely unfair to be dismissed out of hand by the sanctimonious earl. He paced about his study, as one thought chased another.

Lord Howe completely rejects me as a son-in-law, but would welcome John Claud with open arms. How bloody ironic is that?

I am heir to the dukedom of Abercorn. Any other noble in England would consider it an honor to give me his daughter in marriage! After a moment's reflection he admitted, *Trouble is, I don't want the daughter of any other noble in England.*

James opened the window and leaned on the sill, going over every insulting word Earl Howe had flung at him.

I have given approval for my daughter's marriage to John Claud Hamilton.

James crashed his fist on the windowsill. "God in heaven, both of us must have asked Anne's father for her hand in the same week, and the earl has given his consent to my brother!"

Lord Hamilton, who was never at a loss when presented with a problem, found himself with a dilemma on his hands that would be hard to resolve. Of course it was all the more difficult that John Claud was his brother, and not some random suitor. *Difficult perhaps, but not impossible,* he vowed.

Though the hour was late, James retied his cravat and donned his jacket. He took a hansom cab to Hampden House, and opened the door with his own key. Inside, the house was quiet and in semidarkness. He was on his way to his brother's bedchamber when he spotted a light coming from beneath the library door. He quietly opened it and found John Claud sitting behind the desk.

"I see the member from Londonderry is burning the midnight oil to catch up on his parliamentary paperwork. Politics comes with responsibilities. You'll soon get used to it."

"What the devil are you doing here at this hour?" John Claud asked warily.

"I came to see you."

John Claud threw down his pen. "What's this about?"

"A few days ago I asked Lady Anne Howe to become my wife. She said *yes*."

John Claud jumped to his feet. "Damn you, James. I proposed to her the day I returned from Ireland at the Royal Academy of Arts."

James closed the distance between them. "And I believe her answer was *no*." He placed his hands on the desk and leaned forward. "In spite of her refusal, you have somehow managed to get her father's approval."

John Claud sneered. "Earl Howe has made it plain that he has chosen *me* for his daughter's husband."

"That is irrelevant. Lady Anne has not chosen you for her husband. She has chosen me. Tomorrow, you will go to the earl and withdraw your offer."

"And if I refuse?"

"I'll beat the shit out of you." James reached across the desk and grabbed his brother by the throat.

Rising fear caused John Claud to gabble. "I didn't ask him for his daughter's hand. I told him I'd proposed to Anne, and admitted she hadn't accepted me."

James loosened his hands and demanded, "Then why did he tell me that he had given approval for his daughter's marriage to John Claud Hamilton?"

"Oh my God, you asked him for Anne's hand in marriage, and he *refused* you?!" John Claud began to laugh. "Well, well, James, it seems we are at an impasse. She won't become my wife, but without her father's consent, she won't become your wife either!"

The look of contempt James gave his brother would have shamed a more ethical man, but John Claud relished his role of *dog in the manger*.

The library door opened and their mother looked from one son to the other. It was obvious they were having an altercation of some sort. She knew that when young men engaged in heated quarrels, the source of their conflict was usually a woman, and she was almost certain it was Anne Howe. In her wisdom, however, Lady Lu knew better than to interfere between brothers.

"I apologize for disturbing you, Mother. I was just leaving."

"Apology accepted, James. Make sure the door is locked."

Two dozen invitations to Princess Alexandra's garden party had been issued and accepted by the leading ladies of the *ton*. The number of guests who arrived, however, was greater than twenty-four, as Anne and Frances had predicted, since both mothers and daughters of those invited had begged to be included.

Anne was delighted when her mother arrived, driving her own carriage. She took great pride in formally introducing the Princess of Wales to Countess Howe, and was particularly pleased when Alix asked her mother to sit at her table.

Anne and Frances greeted Caroline Chandos, who came with her widowed grandmother, the Dowager Countess of Harrington, in tow.

"Thank you so much for the lovely invitation. My grandmother is simply dying to meet Princess Alexandra."

"How do you do, Lady Harrington. If you come with me, I'll present you now." Anne hid her amusement. *No doubt the dowager will sing the praises of Caroline in hope the Princess of Wales will appoint her as a lady-in-waiting.*

The prime minister's wife rubbed shoulders with the Duchess of Abercorn, and her titled daughters Harry and Trixy, the Countesses of Lichfield and Durham. Even thirteen-year-old Maud had persuaded her mother to let her attend the tea party.

Frances led them to a table beneath a chestnut tree, and rolled her eyes. "I warrant there are so many Hamiltons here, there won't be enough cucumber and watercress sandwiches for the other guests."

Lady Lu waved her hand. "Then let them eat cake, darling."

Anne and Frances greeted their friend Florence Hastings, who had arrived alone, and invited her to sit with them at their table.

"I was hesitant about coming to the garden party today. I feared everyone would be gossiping about my husband. The rivalry between Henry Chaplin and Hastings has intensified to an alarming degree. Last week at Tattersall's auction they were trying to outbid each other on a racehorse called Hermit. It turned into a bidding war between the two of them. Hastings bid the astronomical sum of *two hundred thousand pounds*; then Henry Chaplin, determined to outdo him, offered *two hundred and fifty thousand*."

"Well, think of the money your husband saved," Frances said.

Florence pressed her lips together. "The Prince of Wales cheered when Henry Chaplin outbid my husband for Hermit. Hastings has been in a drunken rage ever since."

"I'm so sorry, Florence. Frances and I should never have encouraged you to marry him. We thought you were in love with each other."

"Hastings didn't love me. It was rivalry, pure and simple, that was driving him. I don't think men are capable of love."

You're wrong, Florence. Anne thought of the rivalry between James and John Claud, and dismissed it immediately. "I'm glad you decided to come today. An afternoon with your friends is just what you needed."

Florence smiled brightly and shook off her cares. "This Thames-side villa is so inviting. It's the perfect place for a garden party."

The tables were set with fine Irish linen, Georgian silver, exquisite Meissen porcelain with its delicate birds and butterflies, and Venetian crystal glasses. Every table had a large centerpiece of fragrant flowers cut that morning by the proud head gardener, Harry Hargrave, and artistically arranged by Lady Elizabeth. And at each place setting was a delicate camellia from the conservatory.

All the fashion-conscious ladies had ordered new gowns for the occasion, but all agreed that the Princess of Wales, wearing crisp white muslin, whose sash matched her blue silk parasol, had never looked more elegant. One or two of the ladies speculated, behind their fans of course, whether Princess Alexandra was already with child. It would certainly explain why she was spending the summer in such a tranquil setting, rather than accompanying the Prince of Wales on the racing circuit.

The guests strolled about the Italian gardens, admiring the sculptures of the naked Roman gods, and exclaiming over blossoms in the orange orchard. Most were agog over a visit to the pagan temple dedicated to the goddess Venus, where sandalwood incense burned on the altar and a pair of colorful lovebirds flitted about among the whimsical wind chimes.

Lady Lu declared to her daughters, "Venus is the goddess of love, beauty, and fertility. Thankfully, we have all three." On the way out of the temple, she spied Lady Anne, who was wearing a gown of leaf green muslin and carrying a white silk parasol. "My dear, you look absolutely beautiful. You are radiating happiness."

"Thank you, Your Grace. I do feel exceptionally happy today." She smiled at James's mother, knowing it wouldn't be long before the Hamiltons learned her secret. *Perhaps Lady Lu has already guessed.*

The guests seemed reluctant to leave and the sun had begun its descent before the ladies decided to take their leave. Anne spied her mother entering the villa with the princess and hurried to catch up with them. When she saw Lady Elizabeth sorting through the post, she said, "I heard so many compliments about your lovely flower arrangements. They made the tables look delightfully festive."

"Thank you, my dear. The tea party was a resounding success." She held up a few envelopes. "Some of the acceptances are only just arriving. It's a good thing we assumed everyone we invited would turn up."

Anne laughed. "Not many people turn down a royal invitation."

"The post delivered a letter for you, my dear."

Anne's pulse began to race as she took the envelope from Elizabeth. When she saw it was from James, she was filled with joy. *My first love letter!* She tore open the envelope and took out the note, breathless with anticipation.

Her eyes focused on the beautiful script: *My darling Anne.* Her mouth curved as she read the endearment. Her smile faded as she continued to read.

> *It pains me to tell you that when I formally asked your father for your hand in marriage, he refused me outright.*
> *He informed me that he has given his*

approval to John Claud, with whom you've had
an understanding for years. When I informed
him that you had accepted my proposal, he
became adamant.

I deeply regret your father's objection to me,
and will do whatever I can to persuade him to
accept me as a son-in-law. It may take a little
time before we can announce our engagement,
but my resolve is firm, and I know I will prevail.

You are my every desire. I will not allow
anything or anyone to come between us.

Anne gasped and closed her eyes. The pain in her breast was so acute it felt as if her heart were being crushed.

"Are you all right?" Elizabeth asked.

Anne opened her eyes. "No . . . yes. Please excuse me, I have to find Mother." She hurried through the Summer Parlor and found Alexandra and her mother in the pillared drawing room. Clutching her letter, she looked from one to the other. "Your Highness, I would like your permission to return to London with my mother. I need to speak with my father on a most important matter."

"Of course, Lady Anne," Alexandra said, gracious as always. "You don't need my permission to visit your home."

"Thank you so much." She turned to her mother, saw the startled look on her face, and hoped she wouldn't start asking questions until they were in the carriage.

Anne's emotions were in such turmoil she didn't hear her mother thank the princess for the most enjoyable garden party she had ever attended. As the pair walked toward the stables, she put the letter back in its envelope and warned herself to calm down. Anne was deaf to her mother's questions. *This has to be a simple misunderstanding. Once I explain matters to Father, all will be well.*

Anne sat perched beside her mother as she drove the small carriage down the Great West Road to London.

"Is the letter from your father, darling? Are you keeping something from me?"

"No, no, it's not from Father. But I need to talk to him, urgently."

Lady Howe sighed. Anne was acting strangely, and didn't seem willing to confide the reason she needed to dash home to London to talk with her father. She picked up the pace of the horse and schooled herself to patience.

When they arrived in Grosvenor Square, Anne pressed the letter into her mother's hand. "Read this, it will explain everything." She picked up her skirts and hurried into the house.

"Father, Lord Hamilton has asked me to be his wife, and I have accepted his proposal."

Richard Howe stared across his library desk. His daughter's green muslin dress and her red curls emphasized the Irish blood of her mother, and at the moment it annoyed him beyond bearing.

"I forbid it!"

Anne raised her chin, dug her fists into her hips, and demanded, "Why?"

"I can think of no young noble with a more unsavory reputation. He is unfit to be the husband of any daughter of mine."

Anne was stunned. Then she remembered the things he'd said at the Royal Academy.

"The prince surrounds himself with dissolute friends." Hellfire! He was talking about James.

"John Claud Hamilton is the young man I have chosen to be your husband. He's been devoted to you for years—he is like a son to me, and it has always been understood that you would marry."

"I assure you it has not been understood by me! I think of John Claud as a friend who is almost like a brother to me. I have no intention of marrying him, and I have recently made that quite plain to him. If he insinuated anything different, he was lying!"

"John Claud was completely honest with me. He told me you had not accepted his proposal, but that he had high hopes."

"He has no hope in hell!"

The earl rose to his feet. "How dare you stand before me, swearing like an Irish washerwoman?"

"No *bloody* hope in hell, and neither have you. I am in love with *James* Hamilton, and I intend to be his wife."

"I will never give my consent, and that's my last word on the matter."

Anne spun on her heel and dashed from the library. As she flung the door closed, she knew she was angrier than she had ever been in her life. She saw her mother standing in the hall and Anne followed her into her sitting room.

"He has a closed mind!" In complete exasperation, she threw her hands in the air. "He refuses to listen to reason!"

Her mother handed back her letter. "You didn't go about things very well, Anne. You are going to have to learn to handle the male of the species much better than that if you want to get your own way."

"I was being honest. I told him I refused to marry John Claud Hamilton because I was in love with his brother James."

"You don't get anywhere being honest with a man, darling, especially a peer of the realm. They believe their word is law."

"You mean I shouldn't have lost my temper."

"You catch more flies with honey than with vinegar. Raising your voice and railing against him will gain you nothing. Believe me, Anne, I speak from experience. You must learn how to get what you want in this world."

"But how?"

Anne's mother shrugged a shapely shoulder. "There *are* ways. . . . Manipulation, negotiation, you often have to give something to get something. Everything has its price."

"That sounds so cynical."

"Life has made me cynical, darling."

"Mother, will you plead my case for me? Will you try to persuade him to change his mind? You know how to get around him."

"I'll try my best, Anne. But these things take time. My advice is to go back to Chiswick and try to be patient. If you stayed here, it would just exacerbate the matter."

"I certainly won't stay here. I'll sleep at Marlborough House tonight and return to the villa tomorrow."

"I think that's a wise decision, my dear."

"He's very angry. Will you be all right?"

"Don't worry. I know how to placate him." She rang the bell for Jenkins. "I'll get the coachman to drive you to Marlborough House."

Anne gazed at her reflection in the mirror on the wardrobe door. The muslin dress that had made her look so vivacious that morning was no longer crisp. It was limp, exactly the way she felt.

There was a knock on the door, and when she opened it, she recognized the chambermaid, who had come to see if Anne would like a late supper tray brought up. "That's very thoughtful, Mary. Princess Alexandra held her garden party today. I've had my fill of sandwiches and iced cakes. Just bring me whatever is handy in the kitchen—some soup, perhaps. But first, what I'd really like is a bath."

Anne lay in the scented warm water, feeling lethargic after her outburst of temper earlier in the evening. Her heart was heavy, and she just wanted the world to go away.

Her father's words about James filled her thoughts and a wave of disgust swept over her for the earl's hypocrisy. *When scandal erupted about his affair with Queen Adelaide, he ruthlessly used my mother as a pawn. He knew she was carrying his son's child and arranged for him to be shipped abroad. Then it was all hushed up. Yet he accuses James of having an unsavory reputation!*

I should have thrown his hypocrisy in his face. Yet she knew she had kept silent for her mother's sake. She loved her deeply, and could never betray her.

Eventually, the water lulled her and reminded her of their sojourn in the Roman bath. *Thank heaven I grabbed the pleasure when it was offered. We may not get the chance to be alone again for a long time.*

The water was almost cold by the time she summoned enough energy to climb out of the bathtub and dry herself. She put on her bed robe and returned to her chamber. A few minutes later, Mary brought her the soup. When she lifted the lid of the silver tureen, she saw that it was leek soup. Her memories brought a lump to her throat; then she smiled through her tears. *Oh James, my love, it's as if you've conjured this for me!*

When Anne finished the soup and the warm bread rolls, the forlorn emptiness inside her had lessened to a marked degree and she was beginning to feel hopeful again.

She picked up his letter from the bedside table and went over to the desk. She dipped in her pen and began to write.

> *My darling James,*
> *When I got your letter I was filled with happiness. When I read it, my heart stopped beating. I was outraged that my father refused your honorable offer of marriage.*
> *I immediately left Chiswick and returned home to confront him. I told him that I had accepted your proposal, and when he said he expected me to marry John Claud, I made it plain that would never happen.*
> *When he refused to listen to me, I left in anger. Mother promised to plead my case, counseled me to return to Chiswick and exercise patience.*
> *Your firm resolve gives me comfort and hope. James, please know that you have all my heart. Yours alone,*
> *Anne*

Chapter 22

"I got your urgent note and came immediately. Is something amiss, Your Highness?"

"No, no, James, nothing amiss. I just wanted to share some ideas I've had."

James thought ruefully of the unfinished paperwork he'd left on his desk at White Horse Street to come rushing to Marlborough House at the prince's summons.

"Sykes's country estate in Doncaster is exactly the sort of place I need. The house is large enough to accommodate all his friends, and the property is unbelievable—thousands of acres where he breeds horses and dogs, and the hunting is spectacular. I don't mind admitting how much I envied him by the time my visit was over."

"A hunt every day and a house party every night, I take it?"

"Exactly!" Teddy was oblivious to the mocking tone of his friend's voice. "First night on the journey home, Carrington and I stayed at King's Lynn in Norfolk, and it suddenly occurred to me that Sandringham, the country estate my father purchased, was in Norfolk County. When I made inquiries, I learned that it was less than seven miles away!"

"So I assume you decided to pay Sandringham a visit."

"I did indeed, James. The place is ideal for my needs. More rooms than I could count and it sits on twenty thousand acres of prime hunting land. It's an absolutely perfect residence for the late summer and autumn months. I shall be the envy of all my friends once they see it. They'll kill for invitations to Sandringham."

"I hate to throw cold water on your plans, sire, but you will need Her Majesty's permission to stay at Sandringham."

Teddy cleared his throat. "Yes, well, that's where you come in, James. I thought perhaps your father could broach the subject with her. Abercorn has always had great influence with the queen."

"Next time I am at Hampden House, I will mention it to him."

"James, it is already July, and I'd like to be at Sandringham for the month of August. There's only a skeleton staff of royal servants. We'll need to hire a full staff and stock the stables and buy hunting dogs before I can send out invitations to my friends."

When you say "we," you mean "me." In your mind it is already a fait accompli. "Since it is July, I take the liberty of reminding you that it is over a month since you've seen Princess Alexandra. A visit to Chiswick would not be remiss."

"You're right, of course. We'll go tomorrow, right after we drop in at your father's office. You don't mind driving, do you, James?"

"Not in the least." *I haven't seen Anne for almost a fortnight. I'm starving for the sight of her.*

James had replied to the note Anne had pushed under his bedchamber door at Marlborough House. They had missed each other by hours, and when he read that she had been there the night before, his imagination played a game of *What if?* When he wrote his reply, however, he told her that he was glad she had returned to Chiswick. He wrote that though it made him happy she had informed her father of her intent to marry him, he advised that she would be wise not to confront him again. He emphasized that they must both exercise patience and assured her again that his resolve was firm and he would prevail.

"James, I have every hope that Abercorn will prevail with the queen. We'll get Christopher Sykes to provide the horses for Sandringham from his Doncaster breeding farm."

"Well, it is by no means certain that she will give her permission, but my father does have excellent diplomatic skills." James changed the subject. "Have you forgotten about the plans you asked me to make for the Cowes yacht races, Teddy?" He steadied the horses as the road curved at the bend of the Thames.

"Of course not. I'm looking forward to it. Did you have the 'Prince's Cup' made?"

James nodded. "It's ready at the silversmith's. But Cowes Week is in August. You can't be in two places at the same time."

"Cowes Regatta starts on the first Saturday, which happens to be the first day of August. We can sail over on Friday, July thirty-first, present the cup on Saturday, sail back on Sunday, and go straight up to Sandringham."

"Providing Her Majesty gives you permission," James cautioned. *You are so accustomed to getting your own way since you became a married man, you simply take everything for granted as your due. There's always someone to do the donkey work for you. There are times when you are insufferable. I warrant I preferred the old, unsure, long-suffering Teddy.*

James drove through the gates and stopped the carriage in front of the villa. When the Prince of Wales alighted, he drove to the stables, then strolled back through the lovely Italianate gardens, remembering the pleasure he'd enjoyed on his last visit.

"Edward, I must thank you for finding this villa. It is so tranquil here in Chiswick. It's one of the happiest summers I've ever had."

Teddy's gaze swept over Alexandra and for the first time he realized she was an attractive woman. His eyes lingered on her breasts, which seemed quite shapely. He closed the distance between them, and drew her into his arms. His hand came up to fondle her breast; then for good measure he cupped the other one.

Alexandra's breasts were tender and she tried not to flinch. She reminded herself that she had been free of his demands for well over a month, and this intimacy was a relatively small price to pay.

"I hope you won't be disappointed, but our plans have changed for Cowes. Instead of spending the entire week on the Isle of Wight, we'll only stay for the weekend. We'll sail over on the last day of July, when the lease expires on this villa."

Alix pulled away from him. "I'd rather you went alone, Edward. Sailing, especially crossing the Solent, makes me violently sick."

His wife's attraction quickly faded and Teddy lost his erection. "Just because you were sick last time doesn't mean it will happen again."

"I'm sorry, Edward, I seem to be prone to bouts of nausea lately, especially in the mornings."

Something clicked in the Prince of Wales's mind. His wife's rounded figure, coupled with her morning sickness, suggested that she was pregnant.

"My dearest Alix, do you suppose you could be with child?"

The princess blushed, and said softly, "You have guessed my secret."

"But that is wonderful news!" He led her to a comfortable chair. "Why ever would you wish to keep it secret?"

"I've been eager to share the news with you, Edward, but once I'm back at Marlborough House, so close to Buckingham Palace, the news will spread quickly. Perhaps it's wicked of me, but I don't want Her Majesty to step in and take over our lives."

"Yes, Mother not only enjoys ruling the Empire; she

insists on dictating to everyone around her. A grandchild would give her an excuse to intrude and foist her ideas of child rearing on us." He took the seat beside her and patted her hand. "The last thing I want for my son is the wretched childhood I had to endure."

"I'm so glad you understand, Edward. Of course, she will know eventually; that is inevitable. But I would love to be able to keep the news private for a few months."

"And so you shall, my dear Alix, so you shall." He surged to his feet, excited to tell her his plans. "On my way home from Doncaster, I decided to take a look at Sandringham, the country estate my father acquired in Norfolk County before he died. To my great delight I discovered it would make a perfect country retreat for us. The house has a great number of rooms and private suites, and it sits on twenty thousand acres of prime hunting land."

"A house in the country sounds wonderful, though I'm not sure where Norfolk is. There is a map in the study; would you show me?"

"With the greatest pleasure. Lead the way, my dear."

"This statue reminds me of you." Anne traced her fingers along the marble thigh of Apollo. "When I feel lonely for you, I come into the garden to admire him."

James caressed her cheek. "Legend has it that Cupid shot him with a golden arrow. We have that in common at least."

"In your last letter you cautioned me to be patient because you will eventually prevail, but I despair of my father ever relenting, James."

"I have written to him, asking for another chance to plead my case. Though he hasn't replied yet, you mustn't give up hope, Anne." James pulled her into his arms and she rested her head against his chest, drawing strength from his optimism. When his sister Frances approached, James continued to hold Anne close.

"I'm sorry to intrude, but Teddy sent me in search of you. He and Alix are in the study looking at a map, and

I'm afraid he needs your help to find what he's searching for."

James took Anne's hand. "Come on. For a man who attended Oxford and Cambridge, the prince has very little to show for it."

When they entered the study, known as the blue velvet room, they saw the prince poring over a library table with a huge vellum map spread out on its surface. "James, Sandringham has now become an absolute necessity. Alexandra is in need of a country retreat for the next few months, away from the prying eyes of Her Majesty."

Since there was only one explanation for the prince's words, James congratulated the royal couple. For the first time in his life, Hamilton felt envious of the Prince of Wales.

"Would you show Alix where Sandringham is located?"

James moved around the table. "This is a rather ancient map when Norfolk was part of East Anglia. Sandringham is on the sheltered coast of the Wash. It's perhaps ninety miles from London, as the crow flies."

The prince beamed. "But only thirty-odd from Newmarket."

"It sounds wonderful. Though I don't look forward to the long carriage ride, I should be able to stay put until the end of September."

James refrained from mentioning to the princess that the queen's permission was needed, but before he and Prince Teddy departed, he took Anne and his sister aside and explained the situation.

"Don't worry, James. Father will work his usual *Hamilton magic*," Frances declared.

James brushed his lips across Anne's brow. "I could use some of that *Hamilton magic* myself."

After Prince Edward and James departed, Anne told Alix that her husband would need the queen's permission to stay at the Sandringham Estate.

"Oh dear, Edward might as well stop wishful thinking. Why is there always a bee in the ointment?" Alix lamented.

"A *fly* in the ointment," Anne corrected, "although bee is most apt in this case, namely, a *queen bee*!"

"Your Majesty, I always hesitate to intrude upon your privacy, so allow me to express my gratitude for granting me an audience."

"You seldom intrude, James." Victoria set aside the dispatches she had been reading and indicated the chair beside her desk. "Do sit down."

"Your Majesty, I have had a confidential inquiry about Sandringham Estate in Norfolk. The law firm of Fulbright and Irwin represent a client who is interested in purchasing the property."

"My dearest Albert bought Sandringham as a country retreat. I wouldn't dream of selling it."

"I perfectly understand your sentiment, ma'am, but I would be remiss in my duty if I didn't point out the enormous cost of running a vast country estate that no one in the royal family ever visits."

"Some other solution must be found. I could never sell something that was precious to my beloved husband."

"Perhaps there is a way to lighten the queen's privy purse. From time to time the Prince of Wales has shown an interest in acquiring a country estate that offers good hunting. If he were given the use of Sandringham for the summer and autumn months, the upkeep could be paid out of his trust fund from the duchy of Cornwall. Prince Edward has amassed a sizable fortune over the years."

"That is an excellent suggestion, James. I knew you could find a solution if you put your mind to it." Victoria leaned forward and lowered her voice. "It will get Bertie away from his dissolute friends in London."

"You won't believe it, but Her Majesty has sent a carriage so you won't miss your monthly audience with her." Anne closed the chamber door so their voices wouldn't carry to her sister Emily, who was waiting below to escort the princess.

"I hoped being at Chiswick would excuse me from my dreaded command performance." Alix licked her lips nervously. "I should have known better."

"I'll invite my sister to stay for lunch. That will give us time to devise an outfit that drapes your figure, so the queen won't suspect you are carrying a child."

"Thank you, Anne. I hate to ask, but will you come with me to London?"

"Of course I'll come. You'll need a buttress against Emily."

Anne searched through Alexandra's wardrobe and then her own and finally chose a dark blue silk tunic that, without its sash, could be worn loose. Then she hurried below to join her sister for lunch, while Frances helped the princess with her toilet.

The lunch table had been set in the Summer Parlor on the ground floor, where Anne joined Emily, who was being entertained by Lady Elizabeth. Anne was wearing a white sprig muslin dress embroidered with blue forget-me-nots, and was ready for her sister's usual critical remarks.

Emily, however, was bent on discussing a far more personal subject. "The entire family was shocked at your outburst of temper with Father. Surely you know that he has only your best interests at heart? It is a father's duty to prevent a daughter from ruining her life, no matter how impulsive, willful, and headstrong she is."

Anne was momentarily taken off guard.

Elizabeth excused herself. "I'll just go and see what's for dessert."

"I thought my disagreement with Father was private. But obviously when I hit the monkey, the whole bloody zoo came out!"

"How *dare* you use such crude language to me?"

"I'll give you crude language. You are a jealous, vindictive snake in the grass. I warrant you almost swallowed your viperous tongue when you learned that James Hamilton asked me to marry him."

"Hamilton was always a depraved libertine. I informed Father that when I was a debutante, he tried to seduce me."

You vengeful bitch! You are the reason Father hates James. Anne threw back her head and laughed. "You are almost three years older than James. The way I heard it was that your pursuit of the fifteen-year-old was nothing short of shameful."

Emily's eyes narrowed. "Enjoy your little laugh at my expense, but I shall have the last one. Father will *never* give his consent."

On the carriage ride from Chiswick to London, the Princess of Wales, buttressed by Anne and Frances, chatted happily about the success of the recent garden party, while Emily sat in aloof silence.

When they arrived at the palace, the queen's lady-in-waiting marched ahead of the others and disappeared into the Audience Chamber, leaving the trio from Chiswick in the anteroom. Emily was gone for some time before she reemerged with a look of consternation on her face.

"Your Highness, since it is five o'clock teatime, Her Majesty graciously invites you to her private sitting room." She added, "This is a privilege not extended to many."

"Thank you, Lady Emily." Alexandra was surprised, but maintained her usual calm, serene demeanor that kept her thoughts and emotions well hidden. "Would you be good enough to order tea for my ladies while they await me?"

When Emily sketched the briefest of curtsies, it occurred to Anne that her sister was beginning to look like the sovereign she served.

When Princess Alexandra was shown into the queen's sitting room, she found her presiding over a well-laden tea table with enough sandwiches and seedcake to feed a dozen. She sat down in a chair that was slightly more comfortable than the one in the Audience Chamber. Victoria poured the tea, and a maid brought Alix the cup and saucer; then, at a nod of dismissal from the queen, the maid bobbed a curtsy and departed.

The princess took a few sips from the teacup, then arose and set it back on Victoria's tea table. She politely declined the sandwiches and cake.

"You should eat more, Alexandra. You are far too thin."

"Yes, Your Majesty." Alix inwardly sighed with relief and mentally thanked Anne for suggesting the loose tunic that hid her breasts.

"I hardly need ask if you are fulfilling your paramount duty as the Princess of Wales. Yet it is no surprise that you have not yet conceived when you and my son lead completely separate lives."

Alix opened her mouth, then closed it again, unable to offer a suitable reply.

"We have decided these unnatural living arrangements cannot go on. The royal family has a country retreat in Norfolk. I shall inform my son that he is to take his wife there for a few months, and hope that the conjugal atmosphere will produce results." The queen brushed crumbs from her black skirt. "Do I make my meaning clear, Alexandra?"

"Perfectly clear, Your Majesty."

When the princess rejoined her ladies-in-waiting in the anteroom, her serene smile was still in place. On the inside she was bubbling with happiness, but decided that she would wait until she was free of Buckingham Palace before she shared her amazing good fortune. It was almost dusk as the trio left the oppressive building and walked toward the waiting carriage.

"Was it very bad, Alix?" Anne asked with sympathy.

"Yes." The princess took a deep breath. "And no." Alix broke into a smile and instructed the driver to take them to Marlborough House.

When they were safely inside the carriage, she did a fair imitation of her dour mother-in-law. "I hardly need ask if you are fulfilling your paramount duty as the Princess of Wales. Yet it is no surprise that you have not conceived when you and my son lead completely separate lives."

"Thank heavens your secret is safe!" Anne let out a sigh of relief.

Alix laughed. "That's not the best part. Listen to this," she said, continuing her impression. "We have decided these unnatural living arrangements cannot go on. The royal family has a country retreat in Norfolk. I shall inform my son that he is to take his wife there for a few months and hope the conjugal atmosphere will produce results. Do I make my meaning clear, Alexandra?"

Anne and Frances whooped with laughter as the carriage pulled up at the front of Marlborough House.

Princess Alexandra eagerly opened the carriage door herself. "I can't wait to tell Edward the wonderful news."

That night Anne decided to have a tray brought to her room. She was pleased that Alexandra's problems had melted away, and wished with all her heart that her own plans could have a happy ending.

The encounter with Emily today had upset her, though she refused to dwell on it and had managed to push it aside as she accompanied Alexandra on her dreaded visit with the queen. But now that Anne was alone, a feeling of hopelessness stole over her as Emily's words echoed over and over in her head: *"Father will never give his consent."*

Anne picked at the food on her tray, then shoved it aside and ate the chocolate dessert. She suddenly began to laugh. *Emily was right. I am impulsive, willful, and headstrong. From now on I will make my own decisions. I refuse to let others destroy my happiness. Right or wrong my fate will be in my own hands!*

Chapter 23

A nne brushed her hair, donned a cloak from her wardrobe, and left Marlborough House. She walked to Pall Mall and took a hansom cab to White Horse Street. It was a short ride, but with each passing moment her excitement grew. She knew she was burning her bridges, but she simply didn't give a fig. *The heart wants what it wants!*

She rang the doorbell and thought it one of the loveliest sounds she'd heard in a dog's age. When Lord Hamilton's manservant answered the door, she gifted him with a dazzling smile. "Good evening. Grady. I will announce myself, so make yourself scarce."

Anne brushed past him and ran up the stairs. She threw open the library door and stood silhouetted in the frame.

James immediately stood up from his desk. "Anne, is something wrong?"

"Nothing is wrong—I simply couldn't bear to be away from you for one more day . . . or one more night."

"My sweetheart!" James moved from behind his desk and she ran into his arms. He picked her up and swung her around. "The sight of you fills my heart with joy." He took possession of her mouth in a long, lingering kiss, then set her feet back on the carpet.

"Has your father changed his mind?"

"Of course he hasn't changed his mind." She removed her cloak and threw it on a chair. "This is *my* decision. Why on earth did I wait so long?"

James brushed the backs of his fingers across her cheek. "My precious love, think carefully. If anyone finds out, your reputation will be ruined for all time. There's no going back. Are you sure about this?"

"I've never been more sure of anything in my life."

He let out a slow breath. "Thank God, I couldn't talk you out of it." He took possession of her hands and brought her fingers to his lips. "Now, first things first, my impetuous beauty. Have you eaten dinner?"

Anne laughed up at him. "I had dessert."

"Did it kill your appetite?"

"Not for a minute. I'm ravenous!"

"Come." He led her to the kitchen, and when he opened the oven door, the appetizing aroma that filled the air made her mouth water. She watched him take two dinner plates from the Welsh dresser and set them on a serving tray. He added linen napkins, silver forks, and a crystal saltcellar. Then he cut into the flaky crust of the steak and mushroom pie and put a heaping portion on each plate. "Food for the gods," he promised.

James picked up the tray and led the way to the drawing room. He set the food on a small table and pulled up two comfortable easy chairs. Then he poured them each a glass of red wine. She sat down immediately and picked up her fork. James sat facing her. "I've always loved watching you eat."

"I cannot imagine why."

"When you enjoy something, you always lick your lips, and that is enticingly erotic. Your appetite for food and the delight it gives you is a damn good measure of the enjoyment you'll take in other pleasures of the flesh."

Anne laughed merrily. "Pleasures of the flesh. That's what I *really* came for, Lord Rakehell. I fully intend to seduce the seducer!"

She devoured the steak and mushroom pie, licked her

lips, drained her wine, then came around the table and sat in his lap. "Now I'm ready for my dessert."

He pulled her against his hard body. "And I'm more than ready to serve you, my insatiable beauty."

Her breath caught in her throat as she melted back against him. His voice was rich, dark velvet, inviting, luring, compelling. The heat from his body leaped into hers, scalding, shiver inducing. Her heart raced in her breast as his lips whispered and lightly grazed her ear, and her pulse went so faint, she thought her heart had stopped beating.

He kissed her hard and swift, then stood up from the chair, put his arm beneath her knees, and lifted her against his heart. He carried her into his bedchamber and sat her down on the edge of the wide bed. An urge to ravish her immediately flooded over him while she was willing and eager. They'd get the pain behind them. But he checked himself with an iron will. He knew he must teach her how her body could give her pleasure, and how his body could increase that pleasure and bring her fulfillment.

James knelt before her and removed her shoes; then he reached beneath her sprig muslin and petticoat, slid his hands up her long legs, and slowly pulled off her silk stockings. He lifted her foot and pressed a kiss to her delicate instep; then he repeated the intimate gesture with her other foot.

Anne reached for the buttons on her dress.

"No, love, let me have the pleasure of undressing you. Though I've imagined doing it a thousand times, the reality is far more arousing to my senses than I ever dreamed possible." As he lifted off her dress, he closed his eyes. "I can smell forget-me-nots; I can taste forget-me-nots." When he opened his eyes, he grinned in appreciation. "To my great delight, your taste in undergarments borders on the indecent." Her pink nipples thrust temptingly through the centers of a pair of forget-me-nots embroidered on her lacy busk.

"When I'm designing underclothes, my imagination runs riot."

"At the moment, it is my lust that is running riot."

She licked her lips and murmured, "How devastating for you."

Anne's playfulness was one of the things he loved most about her, and he knew that he must do nothing to inhibit her the first time they made love. He reached behind her and undid the laces on her busk; then his hands gently cupped beneath her breasts, lifting them so that the pale curves swelled up from his palms. He dipped his head and blew his warm breath over the pink nipples, then touched each one with the tip of his tongue.

As they ruched into tight little buds, she drew in a quivering breath as threads of hot desire shot down through her belly, then all the way to her woman's center. She felt him shudder at the soft thrust of her nipples against his fingers.

"I want desire to build in all your lovely, scented, secret places."

"And I want you to be gloriously seduced."

He removed her busk; then his fingers unfastened the ribbons at her waist that held her petticoat in place, and he lifted it off over her head. She sat before him in only her drawers, naked to the waist. He cupped her upthrust breast with reverence. "You are as exquisite as I always dreamed you'd be."

"I want us to be naked together." She reached out her fingers to unfasten his shirt and brushed her palms across the hard, sculpted muscles of his chest.

"Then Lady Anne wants what I want," he teased. He pulled off his shirt, then removed his trousers along with his linen undergarment.

"Wouldn't it be wonderful if we always wanted the same thing?" Her eyes found his male center that jutted impudently from its nest of black curls.

James rolled his eyes. "Even your drawers are saucy. They are such fine lawn, I can see right through them to the red curls on your mons. Are you ready for the unveiling, Lady Godiva?"

Her eyes sparkled with mischief. "Just a minute."

Anne climbed up and stood on the bed, so that when he removed her drawers, the fiery curls between her legs would be at eye level. She saluted him and said, "Ready when you are, m'lord."

James grabbed for her and they went rolling across the bed, laughing like uninhibited children. When he came over her in the dominant position, his laughter faded, as he stared at her mouth hungrily. "It feels like I've waited forever."

"Not nearly as long as I've waited, you elusive devil. You stole my heart when I was twelve, and left me in a walking trance of hopeless infatuation."

"Such a long time," he teased, "you must be all of fifteen or is it fourteen?"

She pulled his hair. "I'm nineteen . . . I think. In any case, I'm old enough for you to make me a woman. If you're willing."

He nuzzled her neck. "I'm willing, ready, and able."

She reached between their bodies to glide her fingertips along his engorged cock.

"Mmm, I can feel that you are, m'lord. Teach me about foreplay, James."

He brushed the disheveled curls from her brow. "Even kissing has its own foreplay."

"Oh, good. I love it when we kiss."

"The different kinds of kisses are infinite. Let me show you." He lifted her hand and placed a kiss on each finger; then he opened her palm, placed a kiss in the center, and folded her fingers over it to keep it hidden.

They exchanged a hundred kisses. He began with tiny, quick kisses to her temples, eyelids, and the corners of her mouth. His lips kissed her hair, traced along her cheekbone to her ear, then down against her throat. She could not wait for his mouth to take possession of hers, and when it did, she longed for the kisses to lengthen.

For a whole hour, they lost themselves in slow, melting kisses. Their naked bodies pressed together, hot and sweet with passion, as the rough, soft slide of their tongues lit forbidden fires that snaked through their veins, awakening a thousand silken pleasure points. Slowly, his hands came up to cup her face; then his lips traced every enticing feature from temple to chin.

Anne duplicated his caresses, cupping his face, and setting her lips to cherish the planes and hollows of his dark beauty. Then his lips moved to her throat and shoulders, feathering kisses, nibbling her silky flesh, whispering love words.

By exploring and tasting her slowly, sensually, he was arousing and heightening all her senses. She nuzzled and whispered against his chest, inhaling the heady male scent of him, until she was ready to scream with excitement.

"Sweetheart, your legs are so deliciously long, they were made for wrapping about a man." At his inspired suggestion, she wrapped her long legs about his waist, crossed her ankles behind his back, and squeezed.

As he groaned with sheer pleasure, she swept her arms about his neck and kissed him deeply, thrusting her tongue in and out in a gesture that mimicked how she wanted him to thrust his body into hers.

"Not yet, love. You think you are ready, but I must make sure." James slid his warm hands down her silken thighs and caressed the soft skin; then he cupped her mons and she arched into his hand as he teased the tiny folds with one strong finger. He stroked in and out until he felt her begin to get slippery.

Anne gasped with pleasure. "That feels so exciting. I love the feel of your hands on my body, James."

He lay back and rolled with her until she was in the dominant position above him. He positioned his hard length in the hot cleft between her legs. She moaned with need and moved her slippery cleft up and down his long, hard shaft. Her head fell back and her throat and breasts arched with her sensual movements. She was becoming fully aroused and began to kiss him wildly.

"Lower yourself onto me, sweetheart. Take your time. Only do what makes you feel wonderful. Stop if you feel I'm too big."

Anne, almost panting with need, slid over him and pressed down until about half of his erection was buried inside her. She felt so hot and tight that James almost came out of his skin. He rolled her gently, so that he was now on top of her and she lay captured between his thighs. He thrust down until he was seated to the hilt. Then he remained motionless to let her get used to the fullness inside her.

Anne drew in a quivering breath, amazed that they were finally joined as one.

James whispered hot love words. They poured over her, making her melt. Then he began to move, slowly and firmly at first; then taking his cue from the pleasurable cries she made, he began to thrust faster and deeper. He felt the hot, wet pull of her around his throbbing sex, and then he felt her climax.

He arched above her, felt his seed start, and withdrew immediately. He cupped her mons with his warm hand and held her until all her delicious pulsations were finished.

Anne buried her face against his chest and heard his heart beating wildly. They lay still, savoring the sensual feel of their bodies entwined together, breathing in the delicious male and female scent of their mating, and tasting the potent wine of their kisses.

The wonder of being together kept them from sleep. Neither of them wanted to waste one minute of the joy of lying together in the wide bed. They whispered, and caressed, and laughed, and licked, and kissed with such abandon that they were amazed when dawn began to lighten the sky.

James slipped the gold signet ring from his little finger and placed it on her ring finger. "With this ring, I thee wed. With my body, I thee honor. Darling Anne, I'll love you forever. Thank you for the precious gift you gave me."

She stretched languorously. She had never felt like this before, never even dreamed what it would feel like to have her heart overflowing with happiness; her body replete from his loving.

James lay on his side, head propped on his hand, and gazed at her, entranced. "You are so beautiful, it's sinful!"

Anne blushed. "You make me feel beautiful. I suppose I need a bath, but I don't want to wash your scent from my skin."

James sat up, then knelt behind her and pulled her against him. "Don't worry," he whispered, and bit her ear. "I'll put it there again anytime you like."

"In that case, I will have a bath. Is your tub big enough for two?"

"Only if I hold you in my lap."

"I wouldn't have it any other way." She watched as he rose from the bed in all his dark, naked splendor. The muscles of his chest, covered by black hair, and his thighs, thick as tree trunks, looked more solid than rock. His superb masculinity made her feel extremely delicate and feminine. In that moment, she felt pity for every other woman she knew, especially Alix.

"Oh, I forgot to tell you. The queen has given her permission for the prince and Alexandra to go to Sandringham."

James clenched his fists and cursed under his breath. "Damnation, any minute now a messenger will arrive to summon me to Marlborough House. Being at the beck and call of the Prince of Wales can be bloody inconvenient."

"Don't tell me you will have to go to Norfolk?"

"I'm afraid so, sweetheart. And most likely I'll have to leave today. Teddy wants to be there for August. I'll have to hire a full staff of servants, buy horses and hunting dogs, as well as grooms to look after them. Since he wants to show Sandringham off to his friends, the place will have to be stocked with food and drink, and all the amenities that a royal prince of the realm is expected to provide."

"James, thank heaven I followed my instincts and came to you last night. If I'd waited just one more day, you would have been on your way to Norfolk."

He came to her and threaded his fingers into her hair.

"I won't see you again until August. It will seem like an eternity." *Unless, unless . . .* An idea came to him. *If I have only half the persuasive gifts of my father, I should be able to pull it off!*

"Let's hurry with that bath, my beauty. Time is of the essence."

At Marlborough House, Anne slipped upstairs to her room and changed her clothes. She took the gold signet ring from her finger, threaded it onto a fine gold chain, then fastened it around her neck. The ring, now hidden beneath her dress, came to rest between her breasts. She then hurried downstairs to join Princess Alexandra in the breakfast room. "I'm so sorry I'm late, Your Highness."

"You're not late, Anne. I only just arrived myself. Edward couldn't stop talking about Sandringham. He's already making a list of guests he wants to invite."

"Where's Frances?"

"While we're here at Marlborough House, she decided to get the maids to start my packing for Sandringham. Then she's going to pack her own clothes. That way we will be able to leave from Chiswick, and won't have to return to London."

"That's a marvelous idea." Anne selected a russet apple from the fruit bowl. "I'll go up and get my own clothes packed."

"I'll be up shortly. This is the first day I've been able to face breakfast for weeks."

Just as Alexandra was finishing her second cup of chocolate, James Hamilton arrived in the breakfast room.

"Good morning, James. I must thank you for all you do for us. I know that Edward has charged you with the responsibility of making Sandringham Estate ready for our August arrival."

"It will be my pleasure, Your Highness. I will make sure you have a couple of well-mannered riding horses that are worthy of you. I feel comfortable selecting household servants, cooks, and kitchen staff, but personal maids who will serve you are a bit out of my range of expertise. I think perhaps that if one of your ladies accompanied me, she would be much better suited to this task."

"That's an excellent idea, James. She could also make sure Sandringham has enough linen and other amenities that would make our guests' wives comfortable. I'm sure your sister Frances would be happy to accompany you."

James stared at her, for once at a total loss for words.

Suddenly, Alix began to laugh. "I'm teasing you, James. I know perfectly well which lady you would like to accompany you. As a matter of fact, she's upstairs packing. I assume you're leaving today?"

His eyes glittered with amusement. "You assume correctly, Your Highness."

Chapter 24

"When Alix asked me if I would go with you to San-dringham to select some suitable maids and make sure the estate was ready to receive female guests, I couldn't believe my good fortune. Then it began to dawn on me that you likely put the idea into her head."

James grinned as he tooled his horses along the Great North Road. "*Mea culpa*. However, I think that the Princess of Wales is a romantic at heart. The idea of throwing us together seemed to titillate her."

Anne threw him a saucy glance. "It certainly titillates me."

"Then I take it you have no regrets, sweetheart?"

"My only regret is that it took so long. I should have gone home with you the night of the masquerade ball."

"Memories of that night will stay with me forever. You told me that I would never offer you marriage, but I proved you wrong, my beauty."

"Marriage isn't as important to me these days," she said lightly.

His face turned serious. "It is extremely important to me, Anne. I want you to be my wife more than I've ever wanted anything before. Trust me to find a way."

When they reached Cambridge, James decided to stop for lunch at the Eagle, an inn that had been built in the sixteenth century. Afterward, while the horses were watered and rested, they went for a walk along the River Cam. It was busy with punts being poled by university students, whose carefree laughter filled the sunny afternoon.

James and Anne strolled along the riverbank with their arms about each other. "This is such a lovely place, and the best part of being here is that no one knows who we are."

He dipped his head to kiss her, but that only whetted their appetite for more, so they stretched out on the grassy bank, trying to satisfy their need to touch, and whisper, and embrace in the glorious sunshine.

Finally, James sat up. "Come on, if I don't stop, I will get arrested for indecent exposure."

Anne looked up at him and laughed. "I thought it was called outdoor fucking."

James rolled his eyes. He loved her bawdy humor. "Though difficult, it will be prudent to wait until dark."

They entered the Sandringham Estate grounds through wrought-iron gates, then continued along a winding driveway for at least a quarter of an hour before the house came into view. When they first saw Sandringham, the sun was setting, and it made the soft red brick and stone look warm and inviting.

Anne gazed at the bay windows, towers, and gables. "Oh, James, it's lovely! It's more manor house than palace. I think Alexandra will be enchanted."

"It's no wonder Teddy was excited when he saw the place. Will I let you off at the front door, while I go and stable the horses?"

"No, no. I'll come with you; then we can enter together. For the next couple of weeks, let's pretend it's ours!"

"We don't need to pretend, sweetheart; it *will* be ours."

While the carriage was stopped in front of the house, James unloaded their trunks, then drove on to the stables.

The stable block was large, with its own coach house, and pigeon lofts above. James noted that there were both large and small carriages, as well as coach horses to pull them, but there was a dearth of riding horses, a situation he would have to rectify. He spoke with the stableman, Daniel Hingham, and made sure there were oats for his matched pair.

When James and Anne entered the house, they were met by the housekeeper, who bobbed them a curtsy and told them her name was Roydon.

"I'm delighted to meet you, Mrs. Roydon. I am James Hamilton, an envoy for the Prince of Wales, and this is Lady Anne Howe, who serves Alexandra, Princess of Wales, in a similar capacity."

"Pleased to meet you, milord, milady. I had the honor of meeting His Royal Highness when he visited Sandringham."

"Prince Edward was most impressed by the estate. He and the princess have decided to make Sandringham Estate their country home. They will be arriving in early August, and Lady Anne and I are here to make it ready to receive them."

Mrs. Roydon looked worried. "Will they be bringing their own servants, milord? I only have a skeleton staff."

"We will be hiring a full staff of new servants, and your help will be invaluable to us, Mrs. Roydon. Of course they will all report to you in your capacity as head housekeeper."

When Mrs. Roydon lost her worried look and began to preen, Anne thought, *James has such diplomatic skills he could charm the ducks off the pond.*

"Does Sandringham have a cook?" he asked.

"Not a professional cook, milord. My daughter Ethel and I prepare the meals." She hesitated. "Beggin' your pardon, but we aren't prepared to serve nobility, such as yourselves. We're braising some herons that Mr. Hingham shot on the mudflats."

James smiled. "Heron is a delicacy to anyone from London. We don't need a formal tour, Mrs. Roydon.

Lady Anne and I will enjoy exploring Sandringham ourselves."

The housekeeper bobbed another curtsy and hurried off to the kitchens to spread the amazing news, and see what else she could find in the larder.

"Just look at this great main hall, it's longer and wider than any I've ever seen," Anne exclaimed. "And the walls are painted in Alexandra's favorite shade of blue."

"The carpet is rather magnificent. All this space will accommodate some sofas and at least a dozen more comfortable easy chairs."

On the right of the great hall they passed by the library. The bookcases, desk, and chairs were light oak from an earlier time, and a welcome change from the dark, heavy Victorian furniture that was now in fashion.

They passed through a morning room, whose pale gray walls were painted with Highland scenes. "I wonder how many rooms there are."

"Well over a hundred, I warrant, and far too many to visit tonight. I have other things I intend to explore," James declared. "Let's go upstairs and take a look at the bedchambers, before it gets dark."

To their delighted surprise they found that the east wing had many adjoining bedchambers. "How very convenient," James teased. "It's as if the house has been waiting to welcome us."

"I like this room with the ivy-framed windows, and pale green carpet." When Anne pulled back the covers to check the bed linen, she detected the fresh scent of lavender.

James opened the adjoining door and they entered the other chamber together. The wide bed and heavy mahogany chest and wardrobe declared it a man's room. James drew Anne into his arms. "Custom-made for lovers."

After a lingering kiss, he firmly set her aside. "I'll go down and get our trunks. I don't imagine Mrs. Roydon is up to hauling luggage. I'd better employ a couple of strapping footmen. Teddy travels with two valets, but they're too prissy to lift anything heavier than a shoehorn."

An hour later James and Anne, sitting across from each other, were served dinner in a small family dining room with an open hearth. They hadn't the faintest idea if they were eating heron or horse, since all they could think of was the moment they could withdraw from the world, shut their bedchamber doors, and carry on where they had left off the night before.

Their anticipation grew apace with each minute that ticked past. When their fingers touched across the table, heat leaped between them and they felt as if they would go up in smoke. James made love to her with his eyes, caressing her sensual lower lip with his smoldering glance. He hungered to take the pins from her hair and have the red-gold mass slide through his hands. Anne felt the unmistakable heat of arousal at the curve of her belly. When Mrs. Roydon brought them dessert and Anne didn't touch it, James knew that the only thing they hungered for was each other.

"You go up first. I'll have a word with Hingham at the stables." James made a point of thanking the house-keeper for dinner, then bade her good night.

When he arrived at the stables, he checked on his horses. He saw that they'd been fed and watered and were settled for the night, so he joined Daniel Hingham in the carriage house. "Soon, most of the stalls will be filled, so we are going to need grooms to tend the horses and stablemen to keep the place clean. We can use boys to polish the harness."

"There's two dozen empty stalls, Lord Hamilton," Hingham pointed out.

"Yes, and we'll likely put them all to use. The Prince of Wales prefers to be surrounded by his friends, all of whom will be expected to be provided with a mount for hunting. The prince has a friend in Doncaster who owns a breeding farm. In a couple of days horses will be arriving and you can help me sort the grand from the bland. In the meantime, let it be known that Sandringham will be employing stablemen."

Hingham touched his cap. "Right ye are, milord."

*   *   *

Upstairs, Anne opened the windows and lit the lamps in both bedchambers, and left the adjoining door open. Then she unpacked and hung everything in her wardrobe. When there was still no sign of James, she undressed, donned a white silk nightgown, and slipped into bed to wait for him. The anticipation made her breathlessly excited, because she now knew that the reality of his loving was a thousandfold more thrilling than her daydreams had ever been.

When she heard a noise in the adjoining chamber, Anne felt her toes curl. Next thing she knew, James lifted off her covers, swept her up in his arms, and carried her through to his room. He stood her on his bed and turned up the lamp. "I'm hungry for the sight of you, and starving for the feel of you."

She saw by the lamp's glow that he was already naked, and wrapped her arms about his neck. Then she felt his strong hands slide up inside the silk nightgown to caress her legs and thighs, and come to rest possessively on her bottom cheeks.

"Your bum is deliciously round and firm. I'm tempted to lay hands on it whenever you are within touching distance, no matter who is there to see. I'm constantly having to tamp down my desire."

"Now you don't have to," she said breathlessly, "and neither do I."

James lifted off her nightgown and let it drop on the carpet beside the bed. His hands moved to her waist and he pulled her toward him so that he could kiss her belly. She shivered as the tip of his tongue circled her navel, and dipped inside. Then he drew back so his eyes could focus on the red-gold curls that covered her high mons. "You have no idea how often I've pictured your honeypot, and longed to taste it."

She drew in a swift breath wondering if he was serious about doing such a wicked thing, but before she had time to exhale, James dipped his head and slid his tongue into the sensitive cleft at the tip of her mons. When he began to lick her, a surging wave of arousal made her arch into his possessive mouth. She opened to him without regret or reservation and allowed him to thrust into her honeyed sheath. The rough-soft slide of his tongue made her cry out as the exquisite sensations made her breathless with passion.

James felt fire snake through his groin as her cleft opened to the satin slide of his tongue and he felt his cock begin to throb. He withdrew his mouth and blew on her curls. She laughed down into his dark face, falling more in love with him every minute.

"Enough foreplay, my beauty, ready or not, I need you now."

"Ready when you are, milord."

He pulled her down on the bed. "Wrap your legs around my back." He thrust into her hot center, and then he kissed her. His lips were firm, slanting across her mouth, caressing, coaxing, molding, generously giving and selfishly taking all at the same time.

His tongue plunged into her honeyed mouth, moving in unison with his hard cock, and the hot driving thrusts made her writhe and moan as he unleashed the fierce desire that had been riding him for months.

Tonight her climax came hard and fast; then she was stunned when she became aroused again, almost immediately. This time the pleasurable sensations went on and on as she slowly climbed to a peak, and then the night exploded in hot shuddering tremors and she lay beneath him in wonder as she realized she could feel his heartbeat inside her own body.

They clung together in the warm nest they had thrashed out in the massive bed, savoring these precious moments when they could lie naked together. She smiled across the pillow into his eyes. Strangely, she felt no guilt that they had become secret lovers. Anne was filled with a sense of rightness and perfection, and the overwhelming contentment that filled her heart.

With his body curved about her back, her bright head tucked beneath his chin, Anne finally drifted off to sleep.

Next thing she knew, it was dawn and James was carrying her back to her own bed. When she protested, his lips brushed the disheveled tendrils that curled on her brow. "You never know who might be about at an early hour, especially once the house is filled with servants."

Suddenly, her eyes flooded with tears and she buried her face against his shoulder. "James, you wouldn't have to do this if I'd been able to get my father's permission for us to marry."

"Hush, love, hush. The only thing that matters to me is that you love me." Incredibly, it was true. His heart was singing. His senses were dizzy from her close proximity. He kissed the tears from her eyes; then he kissed her mouth, realizing that by nightfall he would be starving for her.

"Today I plan to visit all the nearby villages to get the word out that we will be hiring a large indoor and outdoor staff for Sandringham," James announced when Mrs. Roydon served breakfast in the small dining room with the open hearth.

"I would like to pass the word among my relatives, if you have no objections, Lord Hamilton. I have a large family of brothers and sisters who would give their eye-teeth for a chance to work at Sandringham."

"I would greatly appreciate it, Mrs. Roydon. You can tell them that we will pay better wages than any of the other estates in the vicinity, and while we're on the subject, I imagine you would welcome a rise in pay yourself."

"Oh, your lordship, how very generous you are." The housekeeper was all smiles.

"Much as I would like to see the surrounding villages, I have decided to stay at Sandringham today, Lord Hamilton." Anne and James made a point of addressing each other formally to allay any suspicion that they were lovers. "I need to make myself familiar with the layout of the rooms, and take stock of the linen, the tableware, china, and silver. I'll also need to see the servants' quarters to make sure there is adequate accommodation for a large staff." Anne stood up from the table. "I believe I'll start with the kitchen, pantry, and larder, if you'll be so kind as to lead the way, Mrs. Roydon."

Anne decided to make notes as she toured the myriad rooms. She also made a list of things that must be purchased immediately, and another list of things that could be acquired in August and September, while the royal couple was in residence.

The housekeeper provided her with all the sources of food provisions Sandringham would need, since it had no home farm to supply it, and the prince expected seven-course meals. Since they were on the coast, fish and shellfish would be no problem, but they would need a reliable source for milk, eggs, cheese, poultry, beef, and lamb. Of course, once Prince Teddy and his friends arrived, their hunts would provide the table with an abundance of game and fowl.

"We'll need the services of seamstresses right away. I'll design a simple gray dress with white aprons and caps for the maids, but we'll need people to sew them. Are there any tailor's shops in the vicinity?"

"I think you'd have to go to King's Lynn for those services, Lady Anne."

"Well, that's no great distance. But we would need them to stay at the estate for a few weeks. We cannot send all the new staff we will employ to King's Lynn." There were so many things to think about that Anne's mind was racing ahead. Not only were there products the household would need; there were things the staff would require. She also had to keep in mind items that both male and female guests would expect, and most important of all she must focus on the comfort of the Prince and Princess of Wales.

"Mrs. Roydon, it would be a great help to me if you'd make a list of items you'll need such as silver polish, beeswax to make the furniture shine, and vinegar to clean all the windows. In the meantime, I'll be off on my tour of the house."

Anne was pleasantly surprised when she arrived at the master suite on the second floor. It consisted of two large bedchambers, two dressing rooms, a bathing room, and a sitting room. Since it was freshly decorated and had new bedroom furnishings and hangings, she surmised that all had been done after the late Prince Albert had purchased Sandringham.

In the afternoon, Anne decided it would be better to tour the rest of the house with James. She went outside to view the lake to the west of the house, and walk beneath the ancient oak trees. When she discovered an enchanting walled garden behind the house, she longed for James to explore it with her. She decided to curtail her exploration of the gardens until they could do it together, and walked across the grounds to Sandringham's own parish church, St. Mary Magdalene. She was enthralled to discover a host of carved, painted angels, and knew at the first opportunity she would bring James to see them.

"I hope I'm in time for dinner. Something smells good, and I've lots to tell you."

"It's partridge tonight. Apparently the estate is teeming with game."

"That will make Teddy happy, I'm sure." His eyes licked over her, telling her in unspoken words that her presence made him happy.

"The house is amazing. I want to show you the master suite, but I left a lot of chambers unexplored so we could see them together. The gardens are fascinating also, but each time I discovered something, I wished you were there to see it with me."

"Pleasure shared is pleasure doubled," he murmured with an insinuating wink.

Mrs. Roydon served them the partridge, along with roast potatoes, peas, and watercress salad. Anne ate the bird with her fingers, and James watched in fascination.

"It's delicious, but Ethel is only used to preparing one course, which will be totally inadequate for the prince. I think you should write and advise him to bring his chef."

"That's the only solution. I want to advise him about the convenience of traveling by train, as well. It takes less than five hours from London and would be much more comfortable for Alix than being jostled about in a carriage."

"Did you make any progress today?"

"I visited the villages of Heacham and Hunstanton. I stopped at all the inns and public houses to spread the word that Sandringham Estate would employ any and all who were willing to work for royalty."

Anne laughed. "We'll be inundated by scores of villagers."

"We'll need a score of servants to run this place. It's a good thing Teddy's coffers are full. I put in an order for ale to be delivered every week, but things like champagne, and even a good claret will have to be ordered from London."

When the housekeeper left the room, James reached for Anne's hand across the table. "When you were licking your fingers over your partridge, I wanted to sit you in my lap and feed you." He took her hand to his mouth and bit her fingers.

She took her hand back quickly. "Biting isn't allowed." Her eyes sparkled with mischief. "Licking, however, I might consider."

"I'll hold you to that, Lady Anne."

After dinner they walked through parts of the house they hadn't yet seen. On the ground floor they discovered a billiard room, a smoking room, two gun rooms joined by a weapons corridor, and a long bowling and skittles alley. Down the opposite side was a ladies' gallery for walking, with fine paintings and portraits on the walls.

"Tomorrow, I am taking you to pay a visit on our neighbors at Houghton Hall."

"Who are they?"

"Houghton Hall was built by Sir Robert Walpole, Britain's first prime minister. His descendant George, Marquis of Cholmondeley, and his wife, Susan, live there now. It's only fitting that we tell them the Prince and

Princess of Wales will be taking up residence for August and September."

"What's the real reason we are going?"

"Do you suspect *all* my motives?"

"Of course not—just most of them."

"Walpole constructed the mansion and supposedly filled it with magnificent treasures, yet the estate today provides a relatively small income. The marquis just might be open to selling off some of their fine possessions."

"I can't wait to see Houghton Hall. Are there any other country estates in Norfolk?"

"Actually, yes. Walpole's younger brother Horatio built Wolterton Hall, but it's a bit farther afield in Norwich."

"Then for the time being I'll cross that one off my list of things to do, and before you ask, I really do have lists."

"For everything?" James rolled his eyes suggestively.

"Come to think of it, yes. But my imaginary list is too scandalous to put on paper."

"Ah, it must include some of that licking you mentioned," he teased.

"You'll just have to wait and see, won't you?" Anne changed the subject. "While it's still dusk, and before it gets completely dark, let's go outside. There's something I'd like to show you."

Anne led the way to the back of the house and opened a wooden door in a stone wall. "This is a walled garden. It's so completely private in here, it must have been designed for lovers." The fading light and shadows lent the garden a romantic aura, and the night-scented flowers were giving off their exotic perfume. "You can hear the fountain that splashes into a water garden. It's too dark to see now, but beneath the lily pads the water is teeming with tiny colored fishes."

James drew her into his arms. "The garden is telling me it's been too long since it's been asked to hide secrets of love." Just then they heard the night song of a nightingale.

Anne opened her lips to receive his kisses. The lovers clung to each other, kissing, whispering, touching, tasting. As their passion mounted, everything faded away until there was just the two of them, alone in paradise. "I wanted to show you the intimate stream walk I found, but I'll save that for tomorrow night."

Reluctantly, they left the walled garden and returned to the house. "You go up first. I'll go into the library and write that letter to Prince Teddy."

When Anne got to her bedchamber, it occurred to her that she should write to her mother and let her know she was at Sandringham, in Norfolk. She lit the lamps and sat down at the small writing desk. When she neared the end of the page, she wrote: *I likely won't see you until the end of September, but hope and pray that by that time you will have been able to work your magic and persuade Father to change his mind.*

When James came through the adjoining door, he was delighted that Anne was still dressed. Removing her gown, admiring her provocative underclothes, and pulling off her silk stockings was a ritual he loved. Tonight he decided to do it in front of her tall mirror to double their pleasure.

When the mirror reflected their naked bodies, emphasizing the contrast between male and female, hard and soft, large and small, dark and fair, they became immediately aroused and James knew they would never make it to his bedchamber. As always it became a wild, erotic love ritual, burning, thrusting, surging, pulsing, throbbing. James was all rippling muscle, all rampant, driving male. Anne was all silken, liquid heat, all scented, sultry sensuality. At their mutual, bursting implosion, lust melted into delicious, overwhelming love.

James cradled her against him with one powerful arm, while his fingers brushed the clinging tendrils of hair from her temple, then traced the lovely curve of her cheek and throat with his tongue.

At dawn they awoke in each other's arms, strands of red-gold hair entangled about James's throat. James groaned as he contemplated returning to his own bedroom. "When we are married, and sleeping in our own chamber, we will have a long, lip-licking breakfast in bed every morning."

"Followed by a lovely warm, scented bath," she murmured huskily.

Chapter 25

"Lady Cholmondeley, how generous of you to see us on such short notice." James took the slim woman's hand to his lips. His warm brown eyes conveyed the unmistakable message that though she was crowding sixty, he still found her attractive.

"Lord Hamilton, you may call me Lady Susan. *Cholmondeley* is such a mouthful." She smiled. "Even in the wilds of Norfolk, we have heard that the Prince and Princess of Wales will soon be in residence at Sandringham."

James knew that the news had traveled through the grapevine of servants. "Lady Susan, I'd like you to meet Lady Anne Howe, Princess Alexandra's most trusted lady-in-waiting, who has come to make sure everything is in readiness for Her Royal Highness."

"I'm delighted to meet you, Lady Anne. I am hopeful for an invitation to meet Princess Alexandra. Alas, this is likely our last journey to Norfolk. My husband's gout prevents him from walking or even riding these days. He will be much more comfortable at Cholmondeley Castle in Cheshire."

"I'm so sorry the marquis has problems with his health, my lady."

"Well, his legs may be impaired, but his *upper works*

are still functioning. George is in the great hall by the fire. Do come and meet him."

James and Anne followed Lady Susan into the hall and were greeted by the marquis, who was about seventy and sitting in a bath chair. "Hamilton? Now, let me see, you must be the Duke of Abercorn's heir. What?"

James smiled. "Absolutely right, your lordship. You must have sat with him in the House of Lords."

"Yes, your father is a good Tory, like myself."

During the next hour, the two men shared whiskey, and the ladies drank sherry. When James calculated that the marquis had imbibed enough to make him mellow, he broached the subject of being in the market to purchase furnishings for Sandringham. Since price was no object, James soon acquired two blue upholstered sofas, and eight leather armchairs.

When Anne admired two cherrywood writing desks, and a nest of matching tea tables, she was not surprised to hear James make an offer that was instantly accepted. But she had never expected him to talk them out of the beautifully polished grand piano.

"We have no children to whom we can leave our possessions," Lady Susan explained. "I'm quite tickled at the idea that Princess Alix will be playing my piano."

"What about silver services and things in that line? I noticed that Sandringham is singularly lacking in fine silver."

Lady Susan drained her fourth glass of sherry. "We have two full sets of silver services, complete with tureens and chafing dishes, that are packed away. We never use them because they are monogrammed with *W* for Walpole."

"I'd be happy to take them off your hands. Just name your price."

Anne smiled her secret smile. *James, you are so clever. W for Wales!*

"When will the royal couple be arriving?" Lady Susan inquired.

"Early August. They are hoping to stay for two full months."

"I wouldn't recommend them staying past the end of September. By October, we get the worst of the gales here on the coast."

"Thank you for the warning," Anne declared. "I shall pass your advice on to Princess Alexandra. And I won't forget about your invitation, Lady Cholmondeley."

As James and Anne walked to their carriage, she began to laugh. "You are a bloody marvel. When you offered to buy or rent any saddlery they could spare from their stables, I was dumbfounded."

James grinned down at her. "I'm about to acquire two dozen saddle horses. What the hell good are horses without saddles?"

On the way back to Sandringham, James drove through Heacham, secretly anticipating a reaction from Anne.

"James! Stop the carriage! Lavender fields stretching for miles. I never saw anything quite so lovely. Just breathe in the heavenly scent."

"When I saw them yesterday, I knew you would be enchanted."

"We must buy some. Now I know why the bed linen smells of lavender."

"If you start talking about bed at four in the afternoon, my beauty, how do you expect me to last until dark?"

"Oh, I just had a decadent idea, Lord Hamilton. How would you like to make love in a field of lavender?"

My God, she is so uninhibited. I absolutely adore this woman.

The following day, two dozen horses arrived from Sykes's breeding farm. The grooms who accompanied them put them in a large pasture behind the stables. "Lord Sykes sent more horses than His Royal Highness ordered with instructions to choose the ones you like and we'll take the others back to Doncaster."

With the help of Daniel Hingham, James checked the horses' teeth, fetlocks, and gait. He could tell that Sykes had chosen quality animals. The majority were hunters, but there were also half a dozen easy-gaited palfreys suitable for ladies. "Please thank Lord Sykes on the Prince of Wales's behalf. We'll keep all of them."

For the next few days, both men and women arrived at Sandringham Estate seeking employment. James interviewed all the men and hired any who had experience as stablemen, gardeners, or gamekeepers.

Anne, with the help of Mrs. Roydon, interviewed the women. Most of them were hired as housemaids, kitchen help, or laundresses, but Anne kept her eyes open for girls who were well-mannered and neatly groomed, who could serve Princess Alexandra in a more personal capacity.

Anne compared notes with James and reminded him about the need for uniforms. He agreed to drive her to King's Lynn the next morning. "While you are employing seamstresses, I'll try to find a couple of experienced carriage drivers. We should be back by afternoon when the furnishings from Houghton Hall will be delivered."

By the end of the first week, Sandringham Estate was busy as a beehive. All the furniture was being polished, the linen sheets on all the beds were changed, and the chambers plenished with toiletries, writing paper, towels, and chamber pots.

As James carried Anne back to her own bedchamber early one morning, he teased, "I thought you were simply a decorative female. I hadn't the faintest idea you had a domestic side. You will make someone a hell of a good wife."

"Mmm, if I ever decide to marry," she teased back.

"I think you need a break from all this domesticity, sweetheart. I'll saddle a couple of horses and we'll explore all twenty thousand acres of the estate. Who knows what secrets we'll discover."

"That sounds wonderful. I am ready to cast aside duty for frivolity."

He caressed her bare bottom. "You're always ready. That's one of the things I love most about you, my beauty."

An hour later they were riding around the large lake

that lay on the west side of the house. "I fancy another swimming lesson. I'd love to challenge you to a race from one side of the lake to the other." Her mouth curved in a smile. "I have visions of winning."

"By distracting me with your provocative undergarments?"

"I couldn't win unless I took advantage of your vulnerability. You would have to reveal the secret of your great strength. Playing Samson and Delilah could be most diverting."

"I believe debauchery appeals to you, Lady Anne."

"At heart I am a sybarite."

"So I discovered in bed last night."

"Your compliments always make me feel extremely feminine and desirable." She urged her palfrey into a trot. "Let's go this way. I want to show you the intimate stream walk. Like the walled garden, it must have been designed for lovers."

The tree-lined path followed a babbling stream that led from the lake. Rustic benches were tucked into alcoves between flowering rhododendron and fragrant rosebushes. Marble statues of naked nymphs and cherubs in playful poses peeped from borders of exotically scented flowers.

The path took them down a lush green dell where natural springs bubbled up through the grass, which was carpeted with marsh marigolds and water irises.

Anne gazed at the lush beauty before them. "This is an enchanting place."

"It reminds me of Barons Court in Ireland. I promise to take you there someday."

"Sometime . . . somehow . . . someway . . . someday," she said wistfully.

"Darling, don't be sad. I promise it will happen."

Anne tossed her hair over her shoulders, determined to banish the darklings. "Lead the way, James. There's lots more to see."

The estate encompassed over thirty square miles of woodland and heath. When they reached the open stretches of rolling hills, they galloped full out, sending coveys of woodcocks and grouse into the air. When they slowed to ride through the woods, they laughed as they encountered startled herds of deer that lifted their heads, then sprang off through the leafy green branches. They in turn disturbed flocks of warblers and brilliant golden orioles.

The acres of the estate were dotted with small lakes and ponds that attracted abundant small creatures such as rabbits, hares, stoats, weasels, and foxes, as well as ducks and wading birds.

James and Anne drew rein beside a rocky stream. They dismounted and allowed their horses to crop the tall grass, while they sat down on a fallen oak to enjoy the lunch that Ethel had wrapped up in a linen cloth. Laughing, they fed each other buttery scones, dried sausages, cold partridge, apples, and cider. Anne was thrilled when a curious red squirrel approached and boldly snatched the piece of scone she offered.

James brushed back her fiery curls and kissed her brow. "Even the *cratures* cannot resist you." He plucked a wildflower and tucked it behind her ear. "Queen Anne's lace."

In the afternoon they rode along the tidal mudflats of the Wash, then galloped across miles of empty sandy beach. They dismounted to wade in the surf and poke about in the tide pools, finding jellyfish, tiny crabs, and cockles. Then, hand in hand, they strolled along the shore watching terns and oystercatchers run before them, picking up crustaceans that the sea had left behind on the glistening sands.

They had heard about the glorious sunsets of the Wash, but as they stood together watching the bright golden sun sink toward the sea, the sky turned pink, then red, then deep purple. James and Anne were left in awe at the magnificent spectacle of nature they had witnessed. At the last moment, the sea swallowed the sun, and left them in complete darkness.

Back at Sandringham, during dinner, they discussed the things that still must be done in the short time that was left before the royal couple and their guests would be arriving.

"Tomorrow I have to visit a couple of kennels that have hunting dogs for sale." James finished his ale. "This stuff isn't bad. I should order a few more barrels."

"I have to make sure the uniforms are finished. Then I have to teach all the servants about the bellpull system. Some of the younger girls have never been in service before."

"We've accomplished quite a lot, though I'm sure there are things we've overlooked."

"I'm too tired to think about it. I had such a wonderful day today." Anne yawned. "The sea air has made me soporific."

"How I'd love to carry you up to bed," he murmured low. James cleared his throat as a new serving maid came in to clear the table. "I shall see you in the morning, Lady Anne. Good night."

"Good night, Lord Hamilton." Anne looked at the earnest young maid and didn't have the heart to tell her that she should not clear the table until the diners had left the room.

An hour later when James came through the adjoining door into Anne's chamber, his mouth curved tenderly when he saw that she had fallen asleep. He undressed quietly and slipped into bed beside her.

Without opening her eyes, she whispered his name. "James, my dearest love."

He enfolded her against his heart. "Go to sleep, sweetheart."

Grosvenor Square, London

"Her Majesty has informed Alexandra that she will no longer tolerate her living apart from Bertie." Emily gave her stepmother a triumphant glance. "Anne's idyllic days at the villa in Chiswick will soon be over."

Lord Howe's daughters from his first marriage were

at Grosvenor Square for dinner with their father before Adelaide and Georgiana departed London to spend August at their country homes.

"So long as the royal couple live separate lives, Queen Victoria realizes there will be little chance of Alexandra producing an heir to the throne," Emily continued.

"But surely the queen doesn't expect the princess to spend August in London?" Adelaide felt rather sorry for Alexandra.

"Her Majesty has informed her daughter-in-law that she and Bertie will be going to Sandringham, the country estate in Norfolk that her dearest Albert acquired before he died. She made it plain that she expects Alexandra to be breeding when she returns."

"Oh, that's splendid news. Sandringham is only thirty-odd miles from Apethorpe Hall. I fully expect an invitation for Fane and me."

"Norfolk is lovely in August and September. I'm sure the princess will be taking Anne with her," Georgiana remarked.

Earl Howe threw down his linen napkin. "I don't like the idea of Anne going to Sandringham. The prince will be inviting his dissolute friends and the very atmosphere will be conducive to licentious behavior."

Lady Howe felt her stomach knot. Only this morning she had received Anne's letter that she was already in residence at Sandringham. "Richard, surely you're not implying that Adelaide and Fane are dissolute because they are friends with the royal couple?"

"Of course not. But Anne's situation is entirely different. She's an unmarried lady."

And whose fault is that, you hypocritical swine? "I have every confidence that our daughter Anne will conduct herself with propriety at all times."

"I tend to agree with Father about Sandringham." Emily's face was set in lines of disapproval. "Anne will be exposed to the licentious behavior of the prince's close friends, such as James Hamilton."

You envious bitch! "If I remember correctly, Emily,

you panted after James Hamilton shamelessly when you were a debutante."

Emily's cheeks flamed. "He tried to take advantage of my innocence."

Her stepmother smiled. "How fortunate you were able to fight off his advances."

It was two hours before the earl's daughters said their good-byes and departed. Lady Howe sat in her dressing room and reread Anne's letter. The last sentence tugged at her heart: *I likely won't see you until the end of September, but hope and pray that by that time you'll have been able to work your magic and persuade Father to change his mind.*

She looked into her mirror and spoke to her reflection. "I was going to try to work my magic tonight, but there's little chance of my persuading him to change his mind now that Emily has planted her poisonous seeds."

Anne and James are alone at Sandringham. Knowing the frailty of human nature as I do, I'm not naive enough to believe they won't become lovers.

Lady Howe desperately wanted her daughter's happiness. Anne and James Hamilton had fallen in love, and the only person that prevented them from marrying was Richard Curzon-Howe, the same hypocritical swine who had deprived her of a happy marriage.

What if I told James the scandalous secrets of my marriage? If he confronted my husband and threatened to divulge what he knew, I'm sure Richard would capitulate.

Sandringham, Norfolk

"James, this is the end of our idyll. They'll be arriving tomorrow and we'll no longer have Sandringham to ourselves." Anne lay in his arms, her lips bee-stung from the kisses they'd shared, her body replete from his passionate lovemaking.

"It's not the end, sweetheart." He brushed his lips across her brow. "Our love is without end."

She pressed her cheek against his heart. "How can I bear to share you with others?"

"We will endure the days because of the promise of our nights. I will count the hours until we can withdraw behind closed doors and lock out the world each night."

Anne made a determined effort to push away any bad thoughts. "I'm just being fanciful. Our time together has been precious. I've never been happier. I refuse to let selfish thoughts steal my joy. When I wrote to Mother, I asked her to work her magic and persuade Father to change his mind."

His arms tightened. "When we return to London, I'll ask him again. I'll never take no for an answer."

Anne was on the verge of telling James about her parents' marriage. *If I give him ammunition against my father, I know he won't hesitate to use it.*

"James—"

"Yes, love?"

A picture of her mother came to her full-blown, and Anne knew she loved her too much to betray her. "Good night." She kissed his heart. "Dream about me."

"I always do, my beauty."

Chapter 26

"I'm so glad we came by train. I thoroughly enjoyed the scenery. We passed wheat fields ablaze with poppies, dozens of medieval churches, and rolling green hills dotted with sheep." Princess Alexandra smiled happily at Anne, as the carriage made its way from the railway station. "I can't wait to see Sandringham."

"All is in readiness for you," Anne informed her. "The chef from Marlborough House arrived yesterday with a mountain of pots and pans, and already the aromas coming from the kitchen are mouthwatering—a marked improvement from when I first arrived."

"My nausea has disappeared, so I'll be able to eat again."

"You look wonderful. You appear to be blooming with happiness."

Alix laughed and patted her belly. "I'm brimful of baby."

The carriage rolled through the gates, and the princess eagerly watched for her first glimpse of the country mansion. When the enormous redbrick and stone house came into view with its towers and gables, the princess exclaimed, "Oh, it's absolutely perfect! I know I'm going to be happy here."

"Did Frances come with you?"

"Yes. She insisted on waiting for all the baggage to be unloaded from the train. She was determined that my husband's luggage would not take precedence over mine in spite of the fact that Edward's valets think they rule the world."

"We'll get you settled and everything unpacked before the weekend, when your guests start to arrive."

"They're Edward's guests, not mine. He's the one who'll have to entertain them. Do you suppose we could serve dinner at seven rather than eight? I get sleepy very early these days."

"That sounds like an excellent idea. I'll get James to suggest it to His Highness."

Anne helped Alexandra from the carriage, eager to see the Princess of Wales's reaction when she entered the great hall.

The entire staff, wearing their new uniforms, was waiting in the entrance hall to welcome Princess Alexandra when she stepped through the front door of Sandringham.

"This is Mrs. Roydon, the head housekeeper." Anne brought her forward.

"Your Royal Highness." Mrs. Roydon curtsied, and the entire staff followed suit.

"I thank you all. I would like our country home to be a comfortable, relaxing place. I insist we dispense with the formality of curtsying and bowing."

The servants moved aside and Alix got her first glimpse of the great main hall.

"Oh, Anne! It's absolutely perfect. It's so spacious and inviting." She walked into the room and stopped. "Is that a piano?"

"I knew you'd like it."

"It pleases me beyond belief. I can see how much work you've done."

"It was a labor of love. Lord Hamilton of course deserves most of the credit."

Alix whooped with laughter. "Lord Hamilton, is it? And I suppose he addresses you as Lady Anne!"

"Come, let me show you the master suite. It has two bedchambers separated by a sitting room. It also has two dressing rooms and a lovely bathing room."

Alix leaned toward Anne to speak confidentially. "Sounds delightful. There is no longer any need for Edward and I to sleep together." Her eyes sparkled. "That makes us both happy."

From the moment the Prince of Wales arrived, he monopolized James. "The first item on the agenda is the horses Sykes sent. Let's take a look at them. I've invited Christopher to join us, so if he's palmed off any nags, he can damn well take them back to Doncaster."

James was confident that Teddy would be pleased, and waited patiently for him to decide on a mount for himself. The prince examined every animal, even had the grooms saddle a few so he could try them out, but in the end he chose a big bay gelding similar to the one James had bought him in Newmarket.

Next, Teddy inspected the pack of eighteen hunting hounds James had acquired, and declared them an excellent choice. "I want to get all the guns unpacked. I've invited Aylesford, Mordaunt, and Manchester, all avid hunters. Wait until they see Sandringham's gun rooms—they'll be pea green with envy."

James knew Manchester had not been invited for his hunting skills. He had been invited because his beautiful duchess was the mistress of Lord Hartington, Teddy's bosom pal who attended the races with him.

"Who else will be coming?"

"Well, Hartington of course, and Blandford Churchill. I forget who else. Oh yes, Charles Beresford, who was at Cowes. Henry Chaplin's coming, so I didn't include Hastings, his great rival."

"What about Carrington?"

"Charles accompanied me. I left him at the train station to make sure the guns were unloaded. He invited his latest lady friend—daughter of Baron Suffield, I believe."

"I'd better make sure everyone's name is posted on their bedchamber door, so there are no embarrassing mix-ups after dark," James remarked cynically.

Teddy winked. "Damn good idea, James. What would I do without you?"

Anne and James awoke each morning before dawn. It was the only time they had to talk privately before the demands of the day took every waking moment.

"The princess has truly fallen in love with Sandringham, both inside and out. She enjoys the freedom of riding every day, she walks the pair of spaniels that Lady Cholmondeley brought her as a welcoming gift, and she takes delight in filling the rooms with flowers and plants."

"Sweetheart, most of the credit goes to you for making it feel like a home, not just a house. It's a miracle to me how you trained the servants in such a short time."

"The young Norfolk women are so eager to learn, and they consider it an honor to be serving the Princess of Wales. I'm relieved that the prince took your advice and brought the chef from Marlborough House. The servants are in awe at the number of courses served at dinner every night. They secretly believe it the height of extravagance to serve oysters, two soups, whole salmon and turbots, sirloin of beef, saddle of mutton, along with turkeys and woodcock, and I agree with them."

"Teddy eats and drinks so much, he's getting rather portly." *His appetites are becoming rapacious for sex as well as food.*

"All the guests drink too much. It's fortunate that Alexandra's bedchamber isn't over the great hall. The racket they make at their nightly parties is scandalous, and sometimes they last until dawn."

"I'm glad that you and my sister retire with the princess shortly after dinner."

"Alix needs rest, and she has absolutely nothing in common with Teddy's friends. Lady Sarah Mordaunt is particularly vulgar and silly after a couple of glasses of champagne."

"She's young," James excused, "and Sir Charles likely doesn't give her the attention she craves."

"Doesn't he sit in the Commons with you?"

"Yes, but I can't like the man. He's been particularly ruthless with his Warwickshire tenants. He put them out of their cottages for joining the Labourers' Union."

"Why on earth does the prince like him?"

"Mordaunt is mad about hunting and shooting." *And Teddy is mad about Sarah.* James threaded his fingers through Anne's disheveled curls and lifted her face for a last kiss. "It's past time for me to seek my own chamber, sweetheart. I can hear the servants up and about."

One night during the last week of August, Anne lay in bed unable to sleep. The hour at which James was retiring had gotten later and later as the month progressed. The prince and his friends spent their evening hours bowling in the skittles alley, followed by endless games of billiards, and finally gambled for high stakes at faro or baccarat.

I'm so thankful that Alexandra is oblivious about how her husband and his friends entertain themselves after dinner every night. Her serene demeanor never changes. She is unfailingly polite to everyone, yet distant. Her health is blooming, she's thrilled about the upcoming birth of her child, she loves her animals and Sandringham, and that is all she seems to need to make her happy.

Anne's thoughts strayed to the female guests. *Cecelia Suffield is well-endowed; I suppose that's one of the reasons Charles Carrington is attracted to her. I can hardly believe that her family approves of her visiting Sandringham when she is unmarried.*

Anne turned over in bed and thumped her pillow. *I am being a hypocrite. My family wouldn't approve of my being at Sandringham if they knew what was going on between me and James.*

She pictured Edith Aylesford and Sarah Mordaunt. *Neither of them can keep their hands off any man who comes near them, especially James. At least the Duchess of Manchester seems to be faithful to the Marquis of Harting-*

ton, Anne thought cynically. She pictured Mina Gardner, who was engaged to Lord Charles Beresford. *She's so childish, constantly playing practical jokes on everyone, and her laughter borders on hysterical.* Sir Christopher Sykes had brought a lady called Liz Edgerton, whom he had introduced as his cousin. *Kissing cousin, if you ask me!*

Anne's thoughts moved to Henry Chaplin. *The viscount is oblivious when the females try to flirt with him. I suppose his heart still belongs to Florence Paget. He seems like such a decent young man, apart from his obsession with racehorses.* Anne yawned, and began to drift into sleep. *I wish Florence had married him instead of Hastings.*

James undressed slowly and lay down on his bed, deep in thought. Try as he might, he could not condone the profligate morals of the Prince of Wales. Teddy was having sex with at least two of the married women whose husbands he'd invited to Sandringham, and James suspected that one of them, Edith Aylesford, was also servicing the wealthy young Marquis of Blandford.

James knew that Louise, Duchess of Manchester, was putting horns on her acquiescent duke every night with Lord Hartington. Behind their backs they were referred to as the Duke and Doxie. *The adultery going on at Sandringham sickens me.*

James Hamilton's own behavior was pricking his conscience unmercifully. If he was being honest with himself, he realized that he left his own bed the moment his chamber door was closed. He knew it was time he faced the facts and acknowledged that he was compromising Anne's reputation. Just because it was a secret liaison did not make it right, and he could not bear the thought that he was placing her in the same league as the loose females who were enjoying the hospitality at Sandringham.

Anne was awakened by a noise she thought must have come from the adjoining bedchamber. She turned up the lamp and waited for James. When he did not come, she got out of bed, walked across the room, and opened the door.

James saw her silhouette framed in the doorway. "Anne, come and sit down, I have something to tell you."

She walked slowly to the bed and sat down beside him. "Whatever time is it?"

He took her hand. "It is time that I stopped compromising you, sweetheart. I'm coming to despise myself for doing so. You deserve so much better of me than playing musical beds. Parliament opens in a couple of days, so I've decided to return to London."

"You're leaving early?" she whispered.

"If I stay at Sandringham, the temptation will be too great for me to resist. Prince Teddy, surrounded by his friends, certainly doesn't need me." He touched his lips to her brow. "Our situation is intolerable and cannot go on. When I get back to London, I will press your father to change his mind."

"We'll be separated for a month. How will I endure it?"

"September will be over before you know it. In the meantime, I will do my best to resolve our difficulties." His fingers brushed away her tears. "Don't be sad, my darling. It breaks my heart." He lifted the covers. "Come into bed and let me hold you."

London

From the moment Parliament opened, James's uncle Lord John Russell, the foreign secretary, had to deal with the American Civil War. The Confederate army had ordered built two ironclad rams in Liverpool, and they were now ready to be delivered.

It took the foreign secretary a full week to persuade Parliament to detain the ironclads. Then it took another week for the British forces to stop the shipment of the two ironclad vessels from Liverpool. This effectively dashed the Confederates' hope for support from Britain.

It was the middle of September before James was free to attend to his personal affairs, and he penned a letter to Earl Howe, asking for an appointment. Another week went by, and when he had received no reply, James called at Grosvenor Square.

He presented his calling card to Jenkins, and was surprised to be shown into the drawing room, where he was greeted by Anne's mother.

"Lord Hamilton, how lovely to see you. I thought you were at Sandringham."

"I returned for the opening of Parliament. I wrote to Lord Howe and asked if he would see me. When I received no reply, I decided to pay a call on him."

"My husband is not at home at the moment. Lord Hamilton—James, please have a seat. Perhaps it's best that Richard is not here. A confrontation would gain you nothing."

"Lady Howe, my situation is intolerable. I am determined to do everything in my power to convince Anne's father to change his mind and agree to our marriage."

The countess gave James a look of speculation. "What you need is leverage. Has Anne never confided the story of how I was used as a pawn and forced into a loveless marriage?"

His brows drew together in a deep frown. "I assure you that Anne has never divulged anything of a personal nature about your marriage, Lady Howe."

"I'm surprised. If you knew the details, perhaps you could use them as leverage to persuade Richard to give his consent."

James stiffened. "You are suggesting blackmail."

The countess smiled. "And is blackmail against your moral code, Lord Hamilton?"

"Not at all, in certain circumstances. But I would hesitate to use it against my future wife's father. The breach might never be mended, and Anne may never forgive me if I used information about you to gain my own ends."

"To put her happiness before your own proves that you love her. Give me a few days, Lord Hamilton, and I will see what I can do."

"I thank you with all my heart, Lady Howe." James took her fingers to his lips.

*   *   *

"Darling, I have to talk to you about Anne."

Leicester Curzon-Howe kissed the beautiful woman he had loved for years, led her into the sitting room, and poured them each a glass of claret.

"At the end of June, Lord James Hamilton proposed to Anne and she accepted him. When Hamilton came to ask Richard for her hand, he flew into a rage and refused to give his consent."

"What was his objection?"

"He objected on *moral grounds*, for Christ's sake!"

"His hypocrisy is stunning."

"Anne and James are deeply in love. When I spoke with Hamilton a few days ago, I decided that my daughter's happiness was far more important than my own. I wanted to divulge things about my marriage that James could use to gain Richard's consent. But he refused to use information about me because it would hurt Anne."

Leicester rubbed the back of his neck. "Darling, there's something I haven't told you. Anne came to see me when she returned to London from the Isle of Wight. She told me that she knew Montagu was my son, and asked me point-blank if I was also her father."

"Good God, why didn't you tell me? Whatever did you say?"

"I told her that was not possible, that our love affair ended over twenty years ago when you married. She waved my words aside impatiently and told me that she had overheard us in your bedchamber. It must have been when Richard went to Gopsall."

Lady Howe's face went white with shock.

"I told her that I would never do or say anything that would hurt her in any way, and I meant it. When she demanded the truth, I told her that I didn't know if she was my child, but for her own peace of mind it would be best to think of Richard as her father."

"Leicester, whatever shall I do? My daughter's happiness is the most important thing on earth to me."

"*Our* daughter's happiness is the most important

thing to me, also. I shall take care of it, darling; please stop worrying."

"Leicester, to what do I owe the pleasure of this visit?" Earl Howe leaned back in his swivel chair behind his desk.

"I'm here to discuss Anne's future."

The earl's eyes narrowed dangerously.

"I understand that she has received an offer of marriage from Lord James Hamilton, and that she has accepted his proposal. Why have you rejected his offer?"

"Hamilton's reputation is unsavory. He is reputed to be a womanizer."

"Reputed by whom?"

"Your sister Emily has told me about Hamilton, and the things that go on at Marlborough House."

"Emily has been jealous of Anne since the day she was born. She is a vindictive bitch who glories in being spiteful and carrying tales to you."

The earl's jaw clenched. "Hamilton and the prince he serves are profligate."

"Whereas you and I are merely morally bankrupt," Leicester said with contempt.

The earl leaned forward in his chair. "How dare you? This is none of your business!"

Leicester too leaned forward in a threatening manner. "I am making it my business. I will not allow you to ruin Anne's future. I insist that you withdraw your objection."

"You have absolutely no say in this matter!"

Leicester stood up and smote the desk with his fist. "I have *every* say in this matter. Anne's mother and I refuse to let you destroy her happiness like you destroyed ours. I've let you pretend to the world that you are the father of Montagu and Anne, but we both know that you are *impotent*. I am the last child you ever sired." He modulated his voice, but the threat was implicit. "If you want this charade to continue, you will give this marriage your blessing."

Chapter 27

"I'm truly sorry to be leaving Sandringham. When the guests left in mid-September, we had the great hall and the gardens to ourselves. I was surprised that by month's end, the weather changed overnight. One day I was cutting roses and the next the cold wind was so fierce everything was withered." Alexandra looked out the train window as it neared London. "Edward is happiest when he's entertaining his friends. I imagine he is already planning who he'll invite to Marlborough House for the first party of the winter Season."

"Perhaps when you see the doctor, he will advise against too many parties." Anne had persuaded the princess to consult a doctor as soon as she got back to London.

"I don't want the queen's physician. I want a doctor of my own," Alix declared.

"Our family has been well served by Dr. William Jenner," Frances Hamilton told the princess. "We could arrange for him to see you at Marlborough House."

"That's a very good idea, Frances. I don't want Victoria to be there when my baby is delivered. I plan on telling her she will be a grandmother by March."

"You experienced morning sickness on the way to Newmarket, the first weekend of May." Frances counted on her fingers. "The baby should arrive sometime in January."

Alexandra smiled serenely.

Anne said, "That's why she wants the queen to think her baby will arrive in March."

"I saved you a seat, Lady Anne."

"Thank you, Lord Hamilton."

James stood behind her chair until she was seated in the formal dining room at Marlborough House; then he sat down between Anne and the Prince of Wales. Under cover of the tablecloth, he took possession of her hand and squeezed it.

As was his custom, the prince focused on his food and did not speak until the third course. "It was only a few days after you left Sandringham that Mordaunt packed up his guns and headed back to London. Seemed odd to me that they didn't stay longer."

Perhaps Mordaunt was offended by the attention you paid his wife. "Parliament sits in September, sire. Sir Charles took his seat in the Commons."

"Then a couple of days later, Aylesford and his wife left."

"Aylesford sits in the Lords," James reminded him.

"Ah, yes, I'd forgotten about the government."

James spoke low to Anne. "I paid a call to Grosvenor Square when I got back to London. Perhaps it was fortunate that your father wasn't at home. I spoke with your mother and she promised to see what she could do to make him change his mind."

"Thank you, James. I hope Mother can work her magic."

Teddy helped himself to a brace of roasted partridge he'd shot at Sandringham. "Too bad you allowed duty to call you, James, you missed the fireworks at Newmarket last weekend. Henry Chaplin had his horse Hermit entered, but his trainer said he's come up lame. Chaplin almost pulled him, but at the last minute decided to run him. His archrival Hastings wagered two hundred and fifty thousand pounds that Hermit would lose. When

Hastings lost the bet, the two men came to blows. It was great sport, I can tell you."

"But surely a loss of two hundred and fifty thousand pounds would wipe out his fortune," James said with concern.

Prince Teddy shrugged. "Just deserts for eloping with Chaplin's intended bride."

Anne was deeply concerned about her friend. "I must visit Florence. The Hastings live close-by in St. James's Place. She will be terribly upset over this, James."

"You must be careful, Anne. Don't go alone. Take Frances with you."

"That's a good idea. Will you be staying here tonight, James?" she asked, quietly enough so that no one else could hear.

"Better not, sweetheart. Too many eyes and ears."

"I'm sorry to disturb you, Alix," Anne said, carefully closing the door to the private sitting room. "My sister Emily has arrived from Buckingham Palace. She is delivering a letter from Her Majesty the Queen and insists she's been instructed to hand it to you in person."

"I didn't request an audience with the queen when I returned from Sandringham. I've been expecting a summons all week. Please show Emily in, and order us some tea."

Anne returned to the entrance hall where Emily sat waiting. "Her Royal Highness will see you in her sitting room." Anne was determined to show Emily more hospitality than she had been shown at Buckingham Palace. "The princess has ordered tea."

Alix greeted Anne's sister warmly. "Lady Emily, welcome to Marlborough House."

Emily did not curtsy, but she politely inclined her head. "Your Highness, I bring you a letter from Her Majesty Queen Victoria."

"Thank you so much, Lady Emily. Please sit down and join us for tea." She opened the envelope and took out the letter. "I shall read it immediately."

The serene smile remained on Alexandra's face as she read the missive. As she had expected, it was a summons for her to present herself to Victoria.

A maid wheeled in a tea cart, and Anne brought a small table and placed it beside her sister's chair.

Alix arose and moved to her writing desk. "Do have some tea, ladies, while I write a reply to Her Majesty's letter."

Anne busied herself pouring the tea, then helped herself to a couple of pink iced petits fours so she wouldn't have to make small talk with her sister.

Princess Alexandra dipped her pen in the ink and began to write.

> *Your Gracious Majesty:*
> *Thank you for your invitation to join you at Buckingham Palace.*
> *Because of your generosity in allowing Prince Edward and I to enjoy Sandringham Estate, it gives me the greatest pleasure to share our wonderful news. You may expect to be a proud grandmother sometime in March, next year.*
> *My doctor has advised me to reduce my social activities. I am sure you will understand why my delicate condition prevents me from resuming my monthly audiences with you at Buckingham Palace.*
> *Your devoted daughter-in-law,*
> *Alexandra, Princess of Wales*

After Emily left with her reply, Alix told Anne, "From now on, it will be my decision when I see my dearest mother-in-law."

"Anne, Frances, I'm so glad to see you." Florence invited her two friends upstairs to the drawing room. "I don't want the servants to overhear us, so I won't ring for tea. Will you have sherry instead?"

"Sherry will be lovely," Anne said. "We came because we were worried about you."

"Then you heard what happened at Newmarket?"

"Yes, we know that your husband lost an enormous amount of money at the races."

"It's all my fault—I'm the reason for the insane rivalry between Hastings and Chaplin. My husband's hatred for Henry Chaplin knows no bounds."

"It doesn't do any good to blame yourself, Florence," Anne said firmly. "If he's angry and drinking, you shouldn't stay here. Perhaps you should go home."

Florence laughed bitterly. "I reached out to my father, but my stepmother rules the roost. She said that I made my bed and now I must lie in it."

"You never should have let your heart rule your head, Florence," Frances admonished. "Blandford Churchill was at Sandringham, but I made sure I kept him at arm's length."

"But, Frances, your brother James was at Sandringham. Blandford wouldn't dare make improper advances to you," Anne pointed out. "Florence, I too allow my heart to rule my head. The heart wants what it wants, right or wrong."

"You mustn't worry about me. Hastings isn't here. He's gone to the Doncaster races to enter his horse Lady Elizabeth in the big race. He hopes to recoup his money."

"Well, I hope for your sake that he does. But high-stake wagers are addictive as well as dangerous. Please take care of yourself, Florence. If you need our help, Frances and I are only a short distance away at Marlborough House."

"I love you both. Thank you for caring about me."

For the next few days, Anne was busy designing dresses for Princess Alexandra that concealed her expanding waistline. "It's not just the style that matters; it's also important to select the right colors and materials," she advised Alix.

"Dr. Jenner warned me against tightening my corset

strings because it could harm my baby. Your looser-fitting designs are far more comfortable than squeezing into the outfits I wore last month."

Anne continually consulted with the sewing women. She took Alexandra's measurements often, and it was no longer necessary for the princess to have constant fittings for her clothes. Anne's days were filled with activities, but the nights seemed empty and endless, especially since James hadn't been to Marlborough House for a week.

I don't just miss him, I long for him. Alix retires after dinner most nights and the evening hours seem to drag on forever.

She had fallen into the habit of bathing around ten o'clock each night, and was in bed by eleven, often lying sleepless, hungry for the sight, feel, and taste of James.

Tonight, when she returned to her chamber after taking her bath, every inch of her craved for his touch and she refused to go one more hour without seeing him. Anne opened her wardrobe, slipped on her fur coat, and departed Marlborough House.

She cut through Green Park, crossed Piccadilly, and was in front of his town house on the corner of White Horse Street in less than fifteen minutes. She ran up the steps, lifted the brass knocker three times, and waited. It seemed to take forever for someone to open the door, and she was startled to see James. "Where's Grady?" she asked in surprise.

"Anne! It's not safe for a lady to be out at this hour. Grady is in bed, where you should be."

She gave him a saucy smile. "That's where I intend to be shortly." She walked past him and ran up the stairs. James followed, his eyes drawn irresistibly to her lovely slim ankles in spite of the fact that he thought her behavior reckless. Anne entered the drawing room and turned to face him.

He had been about to read his post when she arrived, but set the letters down unread. "Anne, it's wrong of me to compromise you. I'm going to put you in a cab and send you back to Marlborough House."

She ran the tip of her tongue around her lips. "Can't I make you change your mind?" She slipped off her fur coat and stood before him naked.

"My God, you are not just reckless, you are abandoned!" He enfolded her in his arms and groaned as his hands came into contact with the soft, silken skin of her back. "I should beat you for walking the streets naked."

"Do you have a rod?" she whispered, and bit his earlobe. "Ah yes, I feel that you do."

He swept her up into his arms, carried her to his chamber, and dropped her on the bed. He stroked his hand down the curve of her back. "Your lovely body has so many places that are irresistible to me."

"How many?"

"At least a dozen."

"Show me where they are."

He lifted her foot. "Your instep begs my kisses." He circled her ankle with his long fingers. "Your ankle is so delicate I can span it." His hand moved up her leg. "Behind your knee is an intimate place I love to touch."

His palm stroked up her belly and he dipped a finger into her navel. "A very private spot. I doubt anyone but me has ever touched it."

"You make me want to purr."

"Now right here, beneath your breasts, the flesh is so tender and silky, I like to nibble it." He traced one finger along her clavicle, then pressed his lips to the hollow of her throat. He dropped a kiss on each eyelid. "I can see the tiny blue veins when you close your eyes."

"That's only eight—show me the rest."

"The red-gold tendrils that fall on your brow always invite my lips." Then he lifted her hair and ran his tongue along the back of her neck. "So private." He lifted her arm above her head to expose an armpit. "So intimate." He touched his lips to the hollow, making her laugh. "And so ticklish."

He slid his hands beneath her bottom cheeks and curled his fingers into the cleft of her bum. "This spot is so sensitive it makes you shudder—it makes me shudder."

She slipped her arms about his neck. "Enough, James. You are torturing me."

He held his breath as the tips of her breasts brushed against his chest, and she wrapped her legs about him. "I'm in a fever of need, sweetheart."

When James thrust inside her, she arched her body as a wave of pleasure swept her from her breasts to her toes. He saw her eyes smoky with passion, her lips half-parted, waiting for his kisses. When he covered her mouth with his, and thrust his tongue in deep, she moaned with pure, sensual pleasure.

He began to plunge savagely with hot, drugging strokes until the night exploded. Fire snaked through his groin and as he spilled, a feral growl escaped his throat. They lay still, pulsating together in a mating that had been almost too intense.

The lovers lay whispering for an hour, enjoying their stolen time together. Then finally, James sat up and swung his legs to the floor. "I must get you back to Marlborough House. You'd better put on one of my shirts. I refuse to let you go back dressed in only your fur. That's too decadent even for me, you little wanton."

He took a clean shirt from his dresser, sat her up on the edge of the bed, and threaded her arms through the sleeves. Then he buttoned it. Then he donned his own clothes.

"Where's your coat?"

"I dropped it in the drawing room." She sighed and got up off the bed. "Do I really have to go?"

"Yes, you really, absolutely have to go. Come on." He took her hand to make sure she followed him. He bent to retrieve her coat from the carpet, and saw his forgotten letters. He held the fur and when she put her arms into the sleeves, he wrapped it about her. Then he picked up his post. "Hello, what's this?"

She heard the sharp interest in his voice. "A letter from a secret admirer," she teased.

"It's from your father." He tore open the envelope and quickly read the note. "He's asking to see me tomorrow at four."

Their eyes met and James saw her apprehension. After his last meeting with Earl Howe, he did not feel optimistic, but he masked his doubt. "It will be all right, love. I promise to be civil and won't lose my temper, no matter the outcome," he assured her.

As it turned out, Anne too received a note from her father in the morning post to come and see him. She arrived home at the appointed hour and was relieved to see James emerge from a hansom cab. Jenkins opened the door and they entered the house together.

"Welcome home, Lady Anne. Your father awaits you in the library."

When they entered the room, Earl Howe got to his feet, came around the desk, and kissed his daughter's brow. "It's good to see you, my dear." Then he held out his hand to James. "Lord Hamilton." He returned to his chair. "Won't you both be seated?"

Anne felt a tightness in her chest, and took a deep breath, bracing herself for what was to come. In spite of her father's civil greeting, the atmosphere felt formal and strained.

James waited politely for Earl Howe to speak first.

"I have decided to withdraw my objection to your marriage. I would prefer that you allow a decent interval between announcing the engagement and the date you set for the wedding. This will give my daughter time to make sure she is doing the right thing."

Anne closed her eyes and let out a long breath of relief. "Thank you, Father."

"Thank you for your understanding, Lord Howe. I, too, want Anne to be sure her decision is the right one." James stood up and the two men again shook hands.

As if she had been listening at the door, Lady Howe stepped into the library and the strained atmosphere seemed to disappear, at least for Anne. "Congratulations, darling. Your happiness is the most important thing in the world to your father and me. This calls for a toast." She moved to a credenza that held a decanter, poured four glasses of claret, and handed them around. She raised her glass. "Here's to your health and happiness."

Anne sipped the wine gratefully. She felt a red rose bloom in her chest as she began to radiate joy. She did not notice that the earl left his wine untouched.

James drained his glass and set it down. He took Anne's mother's hand to his lips. "I truly thank you, Lady Howe." His expressive brown eyes conveyed more than his words. He took possession of Anne's hand. "I think we should drop in at Hampden House and tell my family the good news."

"Yes, that would be lovely," Anne agreed. "Sorry to rush off, Mother."

"Off you go, darling."

Earl Howe said, "In the meantime, I'll have the marriage contract drawn up."

James nodded. "Good day, Lord Howe, Lady Howe." He ushered Anne from the library and headed toward the front door. When they were outside, they hugged each other with relief. "I thank the Fates, or whatever it was that made him change his mind."

"I think it was Mother's magic," Anne declared.

"Yes, doubtless it was her invisible hand that orchestrated the whole thing."

As the couple walked around the corner to Green Street, Anne bethought herself.

"What about John Claud?"

"The young devil will have no choice but to accept it. In any case, he should be sitting in Parliament this afternoon."

When the happy couple entered Hampden House, Abercorn had just arrived home from his office at Buckingham Palace.

James kissed his mother. "As I'm sure you've long suspected, I have asked Lady Anne to marry me, and she has accepted my proposal."

Lady Lu kissed Anne, and embraced James. "I congratulate the groom and offer the bride every happiness. Whatever took you so long?"

Anne bit her lip. "I'm afraid that was my fault, Your Grace. My father withheld his consent until today."

Abercorn beamed. "It's a father's duty to be protective of his daughter."

"This calls for champagne." Lady Lu rang the bell for the butler.

When he arrived, Abercorn informed him, "Champagne for the ladies, and Irish whiskey for James and me."

The four sat down in the drawing room to enjoy their drinks. "When is the happy day to be?" Lady Lu asked.

"Anne's father wants a decent interval between the engagement announcement and the wedding date, to give my bride time to change her mind."

Lady Lu threw back her head and laughed at such an absurd suggestion, but her husband was more practical. "Richard may have a point about a decent interval. It's almost the end of October and the anniversary of Prince Albert's death is approaching fast. The entire month of December will be set aside for mourning, and since our family is close to the royal family, it's only fitting that you hold off the wedding celebration until after the New Year begins." Then he winked at his son. "Of course, the decision is yours."

"I wouldn't want to ruffle any royal feathers." He slipped his arm around Anne possessively. "It will give us time to look for a decent house, with a large nursery."

"It will also give Princess Alexandra time to find a new lady-in-waiting to replace me. James wants me to be a full-time wife."

"But it's what *you* want that should count, my dear," Lady Lu asserted.

Anne's eyes sparkled like emeralds. "I want what James wants."

Lu rolled her eyes. "Good God, she's intoxicated by love. More champagne, my dear?"

In less than an hour they were in the cab on their way back to Marlborough House, holding hands and laughing at their good fortune. Before they arrived, James sobered. "Your father gave his consent grudgingly and I don't want to give him cause to find fault with me in any way. From now on, we must live circumspect lives. No more midnight forays to White Horse Street."

"Respectability must be our God, and no scandal! How on earth are we to achieve such boring, lofty goals?"

"By avoiding temptation and seeing each other as little as possible," James suggested.

"Mmm, take the month of November. I wager that *you* will seek unlawful carnal knowledge of *me*, before I come begging to be bedded."

He laughed into her eyes. "What are the stakes?"

"If you lose because you can't hold out, you must come naked beneath your overcoat."

"And if you lose, will you promise to wear your fur coat again with nothing underneath?"

"You devil, James. So I'm not too decadent for you after all!"

That night at Marlborough House the royal couple congratulated Anne and James and offered toasts to their happiness at dinner. Earlier, a jeweler's box had arrived for Lady Anne containing an emerald and diamond engagement ring. She immediately tried it on, delighted that it was not only a perfect fit, but an exquisite choice. The card read:

> *My darling Anne,*
> *It was impossible to get emeralds more beautiful than your eyes, but I hope the ring pleases you nevertheless.*
> *Yours forever,*
> *James*

Anne kept the ring on her finger and showed everyone at Marlborough House right down to the laundry women and the kitchen potboy.

At dinner she gave James back the signet ring he'd bestowed upon her and that she had been wearing on a gold chain beneath her gown.

"Have you set a wedding date yet?" Alexandra asked.

"We were thinking sometime in January, after your baby is born."

"Anne, that is extremely thoughtful, but you mustn't hold off your wedding until after our child is born. I will miss you so much, but I understand you want to start a family of your own. I promise to start looking for a couple of new ladies-in-waiting right away."

Chapter 28

THE MORNING POST

November 11, 1863

Henry Weysford Rawdon, Marquis of Hastings, died suddenly yesterday, November 10, at his home in St. James's Place. Rawdon-Hastings, a habitué of the racetracks, recently lost a fortune on his horse Lady Elizabeth at Doncaster.

Rawdon's father died when Henry was only two years old, and Henry succeeded to his father's titles upon the early death of his older brother, at the age of nine. Later, Henry inherited his mother's barony at the age of sixteen.

Earlier this year he married Lady Florence Paget. The marriage created a scandal as the bride had been engaged to Henry Chaplin, friend to the Prince of Wales.

Rawdon-Hastings was one of only three to hold peerages in all three kingdoms of England, Scotland, and Ireland.

"Oh my God, Henry Hastings is dead!" Anne passed the newspaper to her friend Frances and sat in shock.

"Wouldn't you know they'd bring up the scandal of

Florence being engaged to Chaplin? Damn newspapers delight in dishing up dirt! I wonder what he died of."

"Florence will be in a terrible mess. I must go round to see her," Anne declared.

"Give her my condolences. I'll stay here with the princess."

"In that case, perhaps I'll stay for a couple of days if she needs me."

Anne packed an overnight bag and explained the situation to Alix.

"Of course you must go, Anne. Take as long as you need. Don't worry about us here at Marlborough House."

When Anne arrived at St. James's Place, Florence was distraught. "Thank you for coming. You're the only one who cares enough about me." She wiped her red-rimmed eyes, but immediately they refilled with tears.

Anne cradled her friend, then sat her down before a warm fire, and propped her feet up on a hassock. "Henry was only twenty-six. Whatever did he die from, Florence?"

"The doctor said it was his heart, but of course it was the drink that killed him."

"I'm so sorry, Florence. Have the funeral arrangements been made?"

Florence nodded. "His funeral service is tomorrow. His sister Lady Edyth, who will inherit his English baronies, is taking care of the expenses."

"That's one burden off your shoulders. I'll stay and attend the funeral with you tomorrow."

"Thank you, Anne. The service is at St. George's in Hanover Square, where we were married. But he's to be buried at Packington Hall, in Warwickshire. I'm not up to going all that way, and I don't believe his sisters would welcome me."

"Of course you're not going all that way. It's unthinkable."

Princess Alexandra began interviewing young ladies from noble families who aspired to become ladies-in-waiting. But she was surprised by a morning call from Lady Sarah Mordaunt. She invited the young Scotswoman into her private sitting room, feeling slightly envious about her lovely figure. In the two months since the Mordaunts had been at Sandringham, Alexandra knew her own measurements had expanded.

"Do make yourself comfortable, Lady Mordaunt. I'll ring for tea, or perhaps you'd like to stay for lunch?"

"Thank you, no, Your Highness. This isn't a social call."

Alexandra had learned to present a serene demeanor to the world, since she had been thrust into English Society, but on the inside her emotions ran riot. Certain people took delight in polite conversation that contained clever barbs, and Alix was always on guard.

"How may I help you?" she asked softly.

Sarah opened her purse, took out an envelope, and clutched it in her hand. Her lips began to quiver, and she spoke in a rush of words. "My husband is threatening to divorce me because of the Prince of Wales's adulterous attentions." She pressed her lips together in an effort to steady her voice. "I will be penniless. . . . I need money." She thrust the envelope at Alexandra.

The princess took it, looked down, and saw that it was addressed to Lady Sarah Mordaunt. She opened the envelope and withdrew the letter. Alix did not read it, but saw that it was signed *Teddy*.

"This is just one of many letters from His Royal Highness. I'm willing to sell you the letters so you may destroy the evidence. I think ten thousand pounds is a fair price."

Without saying a word, Alexandra put the letter back in its envelope and held it out to Lady Mordaunt.

"You may keep that one for free. It is a good example of just how incriminating Teddy's letters are." Sarah stood up. "I'll give you a day to think about it, Your Highness. Please don't delay; our time is running out. I'll be back tomorrow."

"No, don't return to Marlborough House, Lady Mordaunt. I will contact you."

After her visitor departed, Alix sat for a long time without moving, deep in thought, her hands clasped protectively over her baby. Finally she arose and walked slowly to her private bedchamber. She heard someone in the adjoining dressing room and opened the door. She was relieved to see Lady Frances hanging up freshly laundered petticoats.

"Frances, do you know if your brother is here today?"

"I haven't seen him, Your Highness. He's likely in Parliament, or perhaps he's house hunting."

"Of course. It's nothing important." Alix returned to her chamber, and penned a quick note to Lord Hamilton. Then she summoned a messenger and asked him to deliver it to White Horse Street.

A few hours later, when Grady handed James the message from the Princess of Wales, he checked the time. *It's five, the hour when Teddy entertains one of his doxies at Jermyn Street.* He told Grady that he would be dining at Marlborough House. James wanted to speak with Anne about their engagement notice. Because of Hastings's death, perhaps she would rather hold off the announcement for a few days.

When he arrived at Marlborough House, he went straight upstairs to the private royal wing. He spotted Lady Elizabeth and asked her to see if Princess Alexandra could see him. In less than a minute, Elizabeth showed him into Alix's sitting room.

"Your Highness, I'm sorry I didn't get your note until I got home from Parliament."

"Thank you for coming, James. Do sit down." She went to her writing desk, took out the letter, and handed it to him.

He instantly recognized Teddy's handwriting and when he saw it was addressed to Sarah Mordaunt, his dark brows drew together. "Shall I read it?"

When Alexandra nodded, he took the letter from the envelope and read it.

"Her husband intends to sue for divorce. Lady Mordaunt needs money. She's offering me the rest of the letters for ten thousand pounds. I'm so sorry to involve you in this, James, but you are the only one I trust."

"You did exactly right, Your Highness. Did she bring this today?"

Alix nodded. "She said she'd be back tomorrow. I told her not to return to Marlborough House, that I would contact her." She pressed her lips together. "James, I want you to get the letters and burn them. Give her whatever she asks."

"My dearest Alexandra, I will take care of the matter. I pledge it on my honor."

James Hamilton masked his fury until he left Marlborough House. As he strode along Pall Mall, he silently vented his anger. *Teddy should be hanged, drawn, and quartered! The debauched son of a bitch doesn't deserve someone as sweet and lovely as Alexandra. He fucks anything and everything that comes within pissing distance, and as a result his Scottish piece of ass is blackmailing his wife.*

James knew he could do little tonight. Tomorrow morning he would go to the bank. Blackmail could only be paid in cash. He decided the best place to make the exchange was the Jermyn Street town house. A place Sarah Mordaunt was obviously familiar with. He knew his problem would be getting a message to her without her husband's knowledge. Since she'd been communicating with Teddy for months, there must be a way.

James decided against returning to Marlborough House for dinner. It would be difficult to dine with the Prince of Wales and not knock his teeth down his throat.

At noon the following day, Lord Hamilton let himself into the luxuriously furnished town house on Jermyn Street and waited. When he'd left home earlier in the morning, he'd taken Grady with him. After stopping at the Bank of England, he drove to Belgrave Square where the Mordaunts resided, and sent Grady to their back door with a note for Sarah and instructed him to wait for a reply.

At one o'clock, the appointed time, Sarah arrived.

"Good afternoon, Lady Mordaunt. Won't you come in?" James led the way upstairs and offered her a seat in the drawing room.

"Why did she send you?"

"Perhaps because I'm neither as indiscreet nor as gullible as Baron Renfrew."

Sarah tossed her head. "Do you have the money?"

"Money for what?"

"For Teddy's letters."

"How many letters did you receive from the Prince of Wales?"

"Ten altogether." She took the bundle of letters from her purse.

"How do I know you don't have more letters you intend to use for blackmail?"

"I don't have more. I want to get rid of them. I don't want my husband to find them."

"So you believe they're worth a thousand pounds apiece?"

"I need the money. Sir Charles has threatened to divorce me."

"I have a cashier's check for five thousand pounds. . . . If the letters are authentic."

"James, I need—"

"Kindly address me as Lord Hamilton." He held out his hand. "May I see them?"

With a wary look she handed him the bundle of letters.

James noted the dates, and saw that the first letter was from shortly after the first dinner party at Marlborough House. The last letter was dated the first week of October, when the prince had returned from Sandringham. "There are only nine letters here."

"The Princess of Wales has the other one."

"Five thousand. Take it or leave it."

Without a word, she took the cashier's check and put it in her purse.

"Good afternoon, Lady Mordaunt."

When he was alone, James read the letters, and then he burned them.

James attended the afternoon session in Parliament, where everyone was agog over the untimely death of the young Marquis of Hastings. Rumors abounded that Lady Elizabeth, the horse he had entered at Doncaster, had been drugged, and a few members were speculating that perhaps Rawdon had committed suicide.

When James left the Commons, he went directly to Marlborough House, where he was in time to escort the Princess of Wales into the dining room for dinner.

He held out his arm and his warm brown eyes met Alexandra's. "The matter has been taken care of, Your Highness."

"Thank you, James." Her eyes told him how much she appreciated his help.

"It is my honor to serve you, ma'am."

The prince was there before them, and James escorted Alexandra to her seat beside her husband. His sister arrived and James held her chair, then sat down next to her.

"Anne went to be with our friend Florence. Hastings's funeral service was today, so I don't expect Anne back until tomorrow."

James nodded. *I should have been there with her.* "You didn't attend?"

"I didn't approve of her marriage to Rawdon. All that nonsense about following her heart brought her nothing but grief."

"Frances, she is your friend," he said quietly. *Obviously, loyalty isn't as high on your priority list as it is on mine.*

James observed the Prince of Wales downing oysters on the half shell. *My loyalty compels me to warn Teddy what is afoot. He doesn't seem to have a care in the world.*

After dinner, James followed the prince to the billiard room. He waited until Teddy lit his cigar. "Charles Mordaunt is about to sue his wife for divorce. Best stay away from Jermyn Street for the present."

Teddy looked startled. "Surely it's just rumor? Divorce is a drastic step to take."

"But not unheard-of, if he has proof of adultery."

"Proof?" He blew out a cloud of smoke and began to cough.

"Witnesses . . . confessions . . . letters . . . that sort of thing." *I hope you're sweating blood!*

James, hungry for the sight of Anne, after the distasteful day he'd had, left Marlborough House and walked over to St. James's Place.

He was amazed to find Florence and Anne sitting alone in the drawing room. "Lady Florence, please accept my heartfelt condolences for your loss." He took her hands and placed a gentle kiss on her brow. "I expected a full house."

"They left," Florence said sadly. "Only a few came."

"Anne, I'm so glad you are here to comfort your friend." He turned to Florence. "I just stopped by to see if there is anything you need."

"Thank you. I can't think. I feel numb," Florence said helplessly.

"That's shock. You need rest. It won't start to wear off for a few days."

Anne walked to the door with James. "I'll stay tonight and return to Marlborough House tomorrow." She twisted her lovely diamond and emerald ring on her finger. "It feels wrong that I'm so happy when Florence is so sad."

"It's not wrong, sweetheart." He drew her close. "But I'm glad our engagement wasn't announced in the paper just yet. It would have seemed inappropriate." He kissed her tenderly. "Good night, love. Think happy thoughts."

Two days later, the Prince of Wales summoned James to Marlborough House. Teddy took him into the library and shut the door. "I'm in a god-awful position, James. Aylesford told me today that Charles Mordaunt intends to name me correspondent in his divorce trial!"

"Adultery must be proven, sire."

"I cannot be dragged into court! I am the Prince of Wales. It is unthinkable."

"You need an attorney to advise you, Your Highness."

"Attorney be damned. There isn't a lawyer living I would trust. What I need you to do is go to Mordaunt and offer him money, or a knighthood, or whatever he's after."

"He's obviously after revenge." James shook his head. "I have no intention of trying to bribe the man; that would be tantamount to admitting your guilt, and playing right into his hands."

"Then what the hellfire do you propose I do?" Teddy demanded.

"When in doubt, do nothing."

"Nothing?" The prince poured himself a glass of whiskey and downed it.

"You need do nothing, unless or until you are served with papers."

"You think that Mordaunt may not go that far?"

"Sir Charles Mordaunt is ruthless. He put his own Warwickshire tenants out of their cottages when they tried to join the Labourers' Union."

"Most landowners are against unions. What does that have to do with me?"

"Nothing. I was merely illustrating the depth of his vindictiveness. That's why I advised you to keep away from Jermyn Street. And above all, you must have no contact with Sarah Mordaunt," James warned.

"You need have no fear on that score. A pox on the little whore!"

Anne recognized James's elegant writing on the envelope that a messenger delivered. Her pulse quickened as she tore it open and read the note.

My darling Anne,
If you can get away after lunch, meet me
outside Marlborough House. There is a
property I am going to look at and of course I
prefer that we see it together.
Love, James

She hoped the house was in Mayfair, where both their families had always lived, but she knew that James could be unconventional. She decided to wear her fur coat, since the November day was chilly, and there was a cold wind coming off the Thames.

After lunch she emerged from Marlborough House and saw that James was there awaiting her. As he helped her into his carriage, his glance swept her from head to foot. "I hope you are wearing something warmer than last time beneath that fur."

"Lord Hamilton, I am now a respectable lady who is engaged to be married. My days of wanton behavior are a thing of the past."

"I sincerely hope not," he said with a wink. "That would be truly devastating." He drove up St. James's Street, along Piccadilly, then turned onto Park Lane. He stopped the carriage in front of the mansion on the corner.

Anne gazed up at the magnificent stone edifice. "Oh, James, is it really for sale?"

He helped her from the carriage. "It was yesterday, when I made inquiries. They let me have a key so I could show it to you." He unlocked the front door and they stepped inside the elegant foyer.

Anne gazed up at the high ceiling with its exquisite chandelier and sweeping staircase. As they ascended to the second level, she saw that the floor-to-ceiling windows provided a glorious view of the park. "It's a magnificent house, but it's very large, James."

"Yes, it has a ballroom, a massive library, and an entire floor of nurseries. Do you like it, sweetheart?"

"Of course I like it, but it's almost as big as Marlborough House."

"And why shouldn't you live in a mansion, my beauty? One day you'll be a duchess." He led the way to the spacious master bedchamber and opened the door to the adjoining bathing room, whose bathtub was large enough for two.

Anne sighed. "Well, I suppose if you have your heart set on it, I could learn to love it." The teasing light in her eyes belied her words.

"The only thing my heart is set on is you, my lovely." He reached into his pocket for the key, and put it into her hand. "I bought it yesterday."

Anne threw her arms around his neck, and he picked her up and swung her around. When he set her feet back to the Aubusson carpet, she let her fur coat slide to the floor. "Let's christen it!"

An hour later as James drove back to Marlborough House, he said, "We spoke about January for the wedding, but we have to settle on a date."

"I was looking at the calendar and was thinking about the fourteenth."

"The sooner the better. Let's make it the seventh."

Anne smiled. "Seven is our lucky number."

When they drove up to Marlborough House, a footman opened the carriage door.

Anne jumped out and blew James a kiss. "I'll see you later, darling."

The footman cleared his throat. "Lord Hamilton, the Prince of Wales asked me to keep an eye out for you. His Highness asks that you attend him in the library."

Chapter 29

"James, where the devil have you been? I've been waiting hours. I sent a message to White Horse Street and your servant said you were here at Marlborough House."

James recognized Teddy's panic; he'd seen it many times over the years. "Tell me."

"I had a visit from Mordaunt's attorney, Simon Rodkin. The fellow had the effrontery to tell me that I'm being charged with *adultery* in his client's divorce case."

That's what it's called when you fuck a married woman. "You must engage your own attorney-at-law, Your Highness. He will represent you in court if it goes to trial."

"It *cannot* go to trial. *I cannot* go to court. I am a member of the royal family, heir to the *throne*. I will be England's next king. Mordaunt cannot do this to me!"

"Sir Charles Mordaunt is a baronet. He is also a member of the ruling party in the House of Commons. He absolutely can bring a suit against you if he has grounds, Your Highness. You will simply have to deny the charges."

"James, I *did* deny the charges. I told Rodkin that you owned the Jermyn Street town house, and that I had never visited the place. James, if you admit to an affair with the woman, Mordaunt will be able to obtain his divorce without dragging my royal name through the mud."

You cowardly son of a bitch! "Sire, do not ask it of me. I have taken responsibility in the past, but I cannot do so now. I am engaged to be married. It would bring shame upon Lady Anne and her family. I'm sorry, but I'm not prepared to do such a thing."

Teddy looked incredulous at his friend's adamant refusal.

James turned on his heel and strode from the library.

"Many happy returns of the day, Your Highness." Anne curtsied before Princess Alexandra, and watched as Alix unwrapped the birthday present she had designed for her. It was a satin, flared bed jacket in her favorite lavender-blue, embroidered with tiny silver fleurs-de-lys.

The December first birthday celebration was taking place in Alexandra's sitting room. It was both small and private because of her advanced pregnancy, and also because December was the anniversary of Prince Albert's death.

Frances Hamilton dropped into a curtsy. "Happy nineteenth birthday, Your Highness. I didn't design these myself, but I hope you like them."

Princess Alexandra held up the kid riding gloves for the ladies to see. "Thank you, Frances, I cannot wait until I'll be able to ride again."

The personal maid who did her hair gave her tortoise-shell hair ornaments, and her head sewing woman presented her with a tea gown, a fashion that was currently all the rage in London.

The princess was visibly touched by the thoughtful gifts her closest attendants had given her. "I thank you ladies, with all my heart."

The Prince of Wales arrived on the happy scene. "My dearest Alexandra, this is your special day. You know I would prefer to throw you a grand celebration, but this year that is impossible. Please accept my gift as a token of my profound esteem and affection."

Inside the jewel case was a magnificent diamond and ruby necklace with earrings to match. The ladies gasped at the costly present. The princess gave her husband her usual serene smile. "Thank you so much, Edward."

If he was disappointed at her reaction, he did not show it. He beamed at the ladies in attendance, bade them good night, and took himself off to play baccarat.

"Mr. Prime Minister, it has come to my attention that the Prince of Wales has embroiled himself in a sordid affair that will rock the Throne of England if it becomes known."

"Your Gracious Majesty, the Prince of Wales is above reproach. You must pay no heed to wicked rumors."

The queen held up her imperial hand. "You need not defend him. I know what my son is. And the thing that is unforgivable is that the case will come up in the month of my dearest Albert's commemoration. As my prime minister, I command you to make this distasteful charge disappear."

"Your Gracious Majesty, perhaps I could have a discreet word with the chief justice of the Queen's Bench, Sir Alexander Cockburn."

"We forbid it, Mr. Prime Minister. The Crown cannot be open to charges of bribery." The queen's jowls quivered in horror. "In the past, my son's gentleman of the bedchamber Lord James Hamilton has handled these matters discreetly and efficiently. I believe he serves under you in the House."

"He does, Your Majesty."

"That will be all, Mr. Prime Minister."

Lord John Russell, the foreign secretary, arose in the House of Commons, and handed the prime minister a bulletin. Russell remained on his feet while Palmerston read it aloud to the members.

"President Lincoln has announced the Proclamation of Amnesty and Reconstruction to Congress. He has offered full amnesty to those who fought for the Confederacy. Lincoln has also promised that all property in the South, except former slaves, would be restored to their legal owners. He also guarantees that any Southern state

will be allowed back into the Union if they swear allegiance and also agree to abandon slavery."

A great cheer went up from the members.

The foreign secretary held up his hand, and waited for the cacophony to die down. "Only time will tell if the Confederacy will accept."

The gavel came down, ending the session, and James joined his uncle Lord John. "I understand the bitter winter weather has taken a heavy toll on both sides. The suffering must be unimaginable. Let us hope the Confederacy surrenders soon."

The prime minister joined them. "Lord Hamilton, might I have a private word with you in my chamber?"

"Of course, my lord." As James walked past the benches with the prime minister, his thoughts were somber. War was hell, and civil war was heart scalding.

James sat down and the prime minister took his chair behind the desk. "Lord Hamilton, a grave matter concerning His Royal Highness the Prince of Wales has come to my attention."

By God, the old adage is true, hasty news travels fast!

"It seems that Sir Charles Mordaunt is bringing a suit for divorce against his wife, Lady Sarah, and he intends to charge His Royal Highness with adultery. Such a charge is unprecedented in the annals of British history, and we must do all in our power to protect the heir to the throne."

"Mr. Prime Minister, I have advised the Prince of Wales to consult with an attorney regarding this unfortunate matter," James stated firmly.

"Lord Hamilton, I don't believe you grasp the dire consequences of this delicate situation. If the Prince of Wales was charged with adultery in a court of law, he would never sit on the throne. He would never become King of England. Moreover, the scandal would besmirch Her Gracious Majesty Queen Victoria, and might even bring down the monarchy itself."

James sat silently as he digested the prime minister's words.

"Her Majesty summoned me to the palace. She is fully cognizant of her son's involvement in this sordid affair. She commanded me to make this distasteful charge disappear."

James could not dispel the sinking feeling that stole over him. "Have you informed Sir Charles Mordaunt of the grave consequences of his suit?"

"That would avail us naught. He is the injured party and bent on revenge. Her Majesty suggested another solution." The prime minister cleared his throat. "The queen confided that in the past Lord Hamilton had handled these matters discreetly and efficiently."

James realized that he had no choice but to bow to the wishes of the Prince of Wales, Her Majesty the Queen, and the prime minister. Their trifold pressure was akin to being squeezed in a vise. "I will consult with Mordaunt's attorney, Simon Rodkin. If you would consent to be present at the meeting, Mr. Prime Minister, it would lend more authority to my negotiations."

"Yes, I quite see that, Lord Hamilton. And if the meeting took place in the offices of Parliament, that might also lend weight. Do not delay; time is of the essence."

"James and I are going to be living at Number One, Park Lane. He purchased it this week." Anne kissed her mother's cheek. "We've set the wedding date for January seventh, at St. George's, of course."

"But, darling, that doesn't give us time to have a wedding gown made."

"We only want a small wedding, and James doesn't want to wait. So I've decided to wear my white velvet gown with the crystals on the bodice. It has a special meaning for both of us." She tossed her red-gold hair over her shoulder. "I've never been so happy in my life!"

"I'd better send the engagement notice to the newspaper and start shopping in earnest for my mother-of-the-bride gown. Your father has drawn up the wedding contract, so be sure to remind James to come and sign it."

"I know it was you who persuaded Father to give his consent. I'll be grateful forever. It means the whole world to me."

"And your happiness means the whole world to me, darling."

"I must rush. Frances and I are training two new ladies-in-waiting."

"Who are the lucky young women who've been chosen to serve the princess?"

"Lady Caroline Chandos and Lady Diana Beauclerk."

"I remember Caroline Chandos from the Chiswick garden party." Anne's mother rolled her eyes, but refrained from comment. "I warrant you'll be attending the memorial for the late consort?"

"Yes, the queen has ordered us all to Windsor on the fourteenth for Prince Albert's memorial service in St. George's Chapel. Would you believe that Victoria has declared it unseemly for the Princess of Wales to be seen in public because of her pregnancy?"

"So Alexandra is excused from the service?"

"Only from the service in the chapel. Alix has been given permission to wait at Frogmore House until the procession arrives, then join in the prayers at Albert's tomb."

"Ah yes, the Domed Temple that sits in Frogmore's lovely gardens is finally finished. This will be the first time that the queen will be seen in public since Albert's death."

"Well, it's not exactly public; only the family and the ladies-in-waiting are allowed."

"I don't envy you, darling. But look on the bright side—you'll get to see Emily."

Anne threw back her head and laughed. "She'll be in deepest mourning, but it won't be for Albert—it will be because I'm marrying James Hamilton!"

"Counselor Rodkin, if Sir Charles Mordaunt brings this suit, the Prince of Wales is prepared to vehemently deny the charge of adultery," Lord Hamilton declared. "I'm sure that the chief justice of the Queen's Bench will take Prince Edward's word over that of Sir Charles."

Rodkin steepled his fingers and glanced at the prime minister. "Perhaps. But ... Sir Charles will have had his revenge. He will have brought down His Royal Highness the Prince of Wales."

"Which does Mordaunt want most? Divorce or revenge?" James asked.

"He wants both, of course."

"He cannot *have* both," Hamilton said emphatically.

"Then I believe he will settle for divorce," Rodkin said smoothly.

"If you agree to a hearing that is both immediate and private, I will testify that I am the owner of the town house on Jermyn Street. If you charge me with adultery with Lady Sarah Mordaunt, I will not contest it."

"Perhaps both you and the prince are guilty of adultery with the lady."

The prime minister looked outraged. "You cannot have it both ways, Rodkin."

"This is as far as my client and I are prepared to go," the attorney stated. "We agree to a private hearing before a judge to be appointed by the chief justice, in the next day or so. We will charge Lord James Hamilton with adultery, but the Prince of Wales must attend the hearing as a witness. Lady Mordaunt's counsel will need to hear his denial."

James looked at the prime minister, who asked Rodkin, "You swear that His Highness will not be charged with adultery and that the hearing will be private?"

"Absolutely, my lord."

"Set up the hearing, for tomorrow or the next day. I'll inform His Highness." James knew that no matter how private the hearing was, the sensational details would be leaked.

When Rodkin departed, the prime minister said, "The government and the Crown owe you a debt of gratitude, Lord Hamilton."

James went immediately to Marlborough House and closeted himself with Teddy.

"I have arranged a private trial before a judge of the Queen's Bench. I will testify that I own the town house on Jermyn Street. A charge of adultery will be brought against me, and I have agreed not to contest it. You will not be charged with adultery, but you must attend as a witness. When Lady Mordaunt's counsel questions you, you may flatly deny any improper familiarity with the woman."

"I cannot be part of a trial for divorce, James!"

"If you refuse, I rescind my offer to take responsibility for your adultery, Teddy, and the charge will be brought against you."

"You're hard as flint, James!" Teddy's hands shook as he poured himself a whiskey.

And you're soft as dog shit.

Lord Hamilton returned to White Horse Street. He sat at his desk in the library deep in thought for an hour before he picked up his pen and wrote:

> *My Dear Lady Anne,*
> *I respectfully release you from our*
> *engagement.*
> *I humbly beg your pardon for the shame and*
> *embarrassment my actions will inevitably bring*
> *to you and your family.*
> *James Hamilton*

He picked up a whiskey decanter and took a large swallow. A vivid picture of Prince Teddy swilling down liquor came to him. With a foul oath, James hurled the crystal decanter against the wall.

"I had no idea that Frogmore was such a lovely house." The Princess of Wales admired the comfortable furnishings, and the cozy fire in the private sitting room. "The queen suggested I withdraw to Windsor for my month-long confinement, but I rejected the idea because Windsor made me unhappy when I first arrived. Now that I've seen the spacious Home Park, I think Frogmore House would make a perfect retreat."

Lady Frances helped Alexandra remove her black velvet cloak. "When we were children, we spent a lot of time at Windsor riding about the Home Park. The Frogmore gardens look a little bleak now, but in the springtime they are ablaze with color."

"Will you keep an eye on the time for us?" Alexandra asked Anne. "The service in the chapel is supposed to be over by one o'clock; then the procession will make its way to the Domed Temple. I walk a lot slower these days, and I don't want to be late."

Half an hour later, Anne drew back the lace curtains. "I can see them coming now." The princess stood up, and Anne helped her don the mourning cloak she had specially designed to minimize Alexandra's pregnancy.

Flanked by Anne and Frances, the Princess of Wales managed to arrive at the burial place ahead of the procession. They entered the Domed Temple, whose walls were made of Portuguese red marble. Queen Victoria, shrouded and veiled, and accompanied by her black-clad ladies-in-waiting, led the procession. The Prince of Wales followed with his brothers, Alfred, Arthur, and Leopold, who walked ahead of their sisters Alice, Helena, Louise, and Beatrice.

When the Prince of Wales left his siblings and joined his wife, Anne wondered why James was not in attendance. The archbishop began the prayers over Prince Albert's tomb and all present bowed their heads in respect.

The prayers seemed to go on forever and when they were finally over, Anne lifted her head. Though she wasn't surprised to find Emily's eyes on her, she was disconcerted to see the smug smile on her face. Anne glanced at the princess, hoping she was not adversely affected by standing so long. Until Queen Victoria indicated that the service was at an end, all had to remain in their places.

Finally, Her Majesty nodded to the archbishop, spoke to her ladies-in-waiting, then led the procession toward Frogmore House for tea. As Emily walked past Anne, she could not keep the self-satisfied smirk from her face.

Anne and Frances walked behind the royal couple, but when the prince arrived at the entrance to Frogmore, he said, "I won't join you for tea. It's better if just the ladies attend. I'll take my brothers back to the castle."

Queen Victoria and Teddy cannot tolerate each other. Anne took Alexandra's arm and escorted her into the drawing room, where the queen and her ladies were sitting. When the princess was seated comfortably by the fire, Anne took her cloak to the chamber being used as a cloakroom. Suddenly, she came face-to-face with Emily.

"Now you know why Father vehemently objected to your marrying James Hamilton. The scandal is spreading like wildfire!"

Anne raised her chin. "What the devil are you talking about?"

"Surely, you've heard. It's on every tongue that Sir Charles Mordaunt was granted a divorce yesterday because his wife, Sarah, was having an affair with Lord Hamilton."

"That's a vile lie!"

Frances came into the room, and Emily gave her a pitying smile. "How devastating that your brother has brought such shame on your family. Your poor sister Jane will likely lose her position with Her Majesty."

"You unearth scandal like a sow rooting out truffles!"

"Insulting me won't alter the fact that your brother's an adulterer, Frances Hamilton."

Emily pulled aside her skirts as if she feared contamination. "Excuse me, ladies, I must attend Her Gracious Majesty."

"I'm so sorry, Anne. I hoped you wouldn't hear, at least not today."

"Frances, surely you don't believe this?"

"Of course I believe it. I heard it from Charles Carrington last night. James owns a town house on Jermyn

Street where he carried on the liaison. Females throw themselves at my brother. His conquests are legion."

Anne felt as if a cruel hand were crushing her heart. Her cheeks were burning, but when she covered them with her hands, her face felt stiff and cold. *The day I went to confront Leicester, I saw James at a town house on Jermyn Street.* Anne suddenly remembered seeing Sarah Mordaunt and James together at Sandringham. *She was like a bitch in heat. She couldn't keep her hands off him!*

Chapter 30

"Her Majesty and the royal family, with the exception of Prince Edward and I, are staying at Windsor through Christmas and New Year's," Alexandra told Anne and Frances on the carriage ride back to Marlborough House. "Thank heaven, we are excluded."

Anne sat in silence, her thoughts in disarray, her emotions in turmoil. As if in a trance, she exited the carriage, and walked up the steps to Marlborough House. Elizabeth Knollys handed her a letter, and when she recognized the handwriting, hope flared in her heart, yet at the same time her stomach knotted. Anne went straight to her bedchamber and Frances followed her.

Anne tore open the letter and with utter disbelief read the words James had penned. When she finished, she sat down on the bed and let the letter flutter to the carpet. Frances picked it up and read it.

"I warned you again and again. This is what you get when you follow your heart instead of your head, as our friend Florence found out to her great sorrow."

"I . . . I thought James loved me," Anne whispered.

"You wouldn't listen to me, and you wouldn't listen to John Claud."

John Claud's words about his brother came back to

her. *His currency is seductiveness. He's like a graceful leopard ruthlessly stalking one prey after another.*

"From the time James was sixteen, there have been rumors about him. Something was going on with the queen's daughter Princess Vicky that had to be hushed up."

Anne remembered the voluptuous Princess Vicky's flirtatious behavior before Alexandra's wedding. *She was slavering over him.*

"I think you've had a lucky escape. What if you didn't find out about all the shameful secrets he's been hiding until after you were married?"

"Secrets?"

"I shouldn't tell you, but you're my friend, and I can't bear you to be in ignorance. We had a young maid called Jenny a couple of years ago. James spirited her away late one night and took her to our sister Harriet because the girl was having a child. It was a family secret, but I put two and two together."

Anne was stunned. *How could I have been so blindly naive?* Then her innate honesty came to the fore. *I knew he had a reputation as a womanizer, and yet I deliberately pursued him.*

Slowly, she removed her engagement ring and set it on the bedside table with his letter. "I don't want to hear any more, Frances. I'm exhausted."

"Would you like me to have a tray sent up?"

"I don't want food, I just want to go to bed."

"Then get a good night's sleep. You'll feel better in the morning."

I'll never feel better. Long after Frances left, Anne sat rocking herself back and forth, trying to ease the pain of a broken heart.

After drowning in misery for an hour, a feeling of anger began to build inside her. Anne got up off the bed, removed her cloak, and began to pace back and forth across her chamber. The things she had learned about James Hamilton in the last five hours had turned her world upside down. Her temper flared higher with every step she took.

Anne stopped in front of her mirror and spoke to her reflection. "I'm not the one who should be shamed and embarrassed. . . . That role belongs to Lord Bloody Rakehell! I shall go and confront the decadent swine and fling his faithlessness in his face!"

I wonder if what Frances told me about him fathering a child is true. With resolution Anne donned her cloak. *There's only one way to find out.*

"Lady Anne Howe to see the Countess of Lichfield." Her challenging tone dared the footman who answered the door at the imposing St. James's Street residence to deny her request. He opened the door wide to admit her to the entrance hall. "I'll see if Lady Lichfield is free, my lady."

Harriet Anson came to the top of the stairs and gazed down at her visitor. "Lady Anne, do come up. This is a pleasant surprise."

When Anne reached the top of the stairs, she said, "Lady Lichfield, I'm sorry to call at such a late hour."

"Anne, my name is *Harry*. You'll soon be married to my brother." She led the way into her sitting room.

Anne shook her head. "James has released me from our engagement."

"Why on earth would he do such a mad thing?"

"You obviously haven't heard yet." Anne took a deep breath. "Yesterday, Sir Charles Mordaunt was granted a divorce because his wife was guilty of an adulterous affair with Lord Hamilton."

"I shall kill my husband. Thomas sits in the Commons with them. He must have heard and has kept it from me!" Harry declared in outrage.

"Your brother John Claud, and your sister Frances, warned me many times that James was a womanizer. I'm well aware that females throw themselves at him, yet I chose to ignore their warnings."

"Well, you may take what John Claud says with a grain of salt—he wanted you for himself. But I can't understand why Frances would denigrate his character."

"Frances told me about your maid Jenny."

Harry's eyes widened. "James has taken on the financial responsibility for Jenny's child, but I assure you he is not the father."

"Why would James take on the responsibility for another man's child?"

"He has a ridiculous sense of honor about loyalty. He would never betray a brother."

Anne sat stunned. "John Claud?"

"Who else?"

"Thank you for telling me the truth," she said slowly. All Anne's ideas about men had been turned on their head today. She stood up and said absently, "Good night, Harry."

"Where the devil are you going?"

"Back to Marlborough House."

"Well, I know it's within spitting distance, but you can't go alone. I'll get a footman to escort you."

Half an hour later, Anne was back in her chamber, deep in thought. She undressed slowly, and climbed into bed. She went over everything that had happened that day; then her mind went back over all the times she and James had been together. She remembered almost every word they had ever exchanged.

She realized that what his sister Harry said was true: James did have a sense of honor. That's why he had withdrawn from their engagement. He had his own moral code and loyalty was high on his list. It wasn't true that he had fathered Jenny's child, though likely he had never denied it. Anne began to wonder about Sarah Mordaunt. Perhaps that wasn't true either. *I should trust my instincts; they guided me well about John Claud.*

Anne had always listened to her heart instead of her head, and she knew she always would. *I love James. To love is to trust. Without trust there can be no true love.* Anne drew up her knees and rested her cheek against them.

I've always loved James. I've never loved any other man. Anne suddenly realized without a shadow of a doubt, *I never will love any other man.* She slipped her engagement ring back on her finger, smiled her secret smile, stretched out in bed, and fell into a deep, dreamless sleep.

"Good morning, Your Highness." Lady Frances entered Alexandra's dressing room and found Lady Caroline helping the princess to put on her shoes.

"Where is Lady Anne this morning? I'm worried about her. She didn't look well at all last evening when we returned from Windsor."

"I think she's still asleep. I didn't want to disturb her." Frances waited until Caroline Chandos left the room. "Yesterday, my brother released her from their engagement."

"Why would—" Alexandra didn't finish her question. She knew the answer. She closed her eyes at the injustice of it all. "Frances, would you ask Anne to come and see me privately?"

Anne, wearing her lavender velvet dress with lace ruffles at throat and wrist, knocked on the door of the Princess of Wales's private sitting room.

"Good morning, Your Highness. I'm sorry I'm late."

"No apologies necessary. My dearest Anne, I know you were told the shocking details of the Mordaunts' divorce yesterday, but there is something I need to tell you."

Alexandra went to her writing desk and took out a letter.

"Thank you, Your Highness. You are being extremely generous, but there is no need to share your secrets with me. I have come to realize that Lord Hamilton's loyalty is a thing to be prized."

"It is indeed, Anne. You are a very lucky woman."

"Thank you, Alix. Shall we go down to breakfast?"

Anne stepped from a hansom cab at the Parliament building, and drew her fur coat close about her. She went up the steps and handed an envelope to one of the uniformed pages.

"Would you be kind enough to deliver this message to Lord James Hamilton? Here's a sovereign for your trouble."

"Thank you, my lady. I'll see that he gets it at the first break."

A half hour later when the House broke for lunch, the parliamentary page handed Hamilton the letter.

James tore it open and read:

> *My Dearest Lord Hamilton,*
> *If you will meet me at the Westminster Palace Hotel, I will buy you lunch.*
> *I assure you it has a most respectable dining room.*
> *Lily Lamb*

James Hamilton blinked and read it again. Then a grin spread over his face. He strode to the cloakroom, grabbed his overcoat, and stepped outside onto Parliament Square. The December wind swirled about him furiously, but he was totally oblivious to its chill. He ran all the way, his heart pounding in his chest.

When he arrived at the hotel, he could see the lady he loved sitting at *their* table in the *respectable* dining room. The maître d'hôtel led him to the table, provided them with menus, and hastened off for the bottle of claret that Hamilton ordered.

James moved behind her chair to help her remove her fur. "Gray fox shows off your glorious hair to perfection."

She was thrilled by his compliment. "Thank you, my lord."

"Call me James." He draped her fur over the back of her chair and his admiring glance swept over her gown with its lace ruffles at throat and wrist. "Lavender velvet suits you even better."

"I'm glad you like it. I designed it myself."

"You have exquisite taste and an eye for color; I shall add that to the vast store of knowledge I've learned about you, Lily Lamb."

"Yes, you know all my secrets, and I have recently learned some of your secrets, Lord Hamilton." She picked up the menu and began to read.

"I thought we agreed you would call me James. Do you see anything you fancy?"

"Oh, hell yes!" She lowered her eyes to the menu. "I think some leek soup would warm me nicely."

The bottle of claret arrived and James poured the wine. "What else will you have?"

"Steak and mushroom pie," she said decisively. "That's what you fed me before you made love to me for the first time."

His warm brown eyes caressed her face. "What about these secrets you've learned?"

"I've learned that you are a keeper of secrets, James—both your own and the secrets of others. I've also learned that loyalty is high on your list of priorities. From now on I will try to aspire to your lofty ideals."

Anne took out his letter and tore it in half. "I will not allow you to withdraw from our engagement. You promised to marry me on January seventh and marry me you shall."

"It will be my greatest pleasure to do so, my beauty."

"Pleasure shared is pleasure doubled."

James couldn't take his eyes from her; the way she ate was a sensual delight that always aroused him, despite the control he tried to exercise when they were in public.

When the meal was over, Anne leaned across the table. "It would give me great pleasure if you would allow me to entertain you privately, Lord Rakehell." She took out the key to their new house on Park Lane and handed it to him.

James immediately hailed the waiter to pay the bill. "If you'd be so kind, we'd like a bottle of champagne to take with us."

"Dearly beloved, we are gathered together here in the sight of God, and in the face of this congregation, to join together this man and this woman in holy matrimony," the minister solemnly intoned.

*This has all happened before. . . . I vividly remember
every detail. I was standing at the altar in my white velvet
gown and James was standing beside me wearing his
dress kilt of Hamilton hunting tartan.*

Suddenly Anne laughed, and the lovely sound rose
and rippled like wind chimes in the vaulted ceiling of the
church. *It happened just like this in my dream, except I
slapped the archbishop of Canterbury!*

She felt James squeeze her hand, reminding her to
curb her impulsiveness, and she managed to do so until
the minister pronounced that they were man and wife.

James lifted her veil and smiled into her eyes. Then he
drew her close, and as he bent his head toward her, she
closed her eyes and opened her lips in invitation. When
his mouth touched hers, her eyelashes fluttered, and she
whispered his name with longing. "James."

Author's Note

I took poetic license to condense into four years the historical events that took place over eight years. As well, the music hall songs I portrayed came a few years later in the century.

The Prince and Princess of Wales's heir was born January 8, 1864, at Frogmore House, Windsor.

The 1st Duke of Abercorn was appointed lord lieutenant of Ireland in 1866.

Lord James Hamilton and Anne Curzon-Howe were married for forty-four years. In 1885 he became the 2nd Duke of Abercorn and was appointed lord lieutenant of County Donegal, Ireland. Their firstborn son, James Edward Hamilton, 3rd Duke of Abercorn, was a great-grandfather of Diana, Princess of Wales.

Lord John Russell became prime minister of England for the second time in 1865.

John Claud Hamilton married Carolina Chandos.

Lady Frances Albertha Hamilton married Blandford Churchill, whom she later divorced.

Maud Hamilton married Henry Fitzmaurice (Fitz), Earl of Kerry.

Read on for an excerpt from another
exciting and sensual historical romance
from Virginia Henley,

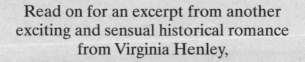

THE DECADENT DUKE

Available now from Signet.

"I *hate* that you are being married today!" Lady Georgina Gordon blinked back tears and threw her arms around her sister.

Lady Louisa looked stricken. "Don't be sad, Georgy. I know you'll miss me, but we shall visit each other often." The bride's other three sisters quickly pulled Georgina away and readjusted Louisa's bridal veil.

Georgina could have bitten off her tongue. The last thing she wanted was for her closest sister to feel guilty about getting married. "Don't be daft! Of course I won't miss you."

Lady Louisa exchanged a glance with her other sisters Charlotte, Madelina, and Susan. "Then why are you sad?"

"I'm not sad." She dashed away her tears with determined fingers. "I'm blazing mad that your wedding day has arrived!"

The lovely, Titian-haired bride looked uncertain. "Georgina, this is supposed to be the happiest day of my life."

"Pay her no mind, Louisa. You know she's as contrary as a cockroach." Charlotte rolled her eyes. "It's bad form to shed tears of jealousy on your sister's wedding day."

Georgina's jaw dropped. "Jealousy? Allow me to inform you that these are tears of pure self-pity. Now that the rabid Duchess of Gordon has bludgeoned poor Charles Cornwallis into making Louisa Lady Brome, I will become the solitary focus of her motherly attention. She will relentlessly pursue every marquis and duke between the ages of nine and ninety until she bags me a bloody husband."

"Charles is marrying me because he loves me," Louisa declared.

Georgina's tears turned to whoops of laughter. "Love has absolutely nothing to do with it. You are a Gordon and rank is the only thing that counts. You cannot deny that Mother set her sights on the Duke of Manchester for Susan and the heir to the Duke of Richmond for Charlotte, and hunted them until she ran them to ground."

"Georgina is queer in the head," Charlotte said dismissively. "It comes from being the runt of the litter."

"If I'm the runt, you are the oldest bitch," Georgina teased.

"*Countess* bitch, if you don't mind."

"Yes, Countess; it all started with you. When you bagged Colonel Charles Lennox, Earl of March and heir to the Dukedom of Richmond, Mother's ambition for the rest of us suddenly knew no bounds. Her thirst for titles became insatiable."

"We cannot deny it," Charlotte finally admitted. "Mother's instincts are more mercenary than maternal. We were all brought up with one aim in life, to marry with the maximum status. And I freely admit that if I were not the daughter of the Duke and Duchess of Gordon, the Earl of March would never have proposed."

"Not marriage, at any rate," Georgina said lightly.

The sisters all laughed at her witticism. She was the adored baby of the family, and the precocious little beauty had been much indulged and pampered by her siblings. The entire brood had had a most unconventional upbringing. Their time was divided between fairytale Castle Gordon in the Scottish Highlands, an elegant town home in Edinburgh, a large unpretentious farm-house at Kinrara beside the wild River Spey, and the spacious mansion in Pall Mall, where they were all presently gathered for the summer wedding.

Jane Gordon swept into the bedchamber and let out a deep sigh of relief. "Prime Minister Pitt and dearest Henry Dundas have just arrived. I also spied the Prince of Wales and the Duke of York making their way through the gardens from Carlton House."

Their arrival wasn't the cause of her overwhelming relief. It was the young groom and his father that she hadn't been completely sure of. The Marquis Cornwallis, a top general in the king's army and member of the Privy Council, had objected to the engagement, fearing the infamous taint of Gordon madness, until the duchess had privately assured him, in the strictest of confidence, that there was not a drop of Gordon blood in Louisa's veins.

"Is Charles here?" Louisa asked.

"What a silly question, my wee lass. Of course yer eager bridegroom is here, as well as yer future father-in-law, the marquis. What great good fortune that the Bishop of Lichfield and Coventry is the Marquis Cornwallis's brother and has agreed to officiate today."

"It will be the wedding of the Season." Georgina winked at her eldest sister.

"The Season? It will be the wedding of the *decade!* An even more impressive affair than they gave the Princess Royal," their mother declared.

Charlotte said dryly, "I believe that is the whole intent."

Louisa reached for her bridal bouquet. "We'd better hurry."

"Nay, that's the last thing we must do. We shall be fashionably late, and make them all wait for a glimpse of the blushing bride."

"I warned my husband to keep his distance from Frederick. The last thing we want is pistols at dawn." Lennox had fought a duel with the Duke of York only months before he had wed Charlotte.

"A wedding duel would guarantee that we go down in the history books," Georgina jested.

Jane Gordon threw back her head and laughed with gusto. "I warrant that graze with the bullet improved Frederick's looks."

"That wasn't the only benefit," Georgina pointed out. "If Lennox hadn't been posted to Edinburgh for his audacity in shooting the king's son, he never would have married Charlotte."

The duchess raised her eyes heavenward and murmured with mock piety, "Amen to that."

"Did your archrival, the Duchess of Devonshire, show up?"

"Not yet, Susan, though I doubt she'll be able to resist."

"A wager!" Georgina announced gleefully. "A guinea says she'll be in the ballroom by the time we make our entrance, and that she'll be sporting the Prince of Wales's feathers atop her wig."

"I'll take that wager," Charlotte declared. "I warrant the Gordon clan en masse is far too formidable and intimidating."

Georgina's wry glance swept the chamber. "You lot certainly intimidate me."

"Little liar," her mother refuted. "Yer afeared of neither man nor beast, Georgy!"

"Enough folderol," Charlotte said firmly. "Let us proceed with the nuptials before the groom has a chance to escape. I shall lead the way."

"Remember to smile sweetly," Duchess Gordon directed, "and though capturing young Cornwallis has earned us the well-deserved envy of the *haut ton*, I order you to banish all traces of smugness from yer lovely faces."

"Dearly beloved, we are gathered together here in the sight of God and in the face of this congregation," intoned the exalted Bishop of Lichfield.

And in the face of the formidable Duchess of Gordon,

Georgina added silently. She glanced at her brother, Lord George Huntly, who had escorted their mother to the place of honor. *He looks so handsome in his kilt.* She returned the devilish wink he gave her.

"Charles Cornwallis, wilt thou have this woman to thy wedded wife?" the Bishop of Lichfield charged.

Charlie looks so young and vulnerable. Georgina felt a rush of pity rise up in her. *We Gordons are a rum bunch—poor bugger doesn't know what he's letting himself in for.* She glanced at the florid face of Marquis Cornwallis. *The groom, already dominated by his father, will now add his wife's mother to the list . . . From the frying pan into the bloody fire!*

The bishop adjusted his purple miter and cleared his throat. "Louisa Gordon, wilt thou have this man to thy wedded husband?"

My sister will make Charlie happy, and coax him from being so timid. Louisa and I had such rowdy fun together—I shall miss her sorely. Georgina's thoughts flew back to the time their mother had taken her two youngest daughters on her now famous Gordon Highlanders recruiting mission. The daring duchess had wagered with King George that she would enlist more soldiers than any of his royal recruiting officers. Dressed in Highland bonnets and the new Black Watch tartan, the beautiful Gordon ladies, accompanied by six pipers, had visited every market and fair held on the vast Gordon lands. They offered a kiss and a guinea to each and every male who would join the regiment.

At some of those fairs the atmosphere was so racy and flirtatious, Louisa and I behaved like teasing coquettes. The braw Highlanders were so eager to taste our mouths, we recruited a thousand men in less than three months.

"Who giveth this woman to be married to this man?"

Proudly attired in his dress kilt, Alexander, fourth Duke of Gordon, stepped forward. "I do."

Georgina watched her father join her mother. *They make a handsome couple. This is the longest they've been together without coming to blows since the last wedding.*

I wish they could stomach each other. I have my father's black hair and my mother's vivacious personality, and God help me, I love them both dearly.

"Forasmuch as Charles and Louisa have consented together in holy wedlock, I pronounce that they be man and wife together. In the name of the Father, and of the Son, and of the Holy Ghost. Amen." Bishop Cornwallis closed his prayer book and bestowed a sanctified smile upon the newlyweds.

Across the ballroom, George, Prince of Wales, murmured to his close friend the Duke of Bedford, " 'Tis a *fait accompli,* Francis, so you may breathe easy. Congratulations on escaping the clutches of Duchess Gordon and skillfully evading the dreaded institution of marriage yet one more time."

"Jane certainly had me in her sights for Louisa, but red hair never did attract me for long. After an initial skirmish, my interest waned. As for being leg-shackled, my brother John's marriage has given me such a horror of wedded bliss that I have vowed to avoid it at all costs."

Prinny shuddered as he thought of his own disastrous nuptials to his cousin Caroline of Brunswick. *I needed so much brandy to face the ceremony that the only thing I recall is my dear friend Francis Russell propping me up.* " 'Tis the world's greatest pity that amore and marriage do not go hand in hand."

"*Au contraire!* Making love to a wife is one of life's sweetest pleasures, so long as I'm not her husband," Russell quipped.

"Lady Melbourne looks particularly ravishing today." Both the prince and Bedford had enjoyed her sexual favors, and each had fathered at least one of her children. Prinny's glance moved to the lady who had accompanied Elizabeth Melbourne, and a heartfelt sigh escaped him. Though for years he had professed his deepest love to Georgianna, Duchess of Devonshire, and had given her a lock of his hair, she always refused to become his mistress. He had been forced to settle for her devoted friendship, which they openly displayed before their aristocratic friends. Prinny raised his eyes from Georgianna's opulent breasts, and they flooded with sentimental tears when he saw that she was sporting the Prince of Wales's feathers. Like iron to a lodestone, Prinny gravitated toward Georgianna, and Bedford followed.

She wafted her ostrich feather fan and sketched a graceful curtsy. "Your Highness . . . Francis . . . I am delighted you both condescended to attend. 'Twill banish our boredom."

The Prince of Wales took her outstretched hand to his lips in a theatrical show of affection. "My dearest Georgianna, I am ever at your command." He bestowed an elegant bow upon Lady Melbourne. "Lizzie, you look charming, as always."

"Ravishing," Bedford said with a leer. "I know a surefire cure for banishing boredom."

"Devil roast you, Francis. Your cure takes nine months," Lady Melbourne drawled. "Do try not to gloat over your bachelorhood. You will be ensnared in the tender trap sooner or later."

The Duchess of Gordon, well versed in protocol, came to greet His Royal Highness, the Prince of Wales, before she acknowledged her other guests. "Such an honor, Yer Highness." Her words were calculated to stress that the honor was his, not hers. Then to prove her point, she dipped her knee and afforded the gentlemen an eye-popping view of her lush breasts.

"Jane, darling," the Duchess of Devonshire gushed, "you've outdone yourself. Young Cornwallis is quite a catch."

Jane glanced at Francis Russell. "You should have seen the one that got away." She slapped her thigh and laughed at her own wit.

The men and Lizzie, thoroughly amused, joined in her laughter.

"Georgianna, dearest, it won't be long before you are husband hunting for yer own daughters. Shall I lend you my rope and teach you how to tie a Gordon knot?"

"My dear Jane, the Devonshire girls won't need a noose," the duchess said sweetly.

Jane Gordon was too good-natured not to laugh at the riposte. "Yer wit is exceeded only by yer beauty," she said generously.

"Dare I hope that you will be serving your magnificent Highland salmon, my dear duchess?" Prinny was almost salivating.

"'Tis the thing that makes a Gordon invitation the most sought after in London—that and our famous whiskey punch." The duke owned a salmon fishery on the River Spey, and the wagons that arrived from Scotland always carried barrels of Scotch whiskey.